THE NEMESIS

Manoranjan Byapari was born in the mid-fifties in Barishal, former East Pakistan. His family migrated to West Bengal in India when he was three. They were resettled in Bankura at the Shiromanipur Refugee Camp. Later, they were forced to shift to the Gholadoltala Refugee Camp, 24-Parganas, and lived there till 1969. However, Byapari had to leave home at the age of fourteen to do odd jobs. In his early twenties, he came into contact with the Naxals and with the famous labour activist Shankar Guha Niyogi. Byapari was sent to jail during this time, where he taught himself to read and write. Later, while working as a rickshaw-puller in Kolkata, Byapari had a chance meeting with the renowned Bengali writer Mahasweta Devi, who urged him to write for her journal *Bartika*. He has written twenty-seven books since. Until 2018, he was working as a cook at the Hellen Keller Institute for the Deaf and Blind in West Bengal.

In 2018, the English translation of Byapari's memoir, *Ittibrite Chandal Jibon (Interrogating My Chandal Life)*, received the Hindu Prize for non-fiction. In 2019, he was awarded the Gateway Lit Fest Writer of the Year Prize. The English translation of his novel *Batashe Baruder Gandha (There's Gunpowder in the Air)* was shortlisted for the JCB Prize for Literature 2019, the DSC Prize for South Asian Literature 2019, the Crossword Book Award for Best Translation 2019 and the Mathrubhumi Book of the Year Prize 2020. The English translation of his novel *Chhera Chhera Jibon (Imaan)* was shortlisted for the 2022 JCB Prize for Literature.

He was appointed chairman of the newly instituted Dalit Sahitya Akademi in Bengal in 2020. In 2021, Byapari was elected a member to the Bengal Legislative Assembly as a Trinamool Congress candidate.

V. Ramaswamy is a literary translator of voices from the margins. Besides *The Runaway Boy*, the first part of the Chandal Jibon trilogy, his previous translations include *The Golden Gandhi Statue from America: Early Stories*, *Wild Animals Prohibited: Stories, Anti-stories* and *This Could Have Become Ramayan Chamar's Tale: Two Anti-Novels* (shortlisted for the Crossword Book Award, 2019), all by the anti-establishment Bengali writer, Subimal Misra. He was awarded the inaugural Literature Across Frontiers-Charles Wallace India Trust Fellowship at Aberystwyth University to translate the Chandal Jibon novels. He was selected for the inaugural translation fellowship of the New India Foundation.

MANORANJAN BYAPARI

THE NEMESIS

TRANSLATED FROM THE
BENGALI BY
V. RAMASWAMY

eka

eka

Published in paperback in Bengali as *Thik Thikaanar Sandhaaney* in 2022 by Eka, an imprint of Westland Books, a division of Nasadiya Technologies Private Limited

Published in English as *The Nemesis* in 2023 by Eka, an imprint of Westland Books, a division of Nasadiya Technologies Private Limited

No. 269/2B, First Floor, 'Irai Arul', Vimalraj Street, Nethaji Nagar, Allappakkam Main Road, Maduravoyal, Chennai 600095

Westland, the Westland logo, Eka and the Eka logo are the trademarks of Nasadiya Technologies Private Limited, or its affiliates.

Copyright © Manoranjan Byapari, 2022
Translation copyright © V. Ramaswamy, 2023

ISBN: 9789395073660

10 9 8 7 6 5 4 3 2 1

This is a work of fiction. Names, characters, organisations, places, events and incidents are either products of the author's imagination or used fictitiously.

All rights reserved

Typeset by Jojy Philip, New Delhi 110 015

Printed at Manipal Technologies Limited, Manipal

No part of this book may be reproduced, or stored in a retrieval system, or transmitted in any form or by any means, electronic, mechanical, photocopying, recording, or otherwise, without express written permission of the publisher.

CONTENTS

The Decade of Liberation

1	Cooking Up a Tale	3
2	Poisoned Life	20
3	The Avenger	34
4	The Great Departure	53
5	An Unequal Battle	68
6	Dandakaranya	84
7	Kusum	96
8	Flight Again	109

Two Jibons

9	Martyrs and the Mighty	129
10	The Jaws of Death	142
11	The Eatery and the Pit by the Pond	160
12	Cycle-rickshaw Riders and Class War in Jadavpur	182
13	The Empire of Water	201

14	A Sanctuary of Lustful Rascals	218
15	The Station Netherworld	236
16	Srimati	247
17	The Temple of the Gods	270

NEW FRIENDS AND OLD

18	*Kamake Khane Wali*	291
19	Gurupado's Liquor Den	303
20	Intimacy and Distance	319
21	The Morgue	334
22	The Accident	353
23	Seth Bagan Lane	369

THE DECADE
OF LIBERATION

1

Cooking Up a Tale

'*Excellent food yields excellent health. Excellent health yields excellent thoughts. Excellent thoughts yield excellent work. Excellent work yields excellent remuneration. Excellent remuneration yields every kind of happiness. Happiness is the means to a long life. It is the backbone of a beautiful and successful life.*' Something to this effect is supposed to have been said by Rishi Charvaka of yore. And so, since excellent food is the source of every kind of happiness—if simple and honest means of obtaining it are not available, it would not be wrong to obtain, extort, claim or collect it by any means whatsoever. Justice and injustice are not based on any prescripts laid down by some edict. It is man who defined them. Whatever is in his interest, is just, and that which is not, is unjust.

A long time ago, on a dark, moonless night, Maran, the boy who sheltered near the crematorium, and was wise and thoughtful beyond his years, had said to Jibon: 'Do you know what's the greatest sin in life? Going without food. The soul dwells in the body. And God, the Supreme Soul, dwells in the soul. When you go without food, the soul suffers. When the soul suffers, God suffers. If you make God suffer, you are a great sinner. You'll be consigned to hell for that sin.'

The fact was that for most of the eighteen years from the time he was born until he became an adult, Jibon had subjected the Supreme Soul to a lot of hunger and affront. He had thereby sinned a lot. As a result, his body had not received adequate nutrition. It had grown imperfectly, like a bonsai. But what he needed to do now was not through strength of body, but rather through strength of mind. After all, strength of mind was all he could hope to have. But starvation extinguished that too. And so, Jibon had now figured out that in order for the lamp to stay lit, he had to ensure that oil was continuously poured into it. He had to obtain food through strength of mind, so his body could heal. If he could do that, he would become strong and capable.

One morning, Jibon walked to the Baghajatin crossing. There were hundreds and thousands of people like him crowding around the place, with hunger in their bellies and hope in their hearts. Everyone was looking for work. For work as day labour. With the wage they would receive at the end of the day for doing such work, they would buy rice powder and return home. The near and dear ones of his family, who were waiting eagerly for his return, would then be able to eat. For some reason, Jibon went and stood at the exact same spot where his father Garib Das once squatted, with his spade and basket. Suddenly a man came and stood in front of him. His name was Dukhe.

Dukhe did not know Jibon, nor could Jibon recognise him. But he should have. Because he had lived for a while on the canalside in Khola-Doltala. Dukhe now lived in a village near there. His father and grandfather were fishermen, drummers and palanquin-bearers. But the canals, lakes and marshes had run dry. There were no fish there anymore. And the electric mic had replaced the playing of drums, just as palanquins had given way to motor cars. Although time eventually took over and bade farewell to everything, no one had been able to make hunger disappear, or bid it farewell. Modern science had not yet been successful in discovering an alternative means of filling the void in the belly.

And so, Dukhe was compelled to come to Jadavpur in search of work. He did whatever work was available. But his favourite work, which he enjoyed doing, was cooking. He was an experienced assistant in the cooking squad of Naresh Chakraborty, a reputed cook of this locality. Dukhe was able to work with Naresh Thakur for about four or five days a month. Although he had to put in four or six more hours than in other jobs, he preferred it because besides his wages, he also got some good food there, and as a result, his children could eat well. That was the unwritten rule in this line—even if they didn't give a lot, they had to give at least enough food for one person. At the end of the day, the cook and all his assistants packed their food into bundles. On such days, everyone at their homes was happy.

Seeing Jibon standing in front of him at the Baghajatin crossing, Dukhe asked him, '*Ei, kaaje jabi*, want to go for work?'

Who wouldn't work for a wage! Jibon replied. 'What kind of work?'

'Cooking. Can you do that?'

'What kind of cooking?'

'For a wedding.'

'But I've never cooked for so many people.'

'You don't need to cook. The cook will do that. You'll assist him, that's all. Like grinding masala, laying the plates, filling water, powdering bread crumbs in the mortar-and-pestle, and so on. We'll show you what to do. Tell me if you can do it. You'll get three-and-a-half rupees, as well as food; you can take it home if you want, instead of eating it there.'

Naresh Thakur's job that day was a big one. He had to cook for five or six hundred people. There were eight or ten kinds of items. He would not be able to do it with the workmen he had. Dukhe had planned to get his son-in-law from the village for the work, but he hadn't been able to come. He was down with fever since yesterday. That's why Dukhe was looking for a helper. He had to take someone or the other along, otherwise his own workload would become unmanageable. This was work which anyone could do, it did not require any special skill or experience.

Jibon said, 'Since you'll show me how, sure, I can do it.' He followed Dukhe to Mahadev Decorators. Naresh Thakur, the cook, was waiting there with his squad. Cooking utensils were being loaded from the decorator's godown onto a van-rickshaw.

The 'caterer' culture imported from abroad had not yet taken over the city of Calcutta. The householder in question still made all the purchases from the market himself, and then employed a professional cook to prepare the food according to an agreed-upon menu. He had his own family members serve the food, and finally, he himself went around the tables to attend to the guests, looking out for who needed more helpings. If he saw any plate empty, he shouted at those serving the food: 'What the hell are you doing? Can't you see the empty plate? Go and serve whatever's required!'

When Dukhe brought Jibon to Naresh Thakur, he asked, 'What's your name?'

Owing to a momentary lapse of alertness, Jibon's actual name and caste-title slipped out of his lips. Hearing that, Naresh Thakur was caught off guard for a moment. But he recovered at once, and told Jibon what he had said to Dukhe one day, 'Truth doesn't feed you. You haven't been possessed by any Yudhisthira that you can't lie! There's nothing wrong with the name you use, but just make sure you mention a high-caste title. After all, it's cooking. If you mention "chandal" and so on, people won't eat what you touch.'

Naresh Thakur hailed from the Rayna region of Burdwan district in West Bengal. He had had more or less good times for half his life. The rest of his life too would have been spent in the same way if it had not been for litigation between brothers. He lost everything in the lawsuit and was left destitute. That was a long story, and now, compelled by circumstances, he donned a thread on his chest, masqueraded as a 'Chakraborty', and earned his livelihood as a cook. From his own life experience, he knew how the lords of caste viewed low-caste folk, and how much they despised them. It was true that adherence to all these notions of pollution and untouchability was much less now than before. A more liberal attitude could be discerned among people of the present generation. But some old-timers still remained. Their outlook had not changed at all, notwithstanding all the calamities of Hindu-Muslim riots and the partition of the country along religious lines.

That day, after work, Jibon had laid out a banana leaf on his gamchha and made a bundle of his food for the night. Because of a sudden downpour, those living far away were unable to attend the wedding. It was almost two miles from the bus stop on the main road to the site in Bikramnagar. It was a muddy road all the way, which got flooded as soon as it rained. Rickshaws were unwilling to ply along it. It was a strange law of the universe that one person's disaster was someone else's windfall! While the householder was lamenting the heavy rain and knocking his forehead in despair, Dukhe, Megha and Srinath were secretly smiling in glee—a lot of food would be left over!

It was half past one at night. When it was pretty clear that no one else would arrive, the householder was figuring out what could be kept and eaten tomorrow after heating, and what could be kept in the fridge and saved for a few days. And he had handed over the rest of the food to Naresh Thakur, saying, 'What am I to do with all this food, I'll have to throw it all away. It's better if you people take it.'

Jibon went home late that night with his bundle, walking through rain. He was returning there after almost ten days. Actually, he had to find his way there. Inhuman circumstances had made him forget the road, the house, and the people at home, who should have been his most dearly beloved and intimate ones. In his parents' eyes, Jibon was a mean rascal, a cruel denizen of hell. And so, Jibon could not go there even if he wanted to. He roamed the city, bearing a burden of grief in his heart. He tramped the streets searching for a way whereby he could find sustenance.

But now Jibon felt as if he had found a feeble ray of hope. If he worked with Naresh Thakur and learnt the job well, then he too could survive, just like so many people in the city did. Jibon wanted to deliver the bundle and convey the news to his parents. He wanted to say: Ma, I have grown up now, I've learnt to earn a livelihood! Look, here's my first remuneration!

It was terribly dark everywhere. And besides, it was raining. Water had leaked through the plastic-sheet roof of Garib Das' shanty, and it was full of slime inside. His siblings had been made to lie down in a slightly dry spot, while the parents crouched in a corner like accursed souls. Jibon reached the front of the shanty and called out: 'Ma, open the door.' After that, he woke up his siblings. He unfolded the bundle in his gamchha, which contained luchis, mutton, fish, chops, pulao, sweets and so much more! Even Garib Das had never eaten such food in all his life.

Jibon's younger brother, Jatan, had accidentally spilt hot water from a kettle on his foot while working in a tea-shop, and so, he was home too, nursing his blistered feet. He looked at the food with astonishment. 'What's this called, Dada?'

'It's called fish fry.'

'And that one?'

'It's called ... wait, let me remember ... it's called chhanar kaliya. And this is called pulao. This thing here is plastic chutney.'

Plastic! With which mugs and buckets were made! Jugol, Jibon's youngest brother, took some on his finger, licked it and said, 'Liar! It's sweet!'

After several years, on this stormy night, amidst darkness, the five people living in the shanty had all sat down together to eat. It was the first time in any of their lives that they had tasted such delicious food. They didn't even know the names of many of the items. But at least today, they seemed to be very happy. As if it was a festive night. As if the night had declared that one person's loss could be the cause of gain for many other people. Well, if one person's loss turned out to be beneficial to many others, then there was nothing bad about that!

⁂

Work became a burden if the person working disliked it. He wouldn't be able to do it for very long. When someone did something out of compulsion, it never turned out well. But Jibon liked his work very much. Each joyful and festive event in the households where he went to work felt like his own. There was laughter and singing. He gradually learnt to cook from Naresh Thakur. He could make curries and kaliyas, koftas and kormas. He became adept at *chorbo-chosyo-lehyo-peyo*, that is, delicacies to chew, suck, lick and drink. Jibon soon became a culinary craftsman who was capable of making everything. And yet, Jibon thought he was merely picking pebbles at the shore of the vast ocean of knowledge.

The art of cooking was the last of the sixty-four arts, but it was an art which knew no limit, something that could never be complete. Jibon learnt that someone had devised a hundred ways of making an omelette, each one tasting different—something he had thought was ready as soon as one cracked an egg on a hot griddle! And then there was someone who knew how to make twenty-two kinds of biryani. He was apparently paid a fee of five thousand rupees, besides the plane fare, to go to some big hotel to prepare a special kind of biryani. Perhaps it was with such delectable food in mind that a disciple of Sri Ramkrishna had said: 'Poetry is most excellent, but even more excellent is music. More excellent than even music are women. And more excellent than that is food.'

Jibon was very keen to learn as much as he could. If he could find out about some big guru of the profession, he would happily sit at his feet to learn.

Jibon had grown up a bit now. He joined Naresh Thakur whenever there was work, and on the rest of the days, he went with Dukhe to dig earth, assist masons and do whatever else was available. His father, Garib Das could no longer work, he lay at home most days. Now that Jibon had started working, food was cooked once a day at home. But he was terribly afraid. What would happen if his father died? Jibon's earnings were so meagre that he wouldn't even be able to get him cremated.

What would he do in that event? Jibon had recently seen the wife and son of a railway porter who had died, lay his body on the road and beg people for alms so that they could cremate him. Jibon had been shaken to the core seeing the dead body. He would never be able to beg like that for anything. And he would not want anyone to have pity on him. What was the use of that? How could anyone give what they did not possess? The very belief that there was ever something called pity or kindness in the world had died in him. When people who were devoid of kindness and empathy flung ten paise towards a pauper, it was as if that money was tainted with disregard, ridicule, contempt and despise. Jibon no longer believed in the thing called kindness.

Take what happened just a few days ago. Jibon and his fellow-workers were all very poor. And so, a kind man had seemingly taken pity on them. But observing his pity, Jibon's whole being had blazed in rage. He had badly wanted to land a tight slap on the face of the babu pretending to be a 'good man'.

By now Jibon was able to handle the work of cooking for a hundred people with one or two assistants. And so, when the pressure of work grew during the wedding season, Naresh Thakur assigned him the responsibility, and sent him somewhere or the other. Jibon had also made a bit of a name for himself as the 'baby cook'!

On the day in question, Jibon and Dukhe had gone to work in a house. After the wedding feast was over, it was time for them to return home with their food bundles. As usual, the two of them had decided to pack the food and take it home. They spread out their gamchhas and laid banana leaves on them. The babus knew they would take it home. They were prepared for that. They put rice and a bit of all the items on the banana leaves. Considering that to be too little, Dukhe could not help saying, 'Please give us a bit more, babu, it's too little.' The kind man responded by saying, 'Just try to eat all of what I've given you and show me! We're supposed to provide food to you, not to let you stuff your bundles!'

Although the babu had given rather small quantities of the food items, the pot of rossogollas was full. It was a large earthen pot, of the size that could hold about three kilos of mishti-doi. The kind man said in a most generous tone, 'Take the whole pot.' Usually, the colour of rossogollas was white. In fact, if it was not white in colour, one couldn't even call it a rossogolla. But the rossogollas in question were more yellow than white. There was a reason for that. When the last batch of guests were eating, sweets had rained on their plates. The friends of the groom had used rossogollas as missiles to assault one another with.

'Hey, serve some on this plate!'

'No, no, no more, please!'

'I can't hear you. You have to eat one more.'

'My tummy will burst.'

'It won't.'

Whatever was eaten, found a place in their stomachs. Whatever wasn't, remained on their plates. Rather than throwing them away, the rossogollas had been picked up and kept in an empty mishti-doi pot. With which the cooks were being remunerated now. Observing that, blood rushed to Jibon's head in a surge of rage. 'What have you given us? We haven't come to your door to beg. We have been sweating from seven in the morning until twelve at night. We're merely asking for the remuneration for our labour.'

'Why are you getting angry? What happened?'

'What happened, you ask! Please have one of those and show us.' The kind babu was flabbergasted. Ashamed at his sleight being caught, he rushed inside the house to hide his face. Another person then handed out two rossogollas to each of them and slipped away. So now they were reluctant to give them any more than two pieces!

That's why Jibon viewed people's kindness with acute disbelief. After all, he had learnt the hard way. He had also been in another house once, and seen just the opposite of such kindness. On that day too, Dukhe was with him.

Their usual routine for a dinner event was to finish all the cutting in the morning, and then attend to all the boiling and frying required. Once that was done, they would eat something, rest a bit and then start cooking in the evening. In this way, the food served was hot, and there was also no worry about the food going bad by late night. So on that day, by the time they finished all the frying and so on, it was two in the afternoon. After washing his hands and feet, Jibon went to ask for food. 'Please give us our food now.'

'Food?' The householder looked surprised. 'What food?'

'Won't we eat?'

'What's it to me whether you eat or do something else?' The householder's simple response was, 'Naresh didn't tell me I'd have to provide food to you people in the afternoon.'

Dukhe muttered timidly, 'But that does not have to be said. We never need to say this anywhere. Everyone knows about it. That's why it's not mentioned specially.'

'I don't know about all that,' the householder said in no uncertain terms.

They had started working at seven in the morning, and hadn't had anything since then other than a few cups of tea. They were famished. And there were piles of food in front of them. The two starving cooks sat before all that food all day and half the night. There weren't even any shops nearby from where they could buy something to eat. They didn't have the option of pilfering any food either, because a man from the household was sitting on a chair in front of them all the time, keeping watch.

⚘

Naresh Thakur was faced with a serious problem today. He had on his hands two big jobs at the same time. If both had been around

Jadavpur, he could have handled it. But one of the jobs was in faraway Duttabagan, and the other in Behala. What was he to do now, he wondered. It was almost like they were at the two ends of the world. Where would he get all the required workers now? And simply getting hands was no good, they needed to know culinary work.

There seemed to be a surfeit of weddings this month. Wedding pandals were to be seen wherever one looked, on both sides of any road. Not a single cook Naresh Thakur knew was free. All of them had two or three jobs in hand on the auspicious dates. Naresh Thakur was at a loss regarding what he ought to do now.

When the job in Duttabagan had come up some fifteen days back, he had confirmed that and taken an advance. But the job in Behala suddenly came up a few days after that. And it wasn't just any ordinary client, but a childhood friend of Mahadev Kundu, the principal partner of Mahadev Decorators. The friend used to live in Jadavpur earlier. He had then built a house in Behala and moved there. But the distance had not affected their friendship. If anything, it had only brought them closer. Mahadev babu had told Naresh Thakur, 'It's my friend's daughter's wedding. There'll be seven or eight hundred invitees. You can't send anyone else there to cook. You have to be there, Naresh. If you pull a fast one on me, you're not going to get any more work from me. Remember that!'

It was Mahadev Decorators that provided Naresh work twelve months a year. He could not afford to antagonize Mahadev babu. But who would handle Duttabagan, a job that involved cooking for three hundred people?

Would Jibon be able to cook for three hundred people?

It was a simple menu. Rice, begun bhaja, dal, fish kaliya, mutton curry and chutney. Jibon was well trained now, he would be able to do it all right. If the menu had chops and luchis, he wouldn't be able to manage.

'Tell me, can you do it?' Naresh Thakur asked Jibon.

But it was Megha, one of the helpers, who replied, 'I tell you, Jibon can do it. Send Dukhe along with him.'

The job was for dinner the next day. Naresh Thakur sent them off that very evening. They could get the stoves and fuelwood and so on ready beforehand. He said, 'When you reach there, tell the babu that Naresh Thakur suddenly came down with fever. That's why he was unable to come and sent us instead. Make sure you tell him that. And when the job's done, ask him for the payment. He's paid an advance of ten rupees, so there's forty rupees remaining.'

The address had been written on a slip of paper. The directions had also been explained orally. They reached the address after an hour's journey by train and a further twenty-minute walk. They had no difficulty in finding the house. After all, it was not in the city, where people living in buildings did not know who lived on the floor above them. Duttabagan was a village. Everyone knew everyone else. And it was a well-off region. Although people did not have loads of cash, they were wealthy in terms of their harvest of paddy, jute, sesame, mustard and so on. Almost every family owned a hundred or a hundred-and-fifty bighas of agricultural land, and to cultivate the land, there were ploughs, bullocks, tractors as well as farmhands and cowherds employed throughout the year. Although the government had enacted a land ceiling law in the mid-1950s, which limited land ownership to about seventeen acres, it was full of loopholes. It was a simple matter to retain the land by registering it in others' names.

Jibon and Dukhe arrived at the ceremonial house in the evening. The compound of the house itself spanned almost three bighas of land. There was a pond, an orchard, a vegetable garden, as well as a cattle shed in the compound. Scattered here and there among the trees and greenery were several pukka and semi-pukka structures. But whatever the condition of the structures might be, there was a large, polished and beautiful courtyard in the middle. The head of the household, the landlord, reclined on an easychair in the courtyard. He did not have the pipe of a hookah in his hand, or else one might have mistaken him for a zamindar in a Bengali film. His bare torso seemed to glisten in the light of the Petromax lamp.

He had a muscular body and a hairy chest. There was a bracelet on his wrist and a gold chain around his neck. And a Brahmin's thread slung arrogantly around his chest.

The landlord had seven sons—which was why the house was also known as *shaatbheyer bari*, or 'seven-brothers' house'—and one daughter. All of them were married. Each of the daughters-in-law seemed to be walking jewellery stores. There were heaps of jewellery on their hands, ears, necks, heads and everywhere else. Jibon had never seen so much gold except in the showcase of a jewellery store.

The house had not yet been decorated. Or perhaps because Jibon was so used to seeing the lights and decorations in Calcutta, he did not know what the usual kind of decoration in such parts was like. There were two people at the entrance, putting up bamboo posts on each side. A gateway would come up there.

When Jibon and Dukhe went and stood before the landlord, seeing the ladles and spuds in their hands, he asked brusquely, 'Where's Naresh? Hasn't he come?' Hearing his voice, Dukhe began to tremble. He remembered an ancient saying of rural Bengal—'*jaar golay dhan, taar kothay taan,* the one with paddy in his granary, has a voice extraordinary'. Hearing his voice, he realised this babu's granary was indeed large.

In trepidation, Dukhe replied, 'He suddenly ...'

'He suddenly fell ill, isn't it?'

'That's what he said.'

'Look there!'

'Where?'

'There!'

In an empty space in front was a pile of lengths of hewn wood, stacked high. That would be used for firewood tomorrow. Pointing to that, the landlord said, 'If the food turns out bad, I'll break one of those on your backs ... Thinks he's too clever ... Thinks he can send just anyone here and get away with it. If he couldn't come he should have said so. Is there any shortage of cooks here! Which of you is the cook?'

Frightened, Jibon pointed at Dukhe, while Dukhe pointed at Jibon. Seeing their nervous state, the landlord said, 'I don't need to know who'll cook. I'll just look at the food. If it's bad, I'll have the skin off your backs, I warn you!'

The cooking area had been readied on one side of the courtyard, under a tarpaulin sheet. Arriving there, Dukhe trembled with fear—who knew what would happen. Hearing that the cooks had arrived, everyone in the house came to have a look. As if a thief had been apprehended, none of those who came had anything nice to say. Everyone seemed to be in a frenzy to thrash the thieving impostors, and to sling them right away on the gallows.

The place given to them to stay the night was an open verandah outside the house. There was a jute field in front of that. If someone crept through the field, there was no way anyone could spot them. Dukhe was unable to sleep out of fear. Later at night, he whispered to Jibon, 'Jibon, hey Jibon, let's run away. One can't be sure about the cooking. Sometimes it's good, and sometimes it's bad. One can't be certain about who Ma Annapurna is annoyed with and when. If things turn out bad, we won't be able to leave this house with our lives intact!'

Full of self-confidence, Jibon silenced him. 'Tomorrow's job can be thought about tomorrow. Only if the food's bad will he thrash us—he won't beat us before that. Keep quiet and go to sleep, Dukhe-da. Have faith in me.'

'But I'm scared ...'

'There's nothing to be worried about. Go to sleep.'

Jibon was no great soul blessed with powers of divine speech. What was the guarantee that his words would turn out to be true and that there was really no need to be frightened! Dukhe was indeed scared. It was almost as if his fear had incarnated into a myriad demons who hovered around him with gaping maws. He was unable to sleep. He stayed awake most of the night.

The cooking began the next morning. Dukhe instructed Jibon, 'You must check each and every item. Get the babu's approval for salt, spice and taste. Don't take the food off the fire until they say it's good. Let's see whether we can somehow get through this calamity by God's grace.'

Jibon knew how to ensure that the food turned out to be excellent. The stove had to burn properly, and the food ought not to get burnt. Salt and spice had to be just right. Everything had to be well-cooked. The cook's sense of application, care and measure was vital. He had to correctly follow the same procedure as during an earlier instance when the cooking was good.

The food did turn out to be excellent. It was indeed a major accomplishment on the part of Jibon at such a young age. The invitees, including those who were seasoned frequenters of feasts, relished and ate to their satisfaction, and praised the cooking. One of the guests also took their address; it was they who would cook for his son's wedding. A smile finally appeared on Dukhe's face, and Jibon felt the weight of responsibility lifting from his young shoulders. But just then, without any prior intimation, an unexpected calamity landed upon them.

⚘

The landlord of the house had seven sons and a daughter. The daughter was married to a man from Jadavpur. The son-in-law was in the transport business. He had a couple of lorries. He had earlier been a mastaan—a hoodlum in other words—who made the locality tremble in fear. He changed his ways after he got married, and became a worker of a particular political party. It was at his son-in-law's sister's wedding that the landlord of this house had tasted Naresh Thakur's food, and decided that he would bring this cook from Calcutta for his granddaughter's *annoprashon* ceremony, where the baby would be fed rice for the first time. But now, the son-in-law from Calcutta had recognised Dukhe.

It was very late at night. In rural areas, it was pitch black at this time. All the guests and visitors had eaten, stuffed paan in their mouths and taken their leave. The light from the Petromax lamps was close to extinguishing. Just then, the son-in-law called out to his youngest brother-in-law agitatedly. Pointing at Dukhe, he shouted: 'You had the cooking done by this fellow! How disgusting!'

The young brother-in-law could not understand what the matter was. He asked, 'Why, what happened?'

'This banchod cleaned our drains day-before-yesterday. You fucker, you got some keowra or katua or scavenger to cook for you without bothering to find out what his caste was?'

This was a dire offence indeed. A person who cleaned drains was untouchable. Let alone touching a Brahmin's food, even coming into his sight was an unpardonable offence. It was not only about what he had done – how he had the gall was the main issue now. After all, this was cheating, a fraud, deception.

The son-in-law's enraged eyes were as red as hibiscus. After having sat in the concealment of the banana grove, downing two bottles of country liquor with hot and spicy mutton liver, his tongue was a bit swollen. His speech slurred. He called Jibon and Dukhe and took them towards the same banana grove, which lay in darkness. 'Come here! Stand straight. Tell me the correct answers to whatever I ask you! First of all, tell me your names! Tell me your dad's name!'

Jibon and Dukhe were illiterate, low-caste, labouring folk. They knew how to dig earth, break stones and harvest paddy. They did not know how to make a garland of words like a skilled wordsmith, and prove truth to be false and falsehood to be true. How could two ordinary bumpkins from rural Bengal do what was possible on the part of a clever, educated person? And so, with just a bit of interrogation, and some ordinary third-degree treatment, they blurted out their names and personal details in distress. It was found out that one was a Keowra, and the other a Chandal. In the caste system, both were untouchable, polluted—people from whose hands water could not be drunk.

The darkness and desolation of the night seemed to exacerbate the son-in-law's caste pride. He possessed physical strength, a mean mind, money in his pocket and liquor in his belly. He dragged the two unfortunate wretches to the middle of the empty field on the further side of the banana grove. The slaps and punches that had rained down on them so far were merely by way of routine investigation. Now the court's verdict was declared: 'Rub your face on the earth and crawl till that jackfruit tree. Keep saying that you'll never enter a Brahmin's kitchen!'

On the way back, neither of them said a word. Jibon and Dukhe didn't even raise their heads to look at anyone. Both of them were scorching to death, each one in his own way, in a secret agony. After a while, Dukhe broke out in a wail, '*Ora kyan marlo re Jibon!* Why did they thrash us?'

Jibon did not know the answer to that. But after a few days, Mahadev babu, of Mahadev Decorators, somehow got the news that they had stolen something and got caught, and that they were thrashed and then let off.

2

Poisoned Life

In 1967, a spark erupted in a village called Naxalbari in north Bengal. Within just three years, it had turned into a widespread prairie fire. Its blazing red flames spread across India. The flames scorched the inertia, cowardice and regressiveness of people as the youth of the society flung away every kind of attachment to self-interest and shed their blood in self-sacrifice. A world-famous leader had likened them to a 'morning sun'.

This time of uprising against exploitation and deprivation, was a terribly hostile one for Bimala, who was a very ordinary village woman. It was a beastly and destructive time. It seemed as if an enormous quantity of poisonous gas had accumulated somewhere deep beneath the soil, and it was that which was now exploding incessantly everywhere. The body of the old society was being bloodied and torn to shreds. The entire city of Calcutta was trembling in fear. The stormy wind of Naxalbari shook the locality of Jadavpur, making everyone shudder. It seemed all the stately buildings there were about to be pulled down and ground to dust. The city folk were living in the grip of terror and trepidation. Irrespective of whether they were employed or unemployed, traders or customers, wealthy or destitute, dark-skinned or fair-skinned, high-born or low-born—the hearts of every kind of person trembled. The destructive and rebellious decade of the seventies had trudged and finally arrived in the city. The dawn of the new decade brought hope for some, and was a cause of anxiety for others. The seventies carved out a special place for itself among all the decades. Unbeknownst to anyone, under cover of the darkness of night, some people, full of conviction, had painted the slogan on wall after wall in Calcutta—*shottorer doshok muktir doshok!* The seventies is the decade of liberation!

Come morning, the relentless, hideous sound of country-bombs exploding began. As the day progressed towards night, the sound went from loud to deafening. The air was thick with the acrid smell of gunpowder. And in the darkness of night, black police vans with beaming searchlights raced through the main thoroughfares. They surrounded one locality after another on the pretext of carrying out search operations, and pounced upon the people there. If they spotted any youth aged between eighteen and twenty-two, they dragged him into the police van. Any youth was now suspect in their eyes, he was viewed as an offender. It was a lawless time indeed.

In such a contagious time, Bimala's eldest son seemed to be changing by the day. He never smiled, never spoke. He seemed to be grave and angry all the time. It was not at all clear why he was angry, or who he was angry with. It was as if he had grown unrecognisably in the span of just a few days. He had become so tall that he could not be measured, and he seemed to have acquired a depth that was unfathomable. And so Bimala was very scared and anxious.

The times were not at all right. As though some kind of inauspicious preparation was afoot everywhere. A frenzy, very similar to the time of the communal riots following the Hazratbal incident, could be discerned among most people. People seemed to be changing somehow. In the way an ant sniffed the air and sensed approaching rain, a poor mother trembled in fear whenever processions of people holding flags aloft thick lathis thronged the nearby lanes and streets and the menacing cries of '*Lorai lorai lorai chai,* We want to fight, fight, fight' rent the air. She seemed to realise that the time of many mothers' laps being rendered bereft was fast approaching.

⁂

Jibon had come home today after a long time. There was no certainty nowadays regarding his movements. Who knows where he went, what he did or what he ate. He wasn't working anywhere now. When he was working, the family's condition had been somewhat sound. Now, once again, they were all in the grip of the octopus called poverty. Garib Das did not get any work nowadays. No one called him for work. He used to sit in front of a ration shop. He carried a load or two and earned a rupee or a rupee-and-a-half, which was too little to feed the family.

Bimala's heart wept seeing her son. What had he done to his appearance? Observing him, it seemed he was in some deep pain. Even if he never said so, it wasn't difficult for his mother to see that he was hungry. There was a little bit of wheat-flour at home, she quickly made a roti for him with that. She gave him some salt and a green chilli to eat it with. Jibon was silent. He ate the roti in silence. Bimala was not so worried about her other two sons; about whether they got enough to eat or not, at least they were in front of her eyes. All her worries were regarding Jibon. His altered, strange behaviour made Bimala very anxious.

⁂

Garib Das's family now had a decent shelter to stay in temporarily. There hadn't been enough space for everyone in the railside shanty, and besides, the railway authorities had also threatened to demolish the shanties if the dwellers did not leave voluntarily. But the new place was large enough for everyone to lie down and sleep.

There was a gentleman who lived in Jorhat, in Assam. The *Bongal khedao*, or 'drive out Bengalis' movement in Assam had turned fierce of late. The homes of Bengalis were being burnt down by the Assamese, they were being beaten up, wounded and even murdered. Seeing the persecution, the gentleman realised that he would not be able to live in Assam for much longer. He would have to wind up his business affairs there and flee to West Bengal. In that case, the foremost requirement was a roof over his head. A relative of his by marriage lived in Calcutta. Through him, he became acquainted with Hemanta babu of Ramakrishnapur, and with the assistance of Hemanta babu, he purchased four katthas of land in Shyampur colony, which was beside Raja Subodh Chandra Mallick Road, right opposite the colony in Ramkrishnapur.

Once the forcibly occupied colonies established by the better off, upper-caste folk from East Bengal obtained government recognition, some people who had also occupied plots in other colonies, retained the plot they liked and sold off the other one. With the money obtained thereby, they were able to complete the construction of their house and make it a fully pukka structure. Some people also kept just a single room for themselves and rented out the remaining three or four rooms, and were thus able to obtain a good monthly income for themselves. It was like the saying in Bengali, *'machher tele machh bhaja',* or frying fish in its own oil, or like eating a couple and putting away a couple in the fridge, thus proving their astuteness. After all they had educated, cunning heads!

So after the gentleman from Assam bought the land, it was time to build his house. He was also a businessman. He left two katthas vacant and began laying the foundation of a two-storeyed building on the remaining two katthas. The vacant space was used to keep the bamboo, bricks, sand, stone-chips and other building materials. He planned to sell the remaining two katthas, at double the price, a few years after building his house. In short, like everyone else, he too would thus end up recovering the construction cost. But who would keep watch over all the building materials while the house was being built? He could not disregard his business and be there all the time. What would happen to all the sand, bricks and stone-chips in his absence? After all, it was a refugee colony. Almost everyone was involved in house construction, so if someone pilfered the materials at night, who would stop them?

Hemanta babu said to him, 'I'll get you a watchman.'

'Is the man honest? Or will he make off with the materials! There's almost two hundred bags of cement there.'

Allaying the fears of the gentleman from Assam, Hemanta babu told him, 'Not everyone can actually be dishonest just because they want to. That requires guts. The person I'm thinking of posting here does not have the guts.'

Garib Das's wife, Bimala, worked in Hemanta babu's house. It was from her that he had heard about the impending demolition of the railside shanty settlement. Where would she go if the shanties were demolished? They would either have to go back to faraway Khola, or rent a room locally for ten rupees a month. If they were allowed to stay on the gentleman's property without paying any rent, wouldn't they do that?

Hemanta babu sent a message for Garib Das through Bimala, asking him to come and meet him. He said to Garib, 'We'll give you a room. There are bags of cement on one side of it, but you can stay on the other side. Keep a watch over the stone chips and sand lying outside. And when the masons are at work, you can work along with them. I know your health is not so good. If you're unable to do it, your son can work. He'll get the wage that everyone gets. Let the shanty beside the rail line remain. If it's not demolished you can go back there later.'

Jibon worked on the gentleman's construction until the lintel of the house had been erected. In between, he also went with Naresh Thakur to cook at feasts for a couple of days or so. The construction work on the house had been halted for a few days right now. But after returning from the ill-fated cooking job in Duttabagan, Jibon didn't go out in search of any other work. He just sat at home morosely. He did not tell his parents, or even his brother Jatan, what had happened. Jibon had never been so grave. What did this sudden solemnity signal!

The decade of the seventies had now swiftly pounced upon this city. As soon as it turned dark, the character of the city that dozed during the day changed, and it suddenly became active. Some people engaged in whispers, while some people walked or ran, fleeing or chasing somebody. A few days back, a body with the throat slit had been found beside the Rajpur Canal. The fact that her son had suddenly grown up and turned grave at such a time alarmed Bimala. No longer did Jibon fear the dark and ghosts and rush to his mother to hide his face in her lap, as he used to when he was a child. No longer did he tremble in fear at the sound of thunder and lightning on stormy days. It would have been so much better had Jibon remained like that. If nothing else, his mother would have been free of anxiety in these murderous times.

⊙⊱⊙

After a while, in a voice tinged with fatigue, Bimala said, 'You don't say anything about where you go and what you do. Your father's grown old. He can hardly walk now, so how will he work? You don't work any more either, so how will the family survive? When you were small, it didn't matter. But you've grown up now. If you still just wander around without a care, what can I say! You went and lived somewhere or the other for a few years ... let's forget about that, but you were working so well for the last few months, and then you suddenly dropped everything. How can we survive if you do that?'

Jibon did not say anything. What could he say? What did he have to say? His mother's plaint was nothing out of the ordinary. It didn't have an answer. But there was in fact an answer, which would make the hearts of all mothers turn to ice.

Bimala was a simple, straightforward girl from rural Bengal. Their bodies grew older, but their minds remained as soft as ever. It was not so easy for one whose heart was as soft as rain-drenched earth to fathom subjects such as the violence and complexity in the world. Garib Das's father had told his son, and he in turn had told his son, Jibon: '*Baapre, khaat khete ja. Kaajer bhoy korish na. Jodi khaat-te parosh, aar kichhu na houk na khaiyya konodin thakbi na.* My dear, work hard, keep working. Don't be afraid of work. If you can work hard, at least you'll never go hungry.' Obeying his father, Garib Das had worked very hard, but he still went without food. Why was that? Who would explain that?

The time when Harkumar Das had repeated to his son what he in turn had heard from his father, was gone now. Perhaps at that time, man had a sensitive mind. But now, mechanical civilisation had transformed man too into a heartless machine. Who cared not for his soul or the Supreme Soul, for sin or good, or heaven and hell. Who lacked morals or ethics. His only attachment was to aggression. As a result of which, the one who had power, only wanted to wring, squeeze, extort from and exploit the people and environment around him, and fill his coffers thereby. He did not care about whether anyone died or cried.

There was a story in the Puranas about the gods and demons churning the sea. The churning yielded a lot of things, the elixir of life was also obtained. But even that did not quench their greed. The elixir would grant immortality if consumed. And yet, even after that, these heartless machines hoped for something greater. They churned the sea again, and then there emerged a deadly poison.

Powerful and greedy people had wrung the society dry, taking everything it possessed. And yet their souls were unsatisfied. Despite sitting on a mountain of resources, they continued to cruelly demand and extort from the body of society. Life was becoming stricken with the poison of hunger, unemployment and poverty. Everything was withering from the poison. That was why from the mountains, dense forests and soil of the terai region in north Bengal, a kind of deadly poison, to which they had given the name 'class hatred', had occupied this city. And it seemed Jibon too had begun to discern the presence of that hatred in his heart.

After a while, Bimala spoke again. Your maijya bhai has left the tea-shop he used to work in earlier and started working in an eatery. His salary there will be five rupees more. If the younger one can also get work somewhere, he'll be able to get something to eat. Why don't you see if you can put him somewhere? Say something!'

Breaking his long silence, Jibon said, 'What can I say? I've worked in tea-shops and eateries. I've seen the whole country. I've begun to hate such work!'

At a loss, Bimala asked him, 'So you're not going to work anymore?'

'What work shall I do?'

After a pause of silence, Jibon continued, 'I worked until my hands and feet began to rot in the water, and yet I did not get paid. After carrying loads the whole month, I was shown the thumb when I went to collect my salary. After burning in the fire and getting boiled in the heat all day, instead of being paid, I had to rub my face on the earth and crawl. I can't accept such work anymore!'

Bimala was stupefied. 'Made you crawl! Who made you crawl?'

'Who else!'

Bimala had no idea what Jibon was talking about. She said, 'What will you do if you don't work? How will you survive?'

Inwardly, Jibon ruminated. Survive! Is living like this called survival? What's the use of living like this, worse than dogs and cats? We have nothing—neither any dignity, nor food for the belly—so what's the great loss if such a life ceases to exist? So many people have so much, their storehouses are spilling over. And our pot is completely empty. No, not exactly empty—there's lots and lots of humiliation and oppression. Where's the need for such a life? This was a life that continued merely because death had not arrived, as if one was alive only because death had disregarded them and turned its face away. A life in which death had to come, not honourably but furtively, like a thief, its face concealed, on tiptoe, silently. Where was the need anymore for such a life? One day, Garib Das too thought the same way. He thought he would throw himself under a train and put an end to his life of humiliation. There was nothing more to be gained by prolonging such a life.

⁂

That was about five or six months after moving to Shyamnagar. Jatan had left his job of washing utensils at the eatery, and was at home. A year-and-a-half or two years younger than Jibon, the boy loved his mother very much. He thought he had grown up now. Now he too could work as a casual labourer and earn much more than at the eatery. Dada had gone awry. Unless he assumed the responsibility of the family, everyone would starve to death. And that is what he did. He assisted a building mason from Murshidabad. Once again, food began to be cooked once a day in Garib Das's household.

It was around the time of Eid. Eid was for Muslims what Durga Puja was to Hindus. The mason had gone home after a year, for eight or ten days. And so, Jatan was without work. None of the boys from *bhadralok* households nearby mixed with or played with them, they did not even speak to them unless there was some necessity. Not having anything else to do, Jatan played danguli with his younger brother, Jugal. He roamed around here and there when he was idle.

One evening, a group of youths from Ramakrishnapur colony arrived at Garib Das's shelter. A person by the name of Sushil had brought them there. They caught hold of Jugal and took him to their neighborhood. Why? What had Jugal done? He had stolen a duck! Who saw him stealing it? No one saw that. Then how was it being said that Jugal was the thief?

A person said, 'One doesn't need to see everything. Everything can be known by assumption.' His logic was simple—for all these years, no one here had anything stolen from them. It was only after these people had come here that thefts had begun. So who were the thieves? If his elder brother had been around, one would have known that he was responsible. But he wasn't here, while Jugal was, which meant that he was the one who had done it. And together with that, this person was also worried about the future. He stole a duck today, and unless he was punished now, he would break a lock tomorrow, and commit a burglary the day after. After all, it is said, *kolagachh kat-te kat-te golakata shekhe,* that while cutting a banana stem, they learn to slit the throat. Something needed to be done before all that!

What needed to be done?

He had to be taught a lesson so that he never stole again.

In order to teach him such a lesson, Jugal was tied with a rope to a lamp post. Then the thrashing began. 'Come on, tell me where's the duck? Did you eat it, or did you sell it? Tell the truth, and I'll let you go. Or else, I'll thrash you all night. Come on, tell me where's the duck?'

These were the youths who caught hold of wandering lunatics, accusing them of being child lifters, and then lynched them. They once thrashed a bus-driver when his brake failed, and sent him to hospital. They set street dogs upon the rag-picking man and enjoyed the show. They gave a bleeding nose to a rickshaw-puller on the pretext that he had asked for too high a fare. They did all this in the name of 'social service'. A group of cunning people had very skillfully perverted the behaviour of such half-educated, unemployed youths of this time. Through various means, they used these budding mastaans for the party's interest, and for their own personal gain. They were made to stand up against those who wrote on the walls, 'The seventies is the decade of liberation!' Because they loved to fight. That was their favourite sport. They only needed a rationale to thrash someone, a pretext, an excuse.

They had found one now. Jugal had stolen a duck. That's why he was being beaten up.

Garib Das had been lying down. When the youths of that neighbourhood called Jugal and took him away, he did not know why they had taken him. His sons worked hard all day so they could get food to eat, they didn't hang around with anyone, so how was he to know what was going to happen when someone took one of them away! After all, people sometimes came to call Garib Das too. A few days ago, a dog was run over by a car and killed at the Jadavpur bus-stand. Following the common procedure of removing the dead dog, free of cost, from their locality, people at the bus-stand covertly tied it to the back of a brick-laden lorry coming from Garia. While returning after unloading the bricks, the rope snapped, and the dead dog lay in front of Sushil's house. Sushil's elder brother came to call Garib Das. 'Garib, please do something! It's lying right in front of my house.' In exchange for eight annas, Garib dragged the dog and threw it in the garbage dump beside the railway line. Garib had thought that the youths were taking Jugal along for something like that, something which Brahmins, Kayasthas and people of the babu class did not handle themselves.

But now they had tied Jugal to a post and were thrashing him. As soon as he heard about it, he lifted himself up. The neighbourhood lay across the road along which buses plied. He ran on his wobbling legs to protect his son. Jugal's lip was cut and bleeding, and he had a hideous black eye. He fell at the feet of the incensed youths and wept imploringly. *'Babugo ore aar mairen na. Polay mor shara dupar kichhu khaite paay nai. Marle moira jabe.* Dear babu, please don't beat him any more. My son hasn't eaten all day. If you beat him, he'll die.'

Garib Das's words lent them stronger grounds for beating Jugal even more. A hungry person had no regard for any ethics or morality, or any rules and laws. It's because he hadn't eaten that he stole the duck. He would sell the duck and eat now.

Someone said, 'He couldn't go to Sandhyabazar to sell it. He was caught before he could do that. The duck is still hidden somewhere. Give it back and take your son away, or else, the thrashing continues.'

How could Garib Das return what had never been taken? Could a father bear to see his son being beaten before his eyes? When another round of thrashing began, he threw himself upon the boy. With his weak frame, he shielded Jugal from the terrible assaults.

Jugal wailed, '*Ami churi kori nai, Baba,* I didn't steal it, Baba.' Blood oozed out of his nose. He was drenched in sweat, blood and mud.

Sushil was the leader of the belligerent fellows. His father had a huge, sparkling garments shop at the Jadavpur bus-stand. He was the second of four brothers. He pulled Garib Das away from Jugal. Sushil consumed milk, butter and raw gram, and exercised at the gymnasium of Manatosh Roy's disciple, Paran-da, He flung Garib on the metalled road with his strong arms. 'Get out from here! Or else we'll thrash you too!'

The inner anguish Garib Das felt as he lay on the metalled road was far worse than the wounds inflicted on his body. He had never imagined that he would one day suffer such abject humiliation. Whenever he was called for any work in the two colonies, Shyamnagar and Ramakrishnapur, he went to attend to it if he was well enough. He did the work diligently. There was no one in the two neighbourhoods as poor as him, and as available for menial tasks. After all the work he had done for them, he had the impression that the babus were fond of him. He now realised, through his aching bones, how misguided that was. Madhai Haldar had told him, '*Babuder bhalobasha aar mosholmaner murgiposha soman. Ei khund khete debe to porkkhone niye golay ponch marbe.* The fondness of babus is like a Muslim who raises chickens. He feeds you grain one moment, and slits your throat the next.'

Sushil's assault had shattered his belief, his illusion of fondness, and ground it to dust. What was the use of such a love-starved, humiliating life? Garib Das rose up and began running like a lunatic towards the railway line. He would lay his head on the railtrack and free himself of the torment of such humiliation. Jibon was not at home at the time. He was waiting at the bus-stand for something. It was about nine or ten at night then. The streets were desolate. Seeing his father running like a possessed man on the desolate road, he stopped him. He found out about everything and took Garib Das back home. He bandaged his father's chafed knee. Jugal returned a short while after that. Because the duck had been found. Where was it found? To the east of Raja Subodh Chandra Mullick Road, was the suburban drainage canal which went past the colony, through Loharpara, beneath the railway line near Garib Das's erstwhile shanty, and continued all the way till Dhapa. The duck was sitting on a dense clump of water hyacinths on the drain. For some reason, it had been frightened and started quacking, and so it was discovered there.

They had taken Jugal away slightly after evening. From then, until nine or ten at night, he was beaten up merely on the suspicion of theft. Hundreds of people from both sides of Raja Subodh Chandra Mullick Road had seen it happening, over the long stretch of time. But no one lifted a finger. No one said—Stop it! Because everyone knew Garib Das was poor, low-caste and an outsider. He did not belong to the neighbourhood. Who cared if he was in distress!

Even if no one else cared, Jibon did. Seeing his father's and brother's bruised bodies, he too wanted to shed blood and finish Sushil off. But where did he have the wherewithal to be able to do that?

And by the time Jibon did have the wherewithal, Sushil got a tumor in his head, bade farewell and departed, plunging his newly-wed wife into the agony of widowhood. He was beyond Jibon's reach.

⚘

Garib Das had returned home now. He had made two trips, carrying the loads of rice and wheat of customers at the ration shop to Narkelbagan, and earned thirty paise from each of them. He tightly held his half-day's earnings in his sweaty right fist, and in his other hand was a bit of dusty rice wrapped in a bundle in his gamchha. A truckload of rice from the Food Corporation of India warehouse had arrived at the ration shop today. One of the sacks of rice was a bit torn. Some rice had fallen on the ground while the coolie was carrying the sack on his head to the godown of the ration shop. Garib had gathered and scooped it up.

He entered his house as Jibon was eating the roti. He said fretfully, 'Feed him, Jibon's Ma, feed your son and make him strong! If he's not strong, how will he work? He's worked hard and come. Get him another roti.'

Garib was scared seeing Jibon now. It was Rakhal Master who had put the fear in his head. 'Do you know, Garib bhai, an idle mind is a devil's workshop. Your son doesn't work, he sits idle. You can be sure he's plotting some nasty design. You don't know what's happening all around. It's all the doing of devious minds. If you put your sons to work, you'll see their heads naturally get back to normal. Your sons don't know how to read and write. Keep them occupied in whatever work they can do. Don't give them a chance, the times are very bad.'

Rakhal Das's fears regarding Jibon were not unfounded. It was quite natural for there to be such fears regarding any youth in the city. Just the other day, it had rained all night, and if it had rained a bit more, the water accumulated outside would have entered his room. Some people were running even in that fierce rain, people were screaming. In the morning, there were two dead bodies floating in the floodwater. Their age, appearance and clothes were all like Jibon's.

What if Jibon got involved in something like that, with people who were not afraid of killing or dying? It was out of that fear that Garib was chiding him. All he wanted was to see his son following the same path that he knew, beyond which he knew nothing. He should go to Baghajatin every morning and get to work. He should buy rice and potatoes in the evening and return home. Once home, he should eat and go to sleep at night.

Jibon finished eating the roti, stepped out of the room and said to no one in particular, 'I'm going.'

'Where are you going?' For some reason, there was a tone of despair in Bimala's voice. 'Hey Jibon, where are you going at this untimely hour! Don't go!'

Who knows what his mother wanted to say, but Jibon, who was about to leave, stayed back. He went and sat down on the pile of bricks outside and gazed at the metalled road ahead.

3

The Avenger

There seemed to be an unwritten rule in the Indian social system that someone who was powerful could oppress the weak, powerless and poor without any hindrance. He could simply do what he wanted. An impoverished father from a south Bengal village close to the border left his ten- or twelve-year-old daughter to work in a babu household. He thought the girl would live better thereby. But suddenly one day, the mistress of the family wanted to burn the girl. She did that too, using a cooking spud heated over fire. She scorched the girl's arm, leg, face and in as many as seventeen places. Of course, it was not done all on the same day, but every now and then, over a whole month. When matters went too far, meaning, when the girl's condition was such that she needed to be taken to a doctor, and some people were thinking of openly condemning it, an officer of the mighty and powerful Indian Police Service foiled all that by saying—'You see my wife has a mental problem, that's why she …'

Surobala Gayen, from the Sunderbans, used to work in a house. The house-owner wanted to have sex with her. He did that too, forcibly, one afternoon. If the wretched girl opened her mouth, his name and reputation would be sullied. So what should he do? He strangled her to death, hung her body on the fan hook, and left for his office or somewhere else, chewing a paan. Nothing happened to him. Because it was proved that the girl had done what any girl did after a love affair turned sour. It was a very commonplace incident. So many incidents like this take place.

The half-crazy schoolmaster in Siliguri had said in bitter scorn—'If a sword is used, the head is severed. But there's no use blaming merely the sword. The neck was also to blame. Because it got severed. Why did it stick out? Why didn't the neck make itself so strong that the sword broke? Why didn't it move itself out of the way of the sword?'

Jibon sat dwelling on such nonsensical thoughts as he watched his youngest brother, Jugal, playing. Jibon loved this boy very much. When Jibon was small, he had no toys to play with. He had neither the opportunity, nor was he ever in the situation of being able to play. And that was still the case. Yet Jibon had bought his brother ten glass marbles, for ten paise. Jugal played with the marbles, while Jibon sat and watched his joyful, smiling face and sought to fulfil his own unfulfilled childhood aspirations.

Everyone who lived around them was more or less well-to-do, they were educated and respectable. They were people whose education, culture and civility taught them to view those who depended upon physical labour as lowly folk, people to be addressed disrespectfully as *'tui'*. They did not mingle with the lowly folk, and the *bhadralok* did not conduct themselves with them in the way they did with their fellow *bhadralok*. And so, Jibon and his family were in something like the situation of a 'boycotted' household in a village.

The plot of land they lived on was quite vacant. Jugal used to play there in the evenings with his younger sister, Anju. The children from the neighbourhood also played there. They would then drive away Jugal and Anju. Seeing their dirty clothes, unwashed appearance and matted hair, the children too realised they did not belong to their class. They were like animals from the wild jungles of Africa who could talk.

In this great land of Bengal, the terms 'low-caste', 'labouring' and 'lowly folk' were all closely related to each other. Those who were low-caste were the ones who carried loads, performed day labour, rode rickshaws and washed utensils in babu households. The people who did all such things were not the *bhadralok*. It was a vital duty of the *bhadralok* to be different from those who were not *bhadralok*. All their thinking and cogitation was confined to that. As a result, through socialisation, children too became infected with such thinking from their very childhood.

A rickshaw-wallah used to take two small girls to school on his rickshaw and bring them back home. One day, those daughters of Devkanti babu were laughing a lot and jabbering away as they sat on the rickshaw. Hearing the delightful chortle of the children, the rickshaw-puller's heart too danced in joy. He wanted to join in their chatter. Forgetting his station, he said in a tone of familiar intimacy, 'Will you come to my house, dear girls?' That was an unforgettable scene. An indescribable look of contempt came over the doe eyes of the girl with a round, moon-like visage. Making an ugly face, the eight-your-old girl had replied, 'You ride a rickshaw, no one will go to your house!' Even that little girl, who could not yet put her clothes on, had learnt that one did not go to a rickshaw-wallah's house, because he and she belonged to different castes.

And so, when five or six children came to play with a cricket bat and ball in the space in front of Garib Das's shed, they drove Jugal and Anju away and took over the whole field. It was true that there was no playfield for children in this neighbourhood. Those who were slightly older went to play in the field in the TB Hospital compound. Where were the smaller children to go? Chased away from the field, Jugal went crying to Jibon. 'Dada, they threw away my marbles. Two of them are lost.' Blood shot to Jibon's head. It was as if his humiliated soul burst into flames. We live here. The one who owns the land has allowed us to stay here. As long as we are here, we have a right over and above anybody else. Who's taken away that right? Who threw away my brother's marbles?

Who had the gall?

There have been plenty of major incidents in the world, which owe their origins to extremely ordinary and trivial incidents. In Jibon's life too, today, a similar turning point had arrived, by way of an apparently trivial incident. He ran into the field, pulled out the stumps and threw them away. 'Get out! You can't play here!'

The children went and wailed to their elder brothers about it. 'He's not letting us play there, he threw away our stumps.'

Five or six of the brothers ran to the field. One of them landed a slap on Jibon's face with great self-confidence. 'Banchod, you have the gall to throw away the stumps! You live in *our* neighbourhood and you try to lord over us! Go and get the stumps! Put them back where they were!'

A slap had landed on Jibon's face. It wasn't just a slap, this was like rubbing salt on a very old, still raw wound. He lost his senses. He forgot where he was, who he was among, and whether anyone would come and stand by him. He forgot about everything. In retaliation, he slapped the left cheek of the son of the leader of the neighbourhood, who was a few years older than him.

It was like a stone hitting a beehive. How could he escape? The five or six of them pounced on Jibon. A veritable storm of blows, slaps, kicks and punches struck Jibon's body. When the boys stopped, a thick stream of blood flowed from his nose and bloodied his chest. His face was badly swollen. When they left after having imparted the necessary education to him, Jibon rose from the dusty field. It was like a poisonous serpent raising its hood from amidst the ruins of some monument. He implored not God, but the devil, for a boon—O powerful one, give me strength, give me courage, shelter me in your bosom! Jibon then ran into his house. There was an axe in the house, the same one with which Garib Das used to cut wood in the forest in Bankura. There, emboldened by the axe,

Garib used to venture deep into the forest. He was not at all afraid of wild animals.

Jibon emerged from the room with the axe in his hand. War had been declared and so there was no question of turning back. He raised the axe and fell upon the violent animals posing as humans. The departing group of boys never imagined this would happen. Being caught unawares, they ran for their lives in whichever direction they could. Some of them went and hid inside their homes. The streets became empty. The doors of houses banged shut. Jibon stopped and looked all around. There was not a living soul anywhere in a radius of fifty feet. The whole place was like a liberated zone. And he was the lord of this zone. The inescapable maze that he had seemed to be trapped in just a little while ago had been smashed with a single blow.

Jibon had suffered a terrible ailment as an infant. And he had never eaten nutritious food. So he was skinny. He was shorter than the average Bengali. But now he felt as if he was taller than a two-storey building. And those whom he had feared so long, didn't even reach his knees.

There are two ways of dousing a fire. One is to pour water on it, and the other is to sprinkle petrol or kerosene. If one poured water, there remained the possibility of it catching fire again later. But in the other case, there was no risk of that. What Jibon had done was quite a bit like pouring petrol. However, the ashes that remained after the fire extinguished, flew around quite a bit for many days.

From amidst those embers, smoke and ash, Jibon commenced another kind of journey.

<hr />

It was almost ten at night. There had been a burst of heavy rain a little while ago. After a whole day of unbearable heat, the cool air was pleasing to the mind and body. Walking slowly along the empty pavement, Vivekananda babu arrived at Sealdah station. He worked in a famous jewellery shop in Bowbazar, whose advertisement graced the pages of the *Anandabazar Patrika* every week. It was in this shop that Maharaj Bhrigu, the nationally renowned fortune-teller, sat three days a week, that is, on Monday, Wednesday and Friday. Today, he had of his own accord told Vivekananda babu, 'Good times are coming for you!' Vivekananda babu walked towards Platform No. 12 in a cheerful frame of mind. The local train to Lakshmikantapur was waiting to depart. He boarded the train. But hey, what was this? Not a single seat was vacant. That never happened. Suddenly, his eyes fell on the seats on the left side of the door. These seats seated four persons, but five people could fit in. Everyone on this route did that too. But he saw that on one seat, there were not five, but four and a half persons. There was a boy of about twelve or thirteen. He was very skinny. He looked like he worked in a sindoor factory because his clothes and body were all covered in red dust. He was asleep on the seat, exhausted after eight hours of labour. Vivekananda babu advanced in that direction. He said in a very kindly tone, 'Boy, please shift a little so I can sit.' Without a word, the boy made place for him, and although the other four persons on the seat were a bit annoyed, none of them said anything. When one commuted daily, one had no option but to put up with such minor inconveniences.

There was a long way to go. Vivekananda babu's initial concern had been about getting a seat. Once that was done, he began to think about sitting comfortably. In a way that no one would know, he gently squeezed his body into place and then leaned his head back and closed his eyes. He had just begun to doze off, when the boy's head suddenly landed on his shoulder. He got a bit angry. He pushed away the head with his left hand. After some time, the head again landed on his shoulder. Once again, he pushed away the head, but this time more forcefully. That was so forceful that the boy's head knocked the head of the man seated on his left. The man cried out in pain, 'Ooh, ooh ...'

He was not one to remain silent. His face too conveyed such a demeanour. In such matters, offence was the prime means of defence. He roared at the sleeping boy, 'Get up! You're banging your head on me again and again. I'm telling you, get up! You can sleep at home. Get up!'

Someone stood up, but it was not the boy. It was another person, from the seat in front. He pinched Vivekananda babu's nose with his left hand and said in the rudest possible tone, 'You get up! This seat is not yours. He took pity on you and allowed you to sit. You don't deserve any pity. You can't sit here anymore since you decided to make him get up in return for his kindness. Get up! Or else I'll drag you up!'

Vivekananda babu had never imagined that something like this could happen. People wearing expensive clothes threatened others, while poor folk heard the threats in silence—that was the norm. What had never happened before had now started happening. But he tried desperately to save face. 'I'm a daily passenger, I travel with a ticket. Does he have a ticket? Travels without a ticket and sits on a seat too! Should people like us buy a ticket to stand all the way?'

'Who asked you to buy a ticket? Take your ticket home with you, wash it and eat it. But get up now! Get up first, and say whatever you have to after that.'

A clear struggle between the two classes of passengers—those who were able to buy tickets and those who weren't—commenced in the railway carriage. Because seventy per cent of the people in the carriage belonged to the poor class, they emerged victorious. Vivekananda babu eventually had to get up.

⁂

The green mangoes used for making pickles had to be immaculate. Mangoes that had fallen due to hail, or those with a mark of some kind, would not last long. The pickle would go bad. Coming upon green mangoes selling cheap in Kolay market, Ram babu could not resist buying five measures all at once. But the problem was carrying it to Sealdah station. After all, hauling twenty-five kilos of mangoes was not a simple matter. There were porters available to carry goods from Kolay market. But what with the charges demanded by the porters, it was like ants eating away the jaggery of profit. The mangoes would no longer be so cheap then. So what was he to do now?

It was an afternoon in the month of Jaishta. There was a pall of unbearable heat everywhere. Mangoes and jackfruits ripened in such heat. But would anyone be alive to eat them! Who on earth would eat the mangoes and jackfruits when everyone was dead!"

Ram babu found someone to help him in his plight. A boy, not exactly a boy, but most suitable to carry the sack of mangoes. He asked Ram babu, 'Do you need a porter?'

'You've got to carry it to the station, what do I have to pay you?'

'Give me a rupee.'

Ram babu was almost on the verge of dancing in joy. This was a third of what the other porters were demanding. He had not expected to find a porter so cheap. But what was the harm in trying to bargain with him? Why not see whether it could come down some more.

'Take eight annas.'

The boy calculated: a loaf of bread cost forty paise, a plate of alur-dam or ghugni cost thirty paise. Eight annas wouldn't suffice. He said, 'If you pay me seventy paise, I'll carry it there.'

'Listen, do something. Carry it to my house. I'll give you a rupee.'

'Where do you live?

'In Vidyasagar. It's not so far away, just a short distance from Jadavpur station.'

'Let's go.'

Ram babu was pleased at his canniness. It would have been a bit difficult for him to walk home in the hot sun with the heavy load. If he had taken a rickshaw from Jadavpur station, he would have had to pay at least two or two-and-a-half rupees.

The boy brought the sack of mangoes alright to Sealdah station, and he carried it to the train as well. But after getting off at Jadavpur station, he began to wobble as he carried the sack on his head.

Who knows whether that was because of the heat or his weakness from hunger. After walking fifteen minutes, he stumbled and fell down. The sack burst open and the mangoes scattered on the road. Damaged mangoes were no longer good for pickles. All his effort and expense had been in vain. Blood rushed to Ram babu's head. He landed a tight slap on the boy's cheek. The boy had just stood up after having fallen. He fell to the ground again with the slap. His lip was cut and began to bleed.

It was about two in the afternoon, the hottest time of the day. It was as if the sky was spewing out fire. The tar on the metalled road, on which buses plied, bubbled in the heat. There was no one on the streets. An indifferent crow sat on a dead tree and cawed. A stray dog sat in the water in a drain and panted with its tongue hanging out. A few labourers were eating their afternoon tiffin in a tea-shop. Suddenly someone emerged from the tea-shop. He had an onion in one hand, and a knife in the other, with which he had been cutting onions. 'Why did you hit the boy?'

Ram babu mumbled, 'My mangoes ...'

'Pick him up.'

But the boy got up by himself. His lip was bleeding. He was drenched in sweat. He had tears in his eyes, anger in his head, and cuss words on his lips. 'You son of a bastard! Why did you hit me!'

The man with the knife shouted at him: 'Be quiet! Don't say a thing.' He brought water from the tea-shop and washed away the blood from the boy's face. Ram babu took out a rupee and offered it to the boy. 'Take it. I gave you my word, so I'm paying you. You don't have to go any further, I'll take a rickshaw and go home.'

The man who had been chopping onions took the money and gave it to the owner of the tea-shop. 'Give him some bread and milk.' After that, turning to look at Ram babu, he asked, 'Why did you hit him?'

'My sack, the mangoes ...'

'Fuck your mangoes! Fuck you! Why did you hit him?'

The owner of the tea-shop intervened in the quarrel. 'Now, now, don't lose your temper.'

'Give the boy five rupees. That's the fine for hitting him. Give it to him.'

'Five rupees! Did I do anything wrong?'

There was a murderous tone in the voice of the man who still had the knife in his hand. 'I tell you, pay him for your own good. Or else—do you see this?' He held out the knife threateningly. 'I'll run it on your throat!'

The tea-shop owner too trembled at the tone of his voice. He said, 'Give it to him, don't invite trouble. Just give it to him.'

There was an anxious apprehension in the tone of his voice, as well as the empathy of a genuine well-wisher, which Ram babu did not have the courage to disregard. He took out five rupees from his pocket. The mangoes were no longer good for pickling. His hard-earned money was lost for no reason.

Mathur babu was in the stone-chips trade. He bought wagons of stone-chips coming in by freight trains, and then sold them by the truckload. He owned several trucks. But he did not possess a motor car. Nor would he ever buy one. He was content to spend the rest of his life wearing dhuti-photua and Kolhapuri slippers, and riding on hand-pulled rickshaws. And yes, he also spoke only in his mother tongue, the dialect of people who lived by the river Padma in East Bengal. All the rickshaw-pullers at the Bondel Road railway crossing knew him well. The rogues did not want to take him. Once, out of breath after walking a little bit, he was compelled to get into a rickshaw. He hailed a passing rickshaw-puller at the Bondel Road railway crossing and got into it. The rickshaw-puller today was not at all after his own heart. He was like an old horse. This half-dead rickshaw-puller, who was bent over, was afflicted with tuberculosis. After going just a short distance, he was exhausted. He was pulling the rickshaw so slowly that it would have been quicker to walk instead. Mathur babu looked at his watch. It was ten past seven. If he could not reach Mudiali Lane by eight, he wouldn't be able to attend to the important task he had to do there. He urged the rickshaw-puller to hurry up. 'Come on, go faster, you *maura*!'

He reached Mudiali before eight, but by the time he finished his work, it was five past nine. There were monetary transactions involved, so it did require some time. From there, Mathur babu went to K.P. Roy Lane, in Tollygunge. And then he went to Jadavpur. He looked at his watch, it was twenty-two minutes past ten. It wasn't so late. He asked the rickshaw-puller to halt at the Jadavpur crossing. He took out some money from the pocket of his photua and counted out eight rupees. For some reason, he also took out eight annas in coins together with that. Possibly as baksheesh. He held the money out to the rickshaw-puller. 'Here, take it, my dear.'

Wiping the perspiration on his neck and brow with a dirty gamchha, the rickshaw-puller asked him in Hindi, 'How much have you given me, babu sahib?'

'Count it and see. I haven't underpaid you.'

'It's not enough. Give me twenty rupees.'

Not ten, or twelve, but twenty in one fell swoop! What the hell does the sattu-eating *maura* bastard think! Is this his thieving land, Bihar! 'Here, take it.' Mathur babu added another rupee-and-a-half to make it a full ten rupees. 'I won't pay you any more.'

The rickshaw-puller took the money in his left hand, but he did not move away. Unless he moved from his spot, it wasn't possible for Mathur babu to get off. The rickshaw-puller's demeanour was like that of the gatekeeper in a railway station. He held out his right hand. 'Give me more.'

'I already told you, I'm not paying any more.'

'You are not giving me alms. I worked, I'm asking for the price of that. Give me ten more!'

'Hey, you *maura* bastard, what's the fare from Bondel rail-gate to Jadavpur?'

'Don't abuse me, babu, talk properly. You went around from one place to another, and then came here—it's been three hours. But you pay me the fare for the direct trip? And then abuse me on top of that! Does the ride come free? You think pulling the rickshaw doesn't require labour?'

The maura was talking too much! Mathur babu was a gentleman. Or at least, no *bhadralok* would hesitate to give him a certificate to that effect. He was a plump man. He had a stapled bundle of rupee notes in his pocket. He didn't pull a rickshaw, he sat on a rickshaw. He could afford to do that. What other quality was required to be *bhadralok*? A rickshaw-puller was misbehaving with a *bhadralok*! It was natural for him to get angry. And he got angry. When someone got angry, he lost his head. Mathur babu did too. Remaining seated in the rickshaw, he raised his Kolhapuri-clad foot and brought it close to the rickshaw-puller's face. 'If you talk too much, I'll kick your face and break your teeth! You maura bastard, you come from Bihar and think you've become too clever!'

'Don't abuse me, babu. Pay me.'

'Pay you? You have a kick written in your fate.' Once again, Mathur babu brought his foot near the rickshaw-puller's face. The distance between the face and the foot was about five inches now. 'What kind of a *bhadralok* are you! If you don't have money, why did you get into a rickshaw? And you raise your foot to kick me! Here, take your money. Buy sweets for your children with it. Tell me if you need some more. I'll give you two rupees as alms.'

Mathur babu raised his foot once again. Once again he stopped it five inches away from the man's face. He was caught in a dilemma. He couldn't decide whether he should transgress that distance of five inches. 'I'll give you one kick and break your face! Talking above your bloody station! Move, move aside! I tell you, move aside!'

Mathur babu's foot remained suspended in the air. He suddenly heard someone's voice. 'If you're your father's son, let's see you kicking him. Kick him first and then talk!'

This was not Hindi. It was the pure dialect from the banks of the Padma! To Mathur babu's astonishment, an undesirable character intervened in the squabble. Beside the road was the pavement. There was a hair-cutting saloon on the pavement. The man had parked his backside on a brick and was having a haircut. The barber's cloth was around his neck. Concealed beneath the cloth, the man had a sharp razor in his hand. Without moving from his position, he shouted at Mathur babu, 'You've been showing him your foot again and again. What the hell do you think? You think you can thieve around as you wish! Do as you please? He's come from Bihar to work. He hasn't come to steal. What did he do wrong? You too came from Pakistan. Why did you come?'

Mathur babu was taken aback. He had never thought a fellow-countryman would oppose him in this fashion. He said quietly, 'It's between him and me. Who are you to speak in between?'

'Whoever I might be, let me see you kicking him! Come on, kick him!'

Mathur babu had never imagined that he would encounter such an ugly problem. But the man also provided him a way out. 'Either kick him or pay him the fare he's asking for.'

The man was no longer alone now. A crowd had gathered near him. They were shouting too—'You have to pay him twenty rupees!'

'Here it is. He took out a red-coloured twenty rupee note and gave it to the rickshaw-puller. He issued a threat with it: 'I know you now! I'll never get into your rickshaw again!' It wasn't clear whether or not the rickshaw-puller reacted to the threat.

⁂

The suburban town of Baruipur had a very special place in the lives of the people of south Bengal. That was where the famous fruit market Kachharibazar was. If you exited the Baruipur railway station and took the road going southwards, you came to a playfield. At different times of the year, various pujas, gatherings and public meetings took place there. The road going past the playfield wound its way behind the police station, and continued till it reached Kachharibazar. Buses plied on the road in front of the market.

There were plenty of large, shady trees on the road beside the playfield. Some eight or ten people had spread out sack-cloths on the edge of the road and sat down under the trees with weighing scales. They bought wheat wholesale. They got the wheat milled into flour and sold that. There was a great shortage of rice in rural Bengal. So poor folk consumed the wheat flour instead.

Every morning, just like trainloads of women arrived in the city from their villages to wash utensils in babu households, some of them also came for business purposes. A group of such women entrepreneurs crowded the front of the ration shops in the city. Whenever any ration-card holder didn't buy his wheat ration, they implored him, 'Dear babu, since you're not buying the wheat, let us buy that.' The babus didn't lose anything in the process, since the women themselves paid the price for the wheat. And besides, they felt good about being generous. Almost everyone yielded to their pleas. These women then sold the wheat to traders, and thus made a profit of eight annas a kilo.

It was afternoon now. A youth clad in a lungi and a T-shirt, who had got off the train and come here, stood under the shade of a tree. It was unbearably hot. Fire seemed to be raining down from the sun, which had now moved slightly to the west after being directly overhead. The scorching wind blowing over the earth was like the hot breath of the serpent king, Vasuki. The youth scanned the environs with doleful eyes. Because of the heat, there weren't very many people around. All those who had got off the train had moved away. A few cows sat in the shade of the trees beside the railing of the playfield, chewing cud tiredly. Spotting a closed tea-shop, the youth went and sat on the empty bench in front of that. His eyes were trained in front of him. Someone was supposed to come there. He was waiting for him.

Suddenly, his eyes lit upon a woman. She had a heavy sack on her head and a small baby in the crook of an arm. Who knows why, but he could not take his eyes off her. He saw the rheum in the corner of her eyes. She was very dark-skinned and terribly thin. Because she was a bit tall, her skinniness appeared even more pronounced. She looked like a palm tree shorn of branches. A small earthen cup hung from her neck. A century's despondency seemed to weigh down upon her dusty and mud-covered body. Looking at her face, one would think she had never had the opportunity to smile or be happy ever since she was born. As if an ocean of tears had occupied every corner of her life, and which could generate a terrifying cyclone at any moment. Grief, poverty, hardship, fatigue and a myriad hardships held her in a python-like grip.

Looking at all these folk, it seemed the great famine of 1943, which claimed three million lives, had not yet ended. No one knew when it would end. The woman seemed to be carrying, all by herself, the agony of all the mothers of the whole world's hungry infants in the crook of her arm. The baby moved from time to time, revealing that it was still alive. Or else, seeing the withered frame of skin and bones, one would have imagined it to be merely the skeleton of a child.

There was wheat in the sack on her head. Putting down the sack she had been carrying in front of a trader, she gasped for breath from her labours. Just then, the baby began to wail. 'O Ma, give me a roti, give me a roti, Ma! Ma, o Ma, give me a roti!'

The woman's chapped lips, her eyes brimming with tears, the rise and fall of her emaciated breasts as she breathed, and her panting as she hauled her body like a load-bearing animal—altogether, the image was a most sorrowful one. She consoled her child weakly, 'Be quiet for a while, dear, I'll feed you as soon as I finish with the wheat.'

The trader was wearing a finely-woven checked lungi and he had a rectangular silver amulet on his neck. He was bearded, chewing paan, and there was cunning in his demeanour. He began weighing the wheat with his hand-held weighing scale. 'Here's one. That's one. ... Here's two, it's two. ... Here's three. It's three ...' Suddenly, the youth sitting on the bench spotted the trader's sleight of hand. It was a major weight fiddle! By this means, the trader was taking from each measure two or two-hundred-and-fifty grams more of wheat than the weight indicated. It was simply theft. And as a result, twenty-five kilos of wheat was weighed as twenty kilos.

After weighing each kilo, the crafty trader emptied the scale-pan on the pile of wheat beside him, thus leaving no option for it to be weighed again. After he finished weighing the woman's wheat, he smiled in satisfaction at his success and looked at the trader beside him. The man smiled back, winked and said, 'Ask for tea!'

When the woman extended her hand and took the money for the wheat, she seemed shocked. She looked like a lifeless clay idol. 'What's this? How can it be!' She had bought twenty-five kilos of wheat for fifty rupees from the ration shop. She should have received sixty-two-and-a-half rupees after selling that. The profit would be twelve-and-a-half rupees. If she bought bread and muri for her son and herself for three rupees, she would be left with nine-and-a-half rupees with which everyone at home would be able to eat rice with kolmi-spinach stew. But now she had a rupee less than the original capital. She had spent that earlier, for some food in the morning.

She looked around vacantly as she held the money in her hand. A look of incomprehension and panic came over her whole being. The baby in her arm was still wailing: 'O Ma, give me a roti.' But the mother's ears did not register any sound. She just stood like a tree struck by lightning. All the trust and belief in her heart, her very breath, had been blown away in the scorching, dust-laden wind.

Her husband had been sick and laid up in bed for the last seven months. He had fallen from a date-palm and broken his leg. The family was reduced to eating once a day, if there was earning for the day. After several days without food, the woman had told her husband, *'Hyago tumi jedi mot deo, to ami etya byabsha pottor kori.* I say, if you permit me, then I'll start a business.'

'You'll start a business?' There was disbelief in her husband's voice. 'You won't be able to do that. People will cheat you. It's not so easy to do business.'

'Don't say no. Just wait and see, I'll be able to do it. Look at Surobala. Her husband's left her and gone, but she's able to look after her four children.'

'So let's hear what business you propose to do.'

'The same as Suro, there's no hassle involved in that. I'll get wheat at the ration shop and then sell it to the traders. There's a profit of eight annas on every kilo. If I do that, we can get some rice to eat. I can't bear to see the baby starving. Tell me, shall I go ahead?'

'You need some capital to start a business, where will you get that from?'

'Suro will lend it to me. She'll keep my nose ring as security. She'll charge an interest of five rupees a month for the fifty rupees. She wants the money back in six months. Won't we be able to pay off fifty rupees in six months? We can do that for sure.'

'Do you know the price of the nose ring? It's two hundred and fifty rupees. Baba had bought it for Ma.'

'It's not as if I'm selling it off! It's only been pledged. I'll get it back alright.'

But now, it seemed everything had slipped through the cracks between her fingers and fallen into the dirt. There was some sign of life again in her broken, crushed frame. She counted the money once again, and then she began to scream: 'What did you measure? How can it be so less? I had it weighed before bringing it here!'

To the youth observing this scene, it was as if some distressed woman's fervent plea was wafting in from a faraway mountain peak. The trader did not think it necessary to pay any attention to that. He lit a beedi indifferently, emitted a mouthful of smoke and said to the trader beside him, 'Want to go for the night show at Showhouse? There's a Mumtaz film running.'

The woman once again made her fervent entreaty, 'Oh dada, dear dada! I'm very poor. Don't cheat me! God will bless you. Just see my child. Hasn't eaten anything all day ...'

Puffing out smoke, the trader said to the woman, with the tone of annoyance with which people addressed beggars, 'I weighed it in front of you, didn't I? You counted, and I counted. Were you blind then? Stop nagging me and go away! Don't make me angry!'

The youth looked at the trader. He too was poor, he wasn't a man of substantial means. From his appearance, he didn't seem to be high-caste either. And that trader was cheating another person like himself. Evidently deceit, theft, swindling and wickedness weren't afflictions of wealthy, high-caste people alone! The woman continued to plead. 'I had twenty-five kilos of wheat, dada. Believe me!'

The trader got exasperated now. 'Will you just leave! Or else I'll shove you and drive you out. What the hell do you think you're saying? You think I cheated you? I don't care about saving a few rupees like that.'

The youth could not take it any more. He rose from the bench, pulled up and folded his lungi, and advanced. *'Aei bhai, kyan maiya manushdare thokaite achhosh! Gorib manush hoiya aar ek goriber kyan kandash? Diya de awr uchit daamta.* Why are you cheating the woman! You're a poor man too, so why do you make another poor person cry! Pay her the correct amount.'

The trader wasn't alone. There were eight or ten people engaged in the same business. They had sworn to stand by one another in bad times. So the trader replied confidently, 'I've given her the correct amount.'

'No, you didn't. I observed you using the scale while I was sitting there. Pay her twelve-and-a-half rupees more!'

The trader now roared out, 'Who the hell are you? Keep your nose out of this! Go back to where you came from, or else you'll be in trouble!'

The youth's tone became grating, 'I tell you, pay her at once.' There was gratitude in the women's tearful eyes.

The trader now lost control. 'See a whore and come to support her! Who the hell are you to intervene in our matter! If you value your own good, get out from here. Or else, I'll thrash you so badly that ...' He didn't get the chance to complete his sentence, because before that, the kilo weight on the pan of the scales landed with force below his ear, where a medium-sized punch could put an end to someone's life. The wheat trader tumbled upon his heap of wheat. A stream of thick blood oozed out. His ill-gotten gains began to flow away with the blood.

The youth could not remain there any longer. The police station was just two-hundred yards away. Overcoming the shock of the sudden attack, the other traders too unitedly prepared to counter-attack. The youth ran ahead. He went past the railway line, the metalled road, the houses and buildings. He could not afford to stop now.

But he did not know that this running would one day land him in a dark prison cell. And before that, it would take him to a veritable slaughterhouse, a pile of unclaimed corpses and the autopsy table in the morgue.

4

The Great Departure

There was a pukka building at the edge of Ramakrishna Colony. On its western side, across the large sewage drain, was Tuberculosis Hospital. There was some empty space on the northern side, and past that, after the sweepers' quarters, was Loharpara. This was the only pukka house here. For security purposes, the householder had a licensed firearm. The house was encircled by high walls. The former owner of the place was a Muslim who refused to sell off his land. However, at the time of the 1964 riots in Calcutta, he had sold the place to the Bhaduris for twenty-five thousand rupees and the assurance of being taken safely to a train.

The Bhaduris were not refugees. They were from some place in the north of 24-Parganas district. They had a lot of land and property there. The owners of such agricultural land were called *jotedars*. The word 'jotedar', like the words, 'police', 'lawyer' and 'trader', was one that provoked hatred. There was nothing wrong with owning agricultural land, but the process of acquiring the land, and the mental transformation of the person as a result of possessing that land, was indeed egregious. Village folk did not consider the jotedar to be one of their own.

The Bhaduris were more-or-less educated folk. They knew about Soviet Russia and the revolutionary China. They had witnessed the Tebhaga movement in this part of the country. For all these reasons, observing the changing behaviour of village folk right from the 1960s, they had sensed the place was likely to erupt in the near future. So they thought about moving to the city. But they did not have enough ready cash to be able to buy land in central Calcutta and build a house there. They therefore selected south Calcutta, where, with the arrival of people of the *bhadralok* class from East Bengal to settle there, education, culture and the whole socio-economic environment had improved significantly. To the north of the road that went from the Jadavpur rail station to the bus-stand crossing was Jadavpur University. Just past that was the Jadavpur police station. The Bhaduris liked the place from the point of view of safety, and bought the fleeing Muslim man's house.

A famous writer and wanderer had said that wherever Bengalis went, the first thing they did was to build a Kali temple. There was a Kali temple here too, on the right side of the Bhaduris' house, beside the big sewage drain. In the evenings, a few boys from this neighbourhood hung out there. One of them was Swapan. He was the most restless, reckless and daring fellow in the twin neighbourhoods of Ramakrishnapur and Shyamnagar. He was the hero of the boys aged fourteen to eighteen. Once he jumped into any activity, he did not breathe easy until he had seen it through successfully. He was only nineteen or twenty years old. But even at that tender age he had astonished everyone by organizing the biggest cultural event of the locality, in which Banashree Sengupta had sung for free, and the two sisters, Rumki and Chumki, had danced. There was no one that Swapan did not know. Everyone from Chinmoy Roy, the Bengali film actor, to P.C. Sorcar Jr, the famous magician, was fond of him.

For some strange reason, Swapan liked Jibon. The two of them sometimes sat and chatted in front of the Kali temple near the boundary wall of the Bhaduris' house. Another boy by the name of

Satindra also used to join them. He had already, at his age, brought out a two-page journal; although after the first issue, no other issue of the journal was published.

The whole city of Calcutta was alight then in the red flames of Naxalbari. There were fierce bomb-battles between the CPI(M) and the Naxalites. One or two people were killed too. Some people were affixing stencilled images of Mao Tse-tung on wall after wall. During this time, one day, while hanging out at the Kali temple, Jibon said, 'I've seen a Naxalite. A real Naxalite!' Satindra looked astonished. Jibon said, 'Yes, a real Naxalite. Whom the police had arrested at Naxalbari and brought to court in Siliguri.'

At the time, a slogan in Hindi was emblazoned across many walls in the city, '*Kanu Jangal Chhutega, Jailka Tala Tutega*', meaning, Kanu Sanyal and Jangal Santhal (two leaders of the peasant uprising in north Bengal) shall escape, the jail locks will be smashed. They had been arrested by the police, while hiding in a jute-field, in 1970. Was Jibon speaking about them?

Jibon said, 'I don't know any names. But on the day they were brought to the court, God, how many hundreds of policemen had surrounded them! No one was allowed to go anywhere near them. I saw them when they got off the police van to be taken inside the court building.'

In the course of conversation, Jibon narrated the whole story of his penniless tour of north India, leaving out only the parts about the humiliation he had suffered. They chatted a long while. Soon it was time for Satindra to leave for school; he was preparing for his higher secondary examination. And Swapan had to go to Palpara, to sit at his father's shop. There were lots of customers in the afternoon; it was difficult for his father to manage on his own.

Satindra, a.k.a. Sati, had left. Swapan too got up to leave. There was a piece of charcoal lying on the ground in front of him. It was probably from the charcoal used during the big yagna ceremony organised at the Kali temple on the previous new moon night. Who knows what Swapan had in mind, he picked up the piece of charcoal and went and stood in front of the boundary wall of the Bhaduris' house. It was a long, white-washed wall, on one corner of which were painted in black four capital letters in English: CPI(M). This was the new method of taking over a wall. No other party had the right to this wall now. It would remain forever under the possession of those who had claimed it first. Whenever they wished, they would express their views here, for instance, announcing a rally or a public meeting, or writing slogans during elections. Using the piece of charcoal, Swapan added the letter 'L' beside the 'M' on the wall.

An 'L'—a letter written with two strokes of a piece of charcoal. No one knew the great danger that those strokes would bring. And Jibon knew nothing at all. After all, he couldn't even read or write his own mother tongue, Bengali. After ceremonially writing the first consonant, ক, or 'Ka', as a child, just before his aborted school admission back in the Shiromanipur refugee camp, he had not written another letter in his life. And besides, this was English—a language from across the shores. But as a result of that 'L' being added by Swapan, the entire wall went from the control of the Communist Party of India (Marxist) to that of their grave enemy, the Naxalites, who had by now formed the Communist Party of India (Marxist-Leninist), or CPI(ML).

This meant that they were now present in the impenetrable fortress of the localities under the CPI(M)'s control, namely, Loharpara, TB Hospital, Chittaranjan Colony, Mistripara, Ramakrishnapur Colony and Anandapalli, and that they had the daring and power to announce their presence in writing on the wall. A widely used slogan of this time was, 'A single spark can start a conflagration.' Who could say that a prairie fire wouldn't result from this spark too?

On one side of Ramakrishnapur, beside the main road, was an ink manufacturing factory. Twelve hundred workers were employed there. The leader of the employees' and workers' union of the factory was Debesh Sen. He lived in Ramakrishnapur itself. While he was walking by on some errand, he spotted Swapan doing his artwork on the wall with great earnestness. But he did not try to stop him. That was not his task. There were other people to do all that. He only did whatever was the duty of a devoted party worker. He immediately informed the party office in the C-Block of Ramakrishnapur. Because there weren't so many people in the party office then, they could not immediately chase the group of youths who owed allegiance to the Naxalites—who were synonymous with fire, who could well be in possession of deadly weapons—and catch them to bring them to justice before the people's court that was held in abeyance until the night. There was a routine procession that evening of the CPI(M)'s youth wing, the Democratic Youth Federation of India or DYFI, with their flags flying high atop thick lathis. The procession of about two hundred youths was led by the six-and-a-half-feet tall Pinaki Sen, whom the whole locality feared. After going around several parts of Jadavpur, the procession returned to the party office in C-Block. Debesh Sen spoke to Pinaki Sen. 'Our security is about to be breached. A wild dog has infiltrated into the tiger's lair!' In all the ten or twelve neighbourhoods nearby, there was no sign of any party other than the CPI(M). They had all been uprooted from the locality. But now the Naxals had entered the arena! It was not at all a good sign.

Pinaki Sen was a farsighted leader. After hearing everything, he decided there and then what had to be done. The appropriate response that would yield adequate political gain, from the standpoint of materialist philosophy. Swapan was a permanent resident of this locality; besides, he was quite popular among the youth. If something was told or done to him, there might be an adverse reaction from the people at large. That may be a trivial matter, but it wasn't desirable. One could try to give him a chance. But the other fellow! What was his name? Jibon. He was a nobody in the locality. Besides, he was very poor. He wouldn't be able to pursue the matter with the police and so on either. He had also quarrelled and fought with various people, and insulted them in the process. There was no hindrance to doing something to such a fellow.

He was the one who ought to be thrashed. There was no way to avoid that. It was simply a political responsibility. Politics came first, and everything else came later. He had to be given such an exemplary thrashing that all those who saw it would tremble in fear even to utter the word 'Naxalite'. As the Bengali saying went, the snake would die and nothing would happen to the stick either. That was the correct step to take in the local political context. There was no other option. 'Bring the fellow here!'

As soon as the general of the army issued the order, a group of soldiers set out to get Jibon, carrying their flag-poles. It had become quite dark by then. Jibon was sitting at Mejda's tea-shop at the bus-stand crossing. There were some other people there too. One of them was Tarak Bag, from the Selimpur basti near the Palpara market, who sold firewood. Before Jibon could surmise anything—a lot like guerilla warfare—the soldiers surrounded him. 'Sen babu asked us to get you.' They tied Jibon's hands behind his back with his own gamchha. It was as if the defeated general of some great battle was being taken to the court of justice of the victorious king.

At this time, there was a new item in currency: tea without milk. Pinaki Sen was sipping a cup of tea without milk, or 'red tea'. There was a lot of 'red' everywhere nowadays. Who knows whether that had affected tea-drinking habits too! Taking a sip, he put the cup down on the table and looked at Jibon, rather like a hunter looking at a trapped tiger.

'What's your name?'

Who knows why, but the six-and-a-half-feet tall, muscular Sen babu's stone-crushing voice made Jibon tremble. He said his name.

'Since when have you been a Naxalite?'

'I'm not a Naxalite or anything like that.'

'Why did you write on the wall?'

'It was Swapan who did that. How would I know what he wrote when I can't even read or write?'

'Where do you store your bombs and pipe guns?'

Sen babu finished his tea as he asked the questions. After that he took a lathi. At one time, he used to play cricket. As if hitting a sixer, he struck the lathi on Jibon's knee. 'How many murders have you committed?' Another blow. 'Tell me, will you ever join the Naxalites again?' One more blow. 'Who else is with you?'

Each question was followed by a blow of the thick lathi made of goran, mangrove-wood. After almost two hours of such treatment, Sen babu thought it was enough. After that a rickshaw was brought and Jibon's limp, bundled body was placed on its seat. Sen babu paid the rickshaw fare. 'Go and throw him in front of the house that's coming up at the Shyamnagar crossing.'

Despite his age, Swapan's younger brother was very intelligent. Realising what should be done in such a time, he ran towards his father's shop in Palpara. He told Swapan about all that had happened after Jibon was taken to the party office. He also told him about what might happen later at night. Swapan did not return home. He stayed for a few days at his uncle's house in Sodepur. And Swapan's father went with Hemanta babu to meet Sen babu at his residence in Mistripara. 'You already know which party I belong to. My son is immature. He committed a grave error after falling into the clutches of that fellow, Jibon. Please spare him this time. I'll counsel him, he'll never do it again.'

Sen babu said, 'Bring him to me. There's nothing to be afraid of. I'll explain things to him.'

Later, at some point of time, Swapan was brought to meet Sen babu. The latter explained matters to him. After that, Swapan became a militant worker of the CPI(M). And, in an incident near the Ram Thakur ashram in Jadavpur, he was shot in the stomach and chest by boys from the Congress Party. He had to have eighty-six stitches after the pellets were removed and was laid up in hospital for two months. But all that comes much later.

Coming back to today, the rickshaw-rider brought Jibon down from his rickshaw, held him and slowly took him till the door of his house, and then left. Jibon went in and lay down. He knew, and his parents too knew, that he needed to go to a doctor. But they did not have the means to be able to do that. They had to console themselves with the hope that since he had survived, his swollen and painful arms, legs, chest and back would heal naturally in time.

Along the railway line that ran straight as a bowstring from the heart of Calcutta to the final reaches of south Bengal, the entire stretch to the north of the three stations, Dhakuria, Jadavpur and Baghajatin, had come under the control of the Naxalite youths. This was a kind of liberated zone of theirs. If the railway line was considered to be the McMahon line, then almost the entire region to the south was under the CPI(M). Only the thirteen municipal wards of Bijoygarh were an exception. All these were under the control of the Congress Party. Armed workers of the party patrolled every street corner in a locality under their party's control. Sometimes their opponents attacked them. Yes, that did happen. One party tried to displace another by attacking them, whether during the day or at night. But at this time, all the fighting was between the CPI(M) and the Naxalites. After these two parties fought each other and were exhausted, the Congress would enter the arena, together with the police.

Palpara, Garfa, Salampur and so on, across the railway line in Jadavpur, were all strongholds of the Naxalites. Tarak Bag, who lived near the rail-side shanty settlement in Salampur, had seen Jibon being taken away from Mejda's tea-shop. He went back to his neighbourhood and conveyed the news to those like him who earlier used to sell firewood, or had been rickshaw-pullers or repaired handpumps, but were all now Naxalites. 'The CPI(M) boys have taken one of us. A very good comrade, I've heard that he went to Naxalbari and wanted to join the battle there. About two hundred people surrounded Jibon and captured him. I think they are going to kill him.'

Jibon moaned in agony all night long. He had a fever too. It seemed he would not survive. Even if he did survive, he would definitely lose the use of his legs for the rest of his life. At least twenty blows of the goran lathi had struck him below the waist. His lower limbs now throbbed in pain, like a suppurating boil. He couldn't even move.

However, the poor were very hardy, they did not die easily. While affluent folk spent a hundred thousand rupees treating some ailment, the poor somehow survived the same merely by sipping hot water and tying amulets around their necks. And so Jibon survived this assault too. After five days, he was able to walk and emerge from the house. He saw that the firewood seller Tarak, accompanied by another person whose name was Nakul, had come looking for him. The handpump repair man, Nakul, whispered to him, 'We can't talk here. We can't stay long either. If someone recognises us there'll be trouble. I'll just tell you one thing. Think about it and decide what you'd like to do. Ashu-da asked you to meet him. Ashu Majumdar.'

Jibon was startled. 'Which Ashu-da?'

Tarak replied, 'There's only one sun and one moon in the sky. Just like that, there's only one Charu Majumdar and one Ashu Majumdar.'

'Do you people know him? Do you meet him? Talk to him?'

'We talk to him, eat with him and sleep with him.'

What were Nakul and Tarak saying! Ashu Majumdar, a brilliant former student of Jadavpur University, the Naxalite leader who was a legend for his exceptional courage! The one whom the police were desperately searching for! These people knew him! And Ashu had asked Jibon to meet him! 'But how did he find out about me?' asked Jibon in astonishment.

'From Rana,' Nakul said.

At the time he worked in Bade Lal's tea-shop, a few thousand bighas of land belonging to Bibhu Sapui and Bihari Mondal had been forcibly occupied, and a refugee colony had been established there under the leadership of Rana Chowdhury. Jibon knew him by sight, but he had never spoken to him. He never got the opportunity. He asked, 'Why has Ashu-da called me?'

Nakul replied, 'Don't you want to take revenge on them for beating you up mercilessly? Tell me, don't you want to?'

'I do.'

'Don't you want to fight those who suck the blood of the poor and pile up a mountain of money?'

'I do.'

'Will you be able to do that by yourself?'

'No.'

'That's why we all have to come together. We have to unite and, beginning from one end, expand our sphere. We have to create liberated zones. That's why you have to go and meet Rana-da. Will you go?'

'How will I go? I'm still unable to walk.'

'Shall I call a rickshaw? If you go there, you'll get medical treatment too.'

'Is there a doctor there?'

'There's everything. Doctors, engineers, lawyers, barristers—what don't we have!'

At that moment that day, Jibon commenced his 'great departure', in the company of Nakul and Tarak. It was as if his destiny pushed him from behind towards his advancement through tempering. Jibon knew inwardly that the path he was walking on was one that knew only destruction, blood and tears. As easy as it was to walk that path, returning was near impossible. The path went through police custody, courts, prison, hospital, the autopsy room of the morgue, and finally culminated in the crematorium. But there was no time to think about all that now. The past was pushing him—move ahead, don't stop!

The whole city, and why only this city, one could say the whole country had been divided into two parts now: one part comprising those who had everything, and another part, of those who had nothing at all.

Between the two was another group, who had something. This group was extremely cunning and opportunistic. They had the gift of education, and so they moved between the two sides and were always on the lookout for where they could gain more from. But the main conflict was between the haves and the have-nots. Standing unabashedly behind the class of those who had everything were the police, the army, law, the judiciary and political parties of all hues. In short, the whole state apparatus. Among the people at large too, no one was neutral anymore. Overtly or covertly, they were standing on one side or the other.

Jibon had realised that abiding by the demand of the times, he too had to pick a side, and with arms in his hand. After coming to the city of Calcutta, Jibon had heard about the Communist Party many times, from lots of people. The colour of their flag was red, the colour of the blood of workers. They fought on behalf of workers, peasants and destitute folk. He too should join them, because he was destitute. But he was unable to decide which Communist Party he ought to join, the CPI(M) or the Naxalites. Which was the real one, and which was the one that only appeared to be the real one but actually wasn't? The incident in Naxalbari, where seven poor Adivasi peasant women were killed, had opened his eyes somewhat. But now, the blows from the red-flag bearing goran lathi determined the path he ought to take.

It was the day after he met Nakul and Tarak. The vast field in Kalikapur, where jackals had once attacked Jibon, was no longer covered by jungle. It was densely inhabited now. There were houses, buildings and structures under construction everywhere. It was there, under cover of the evening darkness, that Jibon met the hero of legend, Ashu Majumdar. A few more boys like Jibon were also there. Ashu Majumdar was taking a class for the boys. Jibon and some others had reached there a bit late. He signalled with his hand for them to sit down on the grass in the field and continued speaking: 'We want to build a classless society, free of exploitation. There will be no inequality and no caste system in such a society. Everyone will have equal rights and enjoy equal respect. Everyone will have the same opportunity to secure food, clothing, education, shelter and healthcare. But how is that to be achieved? It will be achieved only if this rotten society is destroyed and a new society is constructed. The leadership and management of such a society will comprise of labouring folk. That means workers, peasants and people who are politically conscious. Destruction and reconstruction—that is what revolution means. Revolution demands blood. Because in no country has the ruling and exploiting class voluntarily stepped away from the centre of power. But organised groups of people have pushed them out and grabbed power. The example of honesty, courage and self-sacrifice that our great party has demonstrated in a very short time is something rare in India's political history. You are the soldiers of that great party. I hope that by following the path shown by the chairman and great leader, each one of you will grow into a true Communist.'

After that, Nakul spoke. 'Comrade, this is Jibon.' As if he had known him for a long time, Ashu Majumdar asked Jibon to sit next to him. He put his arm on his shoulder. Jibon's whole being trembled in excitement. The man sitting next to him was none other than Ashu Majumdar! He had never imagined that he would be received like this. It was as if his soul, humiliated, deprived and reviled all his life, had finally tasted the elixir of life.

Ashu Majumdar said, 'I have heard about you. It's not the time for talking or hearing now. The war has begun. You are standing in the battlefield. There's only one task now—CM has said that the decade of the seventies shall be a decade of liberation. Why did he say that? He said it because the conditions under which revolution or liberation takes place are now evident in our society. The Chairman has said that this is an era of world revolution. In village after village, peasants are finishing off their class enemies. They are killing policemen, taking away their weapons and building a people's liberation army. Srikakulam has become a liberated zone. That's why CM said that if the struggle advances in this way, the seventies will surely be a decade of liberation. Step into the battlefield, comrade! Employ all your strength to make CM's words come true.' He paused for a while, patted Jibon on the shoulder, and continued: 'You will be with the Palpara group. Rana is the leader of your group. Do whatever he says. And always keep in mind that for a soldier, discipline and obedience are the most important things. Is that clear?'

Jibon said, 'There was something I wanted to know.'

'What is that? Tell me quickly, there's another meeting I have to go to.'

'You said just now that we will fight against those who exploit poor folk. But this fighting between the two parties, with poor people on both sides—why is that?'

'A good question,' said Ashu Majumdar in reply. 'But it's a question that cannot be answered in a simple manner, or in a few words. The state apparatus is a weapon in the hands of one class, which is used to exploit another class. This system of exploitation cannot function without the administrative system. In order to conceal the real nature of the administrative system, it wears the garb called democracy. Anyone can form a political party, contest and win elections and take over the administration. But people won't vote for someone merely because the party exists. For that, the party has to think about how they can win over the minds of some people. And, of course, we have false votes, forcible votes, rigging, buying votes with money, and so on. I won't go into that. I'm talking about people voting out of conviction. So when someone wins the election and comes into power, they cannot advance people's well-being simply by wishing for that outcome. They have to function in accordance with the Constitution, and within predetermined limits. Besides, most of those who win the elections and come into power are not honest in their personal lives. Most of the time, they are affluent folk. They have only one objective in mind, to keep people content by throwing crumbs at them, while protecting their own interests. Now, this party, the CPI(M), who are now a big impediment in our way, hold red flags and talk about revolution. Actually they are stooges of the bourgeoisie in disguise. But they have been able to bring together a very large number of people, everywhere, because people have faith in the red flag, because people want revolution. They have misguided some of their members and been successful in inciting them against us. So when they are attacking us, even though this battle is not at all desirable, we are having to fight them for self-defence. But there's also another side to this, which is to our advantage. Because this battle is taking place in the city, a huge police contingent has to be stationed here. Otherwise everyone would have gone to the villages, where the peasants are finishing off the landlords and zamindars. They cannot do that now.'

Jibon said, 'You've explained the matter, I listened to you, and I understood a bit too. But when something happens to poor folk, I feel sad. There's Kanu, who used to sell fish in the market. He got married just three months ago—and now he's dead.'

Ashu Majumdar responded to Jibon. 'Do you know the parthenium plant? It's poisonous, it even poisons the air. So if you set fire to a large clump of parthenium to destroy it, and within the clump is a tulsi plant, that too will perish. There's no way to save it. We are killing policemen and seizing arms, but the policemen are the sons of our own folk. But they protect the enemy of the people. They kill our people on their instructions. We have a slogan, "*Hotyakarike banchiye rakhar ortho mrityu,*". Protecting murderers means death. Will we be able to survive if we don't act against those who come to kill us, as well as those who provide them fuel from behind? We won't! So we too have to do a lot of things like that, which does make us sad.'

Jibon thought over the matter for a while and then said, 'I have another question.'

'Another question! Didn't I tell you I have to go for another meeting? I'll be back tomorrow. Get down to work, you'll find the answers to all your questions. Read the *Red Book, May the People's War be Long-lived* and the three articles written by our Chairman. All your questions and doubts will be cleared. I have to go now.'

5

An Unequal Battle

Every night in Calcutta now was black as pitch. Every night, fear seized people's hearts. At this time, it was only those who were helpless, recourseless and weak—the cannon fodder of the battle for life—were on the streets. These were people who were ever slaves to hunger. Some of them pedalled rickshaws with their skinny legs, some ran tea-shops with walls made of pieces of matting, some were petty employees of a small factory. Those returning home after work, prayed to their respective deities—Oh Lord, may I reach my destination without mishap! Nowadays, as soon as night descended, a group of trained soldiers from the West Bengal Armed Police descended on the city streets like mad dogs. Their fingers rested on the triggers of automatic weapons. The common people were mere targets in their eyes and consciousness. They only needed a pretext to murder people, spraying them with bullets. Three boys, all of whom were less than sixteen years old, were stencilling an image of Mao Tse-tung on a wall. They were shot to bits for the crime. What else could offer the deathly entertainment that killing people entailed? This was a special kind of carnal pleasure to savour.

AN UNEQUAL BATTLE

Five youths were walking ahead cautiously, trying to find their way in the terrifying darkness. All five of them were hungry. Each of them had a paper packet with muri and telebhaja in their hands. As they walked, they took a bit of muri from the packet and chewed it. Looking at them, one could see they were labouring folk—someone rode a rickshaw, someone repaired handpumps, someone sold firewood. Although they belonged to the weaker section of society, there was no weakness in their legs. They were strong and unfaltering, as if each step of theirs would shatter the earth beneath their feet. Their eyes gleamed like those of an enraged tiger out on a hunt.

They were proceeding towards the place where they would find Mr Pinaki Sen. Information had been received from reliable sources that he was now at his lathe workshop. He went there at this time every day to take stock of the day's work. Eight or ten mistris, or mechanics, worked in this workshop. The workshop still fabricated the same items they used to earlier. However, owing to the political compulsions of the changed situation, they had to make some other items too, like pipe-guns, or single-shot guns, also known as *chhakka*. The members of his party's AG, i.e. action group, needed these badly. This factory supplied arms throughout Jadavpur, and also in south Bengal. Pinaki Sen was the owner of this arms factory. The five youths were going to visit him.

They were walking, but not together. There were three people on the pavement on the left side of the road, and two on the pavement on the right. They each kept a distance of at least twenty feet between one another. They had been instructed to proceed in that manner. So that if the person ahead fell into any danger, the one behind him would be alerted to that and could take appropriate action.

The five wayfarers had begun their journey at the squatter colony along the railway track in Salampur. They walked for about fifteen minutes along the rail track, turned right at the level-crossing, and went past the intersection with the road at the left that headed towards the railway station. They then took the road between the TB Hospital and Jadavpur University, and reached Raja Subodh Chandra Mullick Road. They entered a narrow lane where large vehicles could not ply; only cycle-rickshaws and the occasional taxi entered it. The lane was completely deserted. There were no lights there either. The households living on both sides seemed to be somnolent in some unknown terror. It was as if everyone behind the fastened doors and windows was dead. After all, it was a terribly dangerous time. The doors and windows wouldn't open even if someone was killed at the doorstep. That was what people in middle-class neighbourhoods were like. The five youths walked through the lane and headed towards a triangular junction. There was a small teashop there, run by a Bihari. Two young men sat at the shop and kept watch over the area. There was fear of the police, and of attacks by people from the rival political party. After all, a war was going on. They could not afford to underestimate the enemy. And so, the watch. Pinaki Sen was the local supremo. The responsibility for his safety was among the essential tasks of his party. The two people keeping watch observed the five youths walking through the lane. The secret radar of their sixth sense signalled to them—this could be something out of the ordinary. The five people were walking separately. Their steps were cautious, and there was the same kind of paper packet in everyone's hand! Why was that! Why? They were unable to decide whether or not they should run and inform Pinaki-da to be careful.

They were a bit slow in arriving at a decision. By then the five youths had reached the triangular junction. Their five pairs of eyes gleamed in the darkness. They decided on something by signals. The lathe workshop was opposite the teashop. Pinaki Sen was visible through an open door. The door was only half-open. His white, half-sleeve shirt stood out even in the darkness. He was sitting on a chair and bent over a table, writing something. This was on one side of a verandah. It was a small verandah. Across the verandah was a door. Inside, past the door, were large lathe machines. There were some people working there. Even before any of the boys sitting at the tea-shop and keeping watch could get up and enter the lathe workshop to alert Pinaki Sen, the youth who was the tallest and most dark-complexioned of the five, flung the packet of muri in his hand in the direction of the workshop's open door. Two others did the same after him. The first packet hit the wall on the right side of the door and exploded with a terrible sound. It was clear a country-bomb had been concealed under the muri. The next two packets entered the workshop through the partially open door. One of them exploded, while the other remained intact. The walls of the workshop shook under the impact of the explosion. Smoke filled the whole place. From the smoke came the screams of the wounded and those fearing for their lives, as well as the sound of people escaping. Once the smoke cleared, one could see Pinaki Sen lying on the floor, slightly injured. He had fallen, together with the chair, in a corner on the left side. But where was the mechanic? The one who had been working in front of the lathe machine, whose name was Amar? He was there, but he was on the floor. A bomb splinter had blown away an ear and a part of his head. There was a pool of blood around him. He was still moving a bit then.

As soon as the five travellers flung their country-bombs, they turned and began to run. They went past the bus-stand crossing, and along Station Road, which lay in near darkness, all the way towards Palpara. It took the two boys, who had been caught off-guard by the sudden attack, a little while to recover their senses. After that they too ran, chasing those who had escaped. They fired twice from the single-shot guns they had, but the bullets did not hit anyone. In retaliation, the fleeing group flung their two remaining bombs, which exploded at the bus-stand crossing.

Running through the lane on the left, just past the railway line, one of them said, 'That bastard Sen survived. The poor mistri got caught in between ...'

Another youth at once replied, 'There's nothing to be done. When you set fire to a clump of parthenium, a few tulsi plants will also get burnt.' No one would wait for evidence regarding who had undertaken the attack on his workshop. They all knew that the police would arrive very soon at Palpara. So some twenty boys were sitting ready at the Palpara intersection, and in the lanes and alleys there. They would not allow the police to enter the locality without hindrance. Another group of seven or eight people had been formed in the squatter colony too, who were at the ready, near the signal post along the railway line. Nani, Ananda, Ratan, Haru, Nitai, Goshto, Nakul, Montu and Jibon as well. Each one of them carried a small, innocuous looking, but lethal ball encased in string. That was the country-bomb. As long as it was in one's hand, it was safe. As soon as it hit the earth with force, it could be very dangerous.

⁂

The boundary wall of Jadavpur University was at the rear of the squatter settlement on the western side of the railway line. And on the eastern side was a neighbourhood of affluent folk. Leaning against a wall in the winding lane going through Palpara, and observing the level-crossing in the distance, Jibon waited, alert. His first face-to-face, armed encounter with the enemy would take place today.

They had kept a close watch all night, and at around ten the next morning, the police squad arrived as expected. It was a group of twenty or twenty-five men. Leaving their vehicle at the level-crossing and then walking along the rail track, the khaki uniform-clad squad advanced northwards, the safety catches of their rifles decocked, their fingers on the triggers. One couldn't figure out where exactly they would go. Neither could one surmise where they would conduct search operations, and who they would catch and thrash. But Rana Chowdhury, the leader of Jibon's group, had issued strict instructions: the police should not be allowed to enter the locality. Because if they did that, there would be a massacre. Everyone in the group was as determined. The police would not be allowed to advance.

There had been a bit of rain a little while ago. All the streets were wet. The road in front of the Palpara market was waterlogged. That was probably why the police squad had not taken that road. They had decided to advance in a row. A young man who had secured a police job would enter the neighbourhood through the lane in which Jibon and his associates were keeping watch. He had not yet been confirmed in his job. His officer had declared: 'Perform well and you'll be confirmed in six months!'

Perform well! Jibon was also waiting eagerly to perform well! Such policemen had mercilessly beaten his starving father and dumped him in the dense forest. It was a policeman who had done something so hateful and terrible to him under cover of night. Whenever he remembered it, he felt like dying, or else like killing the man. So today, he was waiting, like a soldier in a bunker, to finally settle scores. The wait was over now; they were coming. The khaki-uniformed police squad entered Palpara from the eastern side. That was the side from which the sun rose. The sun was now directly over their heads. One was a natural phenomenon, and the other was a political one. It was being said that the political sun was the sun of liberation, of not just this country but the whole of Asia. The policemen reached the intersection of the lane, marching to the sound of their boot-clad feet. Jibon saw them from his spot behind a wall and stood up, a country-bomb in his hand. That's it, no more delay! He signalled to his associates—me first! His target was the fat, paunchy, mustachioed fellow, who resembled and had the gait of Jibon's nemesis, the havildar in Lucknow. The man advanced, one step at a time, till he was within fifty feet of Jibon. Now! No more delay! Jibon flung the bomb in his hand on the rail track. It exploded. In the face of the mighty and powerful state apparatus. This was the first fatal attack undertaken by a poor, unfed, powerless boy.

As soon as the bomb exploded, a hail of bullets rained from the other side. And the simple, hand-made country-bombs rained from this side. They made a lot of sound but did little damage. By then, the boys from Palpara, whose group leader was a handsome college-going youth called Katu, had launched a fusillade of country-bombs from the direction of the level-crossing. The plight of the police squad was not unlike wheat being crushed in a mill. In front of them was Rana Chowdhury's group, and behind them was Katu's group. Bombs exploded like fireworks on the night of Diwali. Although there were sophisticated weapons in the hands of the policemen, it was not weapons that fought. It was people. So how could salaried personnel confront fighters who were empowered by the strength of their ideals. Tormented and bedevilled by the recklessly flung bombs, they climbed over the wall and fled towards the police station through the university campus, taking their wounded colleagues with them. But they returned after half an hour. This time there were almost two hundred of them. The boys knew that they would come again, and that the attack would be fiercer. But that did not frighten them. Being the warriors they were, they had steeled themselves to battle to the end.

The police now advanced, firing their rifles, along the road in front of the Palpara market. There was a timber yard behind the Palpara market. To the south of the yard was the rail line, and on the northern side was a large lake. That was where the two groups confronted each other. One group had sophisticated lethal weapons in their hands, while the other group possessed some simple country-bombs, a couple of pipe guns and the stones from the railway track. The former group was fighting to save their jobs, while the other one fought for a revolution. The battle lasted for almost two hours. Gritting their teeth, a few ordinary youths fought an unequal battle, merely by dint of their courage. After a while, they ran out of arms. They had no more bombs or stones. Now they had to retreat. While racing away from the fierce volley of bullets, the leader of the Palpara group, Katu, slipped over a large, wet, moss-covered block of wood in the timber yard. He fell down with a bomb in his hand. The bomb exploded and his right hand was severed at the elbow. That was the only casualty on this side after the two-hour-long battle.

Jibon had left home in the beginning of 1970. The year went by, but it was not so much the winter, summer and monsoon that he went through, as the blood, destruction, tears, dangers, disruptions and corpses that he stepped over in the course of the year. Middle-class boys, who were studying in college and university, read out to Jibon, Nakul and their associates from the Naxalite paper, *Deshabrati* (meaning 'vowed to the nation'), informing them about the various places where revolutionary peasant folk had wiped out the jotedars and zamindars, seized the arms of policemen, and established liberated zones. They had said, 'Whatever we are doing in the city is only complementing the peasants' struggle. If we attack the police and the army, who are the principal upholders of the state apparatus, here, in the city, they'll be busy here. Or else they would employ all their power to destroy the peasants' struggle.'

The Naxalite youths didn't really have any arms to speak of. Yet, despite their limited capabilities, they were fighting a trained force armed with sophisticated weapons merely by dint of the indomitable spirit of their youth. So they suffered great damage and loss. The morgue was full of heaps of dead bodies of youths, each of whom was a rare diamond of idealism and courage.

This was the time when the war of liberation began in the neighbouring country, East Pakistan, and there were many fierce battles. On one side was the Awami League and on the other, Yahya Khan's army. The government of India, under Prime Minister Indira Gandhi, came out in full support of the Awami League, providing every kind of assistance. In the eyes of the Pakistani leaders, India was a Hindu nation and an enemy. In retaliation against India's support to the Awami League, Yahya Khan's army unleashed a programme of murder, attacks, rape and looting on the Bengali Hindus living in East Pakistan. And so, once again, terrified men, women and children began fleeing, fearing for their lives. Once again, Bengali refugees crowded into the border regions of East Bengal, in Bongaon, Taki, Basirhat and so on.

Returning home from work one evening, Garib Das found his brother Shashikanta waiting for him. Shashikanta was the youngest of Garib Das's brothers. Following the partition of India, when people from East Pakistan crossed over to India, leaving village after village deserted, he had refused to leave. Garib Das had pleaded with him time and again, 'Come with me to India. How will you live all alone in this country!'

His reply had been, 'If you want to go, then go. But I'm not going.'

'But how can we be in peace if we leave you behind? What if some danger befalls you! The way the Miyas are incensed ...'

'I don't care what happens. I'm not leaving.'

'Don't be stubborn, bhai, this country is no longer ours. Hindus can't live here any longer. They will hack everyone.'

Shrugging his dark-skinned body, Shashikanta had said, 'It's better to die in the homestead of our ancestors than to live like a king in an alien land.'

Why was Shashikanta in India today, after so many years?

He explained: 'We couldn't stay there any longer. After you people left, there were a couple of riots. But they were not so bad. One time they burnt the Kali temple, and another time, four or six houses were looted. After that everything was more or less fine. But a completely new calamity began this year. Yahya Khan's army arrived from West Pakistan and began killing anyone they laid eyes on. They saw no difference between Hindus and Muslims. After all, they were all Bengalis. Do you remember Mamud's elder son? He's dead. The razakars tied him to a coconut tree and beat him to death.'

'Who on earth are the razakars,' Garib Das asked.

'The razakars are those who support Yahya Khan's army in East Bengal.'

'Why are they killing fellow Muslims?'

'There isn't much of a conflict between Hindus and Miyas now. It's the conflict between Bengalis and Biharis that's dangerous. The Bengalis say they want a separate nation for themselves. The other side says, you won't have that. The Bengalis have the Mukti Bahini, while the Biharis have Yahya Khan's army and the razakars. The two sides are at war. Thousands and thousands of people are dying like ants. There are so many corpses floating in the river that boats are unable to move without hindrance. We managed to escape somehow.'

'Where's the rest of your family? Your son and daughter?'

'I left them at the refugee camp in Taki and came looking for you. I had been to Khola-Doltala. I got your address from our elder brother.'

Garib Das was astonished. 'Is there a refugee camp in Taki?'

'Of course there is! Thousands of people have arrived there. There are no more Bengali Hindus left in East Bengal. They've taken shelter in India. They say, once the war ends, they'll send back whoever wants to return. Those who don't want to go back will be allowed to stay, and they'll get land in Dandakaranya. I've decided I'll go and live in Dandakaranya. I don't want to go back to that country.'

The Dandakaranya resettlement project, initiated in 1956, was still in operation. Despite all the efforts of the government, there had not yet been any significant increase in the number of people who were willing to go to that harsh region. Although some refugees from various camps had been sent there, through various coercive means, a sizeable number of them had been unable to remain there. They had run away and blended into the sea of people of West Bengal. And so, the vast forested region of Dandakaranya was almost deserted. Forest resources worth crores of rupees were getting destroyed, because they could not be gathered for lack of labour. That's why these people were being taken there lovingly.

This time, the government was not making the mistake they had made in the past. Without wasting any time, the refugees were brought directly from Taki to Sealdah station, and made to board the train to Dandakaranya. They were made to get off the train at Malkangiri, Umarkot and Paralkot with the parting line, 'Stay here for as long as you like. The longer you stay the better.'

After a while, Shashikanta said, 'From whatever I can see and hear after coming here, I realise that all of us are having a very bad time. So bad that nothing could be worse. I told our elder brothers, and I'm telling you too—what's the use of remaining here in this condition? Instead of that—listen to my suggestion! Come with me to Dandakaranya. I have a 'border slip' from entering this country. Show that and register yourself in the Taki camp, get in there. When they take us to Dandakaranya, we'll all go together.'

'I've heard there are all kinds of dangers there ...'

'Tell me one place where there are no dangers! I crossed the border and arrived here because of the killings in East Pakistan. But after coming here, I heard that people slaughter each other like goats here as well. So where will I go! I tell you, let's go to Dandakaranya. Let's go and see what lies ahead. We'll either die or survive. Whatever happens to everyone will also happen to us. We'll suffer what's written in our fate. That's as far as my thinking goes now.'

'What did Bor-da say?'

'Bor-da, Maij-da and Saij-da have all agreed. So tell me what you'll do. I can't wait in Taki for very long.'

It was as if Shashikanta was the fabled prodigal son, who at the last moment had arrived with good tidings at Garib Das's door. That very morning, Hemanta babu had spoken to Garib Das, asking him to vacate the place in Shyamnagar. 'I had allowed you to stay here thinking you were a good man. I'm not saying you're a bad fellow. But your son's doings are unacceptable! Just wait and see what happens to him when he falls into the hands of our boys. We can't show any pity to the parents of someone who is harming us so much. I give you three days' time. Leave the room!'

Garib Das said to Shashikanta, 'When Bor-da and Maij-da are going, I'll go too. Let's see what fate has in store for us.'

After a while, Shashikanta enquired about Jibon. 'I heard all kinds of things about him. Where is he now?'

Despair poured out of Garib Das's lips. 'How can I tell you where he is now. Only God knows whether he's dead or alive. I haven't seen him or heard from him for the last ten months. Every once in a while, someone or the other tells me that he's living somewhere in the Salampur-Palpara locality.'

Garib Das's eyes brimmed with tears. 'I don't know whether it's because he was born at an inauspicious moment that my son turned out to be such a black sheep. Only God knows what sin he is punishing me for. It would have been much better if he had perished in his childhood. We would have wept for a few days and then forgotten about him. But now, I will be crying for the rest of my life. He'll either go to jail or be killed.'

Garib Das wiped his tears with his gamchha and said, 'The greatest load in the world that a father can carry is that of his dead son's body. Only God knows whether I will have to carry that load as well.'

Shashikanta said, 'Don't waste any more time now! Come along with me. There's no better way of saving Jibon. No one knows anyone there. Find him by any means and persuade him to come along and begin a new life there.'

Shashikanta stayed back with Garib Das that night. To the sound of country bombs exploding and gunfire, the two brothers lay awake all night, in deep apprehension. The next morning, Shashikanta returned to Taki, while Garib Das left in search of Jibon. The same Garib Das who had once stood firm against going to Dandakaranya had now decided that he would go there with Jibon, and conceal their identities in the darkness of the forests there. That's what he must do. If a tiger chased you to the edge of a river, you had to jump into the river. You wouldn't think about the crocodiles in the water. In order to protect his son's life, an extremely anxious and imperilled father finally considered the terrifying forest to be the safest place now.

⁂

For the next three or four days, Garib Das searched for Jibon in all the lanes and alleys where the Naxalites had their strongholds. He did not have the courage to ask anyone, 'Do any of you know a boy named Jibon? He's very dark-skinned, about five-feet-two-inches tall, and has short hair. He speaks Bengali and there's a scar on the right side of his forehead.' He was afraid that whoever was searching for Jibon might finish him off too for the crime of being his father.. And so, with a spade and basket on his shoulder, looking all around with despairing eyes, he kept tramping through the streets of Palpara, Garfa, Kalikapur, Salampur and Pratapnagar.

His next son, Jatan, had said, 'You won't be able to find him. Let me go and search for him.' Garib Das silenced him with a single retort, 'How can you go? Youths from one neighbourhood don't enter another neighbourhood now. As soon as you do, they'll cut you to pieces. I'm an old man, they won't pay any heed to me.'

Bimala was silent. She only wept. She was filled with remorse. How many Gods and deities had she not prayed to and vowed to fast for to get this son! Who had thought that his life would turn out this way! Perhaps Gagan's Ma had been right when she had said after he was born, that the boy's whole life would turn bitter for want of a drop of honey. None of her children could get any honey, but no one's life had been as bitter as Jibon's. If only they had been able to give him a drop of honey at the moment he was born, the boy would not have become so hot-headed, stubborn and reckless. There would have been at least some kindness, compassion, love and affection in him. Perhaps he would have worked hard and looked after his parents. Now, his heart was hard as stone.

The same day, Garib Das happened to meet Rakhal Master. He said, 'Hey, you're looking for Jibon, aren't you? If you go quickly just now, you'll find him! When my daughter was returning by train, she saw him standing beside the railway line in front of Salampur. If you go there now, you'll find him.'

Garib Das ran along the rail track towards Salampur. Going past the level-crossing, he spotted a shanty settlement of poor folk. There was a crowd of people in front of the shanties. For some reason, seeing the crowd and imagining the worst, he became alarmed. Then he overheard two labourers talking as they walked by him along the rail line. 'Serves him right! He reaped what he sowed. I warned him so many times, but he didn't pay any heed. Let him face the music now!'

Garib Das asked them in a trembling voice, 'What's happening there? Why is there a crowd?'

'A bastard's dead,' said one of the two men, as they walked past him.

'How did he die?'

'With his eyes shut! Did you get that, old man, he died with his eyes shut and lying flat on his back!' Even a person's death could be a subject of amusement for other people. Who was that accursed man who was not mourned even at his death? Garib Das's heart thumped in trepidation. Was Jibon the one who had died? He had chosen to be a traveller on a path on both sides of which lay long trains of dead folk. Just a month or two ago, Garib Das had encountered such a traveller on the road to death. He was crying, while other people laughed. He was asking for water and the people were making fun of him. 'Water! I'll piss in your fucking mouth!' His whole body was covered in blood and yet people were beating him. He had not been able to ask what his crime was, or why people were beating him up on the street. Garib Das had moved away quickly from the terrifying scene.

But there was no way he could move away now. Who knows whose dead body lay here! With wobbling legs, he too went and stood near the crowd. He spotted another labourer like himself, Sona Naskar, nicknamed Kalo. Garib Das learnt from him that it was not Jibon but a rickshaw-driver who had died as a result of excessive drinking. He used to live here all by himself. His wife had left him and gone away somewhere. No, there was no one to shed any tears for him.

Kalo asked Garib Das, 'Buro-da, why are you here?'

Garib thought that he would not tell him. But the next moment, he mentioned the name of the person whom the police and the CPI(M) were looking for. 'Do you know Jibon? I'm looking for Jibon.'

Kalo replied, 'Had anyone else asked me, I would have said I don't know him. But I'm telling you I know him. Why are you searching for him? Was there a hassle with a mason regarding wages?'

'No, no, it's not that.'

'Then why are you looking for him?'

'Jibon is my son.'

'Your son! Which Jibon are you talking about?'

Somewhat embarrassedly, Garib Das said, 'The one whom people know as Chandal Jibon.'

'Is that so? You never told me that he was your son! He's here, he's in this colony. Damodar called him to eat. Do you see the kantha drying on the roof there? That's Damodar's house. Come, I'll take you there.'

Garib Das found Jibon there. He seemed to have become a bit thinner. Actually he could hardly recognise him. Jibon was astonished to see Garib Das there. 'Baba! Is everyone at home well?'

Garib Das wept for a while and told him why he had come looking for him. 'I'm sure it's in my fate to die in Dandakaranya. Or else, why would your kaka arrive after all these years and ask us to go to Dandakaranya, when I had decided not to go there ten years ago? I'm thinking, nothing good has happened here. Let's go there and see things for ourselves, let's see if fate has anything positive in store for us there. We'll go to Taki and register our names. Once we register, they'll give us rice, daal, chira and jaggery. After a few days, they'll take us to Dandakaranya. Come along with us.'

'When will you go?'

'Whenever you say. Shashi is waiting for us, we can't delay too much.'

Jibon could not, at that moment, say he would not accompany them. He knew that in this dangerous time, when the state apparatus had descended on the party youths most cruelly and violently and someone or the other was being killed by them every day, it would not set a good example if he left his companions behind and went away. Everyone would call him a coward who escaped. But if he didn't go, he would lose forever his parents and siblings to the darkness of the dense forests of Dandakaranya; he might never be able to find them again. If they went to that unknown place and fell into any danger, they would not have anyone beside them to lend them courage. Besides, there was no way Jibon could prevent them from going. Where else would they live? And so they had to go. Therefore, Jibon too had to accompany them. After all, if he went and dropped them there, and then did not feel like staying, how long would it take him to return! Jibon was not exactly the kind of self-sacrificing political activist who had given himself up to ideology, and could tie bombs to his body, enter the enemy stronghold and set off an explosion. He was entirely a slave to food. He reasoned, when the issue was revolution in India, after all, Dandakaranya was not outside India. If he got the chance and opportunity, he could establish a stronghold there too! After all, Che Guevara, the darling of millions of youth, left the land of his birth and went away to Cuba for the cause of revolution. So even if my departure is viewed as dereliction today, it need not be the same in future.

Setting aside thoughts about the future, Jibon said, 'I'll go to the Taki railway station tomorrow and wait for you. You people can meet me there. I'll be there for sure, don't worry.'

6

Dandakaranya

Garib Das, his five brothers, and all the newly registered families were kept for about two weeks in a field near the Taki railway station, under a brown tarpaulin sheet, just like in the refugee camp long ago. There were already ten or twelve thousand families there. There was no arrangement for any sanitation or any place for defecation. And so, there was a terrible stench of human faeces around the whole place. Here too, red rice and daal, full of grit and dust, was requisitioned for them. The same rice used to be provided to Garib Das and his fellow refugees a long time ago. They were astonished to find that the warehouses had not run empty! This was the rice about which someone had said, ages back: apparently after three trucks were loaded with rice and daal at some government godown, one truck went to the zoo to feed the animals, one truck went to the prison, to feed murderers, thieves and robbers, and one truck came here to feed all the accursed refugees.

After that, one day, under the instructions of the government, everyone left of their own accord at a specified time, to take the train from Taki to the north section of Sealdah station. A train called 'refugee special' was waiting for them there. It was filled to bursting with the refugees and then it proceeded along a circuitous, less-frequented route. After a continuous journey of three or four days, crossing many hills, forests, rivers, bridges, caves, cities and towns, finally one morning, the train reached Jagdalpur, the principal town of Bastar, the predominantly Adivasi district of the state of Madhya Pradesh. Here, the train was vacated, and the refugees were loaded on trucks. The trucks sped away, each one in a different direction. Garib Das, his five brothers and their family members, were all in the same truck. He had called out all their names and pointed out each family member to the person in charge when the trucks were being loaded. 'Wherever you send us, sir, send all six of us brothers to the same place.' The person in charge acted accordingly. After five of the brothers, together with their families, mistakenly boarded a truck, they were all made to get off and wait for the next truck. That was because the remaining brother and his family could not get into the truck. No more than sixteen families were permitted in a single truck. The truck would go to Malkangiri. That was in the state of Orissa.

Where was the truck that Garib Das and his brothers were in headed? It was going to Paralkot. Paralkot comprised of a hundred-and-thirty-three villages. One or two trucks would go to specific villages. The distance between one village and the next was not less than ten miles. And in between lay the dense forest of Dandakaranya, full of trees that seemed to reach the very sky. The forest was so dense and deep in some places that the sky was not visible. The primitive people of the Gond tribe lived there. One of whose gods or goddesses was named Anga. Who was never satisfied except with offerings of blood. Preferably male blood. So whenever the deity's priests got the opportunity, they sacrificed men to Anga. How many men had been sacrificed, where, and when—not everything about the deep forests was publicised. However, the reports about a few incidents that were known about, for which the police authorities had arrested the priests, made the hearts of all the refugees who had been resettled there tremble.

Four or five hours after leaving Jagdalpur, the truck stopped at a place called Marora, for people to relieve themselves and to have chira and water. One had heard that ages ago, during the time of Emperor Akbar, there had once been a terrible famine in Rajasthan, and large numbers of people from the Marwari community had left their land and set out in search of their fortunes. They spread to various parts of India. One of them had set up a provision store here. The Marwaris indeed deserved to be blessed! There were no people within ten or fifteen miles. There were only mountains and forests all around. The Marwari sat there all alone, with his stock of goods displayed, hoping to do business. Marora, in the middle of a forest, had been fondly named in memory of the region where he was born and left behind. Now there was a *haat* there, once a week. Some other Marwaris like him came with jeeps full of goods to sell, and to buy various forest products, like amlaki (Indian gooseberry), horitaki (chebulic myrobalan), bahera (bastard myrobalan), katira (tragacanth), honey and many more items.

This truck had stopped at a crossroads where the forest office was located. The employees of the office stood on guard to stop the illegal movement of bamboo, timber, tendu leaf and so on from the forest to the neighbouring state of Andhra Pradesh. They also kept watch so that the refugees brought all the way here, with so much governmental effort, did not escape. These refugees were extremely valuable in such regions at this time. That was because they could toil, and they could be made to work for a pittance as wages. When could people be made to work for merely a pittance as wages? When the fire of hunger raged in their bellies. A system had been put in place to create such a situation. All that remained was to put people into the cage.

The truck set off again after a while. The bumpy mud road made its way through dense forest on both sides. The road had been constructed in order to enable the transport of forest resources, like bamboo, timber and tendu leaves, to the city. A cloud of red dust hung over the road. Every person in the truck was covered in dust.

⚬⚬⚬

One truck from Marora arrived a little before evening at a village which bore the number 56. There were two parts to the state of Madhya Pradesh: one was Bundelkhand and the other Chhattisgarh. Bastar was one of the seven districts of Chhattisgarh. Almost ninety per cent of the district comprised dense forest. The forested area was larger than the state of Kerala. Paralkot was the name of a barren, hilly region of Bastar, where the land was rocky, stony and gravelly. This region, spanning parts of both Madhya Pradesh as well as Orissa, which had been brought under the ambit of the Dandakaranya project, was very sparsely populated compared to the rest of India. Because of a high death rate, stemming from the incidence of diseases like malaria, gastroenteritis, dysentery and brain fever, the population growth was less than what was required. But there was a great need for people here. For living beings, with the faculty of intelligence, who were capable of executing labour.

There were many kinds of mineral resources beneath the soil of Bastar district. Like iron ore, coal, limestone, dolomite, copper, uranium, bauxite, corundum, manganese and so on. And above the earth were hundreds of thousands of sal, teak, kino, neel, giri and many other trees that touched the sky. There were countless clumps of bamboo spread over hundreds of miles, which was a necessary raw material for the manufacture of paper. There were thousands of mahua trees here, from whose flowers liquor was made, and whose fruits yielded oil. Liquor and oil which sold for a price. And there were vast forests of tendu, whose leaf was used to make beedis. The tendu leaf trade ran into many crores of rupees. The tendu leaf lobby exercised immense power in the political sphere of Madhya Pradesh. Governments were formed and felled according to their dictates. All this taken together, everything in the forest that could be used or sold, which were collectively called forest resources—

not even a quarter of that could be collected because of the shortage of workers. The people belonging to primitive tribes who were scattered around this region, viewed people of the civilised world as uncivilised, barbaric and oppressive, and stayed away from them. They did not want to come anywhere near the civilised folk. And as far as the people of the civilised world were concerned, the languages of the Gond, Mariya, Muriya, Halbi, Dandami folk were incomprehensible, as was their culture, their religious ceremonies terrifying and their mentality complex. Language is the principal means to express one's thinking. No one on either side had been able to break the barrier of language and peep into the mind of the other. And so, each side remained terrifying to the other.

It was difficult to effectively carry out the activities pertaining to the economic interests of the civilised government with these kinds of people. That was why another group of people were needed, with whose thinking and demands everyone was familiar. Who were recourseless on account of circumstances. Who were compelled to sell their labour for a pittance of a wage determined by contractors, in order to quell the fire raging in their bellies. If they didn't sell their labour, what else could they do in this dense forest? If they didn't do that, they had no option but to wither and die. Anything else was out of their reach.

For this reason, the government had been making all-out efforts over the last fifteen years or so to bring people here. And such efforts had proved futile, time and again. But now, what could not be achieved for so long was finally being achieved. The atrocities committed by the Pakistani army and the razakars turned out to be a great boon for the Indian government. From as long back as 1956, every now and then, a few families from various refugee camps in West Bengal had been brought here. But even with strict vigilance, not all of them could be confined there. They eluded the guards or bribed them, and walked through the forest and escaped, returning to West Bengal, where they sheltered beside rail tracks, or along canals, or on the pavements and railway stations. Some of those who were unable to escape and remained in Dandakaranya, died of starvation, some of malnourishment, some for want of medical treatment, and some of mistreatment. The sun here was fierce, the soil harsh, and hence diseases were widespread. One was gastroenteritis, a waterborne disease, which claimed hundreds of lives. There was no sound arrangement for drinking water here. There were one or two handpumps for a village of a hundred households. Once those were out-of-order, no one knew when they would be repaired. People drank contaminated water from dug-outs and drains and suffered the consequences.

In short, it was a sparsely populated region. The refugees who were being brought here now, were being accommodated in the houses of those who had died or escaped. They would be provided with ploughs, bullocks, fertilizers, seeds, land and houses. But all that would definitely take some time.

Paralkot, where Garib Das and his brothers arrived, comprised of a hundred-and-thirty-three villages of Bengali folk, and also included one-hundred-and-twenty Adivasi villages. Just as the Bengali settlements were referred to by the English word 'village', the Adivasi settlements were referred to as 'bastis'. But each of the Adivasi bastis had a name while the Bengali villages only had numbers. Garib Das had arrived at village No. 56. A hundred houses had been built there by the authorities when the resettlement programme was started in the late '50s, and as many families had been brought and accommodated there; of which seventy families had gone away. Garib Das would now get one of the houses originally allotted to a family that had left. Getting off the truck, Garib Das saw Subol Sutar waiting there, the one who used to live in the tent next to his in the Shiromanipur refugee camp all those years ago. He said, 'Finally you all came too! I can't decide what to do now!'

'What's the problem?'

'How many problems shall I name!'

The house beside Subol's belonged to Sachin Mondal. He was among the families who had arrived initially. Subol called out to him, 'Hey, Sachi-da, this is Garib-dada, whom I know from the time we were in the Shiromanipur camp. He asked me what the problems are! Please tell him about the problems!'

Garib Das pressed Sachin to say something. 'Hey, tell me about the problems. Didn't they provide any land?'

'Provide land!' Sachin retorted wryly. 'They provided land, lots of land. But it's my misfortune that I don't know whether that can at all be called land. One part is at an elevation, while the other part is low-lying. There's water when it rains, and when it stops raining, the water flows away into the drain. How can paddy be cultivated unless there's water standing on the land? Besides there's a white stone, like limestone, a foot or a foot-and-a-half under the soil. When the plough strikes against that, there's a loud sound and sparks fly. How can I farm on such land? What will I harvest?'

After a pause, Sachin Mondal continued. 'But if we plant whatever the Adivasis plant on such land, like some millets called kodo, kutki and mandia, and a horsegram known as kulthi, something grows. You don't need much water for growing such crops, one can make do with a few drops. If you can get used to eating all that rubbish, then you can stick it out here, like us. If you can't do that, there's no option but to escape.'

'The things that you mentioned—does everyone here eat them?'

'What option do they have but to eat it?'

'Don't you eat rice?'

'I do, but only once or twice a month.'

A few days after Sachin Mondal had arrived here, an official turned up. His designation was 'patwari'. He unrolled a map, and using a measuring tape, he showed Sachin Mondal his four acres of land. But it was not a single plot. One plot measured two-and-a-half acres and another one was an acre-and-a-half. On the plot measuring an acre-and-a-half, a small mound straddled almost half an acre. The rest of the land was sloping, like a tin roof. There was not a single blade of grass on it, nor did it look like that would ever spring up, because the whole plot was made up of rock. And the two-and-a-half-acre plot was covered with wild trees, tall as two- or three-storied houses. The trees did not yield any edible flowers or fruits. Nor could the wood be used to make furniture. It could only be used for firewood.

The patwari who measured the land belonged to Bilaspur in Chhattisgarh. But he could understand Bengali. Sachin Mondal pleaded with him, 'What kind of land have you given me, sir! How can I cultivate this land?'

But duty was a very difficult matter. If a butcher paid any attention to the bleats of a goat, it would make it difficult for him to do his job. As he outlined the plot with red on the map, the patwari asked vehemently, 'In what way is the land bad?'

'There are huge trees on this plot, and there's a mound on the other.'

Without batting an eyelid, the patwari said, 'Haven't you been provided with a chopper, axe and so on by the office? Is that for you to only gaze at? Go and sharpen the chopper and axe well and get to work. Cut the trees at the base. Once you've done that, chop it into tiny bits. When that's done, put it all in one place and leave it to dry. With the hot sun we have here, it should be dry in ten days. Then set fire to it, let it burn completely. Then remove the stumps of the trees using your pickaxe and crowbar. Let that also dry and then burn it. Now tell me, what will you do after that? Divide the land into small plots and create boundary ridges so that rainwater does not flow away. That's it, cultivate the land to your heart's content, eat and be happy!'

'How long will it take me to do what you said, saar?'

'How long can it take! If you work hard, it should be done in six to eight months. There's no hurry, do it slowly. Let me know once you've erected the plot boundary ridges. I'll issue the sanction. You'll get the seeds and fertilizer.'

As if he was declaring some good news, the patwari said, 'You'll get a wage for all such work. A hundred-and-fifty rupees to clear an acre of forest, and seventy-five rupees for an acre of boundary ridging. What more do you want? The government is providing two kilos of rice and dal per head every week. That's like additional wages!'

Even after all the good news, Sachin Mondal implored, 'The forest will be cleared one day or the other, but the mound can't be removed. Please change that plot of mine.' As he folded the map and put his papers into an attaché case, the patwari said, 'Changing that is not in my hands. I too have a boss. I don't ask you for a penny. But you'll need to spend at least two hundred rupees to make him agree. If you can arrange for two hundred ...'

'Where will I get so much money! Two hundred ...'

'I know that you don't have it now. That's why I'm telling you to clear the two-and-a-half acres first, and make the boundary ridges. I'll make out a bill and you'll get the money. You can give me the two hundred then!'

A few days later, Sachin Mondal met another official. His designation was 'sevak', or service provider. The patwari had provided his service by allotting land, while this man would serve by providing bullocks. Ploughs and bullocks were vital requirements of farm-work. The sevak sahib was sitting in his quarters, sipping tea, with his feet up on the table, while about twenty newly-arrived refugees were huddled together in one corner of the room, like subjects of third-degree torture. None of them had gamchhas around their necks, or had folded their hands in entreaty, or else, the image of the zamindar's court in olden times would have been complete.

The sevak put down his cup after drinking the tea, instructed his peon to fetch bath-water and looked languidly at the people sitting in the room. After that, he said, 'There are bullocks in the shed next door. You must surely have seen them. If you haven't, go and see them. There are twenty of you and there are also twenty pairs of bullocks. An exact match. Neither more nor less. The person whose name I call out first, will go and pick the first pair. Did you get that? The name I'll call out first!

Hearing the sevak, Sachin Mondal became alarmed. What if his name was called out last? He had seen the cattle-shed on his way here. They weren't really bullocks so much as skeletons of bullocks. Who knows whether or not these bullocks would even be able to walk from the cattle-shed to the village! The animals had arrived last night from Raigarh. They were caked with mud and lowing in thirst and hunger. Their mouths were foaming, their eyes were rheum-encrusted. They seemed to lack the strength to even drive away flies with their tails. If one could select an appropriate pair, maybe somehow or the other one crop could be raised. For the one who did not get that opportunity, it did not appear that he would be able to do anything with the bullocks, except take them to the slaughterhouse. After a pause, the sevak said, 'Now the question is whose name I call out first. Let's see—raise your hand!' Hmm ... Everyone wanted his name to be called out first. 'We can't proceed like this. I'll first call out the name of the person who can persuade me to do that. Do you follow what I'm saying? Just like an empty hand is not taken to the mouth, I can't remember a name with an empty mouth. And so, the one who wants to hear me call out his name first—two hundred! A hundred-and-fifty for the next one, and a hundred for the one after that, and then fifty. I don't want anything after that—it's all completely free!'

Sachin Mondal had sat with his head drooped that day. What could he do! He didn't even have money to buy poison with which he could end his life! He was unable to think of anything. So he sat and stared at the ground, waiting for whatever fate deemed. He had heard about *jungle raj*, but this was the first time he had actually come to know what exactly it was like. There was no justice or ethics here, no law and order. Whoever had power looted the people in whichever way they could. All of them seemed to be heartless, violent man-hunters steeped in greed, while the refugees were like meek prey in their eyes, comparable to goats and sheep. It was wrong to expect any kindness, compassion, favours or gifts from such people. So what could be done? Whatever had to happen would happen! Thinking so, Sachin had surrendered himself to fate.

※

But even Sachin Mondal was considered by some to be fortunate when his was the name that was called out twelfth. After all, there were eight more people after him. Sachin did not want to break the morale of the newly-arrived folk by narrating his story. They would come to know everything by themselves in just a few days.

But Garib Das was eager to find out. 'What will happen to us here? Where will they keep us? I can't see anyone!'

Subol Sutar answered his query. 'You won't find anyone today. They'll all come tomorrow. You'll have to make do somehow tonight. Sachin-da told me that apparently they had to remain under the open sky for six days. I was lucky in that respect. I got my house just one day after I arrived. It will be the same for you.'

For the first time, Jibon took a major decision on behalf of his family. He said, 'When there are so many vacant houses, why should we camp on this field? Let each family occupy a vacant house. Let's spend the night there. When they come tomorrow, they can allot us the houses they wish.' There was nothing wrong with his proposal. Because the next day, at 10 a.m., two or three government employees arrived and allotted the families the houses they had already occupied.

The railway station closest to Paralkot was Durg. It took eight or ten hours to reach there by bus or truck. In 1971–72, when people toiled from sunrise to sunset for two rupees, the bus fare from village No. 56 to Durg was twenty-five rupees. A bus that plied from Durg, via Dalli Rajhara, Bhanupratappur, Badegaon and Kapsee, touched village No. 56 on its way to Pakhanjur and Kelebande. One bus departed from Kelebande in the morning, while the bus from Durg reached Kelebande in the evening. That was all. However, sometimes trucks loaded with timber, bamboo and tendu leaf went by the village. They too picked up passengers for a fare.

As one arrived at village No. 56 along the road from Kapsee, the second house on the left side belonged to Subol Sutar. Where the row of houses came to an end, there was a narrow path on the right side. If you walked for a while along that and passed by eight houses, you arrived at Garib Das's house. On all four sides of the village were hills, forests and some agricultural land. If one walked northwards for a couple of miles through the forest path, one came upon a narrow stream, where the water was knee-deep or ankle-deep in parts, but during the rainy season, it turned into a river in spate. If one walked for about three miles along the stream, one reached Dondi, a village of the primitive people belonging to the Gond tribe. They were still not so accomplished as regards clothing. They had not yet been able to learn how to make thread out of cotton and then weave cloth. Although they did some slash-and-burn cultivation, they did not know how food could be made tasty using oil and spices. They reared cows, buffaloes and pigs, hunted in the forest and gathered wild flowers and roots. That was how they survived. As yet, they had no demands from or complaints against the nation, state or society. They were extremely peaceful, simple and innocent folk. They stayed aloof.

7

Kusum

One evening, when the angry sun of afternoon had begun to subdue its fierce blaze, and a soft breeze from the south began its northward journey, whispering a sweet melody as it touched the green sal, teak and amlaki leaves, carrying along the intoxicating fragrance of ripening mahua flowers, Jibon emerged from his quarters, and gazing at the crest of the bare hill nearby, in the east, he saw to his astonishment that a veritable red fairy seemed to have descended from the sky upon this forested land. And she was looking fixedly in his very direction. She seemed to be smiling and beckoning Jibon. The vermillion glow of the evening sunlight rebounded as it fell upon the red ribbon on her plaited black hair. The golden hue of the sun on the pearl-like drops of perspiration glistening on her face was entrancing. Her large, dark eyes seemed to be sparkling in invitation. A peremptory invitation to self-destruction!

The hill was close by, but one had to cross some farmland, scrub and bushy tracts to get there. One end of the almost quarter-mile long hill was on the road along which buses plied. Because people usually went up and down the hill from that side, something like a path had formed. There was a mahua tree, a few amlaki trees and a wood-apple tree on the crest of the hill. That drew a few people there. Beyond the hill lay dense forest. Sometimes deer, peacocks and nilgai could be seen grazing in the forest. One heard the warbling of birds.

Like a man summoned by a night-sprite to his doom, Jibon climbed up the hill, making his way from the other side, through scrub and bushes, and braving the steep gradient. The hill was not very high. It would have been as tall as an eight- or ten-storey building. Because of this hill, the morning sunlight reached Jibon's courtyard only eight or ten minutes past sunrise. Although the hill was dotted with bushes and clumps, small and large, a part of the hilltop was completely bare and flat. Children noisily played danguli, kabaddi and hopscotch there. As Jibon reached the hilltop, panting for breath, he did actually see some ten- or twelve-year-old children from the village playing danguli there. After all, danguli was a game that required no expense whatsoever. But where was the red fairy with her plaited hair! There was no fairy to be seen. Was it an illusion then? Was it a delusion of an emotionally-charged youth's mind? An indulgence of the imagination? No, how could that be! He had clearly seen the vermillion dot on her forehead, the pearl-drops of perspiration on her face, and the slaying invitation of her eyes. That could never have been an illusion. The way the fairy smiled, as if they shared an ancient intimacy—the thrill within him made Jibon think his very life was about to depart his body!

Breathless after the steep climb, looking all around anxiously and not being able to spot her, Jibon took a deep breath. And then, feeling sad and robbed of hope, he went and sat down on a large rock. He felt an ache in his chest. He felt like breaking into tears.

The children were observing him as they played. They gestured silently at one another in some kind of speechless exchange. It was clear the children were not exactly pleased that he had come. The spark of zest in their play seemed to have gone. Finally, after a while, one of the boys said to him, 'Go away from here!'

Jibon replied, 'You boys carry on playing. I'm just sitting and watching you play, so what's wrong with that?'

'No, go away. It's Didi's turn now. Unless you leave, Didi won't come out.'

'Where's your didi?'

'She ran away.'

'Why did she run away? Am I a tiger or bear? Where's your didi?'

'As if you don't know her! My didi's name is Kusum.'

Kusum! Which Kusum? Subol Kaka's daughter? The girl who used to pout and stick out her lip at the slightest pretext ... her piqued snivelling ... the playmate of his childhood! In all these years, Jibon had never remembered her even once. The storms and gales of the intervening years had made it impossible for him to remember anything. Remembering Kusum's face now, it was as if a strange feeling of affection suddenly leapt through the doorway of his heart. So Kusum was the red fairy! The one who had been calling him!

Jibon assured the boys, 'I won't say anything to her, please call her. Tell her I'm Jibon, Jibon from Shiromanipur. I won't do anything. I'll just look at her briefly and then go away.'

The boy called out, 'Hey Didi, come out! It's your turn now! Jibon-da won't say anything to you. He just wants to see you and then he'll leave.'

There were lots of small clumps of bushes on the hillside, and big black rocks. Who knows which bush or rock she was crouching behind! Jibon tried to frighten her out of her hiding place. 'There are poisonous snakes and scorpions in the bushes and rocks. Once a snake bites you, you won't even have time to ask for water. A person in No. 7 was bitten yesterday!'

Fear of snakes and scorpions was indeed a deathly fear. And there were plenty of those here. Kusum emerged from behind a rock. But she didn't go near Jibon. Standing afar, curving her hip, and raising her eyebrow, she said, 'Bishwo, tell him to go away! There's nothing for him here. I won't play unless he leaves.'

'I'm not harming anyone! I'm just sitting here quietly!'

'Yes, keep sitting quietly. Go and sit where you were all these days ... There's no need to sit here.'

This wasn't anger but wounded pride! Smiling inwardly, Jibon asked. 'Why did you call me here if you wanted to kick me out?'

'Who called you! Hey, Bishwo, boys, did you all hear that? He says I called him! Wasn't I playing with you all? So how could I have called him? God, what a liar! Next he'll call people thieves in broad daylight! I've never seen such a liar in all my life!'

'Are you telling the truth? That you didn't call me?'

Kusum said haughtily, 'I don't have the slightest interest in calling you! Who are you, that I should call you?'

'Am I no one to you?'

Looking in the direction of Bishwo and swinging her plaits, Kusum said, 'If he were really someone, couldn't he find time, even on a single day, to knock on the door of our house? After all, it's been quite a while since he arrived here. Didn't he think it necessary to find out if Kusum is dead or alive? And now he asks, "am I no one to you"! With what face does he say that? So where's the need for me to call him!'

Turning towards Jibon, she again said, 'Go away! You have nothing more to do with me. Everything's over.' As she finished speaking, her eyes sparkled. Her tears were like a torrent of waves, of the unspoken anguish of her young heart.

Jibon felt sad. But he also felt happy. The emotion that arose within him, stirring his heart and mind, was like an unstoppable tidal wave of mixed feelings. No one had ever spoken to him in that way, and with such words. This was not a spoken language, but a language of the heart. Spoken not in anger but with emotion. If one translated the language, not with a dictionary but with feelings, what emerged was beyond explanation. If logic was laid on the autopsy table of the mind and dissected, that could only lead to losing one's way and one's very life.

After a while, when Kusum had quietened down a bit, Jibon slowly said, 'It's been so many years since I last saw you. Where I was for so many years, how I was, what situation I was in before coming here, why I didn't go to your house—if you go on accusing me without hearing or knowing anything, what answer can I give you? You asked me to go away—fine, I'll go away then!'

Jibon got up from the rock he was sitting on, and as soon as he had advanced two steps, Kusum walked ahead a few steps. 'Did you see, Bishwo, did you see the haughtiness? He hasn't lost that one bit! Who does he think he's showing such haughtiness to! I don't go anywhere near such folk. Why would I do that? I've done nothing wrong. Isn't it said, *chorer mar boro gola*, the thief's mother shouts the loudest'! That's the plight of your Jibon-da. He's the one who's wrong, and then he throws his fit of pique! If someone who has human skin on him does something wrong, and then someone says something to him, he listens quietly. Or else, he says, "I was wrong, I won't do that again". If someone does something wrong and admits to it, would people kill him? Wouldn't they forgive him?'

Jibon said, 'I'm sorry for whatever I did. Please forgive me this time. I'll never do that again. Here, I swear thrice!'

Now Kusum came forward without restraint. In her eyes, face and movements was the distinct manner of a victor. No, the divine burbling waterfall of the childhood playhouse had not dried up and become a desert. There was still a trickle beneath the sands of time. And what about Jibon? Jibon just gazed at her in speechless entrancement. She was no longer the forest-dwelling Sita, his childhood playmate. She was now the golden idol of a magnificent queen. King Janak's girl. Whose regal treasures were adorned all over her body. Her hair, eyes, cheeks, lips, chin, bosom, hips ... right down to her feet—she was replete with nature's vast, unstinting assemblage. There was no incompleteness or excess anywhere. Some consummate sculptor had rendered exactly what was needed everywhere.

'What are you staring at?'

'It's been so long since I laid eyes on you. You've grown up so much. It's been so many years since you left Shiromanipur.'

'Yes, it's been almost ten years.'

'Where were you all these years?'

'How can I tell you in a few words the Mahabharata about where I was, and all that I did! Come and sit beside me, and I'll tell you everything.'

Kusum took a deep breath that was like a deep sigh of contentment. 'At least you finally returned! I knew in my heart all along that I'd surely see you again one day. Didn't your heart know?'

Before Jibon could reply, the children called out, 'Hey, Kusum Didi, come and play with us!'

The sun was setting. The gentle light filtered down like latticework through the gaps between the sal, teak, mahua and amlaki leaves. The expansive, dark blue sky was like an umbrella spread over the hilltop. A swarm of pearly birds glided through the sky. Gazing at them, Jibon felt a stormy gust inside that made his heart tremble. How beautiful they were, and how happy! Why didn't people's lives turn out like that? Why were their lives so full of suffering and humiliation? Why did man make people's lives so unendurable?

Kusum said, 'Say something!'

'What shall I say?'

'Whatever you feel like.'

Jibon said, 'I'll tell you about myself later, but tell me about yourself first. Where did you people go from Shiromanipur?'

'We went to Garbeta first. We were there for some time. And then we moved to Ranaghat. That's where we came here from.'

Kusum's tale was not as complicated as Jibon's. Her short life had been a calm one. The blows and counter-blows of the stream of time had not really been able to crush her. And so, there was no scar or wound on her heart, no bleeding. There was only a flawless memory that was entirely secret, entirely intimate, which she had kept hidden in the recesses of her heart, like a pearl in an oyster. If the billowing wind had not blown, it would perhaps have remained hidden all her life. The wind's name was Jibon.

Back in Shiromanipur, Abha and Minati used to live at one end of the row of tents opposite the ones where Jibon and Kusum lived. Abha was the older girl, and Minati was about two years younger than her. One afternoon, when the whole camp was in a gasping stupor in the scorching heat, Abha called Jibon and Kusum, and took them to the vacant schoolhouse. 'Come, let's play husband-and-wife.' Minati was waiting for them at the school. She had lots of clay dolls. But they were fed up of playing husband-and-wife with clay dolls, and so they had brought live dolls along. Abha played Jibon's, that is, the groom's mother, while Minati was the bride's mother. First the groom's mother visited the bride, and then the bride's mother visited the groom. There was all the talk about giving and receiving of dowry and trousseau. Finally, at the auspicious time of dusk, Jibon and Kusum were married, exchanging garlands of round-shaped leaves. The reception at the groom's place also took place. What a feast they had, with dust as rice, together with a chochchori of dry grasses served on banana leaves. A few special guests had been invited, bare-bodied, noses running, their pants torn at the backside. Some had also arrived without invitation. All told, it had been a splendid wedding ceremony in every way.

At the end of the game, before returning to their respective tents, Jibon conveyed to Kusum his right as a husband. 'Remember, from now on you're my wife. Don't forget that! You must do whatever I say! Or else, I'll beat you! You'll obey me, won't you?'

Nodding her head, Kusum had replied, 'I will.'

Was it this that Kusum had remembered? Smiling shyly, she asked Jibon, 'Don't you remember anything from our childhood?'

Jibon replied, 'So much happened in our childhood! Can one ever forget any of that!'

'So tell me.'

'I hit you once. And then you went and told my father, and got me thrashed.'

'Don't you remember anything else?'

'We played Ram-and-Sita once, and went to the forest.'

Toying with a stone using her toe, Kusum said, 'The forest that Ram and Sita went away to was this very Dandakaranya. The Chitrakut hill too is somewhere here, near Jagdalpur.'

Jibon said, 'They were apparently there for fourteen years. I can't imagine how they survived. There's only forests and hills everywhere. Even if we die here, no one will know. Even if some catastrophe ever befalls Bengal, we would never come to know. I used to hear that people were sent away to prison across the sea. It's as if we are languishing in a prison like that. We don't have any news of the country and world. I've had enough even in these few days. I just can't imagine how I can live here!'

Kusum looked up at the sky and then at the earth. After that she said, 'My father too says the same thing. How will we live here? How will we survive here? I ask him where else we'll go. We've wandered here and there for so many years. It seems he's gone crazy. I don't know where he'll take us now. Please ask Garib Kaka to talk to him. To tell him not to behave like a crazy man. There are so many people here—like them, we'll stick it out too.' She paused for a while, and then said, imploringly, 'You mustn't go away, either. You'll stay, won't you?'

There were no habitations within a radius of five kilometres of village No. 56. There was only forest, and more forest, as far as the eye went. And amidst all that forest, it was as if the village lay drooping in grief for having lost kin and country. Laughter, songs, tales, jatras, storytelling, kobir gaan, everything that had been an intrinsic part of the lives of the folk of East Bengal—it was as if all those voices had turned silent, people's mouths having been stuffed with stones. No one chatted or laughed with anyone to their hearts' content. After working hard all day on the fields, as soon as the sun set, everyone returned to their respective homes and shut their doors. The nights here were extremely dark. Night was in fact a matter of dread here. Because that's when wild animals emerged to hunt. It was as if people were hiding in caves fearing for their lives. What kind of life was this where blood-curdling fear pursued them endlessly!

Severe hunger bared its gaping maw here as well. There was only kodo, kutki, mandiya and maize, or else the subsidised, foul-smelling, lumpy rice obtained from the government warehouse. One had to fill one's belly somehow with that and survive, like an animal. Even if one didn't die, surviving like this was agonising. The way draught animals survived ...

Eating, sleeping and reproducing—where was the fullness of human life in that! That's why Jibon was unhappy here. But here was Kusum now! She wanted to tie him down here.

Kusum asked, 'What happened? Why did you turn silent? Say something!'

'Do you like it here?'

'To tell the truth, I didn't like it here earlier. But now, little by little, I'm actually beginning to like it.'

'Why?'

'Why what?'

'Why you didn't like it earlier, but like it now?'

'Shall I tell you?'

'Tell me.'

'Promise me you won't tell anyone!'

'I won't.'

'It's because you've come here. Don't they say, if the mind's happy then all's well with the world. You are here—who do I have anywhere else?'

The children had finished playing. The evening light had turned somewhat ashen. It was time to descend the hill now. As they walked down, Jibon said to Kusum's brother, 'Bishwo, come again tomorrow. I'll teach you a new game.' Bishwo looked at Kusum. A silent approval flashed from Kusum's eyes. As they continued walking, Kusum said, 'I went to your house twice looking for you. Didn't your mother tell you?'

'No, she didn't. But did you tell her? Did you say that you were looking for me?'

'How could I say that! I'm grown up now. Who knows what your mother will think!'

As they descended along the hill slope, Kusum held Jibon's hand the way she used to in their childhood. She said, 'Hold my hand firmly so that I don't fall down.'

⌘

It was the time for mahua flowers to bloom. The air was redolent with their intoxicating fragrance, which brought a strange feeling to the heart, in the way a melancholy but captivating melody did. Mahua flowers bloomed in summer, for about a month or a month-and-a-half. Liquor was made from the flowers. Liquor was an absolutely vital item in Adivasi society, right from birth to death, accompanying every occasion of joy or grief. Mahua flowers were therefore greatly valued. Marwari traders frequently arrived in jeeps and trucks at the haats of Bastar district. Many people of this region gathered mahua flowers from the forest, dried them and sold them to these traders in order to buy their daily necessities.

Jibon was earning a little bit of money now. He went to the forest with his two younger brothers to gather mahua flowers. Kusum and Bishwo too accompanied them. The five of them set out for the forest early in the morning. If they did not get there quickly, birds and animals would gobble up the flowers. Or else someone else would reach first, and claim a tree. It was a tree in a wild forest, and the flowers belonged to whoever laid claim on the tree first. They gathered mahua flowers till ten in the morning, and returned to the village before the sun became fierce. It grew scorching by the time it was noon. The earth radiated heat, and a hot wind blew in the air. It singed one's skin. A few perished too, from sunstroke.

Garib Das had not been allotted any land yet. He had only whatever was provided by way of dole from the government warehouse. His family depended on that. Jibon would return home from his mahua-gathering trip, take a bath, eat whatever was there, and then rest a while. And in the evening, there was play, storytelling and laughter on the hilltop. Amidst the myriad difficulties, this was the only time that afforded a bit of unalloyed peace.

That there was something going on between Jibon and Kusum was no longer a secret. But it was a difficult time. And people were busy with their own matters. It was true that unless that was the case, there would have been a commotion in this rural community over that. Although, by dint of circumstances, people from various places lived together here, and they did not have the luxury to be concerned about who was mixing with whom. This was a blessing in disguise for Jibon and Kusum; the two of them moved around without restraint. They spent time together, they dreamt together. The few girls of Kusum's age in the village—the ones who were considered to be of marriageable age by rural folk, but who were unable to get married because of their present situation—were not entirely unenvious of Kusum's good fortune. And for the young wives and unmarried girls of the village, the affair between Kusum and Jibon was the juiciest topic of discussion.

The social framework was no longer as rigid and inflexible as it had been earlier. Anguish at having left their homeland, hunger and starvation because of poverty, living in an alien land, and the uncertainty regarding the future because of the inhuman behaviour of the government employees—all told, the foundations of the ability of these people to survive any more assaults had become wobbly. Now, the women whose very faces men from other households had never seen, were also running around the fields and forests with loads on their heads, in the same way as, and beside, men. After all, in this insufferable time, poor Kusum too had to go around here and there, to help prepare the leaves for beedi-making, to gather mahua leaves, fetch firewood, and so on. Perhaps she smiled a bit when she encountered Jibon. That was natural at her age, that had to be granted. Thinking so, Subol Sutar too did not say anything to his daughter. And Tulsi? Her hopes were very high.

There was nothing she wanted more than to get Kusum married to Jibon.

One day, Bimala and Tulsi had an exchange about this, albeit indirectly and through innuendo. Both of them wanted to divine each other's opinion on this issue. That day, Bimala had washed and laid out some maize, which she had bought after selling mahua flowers, to dry in the courtyard. She was sitting with a long stick in the shade of a neem tree, guarding the grains from birds. Tulsi quietly came and sat down beside her. 'Bimala Didi, where's Jibon? He's badly required now!'

'Why, what do you want Jibon for? Do you think my son tells me where he goes?.'

'Actually I was looking for Kusum. She left the key of the trunk somewhere. Her father needs the key, he needs to put some papers in the trunk. Do you think the two of them may have gone to the hilltop?

'How would I know?'

The next attempt was by Bimala, and it was like this: 'The places they go to ...' To which Tulsi responded, 'The two of them played together when they were small, they used to fight and bite each other, what didn't they do! And then they were separated for so long. And in the meanwhile, they've grown up. If they go around like this here, people will say all sorts of things. Neither of them understands that.'

Bimala then said, 'Your daughter has come of age. How old is she? Isn't she eighteen? You should look for a match for her now.'

Tulsi said, 'Yes, she turned eighteen this Baisakh. It was on the day Kusum was born that we arrived together at the Shiromanipur camp. She was born in the lorry, remember? Jibon was a little boy then.'

Bimala said, 'We've barely been able to clothe and feed ourselves. Can one bring someone's daughter home and make her starve? Or else, I would have got my son married. In our present circumstances, who'll send their daughter to our house to die?'

'Don't say that, Didi, your son is not a bad sort. His arms and legs are sound. He can grapple with a buffalo. The moment you say so, fathers of daughters will jump and arrive at your doorstep from fifty miles away! If there's no food in your house—tell me which refugee household in Dandakaranya has any!'

'Do you think so?'

'Yes, I do. Just think about what I told you.' After a pause, Tulsi continued: 'You are the boy's mother. What do you have to worry about! And if you do—then what about us? We are the ones who have to worry.'

'Don't say any more! As if your daughter is some ugly witch! People worry for no reason. Or else, there's no count of how many people would have come to your door and laid down their lives.'

Whatever Bimala wanted to say to Tulsi, and Tulsi wanted to say to Bimala—they were simply unable to open up and say now. They only spun a web of words that skirted the main issue. Helpless! People were most helpless. Each day was crossed in a manner whereby nobody knew what would happen on the morrow. One shouldn't hope for something good in such a wobbly life. One shouldn't have beautiful dreams. And so, Bimala and Tulsi waited for a better time. For the earth beneath their feet to get a bit firmer. They could talk then. Jibon liked Kusum, and she liked him too, and that was based on many years of acquaintance.

Even if it was unspoken, the match had after all been formalised in a sense. So one could wait and see for some time.

8

Flight Again

A few days after Jibon and his family arrived in Dandakaranya, the season for gathering beedi leaves ended. After that came the time to gather mahua flowers. Then it was time for the mahua to fruit. Through gathering all these, they were able to earn two or three rupees a day. Together with the bit of assistance provided by the government, they were more or less getting by. But once the fruiting season got over, the additional income stopped, and the family faced the same old hardship. It was at that time that a contractor's truck arrived in the village. They needed labourers.

Every kind of activity relating to development was taking place in Bastar, as well as various other places, all under the aegis of the Dandakaranya Development Authority as well as several more organisations. All of which had been initiated, but remained incomplete for unavailability of labour. Many projects had come to a close too. One of these was the Kharkhara dam, which had been started in the sixties but had not yet been fully constructed. Work needed to be taken up on a war footing in order to complete the unfinished dam. And so, workers were needed. That's why they had come with a truck. Because Kharkhara was fourteen or fifteen miles away, one had to stay there and work. The wages were paid weekly, and there were one or two holidays in the week.

Jibon said to his younger brother Jatan, 'Come, let's go there.' As soon as he agreed, Garib Das said, 'I'll go too.'

'What will you do there? You're an old man, Baba, you're not well either. It's enough that both of us are going.'

'I'll go too. I'll help the two of you in whichever way I can. When there's work available, what's the harm if I can do even eight annas' worth of work?'

Subol Sutar too arrived there after getting the news. Very soon a group of about twenty or twenty-two men were ready, with baskets and spades, pickaxes and crowbars. They got into the truck. After bringing them to the site of the Kharkhara dam, the contractor's manager explained the work to them. A pit had to be dug, ten feet long, ten feet wide and one foot deep. Just that. If just that amount of earth was dug and carried to the dam and thrown there, they would be paid a remuneration of seventy-five rupees. All the labourers there were from East Bengal. They knew the soil of Bengal. But the soil of Bastar district was unfamiliar and unknown to them. This soil was extremely hard and difficult to dig. When those whose hearts had leapt in joy on hearing about the remuneration of seventy-five rupees actually began to dig the earth, and heard the ringing report as spade hit earth, all their joy evaporated. The spade was useless; even when they used a pickaxe, it did not go deeper than half an inch. After a basket of earth was removed, what emerged looked like white limestone, soft, sticky and stony. When that was struck powerfully with a pick, only about a hundred grams of soil and stone could be removed.

Jatan said, 'Dada, what work have we come to? We won't make even two rupees a day here.'

It was Bastar district's infamous period of May-June. The sun was a veritable ball of fire. There was *loo* in the air, the hot wind which scorched the skin. The earth beneath one's feet was as hot as a griddle on which rotis were cooked. One could not stand on that with bare feet. But there was no option—after all, who could afford to buy slippers! After working for a few days in such conditions, Jibon fell ill. His body, fed on Bengal's water and air, was unable to adjust to the new environment. It was said that once someone contracted dysentery, it remained lifelong. The germs of the disease burrowed into the body, and as soon as they found a conducive environment, they rose up again. Jibon had once barely survived this disease. Now it attacked him again. Garib Das returned to the village with the sick Jibon. Jatan remained in Kharkhara. The contractor had of his own accord provided a vehicle on the day they had gone to work. Now Jibon had to make his own way back. What else could he do but return? When he needed to run to the forest every few minutes, what was the use of languishing at the dam site? Bastar was a district that was devoid of water. Owing to the scarcity, the Adivasi folk here wiped themselves with leaves after relieving themselves. As he walked the fourteen or fifteen miles back to the village, Jibon too had to use leaves six or seven times. But it wasn't as if the ailment would be cured as soon as he reached the village. The virulence of the disease only seemed to grow by the day. Eventually, Jibon did not even have the strength to sit up. He didn't have the strength to get up and walk to the field. Garib Das had a few rupees. Finally, he was compelled to take Jibon to Pakhanjor by the bus headed towards Bande. There was a hospital here. The doctor had him admitted at once. Since none of the ten or twelve beds in the hospital was vacant, he was made to lie down on a blanket spread on the floor, and then immediately given a saline drip. The needle was inserted into the fleshy part of his left arm. The previous night he had had about forty painful calls; this night the attack relented after only a single call. Like the relatives of many other patients, Garib Das too spent the night under a tree on the grounds of the hospital. The next morning, when the doctor said, 'He needs to stay here', he told Jibon, 'You stay here, I'll go home. I'll come to take you on the day you are released. The doctor told me that he'll let me know after four or five days.'

Jibon had not fully recovered even after eight days in the hospital. He still passed lumps of white mucus in his faeces; but the doctor issued the release order. There were only ten or twelve beds in the hospital, while the number of sick patients was many times greater. Jibon needed to be discharged so that someone else could be admitted. He had got a bed after spending one night on the floor. Now he had to vacate the bed.

After returning to the village, Jibon was in no condition to go out to work. There was no point in going there either. Seeing that no one could earn more than two rupees a day, after a few days, all the others who had gone to Kharkhara returned to the village. Jatan explained, 'What else could I do but return? What with the hunger after digging with the pick all day, I finish off a kilo-and-a-half of rice every day. That costs a rupee-and-a-half. Add salt, chillies and two potatoes to that. I don't earn enough even to fucking eat! To hell with such work ...'

It was almost a month and a half before Jibon was better. He did not want to stay there any longer. He was sick and tired of seeing the forest all day. He couldn't bear the *jungle-raj*, and the inhuman behaviour of the government employees wielding power. Jibon felt like dragging each one of them into the forest and hacking them to bits there. It wasn't possible for him to do that alone. But where would he get a partner! The hapless refugees were in such terror of the oppression by the autocratic government officials that they lacked the courage even to speak loudly before them about their needs and complaints. Subol Sutar had gone to find out when they might get the land allotted to them. The patwari had silenced him with a single retort. 'We are much more concerned about that than you are! You're sitting idle and eating, go on doing that. We'll tell you when it's time.'

Jibon felt as if he was constantly in unbearable anguish, living among such powerless and weak folk. It had been a long while since he had suffered humiliation without protest. He felt like he was being eaten up from within. As if someone had tied him up and thrown him into a well. As if he was unable to move, and was drowning.

In the vast desert of his troubled mind was a tiny oasis: Kusum. She wanted to hold on to Jibon and survive like a creeper. At the core of all the small hopes, dreams and desires that she harboured was a man whose name was Jibon. It was Jibon who occupied every party of her being. Without him, Kusum felt incomplete, divided, halved. It was because of Kusum that Jibon was thinking of leaving this place now. But he was unable to actually go away. He silently suffered all the hardship, anguish, humiliation, harassment and starvation.

⁂

One day Jibon said to Kusum, 'I don't feel like being here any more. When my father spoke to me about coming here, I had in mind all the fear of the danger I was in back in Calcutta. What would happen if someone vented the anger they had against me on Jatan and Jugal? So I thought it would be better to come away to Dandakaranya instead. If one could at least live in peace, and get by with enough to eat twice a day, that would not be bad. But I can see that I made a big mistake. Everything is just the opposite. Do you know what I think sometimes? I think that in order to escape the frying pan, we have jumped into the fire. I think I'll run away from here.'

'Where will you go?'

'Back to West Bengal.'

'Won't you take everyone else along with you?'

'There's no place there for all of us to live in. I should go alone first. I'll go and arrange for a place for them to stay, and then come back for them.'

'And what about me? Won't you take me along?'

As soon as Kusum's question reached Jibon's ear, it was as if all of Jibon's thinking got jumbled up. That there was something like that, or that there could be something like that, had never crossed his mind. Kusum continued: 'If you leave me and go, my life will be plunged in darkness. How can I live here without you? Believe me, I won't be able to survive.'

'You love me so much!'

Kusum finally spoke her heart. 'In all these days, you never knew how much I loved you. I have loved you since the days of our childhood. I always considered you to be my own. We did not see each other for so many years, but I knew that one day, God would definitely bring you to me. God did heed the yearning of my heart. He brought you back! Now I see that you want to leave me behind and go away.' Kusum began to weep. 'Tell me, tell me you won't leave me. Tell me you'll take me wherever you go. If you don't take me with you, you'll hear someday that Kusum either hanged herself or ate a poisonous fruit and died.'

The breeze at the bare hilltop had stopped. There was a small clump on the hillside, with round leaves, whose fruit was known to be poisonous. A pair of squirrels sat among its leaves and looked astonishedly at the two of them. They seemed to be communicating among themselves. The anguish within Kusum's heart poured out in tears.

'Who else do I have beside you? If I cry, there's no one to wipe my tears away; if I get lost, there's no one to look for me. If you go away, why should I continue to live? What would I live for?'

Grabbing Kusum with his hands and hugging her to his chest, Jibon said to her fervently, 'Don't cry. If you cry, my whole world is shaken!'

'Then promise me you won't leave me and go!'

'Did I say that I was going?'

'Didn't you say that you'd go to West Bengal?'

'You crazy girl, I said that …' Jibon paused, and then continued. 'I only said that I was thinking along those lines. There's a difference between thinking and doing. There are so many things that we think of doing … but can anything get done merely by thinking about it? I have so many enemies in West Bengal, I don't wish to die by returning there now.'

Gazing at Jibon with her large eyes, Kusum softly said, 'Don't play word games with me. Tell me plainly that you won't leave me and go. Swear thrice that you won't.'

'I won't go! I swear thrice'

Trusting him with all her heart, Kusum now placed her head on Jibon's shoulder. In the way a creeper grasps a big tree and survives the storms and gales of nature, she wrapped her two arms tightly around Jibon and simply surrendered herself to fate. The two shores of her heart were washed by the multi-hued waves of youth. Jibon had made a promise to Kusum. But who knew that before the night was over, things would be very different.

Subol Sutar had come to Dandakaranya all right, but he was simply unable to plant roots in this rocky soil. Far from liking the dense, inaccessible forest, it only produced fear in him. His heart wept for the mango, blackberry, coconut and areca groves, for the endless expanse of water, the fish and the soft soil of Bengal. He nursed a secret wish that he would flee from here at the first opportunity. But he never shared this wish with anyone else. If he did, it would only lead to problems. If it somehow reached the ears of the government folk, they would keep a strict watch over him. He prepared for the departure by retaining only the most essential household items and selling off everything else. And then, he waited for the appropriate opportunity to arrive. As soon as the first opportunity arose, he would escape without telling anybody.

The opportunity came that very night. The trucks of the Marwari traders had arrived at the haat in Kapsee, bringing household provisions from Raipur. They were supposed to sell off their goods and return to Raipur. Subol Sutar won over the driver of one of the trucks. 'Will you take me to Raipur?' Subol had earned some money digging earth at the Kharkhara dam and from selling mahua flowers and fruits. Emboldened by that, he negotiated a fare of a hundred rupees for four persons, and boarded the truck. The driver had said that if a few rupees were required to be paid in case they were stopped at a check-post, he would take care of that, and that he would collect the fare only after dropping Subol safely at Raipur.

It was late at night. The government watchmen and all the village folk lay in deep slumber. Subol quietly woke up everyone at home. 'Get up, we have to go.' Kusum sleepily enquired, 'Babu, where are we going, where are you taking us?'

Subol shushed her. 'Be quiet! We are going back to our own land.'

'But we don't have any home or family there.'

'But at least there aren't any hills, forests, bears and tigers there.'

'Did you see any tigers or bears here?'

'Are the sevak, patwari, tehsildar and forester any less ferocious than tigers and bears!' Then he ordered Kusum, 'Be quiet! People will hear you. Start walking quickly. The truck is waiting at the field in Kapsee, beside the haat.'

Kusum was caught in two minds. What was the right thing to do? On one side were her parents and her brother, her entire family; on the other side was the playmate of her childhood and the love of her youth. Who would she leave behind and whom would she grasp? Finally, casting her eyes over the slumbering village No. 56 and her companion in so many joys, the bare hill, she sighed deeply and began following her father with tearful eyes.

❦

The next morning, Jibon found out that Subol Sutar had escaped in the darkness of night. He walked slowly and stood in front of the house. The door was wide open. There was only an infinitude of emptiness inside the room. The floor was full of dust. In a corner of the room was an earthen water-pitcher; beside that was a torn mat made of date-palm leaves. There was nothing else in the empty room. They had not left behind any sign whatsoever of where they had gone.

Jibon felt broken and crushed. Tears streamed down from his eyes. Tears were ignorant, obstinate and foolish. They fell on the dust and trash in the room.

A special quality or flaw of the climate in this region was that it was just as cold at night as it was hot during the day. If the heat of the sun during the day made life difficult, the cold nights made one shiver. This capricious change in weather was difficult for the body to adjust to, and so, people fell ill very frequently.

Today Jibon and his brother, Jatan, were lying on a bamboo platform erected at one end of the courtyard. From faraway came the howls of a pack of jackals and the barks of dogs in response. Who knows why, dogs could just not tolerate jackals. As soon as one was spotted, a pack of baying dogs would begin to chase it. But they never entered the forest. All the bluster was confined to the boundary between the forest and human habitation.

There was no cloud in the sky. Everyone in the area hoped it would rain after the tenth of June. But there seemed to be no trace of that this year. Millions of nameless stars shone in the clear blue sky. Beside them, like a big silver coin, was the round moon. It was probably not full moon tonight, but close to that. One could discern the old hag with the spinning wheel on the moon. Jibon gazed at the moon and stars as the night advanced. He was just not being able to sleep tonight. After Kusum's departure, each day for him was heavy as a rock. It just didn't seem to pass. And night was like a sleepless burden. If he ever dozed off, that was accompanied by all kinds of nightmares. Jibon suddenly became aware that Jatan, who was lying beside him, wasn't asleep either. This brother of his, who was a couple of years younger than him, was like a friend to Jibon. He never felt shy to speak his heart openly to Jatan. He slowly put his hand on his brother's back. Jatan immediately turned towards him and asked, 'How do you like this place, Dada?'

Jibon replied, 'Why do you ask?'

'I don't like this place at all. We were better off in Bengal, even if we were unable to eat. At least all these wretched officials were not there. We're just wasting our time here. What have we gained by coming here? We're still starving. We have no idea when we might get the land allotted to us.'

'I don't like it either.'

'Then tell Baba. Let's run away from here!'

Jibon said, 'There's nothing to be gained by taking off suddenly. Where will we all go and live?'

'Why, we can go back to the canalside in Khola.'

'We can't be sure that people we knew in Khola are still there. Who knows whether or not everyone went away, like us, to different places. But if you agree, I can do something. Let me go first. If I go alone, no one will tell you people anything. If anyone asks, you can say I've gone to Malkangiri for an outing. I'll go and arrange a place for everyone to stay and then send a letter. You all can leave after you receive the letter. If I can't find a place to stay in Jadavpur, there are so many other stations. I'm sure we'll get a bit of place beside the railway line somewhere.'

'In that case, you should go. I can't bear to live here. I heard that people used to be sent to prison across the sea. It's as if we too are locked up in prison for no fault. Send us a letter as soon as you can.'

'Don't tell Ma and Baba, or else they won't let me go.'

'I won't. But please don't go and get involved in any trouble!'

The chapter of forest exile in the absence of Kusum had been unbearable for Jibon. Now, with Jatan's approval, the melody of escape began playing in his mind. He said, 'I'll leave Ma and Baba in your care. Keep an eye on everyone.'

'I'll do that, don't worry.'

<hr />

Having got his brother's consent, Jibon began preparations for his flight. Every year during the months of May and June, the task of collecting tendu leaves was taken up under the aegis of the Forest

Department's contracting system. Villagers squatted in various places, with the leaves they had collected and dried in the sun piled in front of them. Fifty leaves made one bundle. A hundred-and-two such bundles fetched five rupees. The dried leaves were put into sacks and then loaded on bullock-carts to be delivered at the warehouse in Pakhanjur. Once all the sacks had arrived there, they were sent by truck to Dalli-Rajhara. They went to different parts of the country from there by goods train.

Jibon decided that as soon as the truck laden with tendu leaves prepared to leave Pakhanjur for the town of Dalli-Rajhara, he would board it and go there. There was no means of going further than that. One had to take a train from Dalli-Rajhara to Bhilai. One could get trains going to Howrah at Bhilai. At that time, there was a daily train at nine in the morning from Dalli-Rajhara to Bhilai. The same train returned at night. There were no other trains during the day. There weren't very many passengers on this train. Those who travelled by this train were mostly employees of the Bhilai Steel Plant. The train was run essentially for them.

Jibon already had the experience of long journeys by train without a ticket. He was confident he would reach his destination somehow. He had only five rupees on him now; that was all he had been able to save in the months that he had lived in village No. 56. There were no mahua flowers or tendu leaves in the forest in this season. There did not seem to be any other possibility of getting money. Rather, even the few rupees he had might get spent for some reason. And so, if Jibon wanted to return to Calcutta, he had to set out right now. It seemed very risky. He had a mere green-coloured, five-rupee note to lend him any courage or power. But the other Jibon, who resided in Jibon's heart—whose appearance, habits and mien resembled those of Maran, the boy in the crematorium—said to him, 'Perhaps it's a bit difficult and risky, but it's not impossible. Actually there's nothing that's impossible. Anything that is undertaken with courage and determination will definitely be successful!'

Jibon ruminated. If one had adequate provisions and the necessary equipment, one could climb to the peak of a mountain or even cross an ocean. But to reach one's destination without any of that was the real proof of bravery. And so, late one afternoon, without telling anyone, he began walking towards Pakhanjur. At first briskly, then slowly, and finally, almost drooping, he completed the eleven mile journey in the evening, and reached the tendu leaf warehouse.

The warehouse was actually a bit beyond Pakhanjur, in a completely desolate place. There was a thick barbed wire fence around it, and strict vigilance at the entrance. The forest guards took turns, through night and day, to keep watch at the gate. And right in front of the main gate was a board with a notice written in large letters in Hindi and English: 'Entry without permission is a punishable offence'. From afar, Jibon saw that about ten trucks were lined up in the bay inside the fenced area. Porters were loading the sacks of leaves on one of them. Trucks would be loaded like this all night. They would come and go.

The departing trucks started from the bay and stopped at the gate. The guard at the gate examined and signed the relevant papers. The trucks started again, turned right and ascended the incline to the main road. In transport jargon, such trucks were referred to as 'overloaded'. They had to move very slowly, especially when they made a turn. Or else, there was the risk of the truck toppling over. Jibon had observed all this in advance. Like a leopard, he waited near the turning, under the cover of forest, for the right opportunity.

It was about eight in the evening. There was darkness everywhere. One could hardly see beyond a couple of feet. That's when the opportunity arrived. The driver of a truck stopped the vehicle at the main road and got down to piss. This was unimaginable luck! Or else, Jibon would have had to grasp the rope at the back of the moving truck and swing and climb up. If he slipped in the process, there was no way he could avoid getting injured. Without any further delay, like a squirrel, he silently and swiftly climbed up, clutching the binding rope, to the top of the tarpaulin sheet covering the sacks. He then crawled on his chest, like a soldier in a battlefield, to the hollow space of the hood above the driver's cabin, and lay down there. No one would be able to see him there. The journey from Pakhanjur to Dalli usually took three hours. But overloaded trucks, carrying beedi leaves or bamboo moved very slowly, with great caution, and so it took twice as long. Jibon had calculated that he would not reach Dalli before two at night. Once the initial excitement of boarding the truck had passed, he was seized by a great fatigue. Rocked by the moving truck, and soothed by the pleasant breeze at the roof of the truck, he fell asleep.

When he woke up, the truck was still moving. The distant stars in the sky seemed to be moving along with the truck. Something like a shooting star raced through the north-eastern corner of the sky. Jibon began to think about Kusum. Who knows where they had gone. They had not left, even by mistake, any sign or direction, with the help of which his lost love could be found. Thinking about all that, he fell asleep again. When he opened his eyes again, he saw that the vehicle had been parked in the railway yard. There was no sign of the driver or his assistant. Perhaps now that they had completed the journey, they were fast asleep in the driver's cabin. Jibon quietly got down from the rear of the truck. He heaved a sigh, as if he had won a battle, and walked ahead. The Dalli-Rajhara railway station was visible. But it would not be appropriate to go in that direction now. This was not a crowded station like Howrah or Sealdah. In those places, no one looked at anyone else. From his prior experience of living in the station, Jibon knew that in a vacant station there was every possibility of being spotted by the railway police. In that event, if he was taken away on suspicion of being a thief or snatcher, that would be most dangerous. And so, he kept observing the station from afar.

There was a temple a little distance away from the station. From this far he couldn't make out what temple it was. Jibon thought it would be the safest spot. Where else could scoundrels and sinners find a safe place like that offered by pilgrimage sites, monasteries and temples! He walked towards the temple, and spreading out his gamchha on its open terrace, sat down. The priest in the temple had not yet gone to sleep. He was going round and round the shrine, muttering prayers and chants. His appearance was most frightening. As if he had just murdered someone, or was about to do so. But Jibon did not fear or worry about such people. After a while, the priest asked him, '*Kahaan jayega, bachcha?* Where are you going, child?'

Who knows why, but Jibon was now overwhelmed by an imperceptible frame of mind. In a condition where the desire for something, or the fear of losing something, was entirely absent. Impelled by that feeling, he said, 'I don't know where I'll go.'

'Where have you come from?'

Jibon raised his hand and pointed towards the darkness: 'From there.'

'Did you run away from home?'

'I don't even have a home, so where can I run away from!'

The priest didn't say any more, he went away. Once again he went round and round the shrine, muttering something. Jibon wasn't sleepy. When it was dawn and the first light appeared in the sky, he picked up his gamchha and emerged from the temple precincts. He walked slowly towards the railway station.

The station was completely empty at this time. No station in Bengal was ever so desolate. It was as if everyone had disavowed this place and left long ago. There wasn't any tea-stall or even a single vendor, nor any itinerant beggar, or for that matter even a railway employee. Jibon sat all alone in the station, like the caretaker of a cemetery.

People began arriving at the station, in ones and twos, around eight or half past eight in the morning. But even then, there were never more than fifty people there. A tea-seller arrived too, with ginger-tea in a brass pot. But the train just didn't depart. It had been standing there since yesterday, and it didn't look like it would move today either.

This train was supposed to leave at nine in the morning every day. But it was already 1 p.m. now. It ran purely for the convenience of the government employees commuting between Dalli-Rajhara and Bhilai. It was the employees' salary day today. The office would open at 10 a.m. They would collect their salaries and they would board the train only after that. That's why it was so delayed. Finally, the train left at about half past one. After arriving at Bhilai from Dalli-Rajhara, and then taking another train from there, it was almost evening when Jibon reached Raipur.

The Raipur station was not an enclosed, fenced-off and highly protected area like the Howrah or Sealdah stations. Here too there were very few people at this time. Spotting a vacant bench on the platform, Jibon sat down. He was very hungry. He had spent some money in the morning. With the remaining money, he bought and ate something.

At around seven in the evening, the Bombay-Howrah Mail arrived. It wasn't any ordinary mail train; this was the weekly special. Every seat was reserved. The fare was higher too. The comfort and conveniences too were comparatively greater. For the safety and assistance of all the wealthy passengers, within moments, the station was full of hundreds of police personnel, all of whom had suddenly arrived from somewhere. And countless faces of men donning black coats—the dreaded ticket checkers—became visible at every door of the train's carriages. Jibon waited for the train to depart so that he could jump onto a carriage of the moving train.

The train was about to depart, when suddenly, a policeman spotted him. He shouted out in Hindi, '*Saale, yahaan kya karta bey!* What are you doing here, you rascal!' As soon as he said that, he swung his cane on Jibon's backside. Observing Jibon's appearance, the policeman was certain that he must be a thief or pickpocket. He dragged him towards the gate and then gave him a hefty shove. '*Ja, bhaag!* Get lost! If you enter the station again, I'll book you!'

Jibon exited the station and gazed at the train in anguish. The signal turned green. The train would now depart without him. The gatekeeper posted at the gate had observed the treatment meted out to Jibon. Why would he let him enter! So was there no other option? There was. There was a way. If he could jump over the railing, there was definitely a possibility of being successful.

After some time, the whistle was sounded and the wheels of the mail train began to move. There were only a few seconds left. After that it would gather speed. Unless he got on now, it was unlikely he would be able to board the train. Without further delay, Jibon swiftly climbed over the railing. He then jumped into the platform. A sharp, spear-like metal rod on the railing got caught in his lungi. As a result, his descent turned into a fall, and he cut his knee and it began bleeding. But he didn't have any time to pay attention to that. He rose at once and began to run towards the train. He managed to grab hold of the door-handle of one of the moving carriages.

The carriage was like a mobile restaurant. A man was peeling potatoes. He snapped at Jibon: 'What's this? Move ahead!' Jibon did not know that a train also had a mobile restaurant. Neither did he know that one could move from one carriage to another. He went through three of four carriages and then sat down at his favourite old spot, near the door. But he couldn't sit in peace for very long, because this wasn't the Farakka Mail. Within half an hour, a ticket checker arrived, as if he was Yama himself. 'You don't have a ticket? Skip the next four carriages and move ahead. Having evicted the unwanted nuisance from the four carriages he was responsible for, he had no more worries. But why would the person whose jurisdiction Jibon now entered tolerate him? And hence, once again, the barked instruction, 'Skip the next four carriages ...'

Jibon was driven away in this manner till well past midnight, just like a dog. He was tired and exasperated. But it was his good fortune that the ticket checkers had not made him get off the train, the reason being, once this train departed, it did not stop so often.

If he had to be made to get off, they would have to wait for over an hour. So why bother! Another strange thing was that there was no policeman anywhere on the entire train. All their shenanigans were confined only to the station platform.

The caprices of the ticket checkers seemed to abate once it was very late in the night. Tired and hungry, Jibon lay down near a door, amidst all the dust, grime and trash there. For some reason, there was no one at that door. It was wide open. Jibon was soothed by the breeze blowing in. In a little while, he was fast asleep.

⊘

Jibon had no idea how long he slept. Suddenly something heavy hit his head. It felt like a thousand-volt electric current between his eyes, and then everything went black. His whole body was throbbing with pain. Why did this happen? Was it an accident? Which always happened on long-distance trains! Had the train fallen into some thousand-foot abyss? Opening his eyes with great difficulty, Jibon saw that the train was all right, but in front of his head was a booted foot. And it was ready for another assault.

'Get up, you bastard!'

Jibon sprang to his feet. All the soft and gentle feelings that had formed within him after being around Kusum, were shattered now with a single kick on the roaring train in that black night. He looked around him in astonishment. All the passengers were fast asleep. There were no 'eye witnesses' present. Rarely did such opportunities for murder come. He could exact revenge on the whole sordid band of sevaks, patwaris and tehsildars, for all the humiliation and harassment that he had suffered between arriving in Dandakaranya and leaving, by taking on one of them. He looked at the booted man. He was tall and thin. Coming upon Jibon, he had probably realised that he was ticketless and did not have the ability to pay a bribe either. That's why he was in such a rage.

Jibon's eyes moved towards the open door. The mail train was speeding ahead. There was terrifying darkness outside. A sudden shove at this time would make the checker fly away. No one on earth would have a clue regarding his whereabouts.

Jibon didn't say a word. He only took a step forward. But seeing the transformation come over him—his blood-shot eyes, his clenched fist, and the heave of his chest as he inhaled deeply—the ticket checker got scared. He realised what was about to happen. He realised that an enraged murderer was advancing to kill him this dark night. He shot to one side, and then he turned around and ran away.

TWO JIBONS

9

Martyrs and the Mighty

For the past few days, a strange person could be observed roaming around the vicinity of Jadavpur Station. Sometimes he walked along the rail track, and then went and stood near the signal post on the western side. He seemed to be looking for someone anxiously. There used to be a squatter settlement there earlier. Poor but warm-hearted people used to live there. They were rickshaw-pullers, casual labourers, hand-pump repairers and so on. Almost all the womenfolk were maidservants in babu households. Some boys called Nakul, Goshto, Nitai, Montu, Ratan and Haru used to live here. Who loved people, who dearly loved and held the exploited, excluded and poor people close. They were no longer here. No one knew where they had gone. Because a few days ago, on a dark night, the police demolished the squatter settlement and set the huts and shanties on fire. In their view, all those who lived in the colony were criminals. And so, they had to be removed.

Sometimes the strange man walked along the road in front of Palpara and went all the way to Rambabu Bazaar. At one time, this whole locality had been embraced by a group of *agun upasok*, fire-worshippers. Some people called it a liberated zone. Here too, the man could not find anyone he knew. He could only see a few martyrs' memorials dotting the turns and intersections of the road and at the entrance of lanes. The people in whose memory these had been built had said, 'We shall build a beautiful society in place of this filthy, rotten one'. That's why society had turned them from living men into memorials of brick and stone. The stranger did not know, and no one had told him either, that one of the martyrs was the brave youth, Ashu Majumdar. On the day of the elections in 1972, the police got wind of his whereabouts; Ashu Majumdar had gone underground, hiding in a secret shelter in Kalikapur. After that, in a joint operation of the police and paramilitary force, the entire area was surrounded. A gun battle ensued for almost two hours. After a brave battle, a wounded Ashu was apprehended. Some people said he was taken to the police station, where he was tortured inhumanly in order to find out about his comrades. They said they had killed him afterwards. The wandering man did not recognise the memorials, yet, who knows why, his heart shuddered seeing them, and tears streamed from his eyes. If nothing else, they were wonderful people; they loved this soil and its people. After all, it was that love that impelled them to give up their lives.

Sometimes the strange man walked towards the Jadavpur bus-stop crossing. Here too, everything was vacant. The assembly of youth at the crossing, whose faces he knew, was gone. Those who were there now were all warriors of the party of the tricolour, from Bijoygarh. The man was not supposed to know any of them. The army from Bijoygarh had marched into the arena grandly to vanquish the soldiers of the two red parties, the CPI(M) and the Naxalites, who were exhausted after their suicidal, fratricidal battle. Accompanying them was the killing squad of the CRPF, fully armed with automatic weapons. They also had the blessings and assurance of the leader of the party now in power. Almost the entire locality of Jadavpur had been brought under the control of their party. The only areas they had not been able to take over were the region between the TB Hospital and Loharpara, and three or four neighbourhoods in its vicinity. There were the unfortunate strongholds of the CPI(M).

The man roamed around all these localities like a madman. It wasn't at all clear why he was roaming around. He did not talk to anyone. Maybe he wasn't being able to find anyone to talk to. It was as if by dint of not talking to anyone for long, all that he had to say had simply died. Observing him, it appeared he was suffering some agony, as if he was being crushed by his own inner anguish, from which he was unable to rise.

Some people said that human memory was very weak. As a result of the dark clouds cast by the incidents at present, time seemed to be so overwhelming and speedy that it was as if memory, and one's very existence, were all wobbling and sliding, like drops of water on a lotus leaf. Yet, in some people's minds, the scar of some incidents remained indelible. Raghu, a porter in the Jadavpur railway station, who bore such a scar, was certain that the wandering man was none other than Jibon—Chandal Jibon. Going near and taking a close look at him, he said, 'Where were you all these days, bhai? Why do you look like a crow in a storm!'

Jibon replied, 'I was away for a long time, outside West Bengal. Fell sick. Haven't recovered fully yet. Maybe that's why I look ... But let that be. What's happening here? Why can't I spot anyone?'

'Don't you know anything about what happened here?'

'No, I don't. What's happened?'

'I'm meeting you after such a long time. Come, let me treat you to a cup of tea. I'll tell you everything then.'

Raghu used to carry baskets laden with fish on his head from the Jadavpur railway station to the Palpara bazaar. Perhaps he still did that. He had once slipped and fallen with the load, and sprained his ankle. Jibon had massaged his ankle and helped him get up. That's how Raghu became acquainted with Jibon As they sipped tea, slowly and in his own way, Raghu brought Jibon up-to-date about the situation in the locality. Jibon fell into deep anguish. He learnt that the dream of those who had dreamt that this decade would be one of liberation had been cruelly murdered by the helmsmen of the state. And the people who had dreamt that were now grieving the shattered dream, like helpless passengers on a boat without a steersman, who did not know how to swim—wretched, bewildered, lost. There was no clue about where they were or what any of them were doing now.

One group of people had been killed, or else they had been caught by the police and were rotting in jail. Another group was being chased by the police, and were hiding somewhere or the other; they were what was called 'underground'. A third group had admitted their error and taken shelter with the CPI(M). And a fourth group laid themselves at the feet of Indira Gandhi, whose party had been hailed as Asia's sun of liberation. In Raghu's view, the true Naxalites were those who were in jail without trial, under the Maintenance of Internal Security Act, and tried to escape whenever they got the opportunity, and those who had not surrendered to either the CPI(M) or the Congress, and instead gone underground. Raghu's hopes and worries centred around them. He was sure that one of these days, they would make their final do-or-die bid.

Jibon asked Raghu, 'What should I do now?'

'What do you want to do? Do you want to live in Jadavpur?'

'That's what I'd like.'

'In that case, you'll have to join a party, either the Congress or the CPI(M). After all, you're a marked man. You can't stay here otherwise. If you do, you'll get it from both sides.'

'But I don't want to be in any other party. My parents and siblings are in great danger. I have to do something for them before anything else. That's why I came here.'

Raghu said, 'I can't help you with that, bhai. But do something. You know Mona-da, don't you? The brother of the Congress mastaan, Sadhan-da. Mona-da used to be a Naxalite earlier. He lives in the TB Hospital premises now. Go and meet him. Tell him everything, and see if he can arrange something.'

Jibon did know Mona-da. Although Mona-da's elder brother, Sadhan Dey, was a mastaan whose name made everyone in the locality tremble, and was in the coterie of Congressman Subrata Mukherjee, he had never oppressed vulnerable people or extorted money from the poor. That was completely contrary to the prevailing culture of the Congress party at the time. So Sadhan Dey had a different image in the eyes of the common folk. Another factor was that not only had he never participated in the battles between the Congress and CPI(M), but he had also protected quite a few leaders of the CPI(M) from the attacks of the police and the Congress. He used to drink every evening with Shib Chowdhury, the theoretician comrade from Loharpara, in the verandah of the TB Hospital's canteen. For all these reasons, Sadhan Dey was not an enemy of the CPI(M), but more a regular friend. On account of being Sadhan Dey's younger brother, Mona Dey too was not viewed adversely by the Congress workers, as someone to be beaten and driven out of the neighbourhood or whose dead body would be made to disappear.

In the eyes of the police too, Mona Dey was not such a fearful figure, because although he was a vocal supporter of militant action, he was not actively involved. A lot of educated boys like him failed to get jobs and sat in tea-shops and spoke of revolution. But once they got a job, they became entirely engaged in worldly matters. As a result, even after the calamity in the locality, he continued to remain in his neighbourhood despite bearing the Naxalite stamp. He faced no hindrance in his daily routine of going for a morning walk after waking up and then, after his breakfast, going to the station and chatting with his friends there.

That very evening, Jibon went to meet Mona Dey at his usual haunt, the eatery run by Chhechan Sahu, a resident of Arrah district in Bihar.

'Do you recognise me, Mona-da?'

'Yes, I do. But where were you all these days? In jail?'

Jibon replied, 'It was indeed a kind of jail. I came away because I couldn't bear to stay there any longer. I want to live here now.'

'Do that then, what's the problem?' Mona replied casually.

'If I have to stay here, I need to be able to eat twice a day. I need money for that.'

'You know I'm unemployed.'

'Please find me a job somewhere.'

'What kind of job can I find you?'

'After all, Sadhan-da is very powerful. Can't you ask him to put me into any kind of work in the TB Hospital?'

'Will you work as a ward boy in the hospital? Gurumohan babu can't disregard my request. If you agree I'll fix you up there.'

'Fix me up anywhere. I haven't had anything but water for the last four days.'

Mona Dey understood the meaning of Jibon's first request. He needed a job. But he couldn't really comprehend the meaning of what he said after that. He had no idea about the mountain of agony that going without food and drinking only water entailed. Or even if he did, he didn't seem to know what to do about that. After all, starvation did not afflict just one person alone, it was a problem of millions in the country. Revolution was necessary precisely to solve this problem. Once the revolution was achieved, no one would ever starve again. Everyone would have food, clothing, shelter, education and healthcare. Until the revolution came about, one had to put up with some hardship. Mona Dey said, 'I'll talk to Gurumohan babu tomorrow and let you know, alright?'

The government had not yet taken over the TB Hospital. Recruiting people for menial jobs, like those of sweepers, ward boys and so on, came under the purview of Gurumohan babu. The salary of a ward boy at this time was a hundred and twenty rupees a month. It was certain that if Mona Dey spoke to Gurumohan babu, he would get Jibon the job. But presently a long night of hunger lay ahead of Jibon. He was compelled to say to Mona Dey, 'Please ask Chhechan to let me eat once a day. I'll pay him later.'

Mona Dey smiled sweetly and said, 'Not now, I'll tell him later.'

Mona Dey had said he would tell Chhechan before he left. But when he left that day, as well as the following day, he forgot to tell him. Both times, Jibon went to Chhechan's shop to eat, and returned on an empty stomach. Like the earlier four days, these two days too rolled by with Jibon consuming only water.

When Jibon had left this locality and gone away to Dandakaranya, the battle between the CPI(M) and the Naxalites had reached its peak. Country-bombs and bullets rained every day, and hundreds of youth were killed. Apparently some teachers, professors, poets and writers on both sides, people of the intellectual community, came together then and brokered a treaty between the warriors of both sides, that no one would kill anyone from the other camp. This was what gave Jibon some reassurance. He felt safe enough to stay in the Jadavpur station. He thought that if he got a job in the TB Hospital, all his problems would be solved. But it was this belief that later plunged him into danger.

Although Mona Dey forgot to inform Chhechan, he did not forget to speak to Gurumohan babu. But he did that a bit too late, that's all. Jibon went to meet Gurumohan babu at his quarters, which was opposite Mona Dey's quarters. Gurumohan babu asked him to come the following day.

Tomorrow meant the lapse of more time. It meant destruction. Tomorrow meant summons, and death too. But no one knew that this tomorrow was going to be a slice of time that would impart a massive jolt to Jibon's life, to the memory of all the people living in Jadavpur, and to the entire history of the bloody political activity of the seventies.

෴

That night too, Jibon had laid out his gamchha, his constant companion, and lain down in a bit of vacant space beside the tea-stall in front of the ticket counter at the Jadavpur railway station. He had been awake the whole night and fallen asleep just before dawn. He was awakened by the sudden ear-splitting report of a volley of rifle-fire. Opening his eyes, he found that the station looked as if it had been struck by a seastorm, or as if a group of tigers were chasing men. People were running helter-skelter, like mad men, fearing for their lives. The trains in the morning were usually terribly crowded. Thousands of people came from the village to the city to toil. People were running in whichever direction they could. A maidservant girl, who had come to wash utensils in babu households, tripped as she tried to run and blood gushed out from her arms and legs. The spade and basket on the shoulder of a labourer slipped off. The trough of a fish-seller toppled over and the ground was overflowing with water and fish. Hundreds of people were screaming all at once, from all directions. 'Help, help! Oh God! I'm dying!' Within moments, the terrifying storm that blew over the station devastated the morning. Bijoy, the sweeper of the station, was hit by a bullet in the lower abdomen and thrown off the platform in a bleeding state. After quivering like a slaughtered goat for a while, he finally died.

What was the matter? Why did all that gunfire take place? After regaining his composure, Jibon found out that a group of youths who played football had looted the police camp at the station and taken away all the rifles, revolvers and ammunition that were there.

There were seven or eight policemen in the camp. They were unwilling to give up the arms voluntarily and had tried to resist, and so all of them had either been killed or wounded. What happened next was not unknown to anyone. A huge police contingent arrived from Lalbazar, surrounded the locality and began combing operations to recover the stolen arms. A large number of people were caught and taken into custody. Those suspected of being Naxalites were shot. There was no reckoning of how many were killed and how many lay half-dead.

When the attack on the policemen at the camp was underway, a squad of four policemen who had been patrolling the railway line all night had finished their duty and were sitting on Platform No. 2, waiting to catch a train to Sonarpur to return home. Seeing the sudden commotion on Platform No. 1, they had fired at random in an attempt to apprehend those who had stolen the rifles, and one of the bullets had struck Bijoy. After that they had phoned the police headquarters and informed them about the calamity. That's how the huge police contingent arrived from Lalbazar.

A medium-sized contingent had also arrived from the Jadavpur police station by then. They began doing, to the best of their ability, what was timely and also characteristic of the enraged police. In the first push, Kana and Jyote, from Sandhyabazar, and Tapan, from Rajpur, were killed. About ten shops and five or six cycle-rickshaws adjacent to the station were destroyed. There was no count of how many ordinary people were thrashed.

Jibon had to flee from there. The station was no longer safe. But where would it be safe to run away to? Was there any place at all that was safe now? Yet Jibon ran. He ran along Station Road, reached the No. 9 bus-stop crossing, turned right towards the rail track, and then ran in the direction of Salampur. After that he suddenly remembered that the youths had fled with the stolen arms in this direction. The police would surely come here in search of them. He went back to the bus-stop crossing. Walking ahead a bit, he entered the university campus. The turmoil had not yet reached here. Jibon wandered around directionless and spent quite a while there. He then remembered that Gurumohan babu had asked to meet him. The locality had surely become peaceful by now. It should be safe for him to go there now. Perhaps Gurumohan babu would have woken up by now.

The station-side wall of the TB Hospital was a bit broken. The employees who lived in the quarters in the hospital compound needed to go towards the station for various requirements. So the very day after the wall was erected, they had removed some of the bricks on top. The hospital authorities had not repaired that; or else, the employees would have had to undertake the task of breaking the wall again. If one went across the broken wall and walked just a few steps ahead, one arrived at the quarters of Mona Dey and Sadhan

Dey on the left. Not exactly theirs, but their revered father's, who had been a member of the hospital staff. Opposite their quarters was Gurumohan babu's.

Walking slowly and cautiously, Jibon reached the station. It had been about two hours since the incident took place. That meant that even if the blood on the station platform had not been washed away, it had been somewhat wiped out from people's minds. A few people had started walking on the streets again. The police contingent had now broken up into small groups, and they were carrying out search operations in the entire locality. Jibon went through the gap in the wall and stopped in front of the window of Gurumohan babu's quarters, which faced the lane. 'I'm here,' he said.

Gurumohan babu had woken up, brushed his teeth, and was sipping a cup of tea. He was as yet unaware of what the morning had witnessed in the world across the wall. He had heard the sound of gunfire. That was what had woken him up. As he performed his morning ablutions, he had heard the sound of twenty-two gunshots. But such sounds were nothing new. He had heard a lot of that and become used to it too. Finding Jibon there now, he enquired, 'What happened there, boy?'

Jibon said, 'Whatever had to happen has already taken place. Nothing more is happening now. The police have arrived and are firing.'

'What has already happened?'

'Rifles were snatched.'

'Who did that?'

'How would I know that?'

'When rifles were snatched, I think it must be them. After all, killing the police and snatching arms is their line of work.'

'But I believe they aren't around any longer.'

'I too had heard that, but now I see they're very much there. They are the offspring of Raktabeej, can they be destroyed so easily!' He heaved a deep sigh, took a final sip of tea from the cup, and put it down on the table in front of him. Then he picked up a printed form and held it out to Jibon through the grille on the window. 'Take this. Get an X-ray done. Since it's a TB Hospital, you must have an X-ray done. Do you know the X-ray room? It's on the first floor of the Hundred Bed ward. If you show this paper there, they'll do an X-ray. Once I get the X-ray report, I'll do whatever else is necessary and get you the job. I think they must be open by now. If it's not open, wait there awhile. You can go now. I have to go to the market. With all this trouble brewing, who knows what's available ...'

⁂

Jibon took the form and walked southwards. The hospital premises were completely vacant now. The health-conscious youths who gathered at the playing field every morning were not there. The hustle and bustle and din of the hospital employees who had come for the morning shift wasn't there either. The usual crowd of patients on the grass and on the benches on the field in front of the ward seemed to have vanished. The bloody morning, full of the smell of explosives, seemed to have turned everyone's hearts to ice. The police killing was not so frightening; it was a routine affair. But the wheel had turned today—it was policemen who had been killed by people. That was what had made people tremble.

Jibon had not been inside the TB Hospital for a long time, because he did not dare to go there. Long ago, in some forgotten past, or was it in some past life, he used to frequent this place. Although he was unable to come here, he was actually quite happy not to be there, because the area belonged to those who did not consider Jibon to be their friend. But impelled by the terrible hunger in his belly, and emboldened by hearing about the so-called peace initiative, he had come here now. What Jibon did not know was that the condition of abiding by the terms of the peace treaty arose only when both sides were equally powerful. But where one side was weak, the powerful opponents on the other side no longer felt obliged to abide by the truce. There had also been a treaty of non-aggression between Stalin and Hitler; everyone knows how that went.

Under the assault of the state, the Naxalites now had their backs to the wall. Most of them had fled their neighbourhoods and escaped. The few who remained, let alone carry out attacks, were hard put even to defend themselves. And now, on top of everything, was this incident today. The police and the authorities would come down upon them even more cruelly. Those who were apprehended would at once be subjected to an 'encounter'. So there was nothing to fear anymore. There was no need to abide by the terms of the peace treaty any longer.

After leaving Gurumohan babu's quarters, Jibon cut through the hospital grounds. Going past the hospital canteen, the Hundred Bed ward and the sweepers' quarters, he arrived at the culvert at Loharpara. If he had turned left diagonally opposite, and walked for two or three minutes, Jibon would have reached the X-ray department. But before he could do that, a quiet but harsh order reached his ears: 'Halt! Raise your hands! If you try to run, I'll shoot you to bits!' There were trees and bushes alongside the road and in front of and behind the canteen. All the trees had been planted years ago. Two shadowy figures emerged from behind the cover of the trees. Jibon's legs seemed to have turned to stone. He felt the cold, harsh touch of a metal barrel on his spine. Another one, just like that, in the middle of his chest; six poisonous teeth seemed to be peeping at him through the chambers of the revolver's cylinder.

Jibon recognised both of them. They recognised Jibon too. But then, they had waylaid him only because they recognised him. It was a long-standing acquaintance, and a bloody one. One of them was called Nanu. A few days after Jibon had left home and come away to Palpara, one night, Jibon had come as far as the grounds of the sweepers' quarters and attacked Nanu with a country-bomb. The other person was Tapas Dutta. A country-bomb had been flung at him too one morning, at the No. 9 bus-stand crossing. One of the bombs had failed to explode, while the other missed its target and entered a shop.

'Isn't your name Jibon? Come along with us.'

10

The Jaws of Death

Loharpara was not just the name of a neighbourhood, it was a locality of serial terror. It was a name that made even the gutsiest quake in fear. There was a saying in this locality, '*Loharparay je jaay hete shey pherey khate!* Enter Loharpara on foot and exit on a bier!'. There was not a single instance of someone from the opposing party coming here and returning alive. They used to say, 'Why would we bring you here if we had to send you back!' Jibon was being taken to the same notorious Loharpara now.

Had Jibon really walked there that day? Was it indeed Jibon who went there that day? No, he wasn't Jibon. It was impossible to catch Jibon so easily and take him there. He would have resisted right where he had been apprehended, instead of going where death was certain. Nanu and Tapas Dutta dragged a benumbed, insensate, starving, half-dead and dysentery-afflicted body, along what seemed to be the most inaccessible, rugged and difficult terrain he had journeyed through in his life.

Herds of skeletal cows could be seen walking to the slaughterhouse in exactly the same way. The muddy, ashen bodies dragged themselves forward with great difficulty. Every step exhausted them. With every step they shed the urge to live. They did not know where they had begun walking, how many sleepless nights and days they had gone without food, how many bumpy roads they had stumbled over and crossed, or how much more they had to walk. It was as if their weak, exhausted bodies wanted to collapse and roll over on the muddy road. Their legs were simply unable to carry the load of their bodies. And yet there was no option, they had to keep on walking. As soon as their pace slackened a bit, the merciless stick of the infuriated butcher landed on their backs, 'Come on, keep walking!' Their agony was expressed by the foam oozing from their mouths. Big flies sat on their rheum-encrusted eyes. A furtive crow pecked at the wounds and sores on their bodies. Their bodies were so devoid of strength that they couldn't even raise their tails to drive anything away. And yet the poor cows had to walk. They had to transport their living bodies themselves to the slaughterhouse. Jibon now realised how Jesus Christ must have felt the day he carried his own cross on his shoulders and climbed up the hill of Golgotha to receive the death sentence.

The culvert at Loharpara was now crowded with people. How many people might there be? A hundred? Two-hundred? Three-hundred? One couldn't really estimate that. It could also be five-hundred. The sound of a hundred-and-fifty or two-hundred gunshots at sunrise had dragged them out from various localities to their main stronghold. Why was there so much gunfire? Is our beloved stronghold in danger? Has the enemy attacked us? The stronghold provided militant leadership not just in Jadavpur, but throughout south Bengal. If it disappeared, south Bengal would be in danger too. If that was the case, the final reckoning would take place today. Everyone was armed for battle.

But the news had just reached them. No, there was nothing to fear, this involved others. We are safe. So everyone was in a relaxed frame of mind. They were drinking tea. Some people were smoking cigarettes. Some were chatting. That was when Tapas Dutta and

Nanu Das reached the culvert, dragging Jibon. 'I've caught the fucker! A Naxal!'

Although not everyone, but a few people did recognise him. And that recognition was very frightening and dangerous. '*Arey tui!* Hey, so it's you! We got you finally! Sit down, sit down there. Rest a bit. Have some tea. We'll take care of you after that!' There was a small tea-shop beside the culvert. A coal stove was alight, with a tea-kettle at the ready. The owner of the tea-shop had an impassive, stony face. He was a dedicated party worker. He was washing the teacups. He put a spoonful of sugar into each cup. He poured hot water on the tea leaves. And he was rolling the three-nought-three cartridges placed beside the stove to warm them. Everything was happening according to the normal routine. The party had taught him that every job was equally important, and equally honourable. And so, the shopkeeper did not distinguish between cutting bread and cutting the throat. He was equally adept at both jobs.

The work of those who had brought Jibon was over. Whatever had to be done now would be taken care of by the people of Loharpara. This was like a pocket edition of the Indian judicial system. The police would arrest and bring the accused, while the judge would deliver the sentence. And so, Tapas Dutta and Nanu were sitting and drinking lemon tea. The others, who knew Jibon and his crimes, had assembled to discuss what the final fate of the apprehended criminal would be. No one had second thoughts about the fact that the sentence would be death. Loharpara did not know any other sentence. The question was what the procedure of carrying out the sentence would be. They discussed that in a huddle. Some advocated a single gunshot, some others preferred slashing the throat, while some said, stuffing him into a sack and throwing him into the canal would be the simplest.

Jibon was not supposed to hear what they were saying. And what could he do even if he heard? The goat tethered at the butcher shop could see that another like him was slung on the meat-hook. In a little while, he would be swinging there too. What could he do even if he saw that? Jibon had grasped the upshot of the matter now. In one way or another, whatever befell every person at some point of time or another, was about to happen to him.

Jibon was afraid. An icy chill silently gripped his heart. If he had been slapped and punched a bit by now, or had been beaten a bit on his knees with a lathi, he wouldn't have been so scared. If they vented some of their rage through those means, there would have been a chance of survival. But no one said anything. All of them were still burning with anger, and that was most frightening. A pressure cooker had a safety valve so that if too much steam built up, the extra steam could be released. If the steam was unable to escape, the build-up of steam would make the pressure cooker explode.

The people of Loharpara would explode. And Jibon would explode, too, with a hideous sound! Deathly steam surrounded him. They would tear him to bits. Nowadays, those whose crimes were negligible in people's eyes were given a mild punishment and left only half-dead. And the punishment for those whose crimes were very special also had to be commensurate with that. The people at the tea-shop were confabulating about the special punishment that ought to be meted out to Jibon. One after the other, they came and looked him up and down, as if inspecting him. No one said anything. No one even swore at him. They only kept looking at him with the cold, steadfast gaze of a merciless snake.

Pinaki Sen was also among the crowd here. He had once tied Jibon to a lamp-post and thrashed him. A few days after that, bombs had been thrown at his workshop. He suspected Jibon's involvement. Swapan was here too. He was reluctant to face Jibon, and looked at him furtively from afar and paced around restlessly. When their eyes finally met, Jibon called him, signalling with his hands. Come here, Swapan!

Swapan approached Jibon. 'What is it? he asked hesitantly.

'Do you remember you wrote the letter "L" on the wall one day?'

Swapan replied hastily, 'I erased that completely the same night.'

Jibon said, 'Simply by looking at you I know that you erased it. You are all educated folk, you know how to write, and you also know how to erase it. But we know neither to write nor to erase.'

Before Swapan could respond, one of the leaders shouted at him, 'Why are you chatting with him? Go, go and stand guard there!' The man moved Swapan aside and stood in front of Jibon. 'You misguided Swapan and made him a Naxalite, isn't it? You took over our wall! Do you remember, Pinaki-da had given you a warning and let you off? You survived then. You won't survive this time. After all, one can't spare a person again and again!'

Jibon did not speak. What was left for him to say! They were not prepared to hear any plea now. The leader continued, 'How many CPI(M) boys have you murdered till now?'

Jibon did not answer.

'Who were the people involved in bombing Pinaki-da's workshop?'

Jibon was silent.

'Tell the truth! If you tell the truth, we'll let you go! Come on, tell me why you murdered Kanu of Sandhyabazar?'

Jibon shook his head. 'I don't know.'

Enraged, the man said, 'Balak-da is coming. You still have time to admit the truth and apologise. Or else, think of how you would like to die!'

The man walked away from Jibon and went and stood at a distance.

Someone asked him, 'How much longer? I haven't yet had any tiffin, I'm famished!'

The man said, 'As soon as Balak-da arrives.'

'When will he come?'

'He was informed a long time back. He'll be here soon, let's wait.'

Everyone was waiting eagerly for Balak-da's arrival. Balak-da was the leader of the action squad of Loharpara. People said he had committed twenty murders. That his hands were as proficient with knives and daggers as a poet's were with his pen, or a painter's with his brush. Jibon would remain alive only until he arrived. Oh, how beautiful it was to be alive; the flavour of being alive was so unearthly! He had never realised before how valuable and pleasurable each and every breath was.

Jibon's breathing was laboured and rasping. His eyesight was turning hazy. There was a ringing sound inside his head. As if a flute was playing out of tune. The people around him, the blue sky above his head, the moon, the sunlight—the Jibon who was among all these was now free of everything!

Now he had no one and nothing at all. Detaching from all worldly debts and dues, wants and fulfilments, friendship and enmities, his soul had risen very high and taken shelter in the bosom of space. He was sitting, in public, under the sky, in the hot sun, but he had died a long time ago. It was like his dead body had been mummified and placed there.

A person loaded a 12-bore cartridge into a double-barrelled rifle and rested it against the collapsible gate of a locked garage opposite the tea-shop. Jibon wondered—so are they going to shoot me? How expensive each bullet and cartridge was nowadays! Would they be so generous? If they were, that would indeed be good. It was far more comfortable to both parties than slitting the throat, slashing the belly or beating him to death. Both time and labour would be saved.

※

'Aeyi chokra, what was your name, do you want some tea?' Someone asked Jibon, in a very kind tone, 'You can have it if you want. I'll pay for it, do you want some?'

Jibon looked uncomprehendingly at the man. A bhadralok, dressed in a clean dhuti-panjabi, about forty-years-old, fair-complexioned and plump. Gold-coloured, bi-focal spectacles over his eyes, a thin gold ring in his left ear. Plenty of rings on his fingers with ruby, emerald and zircon, and a gold chain with a Baba

Lokenath locket hung around his neck. 'Hey, won't you have some tea? Alright, would you like a glass of milk? You won't have that either? What will you have? Shall I get you some coconut water?'

Someone wanted to dissuade him, 'Benu-da, why don't you stop that! Why are you wasting your time? Why don't you treat me instead!'

Benu-da laughed. He had big teeth. He said, 'You crazy fellow, are you and he the same now!' Affecting a softer tone, he continued, 'He's going to die in a little while. I would have provided him something to eat, some refreshment. After all, we are Hindus. In our religion, offering water to a traveller on the road to death is an act of endless virtue. There's no nobler act than that!'

'That's rubbish! Sin and virtue, religion and duty, heaven and hell are all pure rubbish!'

'I used to say the same at your age. Once you're older, and lose the vigour of youth, you'll know ...'

'But in Marxism ...'

'Look, don't cite Marxism to me! I've been in the Communist Party since 1964. Where were you lot then! Marxism has its place and so does religion and so on. The two are entirely different subjects.' Benu-da paused, scratched his neck with his left hand, and continued, 'Our country is a land of munis and rishis. Bhai, I'm not the kind of stupid scholar who reads two pages of Marxist literature and then casually trashes the ancient vedas and vedanta, which have been around for thousands of years. Benu Gopal Sen does not speak without clear proof. Do you know we have something called tantra shastra?'

The boy who was arguing with Benu Gopal Sen did not want to appear ignorant. He said, 'Yes, I've heard about tantra.'

'You've heard about it! That's right, you only heard about it. But you didn't test it to see the power that's in tantra! If you can bring me a rib of a chandal who died an unnatural death either on a Saturday or a Tuesday—the bone in the middle of the rib cage on the left side—then I can show you how powerful a tantric mantra is.'

Jibon was trembling. His mouth turned dry. What day was it today? Was it a Saturday or Tuesday? So an unnatural death could not be avoided in any way! The slightest possibility of survival would be extirpated! There was a very valuable bone on the left side of his rib cage. This bone was very precious. He had been holding on to it like a leech all these twenty or twenty-two years. After all, it was Jibon's ancestors who were called 'chandal'. It was only sixty-one years ago that the British government had changed their name and replaced it with the more honourable 'Namasudra'. What good was that name! Everyone still considered them to be polluted and untouchable.

Mohan Burman arrived now. Mohan was a close associate of Balak-da, the terror of Loharpara. Was he only an associate? Or was he actually a fierce contender in the competition regarding Jibon's fate? The competition between the two to see who would surpass and defeat the other, who would be the more cruel executioner. If Balak-da was a great artist in murdering someone, then Mohan-da was like a great evil surgeon. If the former was adept at taking a life with minimal time and exertion, with merely a single formidable thrust or swipe, the latter's penchant was to slowly savour the pleasure of making the victim suffer, and killing him in the ghastliest manner possible.

He had a detonator in his hand now. This was used to explode bombs. Its long, thin wire was wound around Mohan Burman's neck. He looked at Jibon for a moment. There was no rage in his gaze, there was only a realisation of the difficulty of his duty. Pity, empathy, love and affection were all very soft feelings. He dwelt many miles away from all that. To guard against being touched by any softness at a weak moment, he surrounded himself with a circle of ghastliness. Because of which, a tale was in currency among the local folk: he did not even need a knife; Mohan Burman could sever a throat with his own teeth.

Now Mohan Burman's eyes were cruel and unblinking, like the eyes of Ismail the butcher, devoid of light and half-shut. Ismail had a butcher shop. When he opened the goat-shed in the morning, he looked at the goats there just like that. After that, he would drag one out, hold it firmly between his legs, and slit its throat with the sharp edge of his knife. That was his daily chore. That was his profession, and his religion too. It could not be called murder by any means.

What Mohan Burman did was also his religion and duty. If the work one did wasn't pleasurable, then it wasn't work but a burden. When work became a burden, man did not want to carry that burden. Mohan Burman had made his work pleasurable. He was impatient now. When would Balak arrive? Should one wait for him at all? Since Balak wasn't here, why not shove the detonator up the boy's anus and explode it? Why waste so much time over one man!

But unless Balak-da arrived ... He was the one who would decide. If his consent was not taken ... The temperature in the locality was rising. Rifles had been snatched, policemen had been murdered—who knows whether or not the police would carry out raids here too. The Baghajatin area was still vacant. If they had to move out of the locality, they had the option of going there. If time was wasted on this fellow, and if in the meanwhile the other option too closed, their plight would be like that of a caged tiger.

What else could be done! In a crestfallen tone, Mohan Burman said, 'Let's wait for another five or ten minutes. If Balak-da doesn't come by then, we'll have to do something ...'

❦

Jibon had been apprehended at eight in the morning. It was about half past ten now. The sun was scorching. There was no shade in the spot where he had been made to sit. The heat assailed him like a volley of spears. Perspiration streamed down like water from every pore of his body. A sudden hot wave ran through his nose, ears and mouth. The scene around him seemed to sway in the air. He could feel the sound of a hammer's blows inside his chest. *Thump! Thump! Thump!* As if someone was breaking stones. Gradually, the lower part of his body seemed to turn numb and bereft of sensation. There was a tingling in the soles of his feet. His eyes burned. A loud crow sat on the branch of a dead tree and cawed. Apparently they could sense approaching death. But had they got wind yet—that a great feast had been organised here?

Now the faces of some of Jibon's departed friends appeared before his eyes, as if on a cinema screen. There were so many names that he wouldn't be able to finish listing them. The one he had been most fond of was Madhai Mondal. Someone had killed Madhai, stuffed his body into a sack, and thrown it into the hogla-reed marsh in Hussainpur. Before the night was over, half of it was eaten up by jackals.

A long time ago, after hearing all the tales about the daring and sacrifice of Bhagat Singh, Master-da Surya Sen and Binoy-Badal-Dinesh, the desire to give up his life too in service of the country had awakened in Jibon's breast. There would be a fierce battle with his enemies. A bullet would hit him exactly in the middle of his chest. Within a few moments, all his agony would be over. His friends would then carry him on their shoulders and bring him to their stronghold. They would touch his dead body and take a vow, '*Shohid tomay bhulbo na!* Oh martyr, we shall never forget you! We shall repay the debt of your blood with blood'. There would be a martyr's memorial on the kerb of some crossing. On Martyrs' Day, men, women and children would raise their clenched fist to the sky and chant the slogan, '*Shohid tomay lal selam!* Martyr, a red salute to you!' But he had not witnessed death from such close quarters then; he had never imagined it could have such a ghastly form.

The fear of death ran a chill down his spine. There was a strange tingling in his navel, on the soles of his feet, and on the palms of his hands. It was as if someone had placed him at the edge of a parapet atop a fifty-storey building. The parapet would break and fall any moment now. He felt an acute thirst, like that of a wanderer in a desert. He would never see his Ma, Baba, brothers and friends again. His parents would most definitely not come to know either.

Who would inform them? Who else, other than Jibon, knew their whereabouts? Ma, Ma, forgive me! Forgive your worthless son, Ma! I remain hugely indebted to you, Ma. I was unable to repay any of that!

Kusum! Why was he thinking of Kusum at this untimely hour? She had gifted him many beautiful moments and days. She had loved him deeply. Had Jibon been able to love her as much? Who knows! The man, what was his name ... Benu Gopal Sen—came up to him again. The one who wanted to offer water to the man journeying to death, and thus accumulate some virtue for himself for the future. 'Ei re, if there's something you want, say it now, when there's still time. Once Balak arrives, you won't get a chance to say anything.'

'Can you give me a beedi? I've never had one, let me try one today.'

'I don't smoke beedis either, re. But since you mentioned it, let me give you a cigarette. Number Ten!' Benu Sen took out a cigarette, gave it to Jibon, lit a match and held it near his face. After that, he turned grave and asked, 'Who do you have at home? Are you the eldest of your siblings? What does your father do?'

He nodded his head, as if in great anguish, as he heard Jibon's reply. 'Chhee chhee! Does anyone act so foolishly! As the eldest son, you should have been working hard and taking care of your parents. Instead of that—what's all this you did? Chhee chhee! Does party work and so on suit poor, impoverished folk? Politics means the policy of a ruler. Why on earth do people like you poke their noses in matters of policy of ruling a land?'

He continued, 'Anyway, whatever had to happen has already happened, there's no use biting one's hand in despair now. If you put your hand in fire you're bound to get scorched. Don't feel sad now. That's why people say, think before you act! Here, tell me your address now. I'll note it down. I'll write a letter later and inform your father.'

Jibon felt uneasy. It was as if words had become mere futile, meaningless sounds—which he had no desire to hear or utter. Who knows why this great benefactor seemed to be even more mean, cruel and poisonous than a snake. Of all the pairs of cold eyes circling around and glaring at him, Benu Sen's gaze and viewpoint could clearly be identified separately. He was not an ordinary person, he was one of those who were exceptional. He was akin to the chief priest of the human sacrifice ceremony organised here! A remorseless, unperturbed disciple of the cult of Kali.

After a while, Benu Sen brought a glass of water from the teashop and poured it on Jibon's head. He said, 'It would have been good if I could have given you a bath ... But there's no time for that now. Let the ritual be followed with just a glass of water!'

In the way an announcer proclaimed a king's arrival at the royal court—Attention! The king is arriving!—a person announced: 'Balak-da is coming!' At once, the gathering of people present there became restless. A hum of excitement arose from among them. 'He's coming! Balak-da's coming!' The waiting was over. The pleasure that everyone was eagerly waiting for would be obtained now. Balak-da was not a man of many words. He did whatever he had to very quickly. A couple of times, even before the person who was to be killed knew anything, he had fallen flat on his face on the dirt. The acclaimed, mighty Balak-da had suddenly thrust his knife and sliced up his abdomen, spilling out his innards.

Jibon's arms and legs had turned inert. His head hummed, as if a top were spinning inside. The breath from his nose and mouth was as hot as fire, like how it was when one had a fever. His body was drenched in perspiration. He had no more feelings, sense, strength or courage. There was no throbbing in his capillaries or veins or arteries. As if all his organs had gone on strike all at once. Jibon's brain had disintegrated under the assault of a mere sound. 'Balakda is coming!'

This was not just a piece of news, rather Yama was arriving with Jibon's death warrant. Jibon imagined in advance his bloody body cut into bits. As his throat was slit, he clutched the earth with the indomitable longing for survival, his final prop. The slime of the earth, grass and blood was under the nails of his hands. Flies sat on the body lying flat on its face in a pool of blackish blood. Crows pecked at it. His eyes were exploding, as if even after seeing the final scene, they stared unblinkingly with the desire to see something more.

Finally Balak-da arrived. But this Balak-da was not the great hero of Loharpara, the one who had committed the twenty unforgettable murders. This Balak-da was a resident of Bijoygarh, and was a senior-ranking, intellectual leader of the CPI(M). He had taken shelter in Loharpara at present, after having been driven out of his own locality by Congress mastaans. Jibon could not recall who exactly had told him that this Balak-da was not as merciless as the iron-men of Loharpara. He was apparently empathic and had a soft heart. It was said that he had let many off after they had been apprehended.

Jibon stood up in a last-ditch effort. He ran and flung himself at the threshold of the mercy of Balak-da from Bijoygarh. 'Dada, please save me! They've brought me here to kill me! Please let me live!'

'Aeyi, aeyi, who are you?'

Jibon suddenly remembered that he had a piece of paper. In the way a drowning man clutches a floating branch or whatever he can find, Jibon now clutched his final prop, the printed form Gurumohan babu had given him. 'I am a TB patient. I've contracted tuberculosis. It's bone TB. I had gone to the hospital to get an X-ray done. See, here's the paper. But they caught me and brought me here.'

Bijoygarh's Balak-da heard Jibon attentively. He looked the strange boy up and down. He was wearing a dirty vest, and had a gamchha wrapped over a pair of shorts. He had a shock of wild hair on his head. Bare feet. Rheum in the corner of his eyes, yellow teeth, and a lifeless rib cage, with the laboured breathing of one who had not eaten for many days.

'Hey, what work do you do? Are you a rag-picker?'

Jibon's appearance now was like that of a rag-picker's; only the sack on the shoulder was missing. He said, 'I used to do that earlier. But I can't do that now. I always have a fever, and when I cough, lumps of blood come out.' Jibon repeated whatever he had once heard from a TB patient. 'The doctor told me to have fish, meat, eggs and milk. Where will I get that? I can't even buy a morsel of rice!'

Balak-da was moved. But it wasn't clear whether it was by Jibon's ailment or his poverty or his Bangaal dialect. 'Who caught you and brought you here? A TB patient, who picks rags for a living. With the disease he has, he'll be dead in a few days. Who brought him here? Who's fond of killing a dead man?'

Nanu and Tapas Dutta came forward. Tapas Dutta mumbled, 'How would I know he was at the hospital for treatment! He didn't say anything earlier, just followed us quietly after we caught him. He was the nasty sort earlier. When I saw him roaming on the hospital grounds, I thought he played a part in this morning's attack. He may well be associated with that gang.'

Balak-da ignored Tapas Dutta. Looking at Jibon, he said, 'Aeyi, go away! Quickly! Once Balak comes, you won't be able to get away! So run!'

It was as if a prisoner sentenced to death had been freed. But was Jibon really free? He could not help doubting. Although he realised that it would be dangerous if Balak of Loharpara arrived, he sat down.

'What did I tell you—run away!'

How could Jibon run away? There was a mountain weighing seven-hundred-and-twenty-seven tons on his feet. The double-barrelled rifle loaded with the Belgian cartridge had not moved from its place. What if someone shot him from the back the moment he walked away? So many people had been killed like that. That was the new fashion as far as killing people was concerned. Of late, it had become quite a popular sport too. Who could say whether the same would not be done with Jibon? Where was the guarantee that it would not happen?

Bijoygarh's Balak-da again said, 'I saw Balak, he was putting on his clothes. Run away before he arrives.'

Jibon did want to get away. But how could he do that? Yes, there was a way! In front of him stood Swapan, the one who wrote the letter 'L'. Only Swapan could act as Jibon's shield. There was no better armour than him now. Jibon hugged Swapan. Wrapping his arms around him like an octopus, Jibon said, 'It's been ages since I saw you! I have no idea how you've been! There's so much I have to tell you! Come, let's have a chat in private!'

Jibon almost dragged Swapan along. Now he began to feel bolder. The rifle would not be fired now. However skilled a marksman he may be, he wouldn't take the risk of wounding one of their own. And Swapan wasn't just an ordinary comrade. Actually he was a half-martyr. He had taken bullets on his chest on behalf of the CPI(M). He had eighty-six stitches on his chest and stomach. Could anyone throw such a valuable comrade into danger?

When Jibon, with Swapan beside him, passed the culvert and reached the sweepers' quarters, he realised he was now out of the rifle's range. He could let Swapan off now. So he said, 'You can go now!'

'What did you want to say?'

'I had plenty to say. Forget about that now, I'll tell you another day.'

Swapan turned around and walked away in the direction of the culvert. Jibon thought he could walk alone now. He was out of the danger zone. That was when, once again, he heard a voice behind him that turned his heart icy. 'Wait! Don't go!'

⁂

There was only one way to survive now. A distance of only fifty or sixty yards lay between Jibon and death. And he had only a few seconds. He had to run. If he could run for his life now, he could escape. There was no other option. Tapas Dutta, who had a .38 calibre revolver, made in China, on his waist, was advancing rapidly. Perhaps he had seen through the fabricated story about having contracted TB. Once Tapas caught him, he would not be able to do anything. Whatever had to be done—had to be done now! But although Jibon wanted to run, his legs seemed to be unable to move. A large police contingent was advancing towards him. They had halted their vehicle at the main gate of the TB Hospital and entered the locality on foot. In front of the contingent was a black, tiger-like dog on a leash. Hot lead shot out of the rifles of the enraged policemen, who were grieving their murdered colleagues. They were terrifyingly bloodthirsty today. They wanted to see a pile of dead bodies in the mortuary of the autopsy department. Who was guilty, or not guilty, was not a matter for consideration. They only wanted numbers. Ten, twenty or as many as possible, in exchange for each of their fallen colleagues.

It was said that when Chengiz Khan's dead body was brought back to his capital city, all the habitations that lay on both sides of the road leading from the battlefield were burnt down. All the people and animals there were killed. Similarly, the advancing policemen were shooting at anyone they came across on their way. They had fired two rounds from their revolvers and rifles in the TB Hospital canteen too, without any provocation. Jibon had heard the sound of that.

Tapas Dutta advanced and put his arm on Jibon's shoulder. It was no longer as tough, harsh and belligerent as it was earlier. It was soft and gentle, like the arm of a dear friend. 'Why are you going there? Can't you see the police coming?'

The warriors of Loharpara too had seen the advancing police contingent. They would defend themselves by any means possible, but under no circumstances would they attack the police; the party had not instructed them to do that. That was the work of the Naxalites. What that lot did was not something that any party which believed in parliamentary democracy could ever do. There were countless lanes and alleys in Loharpara, and there was a jungle on the canalside. All the warriors made off along the lanes towards the canalside. Jibon, Nanu, Swapan and Tapas went through Loharpara and along the canalside, crossed the rail track, walked on the right side of Rajpur, and cut through the field on the northern side of the Baghajatin rail station, to finally reach the ancient banyan tree in Daspara. This was a safe place. There were only empty fields and fish ponds and hogla-reed jungle here. The road leading here was not in a good condition either. Besides, one could climb up a tree and spot anyone approaching from afar. One by one, another fifteen or twenty party workers arrived there. They spent almost the whole day there together, fearing the worst. Who knows why, but everyone seemed to have forgotten that Jibon was not a comrade of their party. It was as if they were all fellow travellers in the same boat on a barren, agitated sea. The only thing they all hoped for was to reach the shore, to touch the earth again.

Jibon was unable to go to the Jadavpur station or TB Hospital again that day. He had not been able to get the X-ray done. He hadn't been able to meet Gurumohan babu either. Seeing people walking on the streets an hour or two after the rifle-snatching incident, Jibon had thought that the situation was slowly returning to normal. But he had been terribly wrong. Train services had not been cancelled. And so, none of the ordinary folk from faraway in rural Bengal, who had got off the train here, knew anything about what had happened. After all, someone who did not know that there were crocodiles in the water would fearlessly get into the water to take a bath. At that time, the carnage by the police had slackened a bit. That had been the stage when they were preparing for a major assault. The way it was still before a storm struck. Once that stage was over, the police divided into many groups and carried out their carnage and combing operations over a vast area—making

Raja Subodh Chandra Mullick Road a border, and then encircling Baghajatin, Santoshpur, Rambabu bazaar and Salampur. As soon as they spotted anyone they considered suspicious-looking, they thrashed him and shoved him into the police van. Sitting under a banyan tree, surrounded by hogla jungle and fish ponds, Jibon and others received stray bits of information about the police operation. No one dared to stir from there.

By the time Jibon was finally able to leave the place and meet Gurumohan babu, and tell him about his calamitous predicament and the reason for not having been able to get an X-ray done, much water had flowed down the sewage drain behind the TB Hospital. There was also a change in Gurumohan babu's attitude. He said, 'You didn't come. I thought you did not want to do the work. And so, I gave my word to someone else. I can't let him down now. Keep in touch with me. If people are recruited later, I give you my word, I'll put you to work there.'

So what was Jibon to do now? He begged Swapan, Nanu, and for that matter, Tapas Dutta too, for money to pay for meals at an eatery. Who could he ask now? He could not think of anyone. Finally, he decided on Balak-da. It was only Balak-da of Loharpara who could come to his aid at this time.

11

The Eatery and the Pit by the Pond

At the end of the line of cycle-rickshaws parked near the ticket counter of Jadavpur railway station, was the Paanch Tara eatery, owned by Chhechan Sahu of Arrah district, which was famous in the locality. The name was the Bengali translation of 'Five Star'. It was Sushobhan Jana, the editor of the wall-magazine in the station's premises, who had coined the name.

Every morning, Chhechan woke up, put a wad of chewing tobacco into his mouth, slung his sacred thread around his ear, and with a water-pot in his hand, sat confidently on the rail track to relieve himself. He did not pay any heed to anyone coming or going that way then. After all, where was the need for that! If the person going by did not have any decency or sense of shame, then that was not Chhechan's fault! After that, he immersed himself a couple of times in the hyacinth-covered pond beside the rail track, to the tuneful chanting of the Hanuman Chalisa, and then returned to his eatery. He drank a glass of pure, unadulterated sattu—brought from his native Bihar—dissolved in water. After that he climbed atop a shoulder-high platform. From there, he kept watch all day over what and how much was being served to the customers. But whichever way he looked, one of his hands always rested on top of the wooden cash-box. It was as if it was not a cash-box but a safe-vault where his very life was hidden. He did not move from there all day, so long as the shutters of the eatery remained open. Seeing his face then, it seemed that even if there was an earthquake, or an epidemic, or a revolution, or even a world war, they were all trivial matters to him. Holding on to his cash-box was of far greater importance than any of that. It seemed that if the great flood arrived and the whole world were to be submerged under water, Chhechan would be clutching the cash-box as he drowned. That was why Chhechan's cook Madhu would say there was glue on the medo's backside. 'The bastard doesn't even go to piss leaving the cash-box there, bhai!' Referring to Biharis as 'medo' or 'khotta', to Odia folk as 'ude', those from East Bengal as 'bangaal', and people from South Bengal as 'ghoti'—was a habit even many refined folk could not rid themselves of; so how could Madhu?

This eatery, with matted walls and a rusty tin roof, owned by the middle-aged Chhechan, was accessible to all the porters, day labourers, rickshaw-pullers, small traders, hawkers, unemployed folk, beggars, rag-pickers and other poor people of the locality. The details about all the items available, and their prices, were written clearly in Bangla on a large board made of a battered piece of metal scrap. The prices here were so cheap compared to all the other eating-joints that it was always full of customers. Sometimes, and especially between 11 a.m. and 2 p.m., there was a long queue in front of it. Wherever there were queues, for instance at the ration shop, or the football stadium, or at a cinema hall or a hospital—it was standard practice for there to be discord and quarrels regarding who was ahead and who was behind. Chhechan Sahu's 'Five Star' was no exception either.

This was in the year 1972. There was rapid inflation in the price of all commodities. Chhechan had no option but to raise the price of his food slightly. The revised price list that was now in effect was as follows:

Rice, first plate	...	Rs. 1.10 (dal free)
Rice, second plate	...	Rs. 0.25 (ditto)
Vegetable curry	...	Rs. 0.25
Egg curry	...	Rs. 0.50
Fish curry	...	Rs. 0.75

N.B.: Rs. 0.10 extra for lemon.

Although it wasn't mentioned on the rate chart, Chhechan provided sliced onions, green chillies and sometimes a bit of vegetable curry too, for the satisfaction of customers, all free of charge.

Chhechan's elder son, Ramlal, was in the trade of buying and selling old newspapers and bottles. He toured various localities carrying a large basket on his head, crying, 'Sell your old bottles and glassware!' He carried a strange pair of scales, made of wooden sticks. Like how Shakuni Mama's dice unerringly produced the score he desired, similarly, Ramlal's scales too rose and fell as per his wish. If he wanted, five kilos could become seven, and seven kilos five. He could do just as he pleased. In the morning, he used his scales to purchase old books, note books and newspapers, and at night, he purchased vegetables. Once night fell, he set out with his basket and weighing scales to Sandhyabazaar. This market was beside the rail track, on the southern side of Jadavpur Station, and as its name suggested, it opened in the evening and folded up just before the last train departed.

When small farmers and traders from the hamlets, villages and markets of south Bengal came to the city fringes to sell the vegetables and greens produced or purchased by them, this was one of the markets to which they brought whatever remained unsold at the end of the day. All the dry, spoilt, wormy stuff, so that they could earn a little more. The later it got, the more eager they were to return home. They became increasingly worried about whether the last train would be cancelled. In that event, they would have to spend the whole night in the station. Only someone who had slept in the station knew how dangerous that was. There were thieves, goondas, drunkards, lunatics and policemen—so many kinds of hassles. Rival political parties could also throw country-bombs at one another. At the very moment when their anxieties were at their peak—Chhechan's clever son, Ramlal, would make his appearance there, like a divine rescuer. He would buy a mountain-high pile of pui-spinach for a mere two rupees.

Two rupees was by no means a small sum in this evening market. One could travel all the way from Sonarpur to Sealdah by train for a fare of half a rupee. Only traders could fathom this. The one who did not, would find that the very next day, his spinach was as good as dung. Dung which was no good for making dung-cakes either. Just as pui-spinach was available, so were rotten potatoes, wormy egg-plant, withered beans, squashed tomatoes, over-ripe bitter gourds and flattened ridge gourds—all available for Ramlal to buy for a pittance. Chhechan also had other means, besides this evening market, for procuring vegetables and suchlike. For instance, some children and old folk from the railside shanty settlement went with bags to Kolay Market, the wholesale vegetable market in Sealdah. It was said that vegetables littered the streets there. They gathered whatever they could find there, or beg for, or even pilfer, and returned with all that in their bags. They kept whatever they needed for themselves, and sold the rest to Chhechan. So every kind of vegetable available in the city markets was to be found in Chhechan's marvellous cooking pot. Bitter gourd, beetroot, carrot and different varieties of spinach were there, and for that matter, it was not uncommon to find even cauliflower there. The cook, Madhu, chopped them all indiscriminately on the long, curved blade of the bonti held down by his foot, and all the bitter gourd, yam, bottle gourd and pumpkin mingled to prepare a great dish.

The dal prepared by Madhu for the Paanch Tara eatery actually came nearly free of cost. It was created by tempering the foamy starch discarded while cooking rice with a bit of salt, a big pinch of turmeric and a few dry chillies. In this regard, Chhechan's conscience was as clear as his argument. 'If you don't like to eat it, bhai, throw it away! After all, I'm not charging you for it. Whether you eat it or throw it away, either way, it's my loss. So what's your problem?'

In the same way that vegetables from the market arrived at Chhechan's eatery, so too was it with fish. That was purchased by Chhechan's younger son, Manilal. The appropriate time for him to buy fish was in the hour after noon when fish-sellers thought about throwing away the unsold fish so as to save on the cost of ice. But while Chhechan served fish, he never served meat. He did that only once, on the day someone's goat was run over by the train, at Garia or Baghajatin. A rag-picker boy had stuffed its remains into a sack and sold it to Chhechan for two-and-a-half rupees.

―⁂―

Jibon came and stood in front of Chhechan's eatery. Chhechan had seen him earlier. He had been talking to Sadhan-da's brother, Mona-da. And he had seen him hovering around the station. Now he had come after taking a bath. He did what he had seen many others doing; he stretched out his right hand in front of the cook, Madhu, and said, 'Bhai, give me a couple of drops of oil. The skin on my arms and legs is so bloody dry …'

Careful that too much did not pour out from the dirty, black, oil container, in which case Chhechan would pull him up, Madhu gave Jibon exactly two drops of mustard oil in the palm of his hand. Jibon rubbed the oil on his arms and legs and went and sat on a dirty bench over which flies hovered. 'Please remove the dirty plate. Give me some water.'

The aroma of the steaming rice served on everyone's plate in the eatery made Jibon restless. It was as if his dozing intestines suddenly began squirming. Jibon had no money on him. What he needed now, if he wanted to eat, was the power of money. Or else physical strength. Jibon had neither of those now. As it is, he had been down with dysentery in Dandakaranya, and besides, ever since he had arrived in Calcutta, he had not eaten properly for a single day. He had not had any rest to speak of either. Such a body did not have any strength. The mind in the body devoid of strength became captive to weakness and meanness. As he loudly ordered rice, his heart did thump a bit in trepidation. Jibon had entered the eatery relying solely on the intention of mischief and cunning. But what if the cunning did not work?

'What happened!'

'I'm scared! What do I do?'

'Scared! Are you afraid of this after all that you've gone through? Are you afraid to order something as trivial as a plate of rice? What can Chhechan do once you've eaten the rice? Will he cut open your stomach and take the rice back? What had you done in Boudi's eatery! Won't you be able to run away like you did then?'

Every person has two mutually opposing selves, one of which is good and the other bad, one brave and the other cowardly. One says, go ahead, while the other holds you back, saying, don't go. Two selves co-existed within Jibon too. A weak power within Jibon was moved by everything in the world that was good, beautiful, fair, just and wholesome. Another Jibon was directed by Maran, the boy—who was no longer a boy—who used to frequent the crematorium in Shiromanipur. He had defined what was good, beautiful, just and wholesome in his own terms. Which, in the eyes of many, was a path of error, dereliction and wrongdoing. Now the two Jibons were having a conversation.

One Jibon said to the other, 'Do you remember what I told you?'

'What was that?' the other one asked.

'Excellent food yields excellent health. Excellent health yields excellent thoughts. Excellent thoughts yield excellent work. Excellent work …'

'You've told me that ten times.'

'Right, so go ahead and order fish curry and rice then. Don't say a word, just eat to your fill. You can't have a good idea when your stomach is empty. Just eat, and after that, whatever has to happen will happen. You can think about that once you've eaten.'

The other Jibon said plaintively, 'You just go on talking, but I can't stop being scared. I don't have a penny on me and I've walked into an eatery to eat. Where have you brought me, O Maran? Why did you bring me here? What if cunning does not work?'

'Be quiet! Don't say a word! What else could I do but bring you here! Would I have let you starve to death! I won't let that happen. Order the food. Eat!'

'What if there's a terrible scene after that? What will I do then?'

'If it happens, let it happen! Survival itself is a terrible problem. So if you want to survive, you have to face some problems. If you can't do that, throw yourself in front of a train. Then there'll be no problems at all from tomorrow. Will you do that?'

'My brother is waiting for me. I don't know how my parents are. It's for them that I want to survive.'

'Then stop thinking about what will happen. Just eat.'

Rice! To eat! Hot, steaming, red, thick-grained rice! One's heart leapt simply by looking at it! Could there be any aroma more sweet and captivating than that of rice! Was there any other fragrance which could mask the arrogance of the thousands of flowers in some splendid garden! What else had the power to grant someone dying the hope of survival! Rice, it was only rice that had the power to boast so.

Six more people had sat down to eat on the long bench on which Jibon was sitting. Madhu was laying the plates from one end. The people seemed to be impatient. They mixed lumps of rice with the assorted dish of potato, pumpkin and spinach, and ate hungrily. It seemed they had not eaten in a long time. As if a severe, yawning hunger gaped from every part of their body. These were labouring folk from rural Bengal, who breakfasted on a seer and a quarter of stale rice, after which they worked just as hard. How could the few grains of rice of a meagre city measure appease the ogre-like hunger in their bellies? A hunger which hounded them from the day they were born!

It wasn't exactly clear what kind of work they did in the city, but it was certain they weren't ordinary labourers. However cheap an eatery might be, daily labourers did not dare to enter one. They crowded around shops that sold tea, bread and alur-dam; they made do with a plate of alur-dam and a loaf of bread for lunch, which cost fifty paise now. Jibon's father, Garib Das, had come down with a stomach ulcer after eating this kind of food, debilitating his body and hastening his own demise.

'Madhu bhai, have you made fish today?'

Concealing the fact that, like the greens and vegetables, the fish too was foraged from the market, Madhu replied, 'The fish today is really good ... absolutely fresh!'

'Then give me a plate of fish curry and rice.'

The first plate of rice with fish curry cost a rupee and eighty-five paise. That was the wage for half a day's work by a daily labourer. But Jibon did not have even five paise in his pocket. He was still scared. The fear gripping his heart made his hands tremble as he weakly lifted the food to his mouth. Who knows what would happen! Who knows how much humiliation lay in store for him if his cunning failed to work. He couldn't really enjoy the meal owing to his fear. Jibon hiccupped.

'Water! Hey Madhu, where's the water?'

Jibon drank some water after Madhu poured it into his glass, and asked for some more rice. Two plates. He ordered half a plate of the mixed vegetables dish, and asked for some fish curry gravy too. After he had eaten and washed his hand and mouth, Jibon asked how much the bill was.

Chhechan calculated the amount and said, 'Two rupees and fifty paise.'

'Note it down.'

Chhechan looked at Jibon with his mouth agape. Jibon made him gape even more when he added, 'In Balak-da's name. Balak-da has said he'll send two or three more comrades here to eat. Make sure there's food for them. He'll pay the bill.'

It wasn't as if Balak-da, or Shib Choudhury, didn't send a couple of people to Chhechan's eatery sometimes; they paid for that too. Although it was delayed, the payment was eventually made. But had Jibon really been sent by Balak-da? He surely had, or else, who would have the guts to use Balak-da's name falsely.

Chewing a bit of the aniseed provided by the eatery as breath-freshener, Jibon climbed over the broken wall of the hospital and walked in the direction of the Hundred-Bed ward. There was food in his belly, so he wanted to sleep now. It wasn't certain whether he would be able to sleep at night.

⁂

A terrifying, dark time was now underway in West Bengal. Indira Gandhi's Congress party had come to power in West Bengal through a farcical election. The Chief Minister was Siddhartha Sankar Ray. Chief Minister Ray had given the police the go-ahead to do as they wished. And they were doing that too. Every day, they killed whoever they wanted to, spinning tales of fake encounters with Naxalites. Eight or ten people died at their hands every day. The poet, writer and columnist Saroj Dutta was picked up from his friend's home, taken to the Maidan and shot to death. It was indeed a difficult time. A great carnage of death was being played out everywhere.

Jadavpur was not spared the carnage either. Both Ajit Dutta of Salampur and Tulsi of Palpara were shot in the same way. Balak-da of Bijoygarh, the one who had saved Jibon's life, was also dead. He was apprehended by Pal babu, the notorious police officer of Jadavpur Police Station, while he was sitting and drinking with a friend one night at the No. 5 bus-stand, near the second gate of the TB Hospital. Instead of taking him to the police station, Pal babu took him to a field in Layalka that lay in darkness. And then the same old procedure. Jibon had once shrivelled up in fear of such a procedure. 'Go, I've spared you, go away!' And then a bullet from the back after advancing ten steps!

Loharpara had so far been fending off the Congress assault, but instructions had been issued now by the CPI(M) party headquarters, in Calcutta's Alimuddin Street, for everyone to leave their neighbourhoods and go into hiding. All the leaders had done that. Only those who had nowhere to go stayed back. Nanu and Babua were among those who had nowhere to go. Babua was from Mistripara, which adjoined Bijoygarh, across the Raja Subodh Chandra Mullick Road. Babua had been to school, but after that he worked as a labourer. He had then become an active worker of the CPI(M). He had also become adept at whatever being 'active' meant right now, that is to say, using pipe-guns and country-bombs.

One evening, Jibon arrived at Nanu's den. Later in the evening, Jibon, Nanu and Babua sat down to snack, spreading a newspaper sheet on the grass and pouring muri and chanachur on it. They were sitting on one side of the field behind the TB Hospital, beside the hospital waste incinerator in front of the sweeper's quarters. All those with whom Babua had worked so long in the party had left their neighbourhoods because of the ferocity of the attacks by the Congress. They had gone away to some safe shelter, leaving Babua behind. He stayed back in Jadavpur, risking his life. Because Mistripara, where he lived, was just next to Bijoygarh, staying there was extremely unsafe. Given the damage Babua had done to the Congress, they would not spare him once they got hold of him. For that reason, even if Babua roamed around here and there during the day, before it turned dark he returned to this spot in the hospital premises. The adjacent Loharpara seemed deserted now. But however deserted it might be, the very name of Loharpara was still one that evoked fear in the people of Bijoygarh. Although the police had entered the locality on a couple of occasions, the Congress goons could still not think of taking it over; they did not have the courage to enter Loharpara.

This section of the hospital compound was close to Loharpara. And the environs there was also such that an attack from outside was not so easy. Even if it did happen, there were plenty of escape routes. That was why Babua was very fond of the spot. He felt safe there. The waste incinerator on one side of the field, beside which they now sat, was no longer in use. When it was in use, the discarded pillow cases, blankets, bedsheets and mattresses used by tuberculosis patients were all incinerated there. The whole area was full of smoke and stench then. Behind the incinerator was a dense jungle of hogla-reed, morning glory, swallow-wort vines and jungle tulsi. This jungle was absolutely foul-smelling, with the excreta of humans, dogs and the pigs raised by the sweepers. On one side of the long strip of land was about a bigha and a half of land enclosed by walls. For some reason, people called that a mosque. Although there was no trace of any mosque there, there were a few beautiful and palatial buildings in which some big folk with important jobs lived.

On the other side of the incinerator was a very long, slimy, filthy, muddy pit full of the garbage and waste-water from the hospital. A narrow path from the front of the incinerator, going eastwards, fringed this pit. A deep fish pond lay to its left. To its west was Raja Subodh Chandra Mullick Road, but to the east was the two-storeyed sweepers' quarters, beside which was the culvert in Loharpara. The sweepers here were more or less getting along, but the dwellings of the ten or twelve households near the incinerator, far from being pukka, lacked even proper roofs. During the rains, there was water and slime inside their shanties.

People did not frequent these parts very much. That was mainly because of the foul environment. The path between the six-foot wide pit and the fish pond, which curved rightwards and hit Raja Subodh Chandra Mullick Road, was used by the sweepers when they needed to go to the shops for purchases. And some drunkards of the lower-class also came there to guzzle cholai. Otherwise, it was deserted all day.

Nanu and Tapas raised fish in the fish pond. There were loads of tilapia in the murky, green water. Some people used the water for other purposes as well. But the pit on the other side could not be used; the green water and slush in it was full of white worms. It was in that foul state because of all the waste-water, saliva, phlegm, mucus, pus and blood that flowed along the drain and reached it.

Nanu, Jibon and Babua were sitting at the end of the field, just before the fish pond. If some undesirable figure walked along the canalside and came this way, from Raja Subodh Chandra Mullick Road, or even if someone approached from the Loharpara side, one could spot them from afar and take the necessary precautions. Babua's eyes were trained on that direction. Babua knew very well that on account of being with the CPI(M), as well as for some personal crimes, the police were frantically looking for him. The police wanted him—dead or alive.

Babua was wearing a white, collared T-shirt and a blue-coloured lungi. He had the build of a twenty-three or twenty-four year old youth. The labour performed by him daylong for his livelihood had given him a strong physique, which came in handy now. He could easily leap off the roof of a single-storey building. He could vault over a seven- or eight-foot-high wall with a single jump. That was why the police had not been able to catch him, despite many efforts. Sitting opposite Babua, Jibon was watching the children who were rapt in their football game in the hospital playfield. They were all the children of hospital employees. Despite the disease-carrying germs going around in the air, their struggle to survive and grow continued. That was life.

Nanu's eyes were trained on the broken building far away, beside the jungle of morning glory, which was once used as a mortuary. His cholai den was there. The capital was Nanu's, while the business was run by Dilip, a sweeper boy. The profits were divided equally between them. Every business had its own characteristics. In the liquor trade, quarrels and fights were normal, everyday incidents. If there was any trouble, the entire responsibility for taking care of that was Nanu's. But for him, the young fellow, Dilip, would not have been able to run the cholai den. People would have drunk and left without paying.

The customers had begun to arrive now. There was some festival or the other in the sweepers' neighbourhood. A pig had been slaughtered in the afternoon. Its meat was being cooked in a large vat. The liquor den was also getting crowded. Nanu was keeping a watch on that. So that nothing untoward happened.

Babua was usually quite cheerful, but for some reason, he was very grave today. He had not said a single word for almost half an hour. After a while, he suddenly said, 'Let's say I die, let's say a bullet hits me on the chest. After all, every day, someone or the other, known or unknown, dies like that. There's no certainty that I won't die the same way today or tomorrow.'

Nanu responded, 'None of us has that certainty.'

'That's what I'm saying. Let's say I got a three-nought-three on my chest. What will happen then?'

'What else will happen? You'll die!' Jibon said abruptly. 'All these days, no one knew of your existence, but your name will appear in every newspaper now. Everybody will know that there was a boy named Babua, a scoundrel. He was shot to death. Good folk die of starvation, while scoundrels are shot to death!'

Babua said, 'That's not what I'm talking about. Whether my name appears in the newspapers or not, or whether or not there's a condolence meeting, or a martyr's memorial—what good is all that to me? After all, my life would be over.'

Jibon said, 'What's the use of thinking about that now? Whatever had to happen has already happened. It would have been better to think about all that before entering this line of work.'

'Why did you enter?'

'Did I enter on my own? I was made to enter this line.'

'Who made you enter?'

'Whose name shall I say? I should blame my fate. That's what brought me here.'

Babua was quiet for a while. Then he said, 'I don't believe there's anything called fate.'

Jibon said ruminatively, 'A lot of educated people like you say that. But I think there's certainly something called fate. It's simply about a sequence of events. One thing happens and so the next happens. Unless the first event occurred, there would be no reason for the next one to occur. One incident that pushes you into the next incident—that's fate.'

Chewing a mouthful of muri, Jibon continued. 'So I've entered this line, fate made me enter it, I'm not sad about that any more. In the same way, I was born and grew up in a manner whereby nothing good could have resulted. I can't tell you how much oppression I have suffered at the hands of people. But at least now I know that no one else can oppress me and get away with that. If I have to die for that, let that be so. It's better to die like that than to die little by little every day, getting beaten by people.'

Babua said, 'Whatever you said is my story too. But someone kills me, or I kill someone, and either I die or he dies—what do we eventually gain by doing all this?'

Nanu joined the conversation now. He said, 'This isn't the time to calculate gains and losses. Stay alive in whichever way you can! If someone comes to kill you, kill him.'

Babua was quiet for a while and then he resumed. 'Pinaki-da asked me to join the party. I could not disregard him. He said, "It will be good for the country and for the people." I began pasting posters on walls and attending meetings and rallies. In the process, at some point I began handling knives and country-bombs. I did not realise then that I was getting trapped in a spider's web. I'll never be able to get out of that and return to a normal life. All those who were with me sensed danger and moved away. But I have nowhere to go. What shall I do? So I remain in the neighbourhood. I survive by playing hide-and-seek with death every day. I don't know when I'll lose.'

Nanu responded, 'Everyone has to die some day or the other. Someone dies a couple of days earlier, and someone a couple of days later. Someone dies lying in bed, in shit and piss, while someone else dies standing up, or running.'

Babua silently chewed muri for a while. And then he said, in a kind of self-absorbed way, as if he was sitting in a cave on some faraway mountain, 'Bhai, whatever you might think, I really want to live now. Believe me, when I think about death, I get depressed. This world, the sky, the soil, the water and the wind are all so beautiful. I'll be gone, but everything will remain! Tell me, won't it remain just the same? There'll still be clouds in the sky. Drops of rain will still fall on the tin roof with the same pitter-patter. People will continue to doze off to that sound. But I won't be there then. I won't hear the sound. Flowers will still bloom in parks and gardens, the flowers will continue to wither away and bear fruit, and birds will still sing their songs from the trees.'

'Where are there trees with flowers and fruits in Calcutta?' Jibon asked softly in jest.

Babua's house had a tin roof. But not everyone was so lucky. Some people's roofs leaked, flooding their homes with foul water, which made their bodies itch. To save themselves from the spray of rain, they wrapped torn sackcloth around themselves and sat crouched in a corner of the hut. They were constantly scared about the rain-soaked, cracked wall suddenly collapsing over them. All these scenes were well known to Jibon. But he did not talk about all that now. As dusk approached, Jibon silently listened to the emotional and plaintive Babua. It was as if an unbounded, deep agitation was emerging from his inner being, which was a lot like some piece of blank verse.

'So think about the last day. Everything's there, everyone's there, only you're not there. Doesn't your heart tremble when you think about it?'

The sun had set a little while ago. The host of reddish hues left behind at the edges of its setting path were beginning to fade now. The feverish patient in front of the Hundred-Bed ward who had been sitting and coughing away, now got up and walked back slowly towards his bed. His dark disquiet was writ large all over his face. Who knows what form the coming night would assume.

'I want to love someone very much now. I wish someone loves me very much. She'll wait for me in all her finery. We'll go for a holiday to some remote place, like a desolate riverbank. We'll walk together, hold hands, laugh, talk, play and run.'

Jibon interrupted him: 'Get married!'

Babua paid no heed to that. He continued. 'If I hadn't got into this path of violence, I would probably have got all the things I said. He heaved a deep sigh. 'I won't get it now. No one will exchange hearts with me. Why would they do that? Tell me, who will knowingly get into a sinking boat! That's why the thought of death pains me greatly, Jibon. I feel as if my life has remained unfulfilled.'

Although Babua's father's economic condition was not so sound, he had at least been able to send Babua to school for some years. Because he was educated, he could express his thoughts in the language of books. His words seemed to be laden with grief over an imminent death. 'If I had loved someone, I would surely have married her as well. If I'd had children, I would have been reborn and continued to live through them. But now? If I die now, everything about me would be over the moment I die. And there won't be any trace of me left in this world. Tell me, what's the use of being born if everything's over as soon as you die!'

Jibon now laughed and said, 'So there's only one problem for you, as far as death is concerned—you didn't get married, and you don't have sons and daughters!'

Babua replied in a tone conveying a degree of anguish. 'I'm twenty-four or twenty-five years old. I've never touched a girl yet. I don't know about the storm that blows in the heart when you touch her. If I die before knowing that, I'll really regret that, re.'

Hot tea arrived in a mug from the cluster of shanties where the sweepers lived. It had been sent by the family observing the festivities. Some clay cups had been sent as well. Jibon drank the tea and flung the clay cup into the pond. He said, 'For me, life is like this cup. As long as there's tea in it, it has value. Once the tea is over—come on, let's throw it away! As long as I'm breathing, I'm here. I'm trying to stay alive. But if my breath departs, what can I do? Let it go! There's so much I didn't get in this life. So now, one more thing is added to that list. What's the option!'

Babua said, 'I'm thinking of going away to some faraway place.'
'Where?'
'Anywhere. A place where no one knows me. I'll change my name and start doing some kind of work. I'll try to live a different kind of life.'

After a long while, Nanu spoke. 'You won't be able to do that, re Babua. I had gone to Medinipur, to my Mama's house. He was too scared to allow me to stay there. Nowadays police informers keep an eye on unknown people everywhere. They'll promptly report you to the police. Don't you remember how Bishu-da got caught?'

Bishu-da was the alias of Bishwanath Roy, who had disguised his identity and was working as a waiter in a restaurant somewhere in central Calcutta. He had been arrested and was in jail now.

Nanu continued: 'I've decided, I don't care what happens to me, but I won't leave the locality. That's like a tiger leaving a forest, or a fish out of water.'

Darkness now began enveloping them. The children had finished playing and gone back home. The sound of some commotion came wafting from the sweepers' quarters. That was accompanied by a melodious voice playing at full volume on the radio. *Jeena yahaan, marna yahaan, iske siwa jana kahaan*'. In a little while, the lights in the hospital, the wards and the streets came on. But the lights were not yet bright; the more dense, thick and fierce the darkness grew, the brighter they would become. The patients who had been walking on the field in front of the ward had gradually gone back to their beds. The doctor would be making his routine round of the ward now.

◈

Nanu, Jibon and Babua were immersed in their thoughts, sitting near the pond at the end of the field in front of the TB Hospital. There was a slight slackening of the alertness of the trio of battlefield soldiers. The darkness too had made it difficult to see too far. And so, they did not notice that the notorious police officer from Jadavpur Police Station, Suresh Pal, had left his vehicle at the main gate of the hospital and was walking furtively towards them under the cover of darkness. People said that Pal babu had unfaltering aim when he fired a revolver. He was such a crack shot that he could apparently shoot an eight-anna coin held aloft on two fingers.

Pal babu had received word through a local informer that a miscreant from Mistripara was sitting in front of the hospital's waste incinerator. He was wearing a white, collared T-shirt. As soon as he got this tip-off, he set out, together with four plainclothes policemen. The five of them had arrived by police jeep. A black van had followed them. Seated inside were twelve uniformed policemen. They were waiting at the main gate. They would enter the hospital premises after five minutes to assist Pal babu.

The five pairs of feet of Pal babu and his four associates scurried ahead silently, past the hospital canteen and the Hundred-Bed ward on the right, past the ward on the left where the young revolutionary poet Sukanta had died, and in the direction of the waste incinerator.

Although the sun had set a long while ago, it was not yet completely dark. This was the slackest and most disorganised time of the day. At this time, it was only people going from one place to another who were around. The five policemen blended into the transient, scattered passers-by and arrived at a spot exactly in front of the incinerator. From where Babua's broad shoulders and white T-Shirt were clearly visible. Nanu was looking in the direction of the incinerator, but the blurry darkness concealed them; it did not allow the faces of the ambassadors of death to be spotted. They were spotted only when the revolver in Pal babu's hand roared and spat fire. With unerring aim, the weapon in Suresh Pal's hand lodged the lead projectile of a .38 bullet in Babua's back. Twice in succession. With a final gasp, 'Aah!', Babua was thrown by the force of the bullet into the fish pond. After a couple of bubbles rose to the surface, and the green water turned a bit red, Babua's body sank to the bottom.

Both Jibon and Nanu had been stunned by the sudden attack. But that was only for a few seconds. After that, overcoming their bewilderment, the two of them jumped into the foul, noxious, maggot-infested ocean on the opposite side. Scrambling and crawling on all fours, they ploughed their way through the hyacinth and hogla and slime, and somehow managed to reach the middle of the pit. They then sat crouched like dead men amidst the slime, with only their noses held above. Time passed by slowly. Slowly the night advanced. But they did not have the courage to move towards the bank. Who knew whether or not the pit had been surrounded!

How would they know, in their circumstances, that the police had come from one direction only, that is from the main gate, and headed eastwards. After Babua was taken down with an unerring shot, they had returned as quickly as possible. Just like Pal babu and his associates had not chased Nanu and Jibon, they had not fished out Babua's body from the fish pond either. Perhaps they were worried about a retaliatory attack on them. After all, Loharpara was nearby. Arrangements had already been made so that they could get away at once. Their jeep had arrived almost as soon as the successive shots were fired. They got into the vehicle and left.

Jibon and Nanu did not know about that. Who would inform them? The Hindu puranas spoke of Puyoda, the special kind of hell of pus, reserved for impoverished labouring folk who lived in filth and were unversed in gracious conduct. Such people fell into an ocean of pus, excreta, urine, mucus, saliva and every other repugnant thing. Jibon and Nanu remained immersed in the middle of that maggot- and worm-infested slime, fearing for their lives every second. The wriggling worms that fed on excreta began biting away tiny bits of flesh from their bodies. Hundreds of black leeches began sucking away the hot liquid of their blood.

A long time ago, Jibon had once gone to the morgue in Sealdah. A girl he knew had quarrelled with her mother and then poured kerosene over body and set herself on fire. He had gone to fetch the body after the autopsy. On that occasion, he had seen a dozen rotten, decomposed bodies in the morgue for unclaimed bodies. Millions of maggots had infested the bodies, and especially the abdomen, where they squirmed and wriggled. The multitude of white maggots jubilantly rose and fell in waves over the innards.

Jibon felt as if he was such an unclaimed body now. He wasn't able to move his hands and drive away the maggots and leeches from his body. He was gripped by a terrible fear. Perhaps a bullet would tear into his head if he moved! A single bullet could turn a man into a corpse in a moment.

Jibon could hear the sound of car horns and of vehicles plying on Raja Subodh Chandra Mullick Road. The double-decker buses bearing the Calcutta State Transport Corporation's tiger imprint raced by, making the road shudder. Near the wall on the other side of the large stormwater drain —on which Swapan had once painted the letter 'L', the 'L' that was a milestone in Jibon's life—Rabindra Sangeet was playing on the radio in some house—*'Ami jwalbo na mor batayone* ... I shan't light a lamp at my window ...' Nothing had changed anywhere in the environs in which two gunshots had been sounded and an insignificant man struck down. So many sounds of gunfire and country-bombs were heard night and day, and so many people died. These were all extremely ordinary incidents nowadays. But as a result of this evening's gunshots, Nanu and Jibon, two ordinary youths from very ordinary households, victims of an extraordinary situation, spent an unbearable night in the slime pit.

After a long time, the moon appeared in the sky. It was a slim crescent moon, like a sliver of coconut. Finally, the whole locality went to sleep and became still. The Nepali watchman in the ink factory nearby sounded the gong twelve times in succession to announce that he was awake. The crickets perched on the hogla and hyacinth leaves of the slime pit, and on the clump of jungle tulsi and swallow-wort vines on the long strip of land beside the wall of the 'mosque', began their nocturnal chorus. It had been six hours since the shots were fired. Jibon thought—I've survived another six hours, despite the circumstances in which I did it. Who knows why, but he considered himself most fortunate. If Babua hadn't shielded him, one of the shots could have ripped his chest apart. In that event, he would not have seen this moon rising. He would not have heard the chirping of the crickets that wafted in the air like a background score.

The withered moon, the glum light streaming down, the meaningless cries of the crickets, the rise and fall of the chest nibbled at by water-snakes, leeches and maggots—Jibon had survived amidst all that. But one thing was clear, there was no way of denying anything. There was no way of avoiding it. Rabindranath Tagore had penned, '... *Ke more thelichhe? ... Dekhilam thami, sommukhe thelichhe mor poschater ami*. Who pushes me? I halted and looked, my past's pushing me ahead '. It was Jibon's past that had brought him here today. The black, accursed, difficult moment in which he had been born. It was the curse of birth that had turned him into a denizen of this Puyoda hell.

After a long time, from across a clump of hogla in the pit— or perhaps from some faraway planet, or a cave in some faraway mountain, or some sea over which a storm had blown, or from the rubble of some dead city destroyed by an atom bomb —the sound of a feeble whisper could be heard.

'Jibon, ei Jibon!'

Jibon too flung a soft whisper in the direction of Nanu's voice: 'What?'

'How much longer will we stay here?' This wasn't a question but a lament.

'What else can we do? We have no clue at all about what's happening. Who knows whether they're still here or whether they've gone away!'

'It feels like the maggots have eaten away the skin of my body!'

'As long as the body's there, the skin will grow back. But can you get your life back once you lose it? If Babua's dead, at least he's more comfortable than us tonight. He wouldn't have suffered for more than a few seconds.'

Once again the two terrified youths looked at the sky and waited endlessly for morning to arrive. A happy night passed by very quickly, but a difficult one seemed terribly long. Although he had made light of the matter, Babua's death had left a major scar on Jibon. All his thoughts were about him, rather than about himself. The way he was struck by the bullets, the way he sank into the water ... Even if he hadn't been killed by the gunshot injuries, he had surely drowned. Although, of the three, he was the one who was the most eager to live. He wanted to love someone, he wanted to marry and raise a family. The two bits of lead that pierced his back had shattered his dreams to pieces.

Jibon wondered: What if one of those bullets had pierced my heart? I would not have been around anymore. I would have become a corpse. A *laash*! That most terrifying word for a living person! The most ghastly word!

At this time, when the only difference between a corpse and the living consisted of a few breaths, Jibon suddenly remembered Babua dreaming of another life and then squinting his eyes in anguish. The mute life within Jibon began to weep uncontrollably. 'Babua, look at me. I've become a corpse too, just like you. A rotten, decomposed unclaimed corpse. Look, a bunch of worms and maggots are biting my flesh away. There's nothing I can do now, re. You, I and all the rest of us, we have the same thing written in our fate—to become a corpse. None of us can do anything about it. There's no deliverance from this. Earlier, hunger ate us away. And now jackals, vultures, worms and maggots will feed on us. There's nothing we can do about it.'

12

Cycle-rickshaw Riders and Class War in Jadavpur

If one listed the names of the ten most wealthy individuals in the Jadavpur locality—whose wealth was in cash—then the one whose name would be above everyone else's was Kanti Dutta. He owned a thousand cycle-rickshaws. His rickshaws plied on every route in the Jadavpur, Kasba, Baliganj, Taliganj and Behala areas, and for that matter, even in Baruipur. He had arrived at Loharpara, in Jadavpur, from Dhaka district in East Bengal, in an impoverished state. But through hard labour and intelligence, he had attained his present standing in a period of twenty to twenty-five years.

His cycle-rickshaw workshop was near the Jadavpur bus-stand, on Raja Subodh Chandra Mullick Road. Four workmen repaired broken rickshaws there all day. To produce new vehicles. As a rule, Kanti Dutta put out one or two new vehicles on the road every month. He did not bother about permits or licenses, although he had earlier paid a hundred or two hundred rupees for that. But now, all the vehicles were unlicensed. He ran his business on the basis of arrangements with the individuals in authority.

When he arrived at the workshop today, at the same time as he did every morning—after his bath, the ritual puja offering to Vishwakarma, and finally, his breakfast—he found someone waiting for him there. Someone or the other waited for him like that every day. But the person waiting today was unlike them. And Kanti babu recognised him too. Kanti babu used to go around all over the place on cycle to collect his rickshaw rents, so he observed what various people did. He felt somewhat uneasy seeing the person who had come to meet him. He was discomfited wondering what he had come for.

Kanti babu picked up a dusting-cloth from a chair, wiped his own dusty chair and sat down. He looked out of the corner of his eye at the stranger seated on the long wooden bench, and waited for a question or response from him. In a little while, Naru, a rickshaw-puller from the stand at Jadavpur station, entered the workshop. He looked at Kanti babu and smiled, and said in a tone of humility, 'You're here!'

Kanti babu smiled back in response, and retorted, 'Where else would I be if not here?'

'I wanted to meet you.'

'Meet me! Only meet me? So you've met me now!'

'No, I mean ... I need to ask you for something.'

'Then say that! Why did you say you wanted to meet me! Say you've come to ask for something. When else do you come, except when you need something? Tell me what you want!'

'I need a rickshaw.'

'Do you want to buy it?' Kanti Dutta smiled wryly, making a jest of Naru's incapacity.

'No, to rent. I want to rent a rickshaw.'

'But you ride Moti babu's vehicle. What happened to that? Have you given it up?'

'It's not for me. There ... ' said Naru, pointing at the person Kanti babu had been discomfited by. He said somewhat embarrassedly, 'It's for him.'

'For whom?'

'For him. He'll ride the rickshaw.'

Kanti babu did not believe him. Given the path these young men had embraced, it was difficult for him to believe they would join those who toiled and sweated, and yet starved or remained half-fed.

The person was none other than Jibon. It was Jibon who had come with Naru to meet Kanti babu. Being a rickshaw-owner, he could rent out a rickshaw to Jibon. Jibon would ride a rickshaw now.

○§○

Almost a month had passed since Babua died. There was a suppressed inner terror in people's hearts and minds, but they wrapped a cloak of normalcy over that, and went about their daily lives. Man sought to survive under all situations. After all, if one wanted to survive under every kind of adversity, one couldn't carry on unless the daily chores were performed.

After Nanu got out of the slime pit, he brushed the leeches off his body and took a bath, scrubbing himself with soap. He had once said that he wouldn't leave his neighbourhood even if he died. But the very next day, he packed some clothes in a bag and disappeared, without even telling Jibon. Ever since the rifle-snatching incident in Jadavpur police camp, Jibon had considered Nanu's den and the hospital field safer than Jadavpur Railway Station. He had become a familiar face to everyone there because he had been going around with Nanu. There was no hindrance to staying there. After eating somewhere, he could peacefully spend the night on the roof of the morgue. But with Nanu gone, the hospital precincts seemed orphaned, alien and unsafe to Jibon.

So where would Jibon stay now? The only place he could stay was the Jadavpur station. But what would he say if the police caught him? The police patrolled the station almost every night nowadays, and they thrashed and took away anyone they spotted there. If he had a rickshaw now, he would at least have an explanation, although whether or not the police accepted that depended entirely on them. 'I live in Khola-Doltala, I drive a cycle-rickshaw in Jadavpur. The last train was cancelled, so I could not return home—that's why I'm sleeping in the station. Here's my rickshaw, I'm no miscreant ...' But of course, at present, in the eyes of the bhadralok, a rickshaw-wallah and a scoundrel were synonymous. Nonetheless, he could at least say something, and have credible proof. Besides, if he drove a rickshaw, if nothing else, the problem of food was taken care of. After all, how long could he continue to rely on his cunning!

When Naru had suggested to Jibon to drive a rickshaw, he had rebelled inwardly. How can I, a man, carry another man! Will I do the work of a horse? But later, Pranab Chakraborty, whom Jibon knew as Pranab-da, had said to him, 'Listen, it's not enough for a man to be merely honest, courageous and militant. He has to be a bit crafty and intelligent, and also learn how to adjust to prevailing conditions. Or else, he won't be able to survive. Think about a factory. People work there. They know they don't get a fair wage for their labour. To top it, the owner misbehaves with them. And yet they work there. What else can they do? Will they quit the job? If they do that, they'll starve to death. They won't earn even the little bit they presently do. The whole society is exploitative, inhuman and oppressive. Those who are powerful and strong torment and coerce those who are weak and powerless. When will this come to an end? When there's a revolution. But does anyone know how many years that will take? In Vietnam, they've been fighting a war for forty years. What if it takes forty years here too? What will you do in all that time? Will you go without food? Can you do that? Don't you remember, they caught you and took you to Loharpara? How were they able to do that? It's because you were sick and starving, because you were half-dead. You could not resist. Would they have been able to take you away if you were strong and in good health? Listen to me, you can't be stubborn all the time. You have to compromise a couple of times. In Lenin's words, one step forward, two steps back. If you take one step forward and two steps back, it looks like a defeat. But why did Lenin speak of taking two steps back? That's called battlecraft. Take two steps back and pause a bit; plan your next move. And then advance! You've run around a lot. Now take a step back and observe, analyse, gather your strength. At this time, that's very important for you.'

Pranab Chakraborty was a boy-catcher. His party, the Revolutionary Socialist Party, or RSP, had assigned him that work, to catch as many boys as possible. He wanted to catch Jibon. And so, whenever he got the time, he called him and talked to him. He spoke to him about various things. Jibon did not dislike him either. It was on his advice that Jibon decided to take two steps back. He was reminded of something someone had said long ago: it's better to bend a bit than to break completely. If one bent, then one could stand erect again when the opportunity arose. But once broken, you wouldn't get that opportunity again.

⁂

As an addendum to Naru's introduction, Jibon looked at Kanti babu and nodded his head to confirm that he would really like to rent a rickshaw.

Kanti babu now said to Jibon, 'Didn't you live near the ink factory earlier?'

Kanti babu was close to sixty years old. The expression *'tui'* did not seem as inappropriate coming from him, as it did when Hemanta babu, of Ramakrishnapur, used to address Jibon's father as *'tui'*. Jibon always wanted to ask—why don't you use *'tumi'* instead? If Garib Das too addressed Hemanta babu as *'tui'*, would he be able to tolerate that?

Jibon nodded his head to convey that they used to live near the ink factory. Kanti babu then asked him, 'Isn't your name Jibon?'

This time Jibon spoke. 'Yes, my name's Jibon.'

'I know you.'

'How's that?'

'I told you I know you. Don't ask me how. But have you left all that?'

'Left what?'

'All the violence!'

Jibon was unable to respond, he remained silent. What could he say?

Inwardly, he wondered—did I at all join, that I could leave! Doesn't one have to join first in order to leave?

Kanti babu squinted at Jibon from above his spectacles and laughed his habitual laugh. A jeer masqueraded as a joke in that laugh, which only suited those who had begun with nothing and reached the great nothingness. He said, 'Since you've come with Naru, I won't refuse—I'll give you a rickshaw. But you have to give me your word.'

'What word?'

'First of all, you have to pay me each day's rent the same day. You can't have any dues. And none of your goonda, scoundrel ways! Work hard and eat, that's all. And keep yourself out of trouble, don't get involved in fights. If you pick a fight somewhere and go to jail—what will happen to my rickshaw? I'll give you a rickshaw tomorrow if you agree not to do any of that.'

Naru replied on behalf of Jibon, 'No, no, he won't do all that any more!'

'It won't do for you to say that. Let him make the promise.' But before he could get Jibon's reply, Kanti babu had to leave his seat to go into the workshop. A workman was calling him. The new rickshaw that was being prepared needed tyres, tubes, rings, bearings, spokes and pedals. The workshop was as large as a hall. There was space to keep thirty or forty rickshaws at a time. On the farther side was a large cupboard. It had been custom-made. All the requisite parts were inside that. When Kanti babu went there to unlock it, Jibon said to Naru, 'I can't take the rickshaw!'

'Why?' asked Naru in astonishment. 'Why can't you take the rickshaw? Kanti babu said he'll give it to you.'

'Didn't you hear him? He said I have to give my word that I won't get involved in any fights.'

'Don't get involved! Where's the need for that?'

'What if someone hits me? Shall I simply stand and get thrashed then?'

'Why would anyone hit you for no reason, if you didn't do anything?'

'People beat others up even if they've done nothing!'

'Don't talk rubbish! Don't they have anything better to do?'

'Answer my question first! If someone hits me for no reason, what shall I do? Just get beaten?'

'No, you shouldn't get beaten.'

'I'll hit them back, won't I?'

'Yes.'

'But won't that mean going back on my word?'

Naru was silent for a while, and then he said, 'Look Jibon, no one's asking you to be like Yudhishtira, the great man of truth. Nod your head to whatever he says, and take the rickshaw. Kanti babu has a thousand cycle-rickshaws. With the rent he gets, he can buy four new rickshaws every day. There's no reckoning of how many rickshaws get stolen or confiscated by the police. Let's say you take a rickshaw, you go somewhere and get into a fight, or there's some other hassle, and you leave the rickshaw and run away—what happens to the rickshaw? It'll be stolen. That does not matter a whit to Kanti babu. Be quiet about whatever you do. Just take the rickshaw now and go!'

Kanti babu returned after taking out the parts and giving it to the workman. He sat down once again in his chair. Naru said, 'So shall I come tomorrow morning?'

'Why?'

'To take the rickshaw.'

'But we didn't finish the conversation.'

'Then finish it.'

'My final word is that I don't want any problems on account of fighting. And there's one more thing.'

'One more? Tell me.'

'I have twenty or twenty-two rickshaws at Jadavpur Station. Some of the men are really good chaps. And some are great scoundrels. Jibon must collect the fares for those rickshaws. I know he can do that.'

Naru said, 'I too know he can do that. But if he has to do that, when will he drive his own rickshaw? How will he pay you your rent?'

Kanti babu said, 'If he does that, then even if he's unable to pay me the fare for half a day or a full day, I'll overlook that. I give my word!'

Jibon said, 'I'll think a little bit about your final condition and tell you tomorrow.'

Before they left, Kanti babu said, 'Have some tea before you leave. You've come so early in the morning.' And he called out to a worker, 'Go to Kumud's teashop and ask him to send three cups of tea and three biscuits.'

༄

The cement warehouse on the northern side of the Jadavpur railway station, just at the beginning of Laskarpara, belonged to Batokrishno Sengupta. He lived with his family in the yellow-coloured, two-storeyed house just adjacent to the warehouse. Bato babu's elder son, Nabokeshto, was an avid angler. Last night, he had gone to the pond with a torch in one hand and a fishing rod in the other. Sometimes the fish raised their heads through a clearing among the clumps of water hyacinths at the edge of the pond, creating bubbles. If one could aim properly and cast the bait, one could get a fish weighing two kilos in a single try. He was so engrossed in catching fish that he did not realise that there was a snake curled up near his feet. As soon as he stepped on it—*Hiss!* The moment he was bitten by the snake, Nabakeshto screamed for help—'Baba, come quickly!' The snake immediately slithered away into the hyacinth-laden pond after delivering the bite. It was impossible to find it. And so, it wasn't clear whether it was a poisonous snake or a non-poisonous one. Batokrishno babu did not take any risk—he did what only an intelligent person would do. He took his son to the banyan tree in front of the Jadavpur railway station, where the cycle-rickshaw-stand was. He would take a rickshaw and reach the hospital.

It was about half past twelve at night then. There were no rickshaws at the stand. The times were bad. Rickshaw-pullers did not have the courage to stay up so late nowadays. Feeling helpless, Batokrishno was imploring God when a rickshaw-puller from the bus-stand crossing suddenly arrived to sleep in the station. Bato babu hurriedly went up to him. 'Let's go, re. Be quick!'

Jalil Mollah had just finished eating at Chhechan's restaurant after a whole day of back-breaking labour. After consuming four plates of rice with a dish of mixed vegetables with potatoes, egg-plant and pumpkin, he was feeling extremely lethargic. He was eager to sleep. He said, 'I can't go now.'

'My son's been bitten by a snake! Please take us!'

A victim of snake-bite. That meant—not just any hospital nearby, one had to go to the Calcutta Medical College. Which was under the jurisdiction of Calcutta, and came under the Calcutta Police. Jalil Mollah's rickshaw wasn't permitted to ply there. If he went there and got caught by the police, his rickshaw would be confiscated. So many such confiscated rickshaws were rusting and rotting in front of the police station. The owner he was renting from would be enraged. Slaps and punches would follow. He would also demand the price of the rickshaw. For a small mistake, Jalil Mollah would lose his livelihood. It was too dangerous. But he didn't say all that. He only said that the police would create trouble, and so he couldn't go.

Batokrishno was still calm and composed. 'Come along. I'll take care of it if someone catches you.'

'But where will you be when they catch me! I'll have to return by myself.'

Batokrishno was beginning to lose his cool. He said, 'Whatever happens, come and tell me tomorrow. You know my warehouse, don't you?'

Jalil Mollah pondered over the matter. How credible was Bato babu's assurance? Lots of people say so many things like that. After all, there was no certainty that he would rush to get Jalil's rickshaw released, simply because he had said he would. Who remembers anybody once the danger passes? Who knows whether his son, once admitted in the hospital, would survive or die. Would he even be in the mental state to take care of someone else's problem? Besides, what guarantee was there that the police would release his rickshaw merely on Bato babu's intervention? He wasn't some MLA or leader!'

Jalil said, 'I don't have any papers for my rickshaw, babu, I can't go.'

Sachindranath, the owner of the tea-stall and paan shop in the station, was about to go home after shutting his shop. Seeing that someone from the neighbourhood was in trouble, he went up to them. 'Ei, why don't you go? It's an emergency!'

Jalil shook his head. 'Didn't I tell you already that I don't have any papers for the rickshaw?'

'Bato-da has said he'll take care of any hassles with the police!'

'Oh, everyone talks big. But once their job is over, there's no trace of them ...'

Bato babu lost his composure now. It was quite natural for someone in his situation to get hot-headed when his son was moaning in agony. He said, 'Don't try to be too clever! Why do you ride a rickshaw if you don't have the papers? You have to go! Won't go? Your bloody baap will go! Come on!'

Jalil decided that the best thing to do was not to waste any more time talking; he ought to lock the rickshaw and go to sleep. He thought to himself, what do I care who got bitten! Why did he step on the snake? Why should I fall into danger because of that? Does anyone ever come forward to help me? The time a mini-bus hit my rickshaw—there were so many babus there, did anyone take me to hospital? No! Instead, they said it was my fault, and so much more! Why should I lose my sleep over this today?

Observing Jalil locking up the rickshaw, Sachi, or Sachindranath Mitra, thought that the rickshaw-puller could be thrashed mercilessly now. Here was a victim of snake-bite. As a result of which, public support would be entirely in his favour. Whoever heard about it would put himself in the shoes of the victim, and elaborate on how grave the rickshaw-puller's misdemeanour was, and how hard-hearted and inhuman he was. Sachi's offence would then not even be noticed. They would see him as a socially aware citizen, anguished at the plight of another.

As the last resort, without giving Batokrishno an opportunity to get any angrier, Sachi landed a mighty punch on Jalil's nose. 'You bastard *katua,* you're trying to be too clever, aren't you? You won't go at a time of danger like this? I'll thrash you so badly, you'll forget your baap's name. Unlock it! Unlock the bloody rickshaw!'

The punch had been a formidable one. Seeing the blood gushing out of Jalil's nose, Bato realised there was no point in saying any more. It was impossible for him to ride his rickshaw now. And so, without wasting any more time, he moved ahead with his son in tow. Perhaps he could find some form of transport at the bus-stand crossing.

❦

The next morning, the rickshaw-pullers at the Jadavpur bus-stand crossing came to know about the incident. Pakhi, Nedo, Kala, Bhime and several others got together and began asking themselves questions. Will we continue to get beaten like this every day? Just because we are poor and have no one to turn to, does it mean that anyone who wishes so can give us the treatment? No, we won't just sit quietly; we'll avenge the thrashing with thrashing in return. The slogan that was on everyone's lips at political rallies was the one all the rickshaw-pullers now yelled out as one—*'Maar ka badla maar hai. Khoon ka badla khoon hai!* Thrashing shall be avenged with thrashing! Blood shall be avenged with blood!'

Sachi or Bato, as well as those who were rickshaw passengers, would look at this matter through their own lens. Similarly, the rickshaw-pullers too would look at it through theirs. *Aarey*, this rickshaw-puller was an old man, he was exhausted after working under the hot sun all day. He was going to sleep. Someone forces him to ride the rickshaw—what the hell do they think? If he doesn't want to go, what's wrong with that? And if he was indeed at fault, a complaint should have been lodged with the union. The union could decide on the matter and punish him. But instead of doing that, he hit him! Aren't we human beings! Have we become cows or donkeys just because we ride the rickshaw? Come on, let there be a final settlement today!

Sachi had gone to sleep late, and so he opened the shop late the next day. He had no fear or regret. First of all, there was a reason for whatever he had done. He had the pretext of responsibility and duty. So why should he have any regrets? And fear? No, there was nothing to fear about hitting a rickshaw-puller! After all, who rode rickshaws? A bunch of low-class and low-caste folk. Who had no money in their pockets nor any strongman behind them. After all, they were thrashed all the time on the streets, with or without any reason. Who does anything about that? Of course, if it had been someone from the rickshaw-stand at the Jadavpur station, he would have felt a bit squeamish. At least their faces were familiar. They came to his shop for tea and beedis. But the man who had been beaten was from the bus-stand crossing and lived in Taldi. And he was Muslim. Sachi hardly saw him. So why should he feel squeamish?

After some time, Sachi was quite astonished when he saw a group of extremely timid men, whose bodies were misshapen from malnourishment, standing in front of his shop. They had cycle chains and axle-rods in their hands. They were not solicitous. Addressing him as *tui*, they asked authoritatively, '*Ei* Sachi, why did you hit Jalil?' It was as if someone had pricked a pin in the balloon of courage that Sachi had been inflating all this while. With an ingratiating smile, he promptly said, 'Anybody would get angry under those circumstances! A boy was dying in front of my eyes!'

'Where's he dying? Go and see for yourself, he's looking after his dad's business and stuffing himself with porotas!'

'One didn't know then that the snake wasn't a poisonous one. The way he was writhing in agony ...'

'So why did *you* hit him? The boy's father could have hit him. Who the hell are you?'

Someone from the crowd of rickshaw-pullers roared, 'Sure, he'll hit him! Hasn't he become a mastaan? A big mastaan! We'll rid you of your mastaani! What the hell do you people think? What do you think we are?'

Another rickshaw-puller, without saying anything, swung the rod in his hand and brought it down upon the glass jars arranged in the front of Sachi's shop. Pieces of shattered glass went flying everywhere. All the biscuits and cakes in the jars fell into the dirt.

That was all that was needed. It was as if everyone had been waiting for the one who would first smash the wall of fear. Now that it had been smashed, why should there be any more doubt or hesitation? Everyone began attacking the shop, the display shelves, the pile of paan leaves and the pot with lime, with whatever weapon they had brought. One person held Sachi by the collar of his shirt and yanked him down from the altitude of his bhadralok-dom— down to the level of a chhotolok, the lowly folk. After that it was as if a storm raged over his body.

<hr>

It wasn't as if Sachindranath, alias Sachi, only stirred sugar in tea and applied lime on paans. He could also smash brilliant fours and sixes using those hands. He was a famed player in the local cricket team. When the boys from the neighbourhood youth association, Shakti Sangha, got the news that their captain had been badly thrashed by chhotolok rickshaw-walas, they descended with their full team, cricket bats and stumps in their hands. The bastards had become too uppity. As soon as it turned dark, they looked the other way when a passenger arrived; they refused to go if there were a few drops of rain; they demanded twice or thrice the fare when there was an emergency. The country had become a bloody den of thugs and swindlers! The bloody gall! They dared to raise their hands against a member of the public. It was all the fault of the party-folk of the neighbourhoods in the east and west. It was their indulgence that had made these bastards so audacious. A proper lesson needed to be taught now. Or else, they wouldn't get off their high horse!

When the cricket team—almost like a procession—passed Batokrishno's cement shop, it was as if his fifty-year-old conscience felt a scorpion's sting. It's because of me that Sachi is in hospital now. This public awakening is on my account. While I'm preoccupied with selling bags of cement! What would people say if I'm so selfish? Even if I'm not leading the way, what's the problem with at least following them? So Bato babu too picked up a lathi and joined the band.

The rickshaw-pullers from the stand at the Jadavpur railway station did not have any role in the events of yesterday or today. It was the rickshaw-pullers from the bus-stand crossing. But Sachi, who was the only one who knew that, was in hospital then. The incensed cricket team wasn't in a frame of mind to investigate the case too deeply. Their arithmetic was extremely simple. When the issue was one of the public versus the rickshaw-pullers, and when the site of the attack was the station—then whoever came in sight there would be the target of vengeance.

The first person they came across was Loha Kartick. The poor man's black face was so villainous that any one would think he had either just killed someone, or was about to do so. After an attack of small-pox in his childhood, he had become fully blind in one eye.

But he rode the cycle-rickshaw like a gale. They had added Loha or 'Iron' to his name because no rickshaw-puller could overtake his vehicle. Kartick was not made of flesh and blood but iron.

The cricket team confronted him. 'Why the hell did you thrash Sachi?' Bats and stumps rained down on his back and on the rickshaw. One man overturned the vehicle. After that it was the turn of Nimai, Gokul and Abhimanyu. Those who were old or middle-aged were spared after a few blows. Those who were able to flee also got away with a few blows. Those who were ferrying passengers were saved. And those who stood and pleaded, 'I didn't do anything, I don't know anything!', were thrashed till they lay on the ground.

❦

When the first incident, involving Jalil, occurred, Jibon was asleep on the overbridge at Jadavpur Railway Station. It was windy there, and there were no mosquitoes. But since the site of the incident was not so far away, he had heard the loud shouting. And so, he had come down to see what was wrong. But Bato had gone by then. There was nothing to be done, other than taking Jalil to the standpipe and splashing water on him.

When this morning's incident, at Sachi's shop, took place, like every day, after finishing his morning ablutions, Jibon had gone to bathe in the lake at Garpa. If he could finish that in the morning, he would not have to worry about it for the rest of the day. When he reached the station, he saw Sachi's shop lying in ruins.

At the time of the third incident, at the rickshaw-stand at the Jadavpur railway station, Jibon was in the field in the hospital premises. It was the day of Sompal Valmiki's engagement ceremony, so he was in the sweepers' quarters. A pig had been slaughtered. Jibon had been invited to attend. Seeing Shibu come running, all bloody, he asked him, 'What happened?'

Gasping for breath, Shibu said, 'Thrashing! The club boys are beating up whoever they can find!'

Jibon ran quickly to the station. But the brawl was already over by then. The line of rickshaws resembled some border village ravaged by war. The final livelihood prop of hapless folk, the cycle-rickshaw, lay broken everywhere. The crumpled, moaning bodies of a few wounded rickshaw-pullers were lying there. Everyone else had fled.

There was no one to come to their aid.

Looking at the scene, Jibon felt as if it was his head, chest, back and stomach that all the lathis and bats had targeted. Loha Kartick writhing in the dirt with his head split open—was none other than Jibon himself. Those who rode the rickshaw all day and then purchased rice and potatoes with the day's meagre earnings so that their aged parents could eat—those like Nimai, Gokul and Abhimanyu—were all various parts of his own soul. Like how the Dalit Dusad Dayaram, who was killed by the Ranvir Sena in a village in Bihar bordering West Bengal, was a part of his soul.

The broken seats of the cycle-rickshaws and their twisted wheels seemed to bear witness to the fact that this was not just an ordinary punishment meted out to a few recalcitrant poor folk in a fit of temporary rage. It was nothing short of a well-planned conspiracy to create an economic blockade, and wipe out the rickshaw-pullers and their families through forced starvation. Jibon's chest heaved in anguish.

The cricket team was moving ahead then. They had vented some of their rage. Whatever remained would be let out at the bus-stand crossing. After all, they were the real culprits. But as they moved towards the bus-stand crossing, they suddenly came to a halt near Chhechan Sau's eatery. Another rickshaw-puller was at hand. Babul was returning after making a trip to the Kalabagan market.

Babul was just sixteen-years-old. Until last year, he had been a student at Aurobindo Vidyapeeth. He did not have a mother. He lived with his father and sister. Last Ashaad, while trying to plough his cycle-rickshaw through a water-logged street, his father had toppled over with the rickshaw and broken his leg. Babul had had no option but to take up the same work, in order to feed his family and pay for his father's medicines. Babul hoped that once his father recovered, he would be able to return to school.

From afar, Jibon observed how inhuman and blind rage was. How ghoulish. All these blind, ignorant youths derived a ghastly pleasure from thrashing to death innocent wayfarers on the suspicion of being child-lifters. They lynched to death any bus-driver involved in a road accident. They incited communal riots and brazenly set fire to the houses of innocent folk. They committed crimes like murder and rape without any shred of remorse.

The cricket club boys pulled Babul off the seat of the cycle-rickshaw, the way a cruel tantrik about to perform a human sacrifice would snatch a child from its mother's bosom. The one with a bat slammed Babul's back with the force of smashing a boundary. Like a slaughtered goat, Babul collapsed on the dirt of the road, crying, 'Ma go!' The batsman raised his bat again. At a loss regarding what he ought to do, Jibon ran and grasped the arm with the bat. 'What are you doing? Have you gone mad?' A youth wielding a stump in his hand answered Jibon's query.

The wall of Jibon's self-restraint was demolished by that assault. All his righteous resolve vanished. He forgot about his parents and siblings. He forgot that he had left everyone in their forest exile and come alone to the city with high hopes.

Jibon felt as if these people were the very ones who had deprived him of honey when he was born. It was these people who had deprived him of his rightful wages and accumulated a mountain of money. It was they who had clutched their sacred threads and declared Jibon to be untouchable. The assault made Jibon realise that it was all these people, who at different times, in different guises, had gone on destroying his community. In order to survive, he would have to counter-attack just as cruelly, and inflict destruction in retaliation. And just after that, it was as if from the rubble of some demolished mansion, a wounded, venomous snake raised its hood. He did what he never did. A foul swear word escaped his lips.

He picked up Chhechan Sau's sharp bonti, used for cutting fish, and charged ahead with it.

Brimming with confidence, the cricket team had advanced towards the bus-stand crossing after hitting Jibon. Their gaze was on the road ahead, their advance was unhindered, but their rear was unprotected. Which was against any battle strategy. By the time they were aware of it, one of them had received a slash on his neck and lay on the ground. The next person, seeing the weapon brandished near his neck, cried out, '*Baba re, mere phel-lo!*', and ran for his life. It wasn't the diminution in their numbers or capability that was the issue, it was their morale that was punctured. Having been suddenly attacked, they fell into panic and without looking back or turning around, they ran ahead for their lives. Their aim was to turn into the alley on the right, cross the rail track and flee to their own neighbourhood.

Seeing Jibon chasing the group with a bonti, the rickshaw-pullers who had earlier fled in fear of being thrashed, and those who had been beaten and lay wounded, as well as some porters and vendors from the station, picked up whatever they could find and ran behind Jibon. They chased the cricket team till the rail track and then returned. But they did not think it was safe for them to be near the station now. Danger could arrive from anywhere, either in the form of a counter-attack, or the police.

⊗

Run Jibon, run and go far away, very far away! This city is no longer safe because there's the red stain of thick blood on your hands. The smell of human blood was most pungent. There was no way this smell could be masked. *It's this scent that the police will follow and find you. First, they'll throw you into the police lock-up and thrash you. After that, they'll send you to rot and die in some dark prison cell. You'll not be pardoned because the dada or mama or kaka of the person you assaulted, or the dada or mama or kaka's friend, acquaintance or well-wishers rules the roost as far as the state and the judicial and political systems are concerned. In their eyes, you have been identified as a wayward attacker. If you love your freedom, if you want to stay alive—flee! You'll be safe only so long as you flee. It's not just the police, the people you attacked and caused bloodshed to are also searching for you like mad dogs. Once they catch you, they won't spare you!*

The public! This entity was formless, shapeless and bodiless. Anyone could do as they wished and get away. *The public is enraged with you. And so you must flee.* That's why Jibon was fleeing. It was an ominous time now. He had to conceal himself among a crowd of unknown people. The company of known folks wasn't safe. Because someone from among the known people could inform the police or the public—here, this is Jibon!

But where, and how far away, would he flee to? He was no longer the small boy who could get into a train without a ticket, and go to Delhi or Bombay, whom the checker would not catch even if he spotted him. Now he had grown up. Now he was of the age at which youths waited in Calcutta's alleys with country-bombs in their hands.

This was the fiery decade of the seventies. No longer was any youth of West Bengal trustworthy in the eyes of the lawmakers. To them, youth were synonymous with bomb-throwers and murderers who revelled in revolution. So as soon as they were spotted, they were hauled up. Therefore, whether he fled to Assam or Bihar, it was impossible to hide anywhere.

Being clueless about where he should go, and which place would be safe to hide in, Jibon began to wander continuously around a certain ambit. Baruipur—Diamond Harbour—Lakshmikantapur—Canning.

13

The Empire of Water

One day, when Jibon, tired after having wandered long, had sat down on a bench at a rail station to rest, a youth just like him came and stood before him. *'Ki re* Jibon! How come you're here?'

Dumbfounded at being recognised, Jibon said, 'I can't recognise you ... Where are you from?'

The youth laughed. 'It's clear that you don't recognise me. Would you have addressed me as *'tumi'* if you had recognised me! I'm Ghalib. We used to play together when you worked at Hem doctor's house—don't you remember?'

Now Jibon remembered. He said, 'We fought over glass marbles once!'

'You remember the fight, but you don't remember that I pinched money from home so we could buy papad or visit the Ghazi Baba fair.'

'I remember! I remember everything! I haven't forgotten anything about those days. Tell me, how are you? And how are Hamid and Javed?'

Ghalib sat down beside Jibon. Seeing his face, Jibon once again felt the warmth of a child's life that had been lost many years ago.

Ghalib said, 'You didn't come even once to our village ... Whatever Hem doctor may have done, we didn't do anything to you. If you had visited us, you'd have found that all of us still remembered you. Anyway, tell me about yourself. What work do you do, where do you live?'

Jibon smiled weakly. 'I don't do any work ... I don't get any work. I don't have any place to live either. I lie down wherever I happen to be at night, whether it's on the pavement, or under a tree, or in the station.'

'How can you survive without work?'

'I don't.'

'What do you eat?'

'I don't eat.'

'How's that? You survive without food?'

'Not without food, I survive on water and air.'

For some reason, Ghalib thought that perhaps Jibon was joking. In an annoyed tone he said, 'Then you don't have any problems! The one who survives on water and air has to be a great man, re!'

Jibon said, 'I once met a sadhu. He told me that he had lived in some cave. He did not eat for months on end. A great man indeed, but I saw that he too stretched out his hands to beg for alms. I'm no great man. I go without food because I can't help it. Forget about all that—tell me about yourself, what do you do?'

'I guard the fishery. I get my meals, and a salary of two hundred rupees a month.'

Jibon had no interest whatsoever in working in a fishery. He said, 'There's a constant fear of death in such work.'

'I know.'

Jibon wasn't lying. He really did not have the slightest interest in working as a guard in a fishery. A fishery was an immense empire of water. A lot of blood and tears, eliciting a history of oppression, was attached to the establishment and expansion of this empire of water. Which could provide much fuel and fodder for the imagination and work of historians, antiquarians and writers of detective fiction.

⁂

The owner of the fishery where Ghalib worked as a guard was one Pratap babu. He also owned two cinema halls and a hotel in Calcutta. He lived in a posh locality. He had contested two elections on behalf of a national political party, although he hadn't been able to win.

Long ago, an ancestor of his had taken seven hundred bighas of land on lease from the government, for pisciculture. The area was undeveloped and remote. A few people belonging to the Keora and Bagdi communities, as well as some Adivasis, brought as contract workers from the forests and hills of Chotanagpur, lived here at the time. These people were considered 'wild'. They eked out a living catching fish and doing a bit of cultivation.

Having found the means to lay his feet on this soil, within a few years, Pratap babu's ancestor became the proud overlord of the entire region. On the strength of a band of men called lathiyals, who were expert in using staffs with lightning speed and lethal effect, and a licensed double-barrelled gun, within a few years, his hegemony came to be established in the region. There was a saying, *Jomi hoy baaper noy daaper*. Land was either one's dad's or grabbed.' Like a python swallowing its prey with its gaping maw, he began swallowing the homesteads and lands of the Keora, Bagdi and other poor folk nearby. By threatening to kill someone, by accusing someone of stealing fish and thrashing him mercilessly, by embroiling someone in a false litigation, by lending someone a hundred rupees and taking his thumb-impression on a paper specifying a thousand—through various such means, he managed to appropriate thousands of bighas of land. As a result, the seven-hundred-acre fishery grew to become so immensely vast that one could not see one bank from another.

And of the low-caste folk who lost their lands, some went to live in railside and canalside shanties, and they descended to the rank of daily labourers and rickshaw-pullers to feed themselves. They sent their wives and daughters to babu homes to wash and clean. Of course, some of those people, who attained the requisite passmarks in the test of obedience, docility and humility, were inducted as salaried employees of the fishery. They were the ones who pulled the nets, cleared away the hyacinths, and cast the oil-cake fish feed. Those among them who were more courageous, guarded the fishery, day and night, with spears held aloft. And some people, having no other option, became thieves in order to survive. Their work involved catching the guard unawares and casting nets in the water.

In order to secure the fish from such fish-thieves, just as the current descendant of that ancestor had increased the number of licensed and unlicensed firearms he possessed, he had also gathered together a number of adept guards who could use the firearms. Pratap babu had declared, 'Make sure that any banchod who steps into the water never sets foot on land again. Cut him to pieces and feed him to the fish. I'll take care of whatever happens after that!'

They did that too. Many of those employed in the fisheries were convicted criminals, who had served prison sentences. Killing and thrashing was their favourite sport. Every now and then, someone or the other went missing on their account. But of late, the matter was not at all one-sided. Now, the guards too became fish food sometimes. The thieves were much more alert than before. One group of them would enter the water, while another group would stand watch on the bank, armed with country-bombs and guns. Someone or the other had implanted in their heads the idea that attack was the prime means of defence. As soon as Pratap babu's guards shone their torches, the thieves aimed at the light and pulled their triggers.

This had become a daily affair now. Both sides battled with guns every night.

But why was Ghalib in such a job? After all, he belonged to a more or less comfortably placed family in the village of Chakla, who had been reared on rice from the paddy they harvested. Why was someone who had been the most educated person in his village in this job of killing and dying?

Jibon asked him about that. 'An educated chap like you, why did you get into this line?'

'I was forced to,' said Ghalib. 'Because you're a friend from my childhood, I'm trusting you when I say this, but don't tell anybody. There's no better place than a fishery to hide. There's water all around, and an island in the middle. If you go and sit on the island, nobody can ever get any trace of you. I ran away from our village and I'm hiding there.'

'Why? What did you do that you need to hide? Tell me!'

'You won't be upset, will you?'

'No, I won't.'

'It concerns Hem Chakraborty.'

'So what of that?'

'He's from your religion.'

'I don't believe in any religion. And the religion in which Brahmins like Hem Chakraborty are at the top—I don't believe in that all the more. I've heard that earlier our religion was Chandal. In the same way as you people are Muslim. Like how the British were Christian. A separate religion. They counted us as Hindu only to increase the numbers of Hindus, so they could stand up against the Muslim majority. We are Hindu in name only. But in practice, they consider us to be untouchable, just like they do Muslims. So tell me, what did you do to Hem Chakraborty? Did you murder him?'

'Worse than that ... Do you remember Hem Chakraborty's daughter? I raped her.'

Jibon was shocked. Blood shot to his head. His whole body began to tremble, and beads of sweat lined his brow. Ghalib! So the most handsome, educated and well-spoken boy of Chakla village was a rapist! There couldn't be a more foul person than that!

Ghalib continued. 'What I did or didn't do—are only words without any value whatsoever. Nobody would believe it either. Because Gayatri went to the police and said that I took her away forcibly and raped her. The police are looking for me in connection with that case.'

'Are you saying they accused you falsely?'

'Did I say that? Gayatri did not lie. But she didn't say the truth either ...'

'I don't understand.'

'Whatever happened was with her consent. I did not use any kind of force. Whatever happened was by mutual agreement. But now she's changed her tune, and says that I took her away by force and raped her.'

Jibon could still remember Gayatri's face. A fair girl with a doll-like face. Because of whom Mrs Hem had hit him with a red-hot ladle. He still bore the scar from that on his forehead. The viper-like daughter of the bloody Brahmin kept saying, 'Chandal, Chandal' whenever she saw him. Jibon had no sympathy for her. But the very word 'rape' made it impossible for him to be objective, or in favour of Ghalib. Without being aware of it, he stood in favour of Gayatri.

Ghalib said, 'You're my friend from our childhood. Whether you believe me or not, I'm telling you what the truth is. I'm not saying that I am without blame. But it was Gayatri who pushed me into doing what I did. Whenever we met, on the road, or by the pond, she used to smile and wave to me. And so love and affection grew between us. Then she told me, come, let us run away and get married. That made me scared. They were so fussy about matters of caste and religion, who knows what kind of pogrom Hem babu would organise when he found out that his daughter had run away with a Muslim. Gayatri told me, "If you don't marry me, I'll consume poison and die. And before I die, I'll write your name in a letter." So what could I do then? I ran away with her. We went across the Matla river, to my brother-in-law's house, and I married her in a proper nikah ceremony, with a maulvi reciting the Kalma.

We stayed there for ten or twelve days. After that, a few people from our village came there and took us back. As soon as we returned, rioting began between the two villages because of us. Hem babu went and filed a complaint with the police. The police came and took Gayatri away. I managed to escape by a mere whisker. I ran out of the back door of the house and fled ... I've told you what I did. If you think I did wrong, then so be it; and if you think I did no wrong, then that's what it is.'

Jibon did not say anything. He did not have anything to say. Ghalib too was silent. The two friends, each one embroiled in his own kind of danger, sat silently beside one another. It was as if their past had begun an evil sprite's ghoulish dance in front of their eyes. Like an octopus, it wanted to crush the life in them with its eight arms. The sun had set by then. Night was descending in the desolation of the rural rail station. Night meant the time for tired folk to rest at the end of the day. And for the fleeing Jibon, it meant counting the hours as his heart beat anxiously. The eyes of night-time were very suspicious. *'Ke re tui?* Where do you live? Why are you sitting here?' If the answers to the volley of questions with which the night advanced were not satisfactory, at once would come the order—'Come to the police station!'

Nowadays, rural Bengal wasn't like it used to be earlier. In those days, anyone could go anywhere without the slightest hassle. Now the times were very bad. Anyone who spotted an unfamiliar face in their area became terrified. Who was this person? Could he be a thief or robber?

After a long silence, Jibon said, 'You told me about yourself, say something about Hamid, Javed and the others. How are they?'

Ghalib replied in a distressed voice, 'Oh, they're also like me. All fine!'

'Your words sound strange. Tell me properly, are they well?'

Ghalib was silent for a while, and then he said, 'Hamid lost a hand in a bomb explosion. And Khaled is in jail. He's serving a ten-year sentence. There's no news about Javed. We don't know whether he's dead or alive. He left saying he was going to Medinipur, and never returned.

It was as if lightning had struck the lives of Ghalib and company and ravaged them. Jibon wondered—why does this happen? Why doesn't something else happen? Why did everyone—Javed, Hamid, Khaled, Ghalib, Jibon, Ganesh, Gopal, Amal and Bimal—rot even before their lives could bloom?!

Ghalib said, 'Do you remember Zuleikha? Khaled married Zuleikha. Within a year, he got a ten-year sentence. Can you imagine what Zuleikha's plight is now?'

'What did Khaled do?'

'Murder.'

'Where? Who?'

'He killed someone in the Kudali area when he went to commit a robbery. He may have done all that earlier, but do you think it was right to do it after his marriage?'

⊂⊃

The picture of Chakla village, and the people there that emerged from Ghalib's long account, was truly a very grave one. The lingering resonance of the Hindu-Muslim riots that had broken out in Rajabazar, Park Circus, Watgunge and many other parts of Calcutta a few months after Jibon had left Dr Hem's employment, also had a violent expression in a few places in the Ghutiari Sharif region. In this predominantly Muslim locality, a group of refugees who had been driven out of East Pakistan had been sheltered in a camp at one time. With no resettlement forthcoming, they remained there. Given their anguish at leaving their homeland, they could never view Muslims as kin, or friends, or their own. Like the mythic subterranean river Falgu, a hostile rage against the Muslim community flowed deep within the beings of these refugees.

A housing colony had come up near the refugee camp. Those who lived there were a group of affluent, high-caste people who, although they had come from East Bengal, were not refugees. Who, out of their caste pride, viewed both the Muslims and the low-caste refugees with the same contempt and disregard. They were clever, and so, whenever necessary, they craftily used both the groups for their own ends.

The central figure of these high-caste folk was Dr Hem Chakraborty. Who was currently the local leader of a political party, which, in principle, did not acknowledge the existence of any difference or division among people, or of fate or God. They said there were two classes of people, one of whom were exploiters, and the other were the exploited. Just as Dr Hem was equally adept at treating humans and animals, and secret as well as public diseases, so too was he artful in posing as an atheist in the party while being a practising Brahmin at home.

Most of the Muslim folk in the nearby hamlet were poor and deprived of education. Hundreds of superstitions resided in the minds of the uneducated folk. Religious sentiments were deeply rooted in them. Fanned by such religious sentiments, in accordance with their religious edicts, they referred to the pig-eating idol-worshippers as kaffirs. Kaffirs were such hellish wretches that even Allah disliked them. And so, they did not let even a shadow of a kaffir fall on them.

The few persons like Nurul Sheikh, Amjad Ali and Rahamatullah, who had broken this barrier and come forward, had returned in deep anguish. It was they who, smarting severely under the insult, had now become crazy with the desire to take revenge on the Hindu community. It was they who were poisoning the minds of Muslim youths. Kill them! Wherever you get the opportunity, kill and wipe out the kaffirs!

The situation now was so bad that if a cow from one hamlet broke its tether and ate another hamlet's crop, or a goat from this hamlet ate the spinach of that hamlet, a fight broke out between the two sides. Sometimes country-bombs and pipe-guns were also used, although some people labelled that as faction fights within the party. Actually it was blind rage instigated by communal hatred.

When there were riots in Calcutta, when fierce killing, attacking, looting and arson took place everywhere, it wouldn't be incorrect to say that there were no political parties present here in the Ghutiari Sharif region. But even then, quite a few houses here were looted and set on fire. One person was killed too. The attacks and counter-attacks that began then were still continuing. It was just that party colours had now been affixed to that, and thus another dimension had been added to the situation.

※

Javed and Hamid were very poor, their future promised nothing more than dark nights. The dadas of the party used that opportunity. By giving them illusions of a happy, beautiful future, they thrust country-bombs and pipe-guns into their hands. For a few years, they were completely engrossed in sloganeering, party meetings and rallies, and employing bombs and pipe-guns. It did not take long for that attachment to wane. They could see that the leaders were getting rich and powerful, while they were exactly as they had been. That's when they turned the bombs and pipe-guns in another direction. From party comrades they turned into armed robbers.

After talking about all this for a long while, Ghalib said to Jibon, 'You've heard everything. Now tell me about yourself. Why are you roaming the streets without food or sleep?'

In the distance, in the middle of the field ahead, stood a solitary palm tree in the darkness. Crowning the tree was a patch of black cloud. It was very peaceful now. But hidden within it were gale and lightning. Looking in that direction, Jibon narrated one incident after another about himself. When he finished, he asked Ghalib a final question: – 'Achchha, Ghalib, you're an educated person. Tell me, why has each one of our lives been destroyed like this? Why is it that nothing good befell anyone? We were born like dogs and cats, and we die like dogs and cats. What was the use of being born a human?'

'I don't know.'

'Isn't it written in any book?'

'Every book says something different. Every scholar has a different kind of explanation. I don't understand all that.'

'So what should one do?'

'There's nothing to be done. Nothing else is necessary now other than self-defence. Stay alive however you can. Eat to your fill in order to stay alive. Don't depend on water and air. What's right and what's wrong can be looked at later. Do you want to work in the fishery? Come, I'll get you the job.'

Thanks to Ghalib, a night and a day went by without any danger. Any news from this empire of water, which was totally cut off from people's lives, took time to reach the outside world. And news from outside reached here only after it had turned stale. Observing the environment, Jibon realised that he could easily spend a few days here free of anxiety. After all, he wasn't alone, many others like him were also hiding here.

By the evening of the following day, Jibon was restless. He felt a strange kind of heaviness in his head. Ghalib asked him, 'What's happened, Jibon? Why are you acting strange?'

Jibon replied, 'I've not had tea since yesterday, that's why I don't feel so good. I think I have a headache. Come on, Ghalib, let's go and have some tea.'

Ghalib said, 'I won't go. I'm not crazy! I have no desire to walk three miles to go and drink tea. You can go if you want. And if you're hungry, come and eat some rice with fried fish, onions and green chillies.'

'Hunger for food is one thing, and thirst for tea another thing altogether. I'm thirsty for tea now. Why don't you come along with me, bhai, we'll go, have some tea and come back.'

Unable to brush aside the request, Ghalib finally said, 'Do I have an option? Okay, let's go. Let me suffer walking six miles in vain!'

'Why in vain? Won't I treat you to tea?'

It was evening. There was only water and more water as far as one's eyes went. One fishery after another. Each one had a different owner. Walking along the banks of the fisheries, the two friends headed in the direction of the rail station. This was an unknown, small, rural rail station in the southern region of the 24-Parganas district, some forty kilometres south of Calcutta. No congested habitations had sprung up around it yet. But that would happen within the next eight or ten years. There was a steady flow of people who crossed the border and came every day, from East Bengal, which was now known as Joy Bangla—Victorious Bengal. This region would be flooded with that immense human tide. There wouldn't be even the tiniest bit of vacant space left.

Earlier, it was the Muslims who were in the majority in this region. Now it was more or less even. But as yet, there had not been any hardening of communal divisions or attitudes, with which riots could be instigated. Despite that, in some quarters, an unrelenting effort was being made. Of course, there were some quarrels and fights. But eventually, whatever happened was a party matter. Most of the Muslims stamped their votes on the Congress symbol. It was the Congress that they saw as their staunch friend. Of the remaining folk, some of them supported CPI, some the CPI(M), and a few households supported the rightist Jana Sangh. All the violence that took place was between the former three parties. But party affiliation never became widespread. It remained confined to one or two hundred people. But the current era was a time of wholesale killing. One or two lives were no lives at all.

The two friends sat on the bamboo bench of a tea-shop with a cup of tea and a salty biscuit each. The shop was at quite a distance from the rail station, close to the level-crossing. As they came walking from the fishery, Jibon picked the first shop they encountered. It was empty. In any case, there were very few people to be seen in these parts. But when a train arrived, there was a bit of a crowd. The people who went to the city for work or trade returned home on such trains.

Dusk had just set in, but it wasn't fully dark yet. Electricity had not yet arrived in this locality. Lamps began to be lit in one shop after another. Kerosene lamps, Petromax lanterns. The twelve- or thirteen-year-old boy in the tea-shop was dark-skinned and skinny, with dirt plastered all over his body. He too lit a kerosene lamp and put it on the table in front of Jibon and Ghalib, and then began poking the coal-fired stove with a thin rod. The fire was dying because there was too much ash. He would put some fresh coal in the stove now.

Jibon finished his tea and put down the empty cup on the table. He took out a beedi from the folds of his lungi. He held it to the fire of the lamp to light it. From the time when, trembling at the fear of death, he had sought to gather some courage with the help of nicotine, it had become his companion. But the boy who was poking the coal in the stove could not tolerate this careless act. Blood rushed to his small head. He struck Jibon's hand with the hot rod in his hand and roared, 'Have you lost your senses? I've just lit the lamp, and you're lighting a beedi with it?'

Customs! Jibon had unknowingly violated rural Bengal's customs, adhered to by one and all. For instance, if one wanted to buy turmeric from any shop here after sunset, one had to ask for 'big'—'Give me an anna's worth of the big vegetable'. If one wanted to buy lime, one had to say, 'Give me the curd for the paan'. If one asked for something by its actual name, the shopkeeper would brusquely reply, 'Don't have it!' The reason was that uttering the names of turmeric, lime and suchlike after sunset was supposedly inauspicious and harmful.

Similarly, lighting a beedi from a freshly lit lamp after sunset was also an inauspicious act. Customers would no longer come to the shop. And if they did, they would drink tea and slip away without paying. If he was asked to pay he would argue and fight. In short, the shop would fall into the gaze of Shani, the God of Justice. Shani was terrifying. King Srivasta turned into a beggar on the street through Shani's blow. That was a story in the puranic tales. Jibon had momentarily forgotten about this custom. That's why he now had a scorch mark on his hand, left by the hot rod.

Seeing Jibon being hit by a mere boy, Ghalib was livid. His chest heaved. He held his breath and waited for a befitting response. He visualised it actually happening the very next moment. A powerful punch from Jibon's fist would land on the boy's nose. He would fall and lie on the dirt on the road in front of the shop. A fountain of blood would gush out from his smashed nose. All his life, Jibon had suffered many insults, many times and in many ways, from many people. He had endured lots of oppression. But the wall of tolerance had now been breached. He could no longer tolerate any injustice or humiliation. Blood rushed to his head in a flash. It would be like firing a cannon to kill a mosquito. Ghalib knew that. And so, he waited for a terrible retribution.

Jibon advanced a step towards the boy, and raised his knee. You bastard! You have the gall! Do you know who I am? I'm the Jibon whose deadly form made people tremble in fear! Chandal Jibon! Go through the pages of the newspaper from a few days back, and see what they've written about me. And you dared to raise your hand against me? Such thoughts were agitating Jibon's head. That's why he had advanced a step. But he stopped at once. He remembered the famous dictum, 'One step forward, two steps back'. After advancing a step, he moved back two steps. He could thrash the boy now if he wanted to. But after that ...? What would happen after that?

Hundreds of train passengers were now walking back home along the road. They would stand in front of the tea-shop to savour the spectacle of the thrashing. Some of them would surely be travelling to Jadavpur. Perhaps some of them knew about the incident of the other day. Suppose someone recognised Jibon now? His hiding here would be in vain. Maybe they would go to Jadavpur tomorrow and tell someone, 'Jibon is hiding in our area'. That information would reach Suresh Pal, in Jadavpur police station, through word of mouth or via an informer. Jibon would be defenceless then. He would get caught. After that would come a long term in prison. With some third degree thrown in for free. Instead of all that, retreating a bit was the best move, all things considered.

After stepping back, Jibon ran his eyes all around to see who might have seen him get hit by the hot rod. No, no one had seen him, there was no other witness except for Ghalib. That meant that although he felt some pain, his dignity had not been harmed in any significant way. No one was laughing at him.

He said, 'Let's go, Ghalib.'

'Where to?'

'Back to the fishery, where else?'

'Won't you say anything? He hit you!'

'He's just a boy, he doesn't understand. Let it be.'

Ghalib walked dejectedly behind Jibon and said, 'You should have done something. That chit of a boy, he had the gall ...! Bhai, if he had touched me, I would have simply smashed his face!'

Jibon did not respond to such talk. But Ghalib continued, 'A bloody child hit you and you accepted that! You couldn't say a thing! How can you work in the fishery with this kind of cowardice? What will everyone say when they hear about it?'

Almost in a whisper, Jibon said, 'Don't tell anyone! Aren't you my friend? Isn't a friend's humiliation your own as well?'

༄

In the simple arithmetic of Ghalib's straightforward, rustic thinking, violence had to be responded to with more violence. But Jibon could not rely on such simple arithmetic. He was still thinking—he had done well not to thrash the boy. A potential problem had been averted cheaply. Or else there was the risk of a major calamity following from that. Who knows what would have happened if he beat him up? The people who would have gathered to watch the spectacle, another name for whom was the public—what if that omnipotent force was swayed in favour of the boy? He's just a boy, so he made a mistake and hit you, but just because of that, should you, a mature person, have beaten him up, and that too in this way? If he did wrong, couldn't you have complained to his father, or if his father was not around, then to the bazaar committee? Or else, you could have gone to the police station and lodged a complaint. But why did you beat him up?

Who would have saved Jibon from public ire in that event? Public ire was a terrible thing. Great big generals had been rocked by public ire. Who had been able to save anyone from its fury? Mighty palaces had been laid low. Why would Jibon be spared? Sometimes a period of helplessness arrives in people's lives, when there's nothing to be done. One has to stand and get beaten at the hands of a weaker opponent. The four-times world champion boxer, Muhammad Ali, whose former name was Cassius Clay, had once gone as a guest to Pakistan on the invitation of their government. There were thousands of Ali's fans there. They welcomed him warmly with garlands of flowers and requested him, 'Show us some boxing!' Unable to disregard their request, Ali finally donned gloves and entered the ring, saying, 'Come on!' What came next astonished the crowd. They saw that it was not any famed boxer of the country, but a boy who was only eight years old, who came forward to box to fight the world champion. What could Ali, who could slay a buffalo with his punches, do with all his strength then? There was nothing for Ali to do then but get beaten. Covering his face with his infinitely powerful arms, he lay fallen on the floor of the ring till the count of ten. He had accepted a knock-out defeat laughingly.

Not like Ali's, but with another kind of defeat, Jibon turned around and walked away. Although today, for the first time, he had been unable to beat his opponent, his mind was not poisoned by self-loathing. Rather, a kind of elation touched every corner of his mind. This was definitely a victory for him. This was a victory in his battle against himself. It was because he could defeat his own rage at the final moment that Jibon was now saved from another new danger.

But what about Ghalib! In his eyes, Jibon had lost. The brave image of Jibon that he had drawn inwardly was smashed to bits. How could a job such as guarding the fishery—in which people were killed everyday—be entrusted to such a cowardly person? If someone was caught stealing just a few fish, the owner of the fishery ordered, 'Cut the bastard into pieces and feed him to the fish!' What would someone who turned into a worm in fear of a child do when there were gunshots from all directions!

No, he couldn't be kept here. If he stayed, it was Ghalib who would be disgraced. The fishery owner liked tigers, not sheep.

The next morning Ghalib said to Jibon, 'The manager babu has sent word that no more people are needed for guard duty. If there's a requirement later, he'll let me know. Come from time to time to check.'

14

A Sanctuary of Lustful Rascals

A silent, still, black, ghoulish night descended upon the metropolis. There was no sign of life anywhere. It was as if all the people were lying like corpses behind closed doors. In that terrifying darkness, a black police van with protective anti-riot mesh sped through the thoroughfares with its two searchlights beaming like the devil's eyes. In the belly of the van were seated twelve men, like bloodthirsty hyenas. They were desperately searching for some people. Once they spotted them, their chests would be ripped apart with bayonets and bullets.

The clock tower in Jadavpur University had just sounded midnight. Earlier, this wasn't considered so late for the city of Calcutta. The last train had left just a little while back, and now there were only a few people in the shops or at the roadside eateries. Bus drivers, taxi drivers, rickshaw-pullers and so on came to eat at this time. But the times were very dangerous now. A fever of fear, of some calamitous dissolution, had taken control of every part of the city. And so, nights nowadays were very deep.

As the night advanced, Anjali Bag's heart turned icier. She was a single woman who lived in the railside shanty colony in Taltala, near Jadavpur station. The broken door of her hut did not allow her to sleep in peace. Anjali's fault was that she was young and single. Her body was attractive too. And so, the advancing night was her gravest problem. Someone was pushing her door, calling her by her name.

Anjali sold illicit liquor. Her husband Kenaram used to work as a porter in the station. At dawn one day, while trying to jump into the vendor's compartment of a morning train, he had slipped and fallen under the train. Anjali had had to open a liquor vend in order to feed herself. She made a profit of eight rupees if she sold four bottles. After paying two rupees to the police, the mother-and-son duo managed to survive on six rupees. Some people were of the view that when a woman could sell liquor, she could sell her body too for a slightly higher price. That explained the push on the door.

Anjali had only one son. She was sending him to a missionary school in Raidighi. He had been promoted to Class Four this year. Anjali had great hopes that by educating him, she would be able to make him a man of substance. Once her son grew up, she would face no more hardship. The Christian father in the missionary school had assured Anjali that the mission would bear all the costs of his education till he completed high school. Fearing that he would turn wayward, she never brought him to the shanty settlement beside the railway line. All the boys of his age here smoked beedis. They engaged in petty thefts, they picked pockets.

Her son was doing well now, so she had no anxieties in that regard. Anjali's anxiety was about herself. As the night advanced, so did her anxiety grow. Because of that, she had shut the door tight with the help of a rope. But right now, it seemed that her fear was standing close to her door and was calling her by her name. At first in a whisper, and then a bit louder, 'Anju, hey Anju!' Anjali thought the voice sounded familiar. Emboldened by that, she asked, 'Who's that?'

'It's me.'

'Who's me?'

'I'm Jibon.'

'Which Jibon?'

'It's me—Chandal Jibon!'

Anjali opened the door, and when she saw Jibon, she froze in fear and astonishment. 'How did you come to this city of death? Why have you come? Get inside at once! Did anyone see you coming here?'

Jibon stooped to enter Anjali's hut, and sat down on one side of the torn, dirty bedsheet laid out on the floor. He asked Anjali, 'What's happening here?'

'What do you mean?'

'Did the police come?'

'Of course they came! They were looking for you like Yama himself! They took a few people away.'

'How's the situation now?'

'The area was very tense at first, for five or six days. But it's a bit better now.'

Jibon laughed. 'How long can the police keep searching! Where do they have the time to work for months on a single case when there are corpses lying around everywhere.'

Jibon paused awhile and then he asked, 'What about that chap? Is he dead or alive?'

'Who are you talking about? Oh, you mean the one you stabbed? Why won't he survive? Is he hand-to-mouth like us? I heard he is being treated in a big hospital in Calcutta. I believe it costs five hundred rupees a day. But Gokul is in a very bad way. He is in the Nilratan Sarkar Hospital. He's not getting proper medicines there. Who knows whether he'll live or die. Do you know Gokul's wife? She has four children. They are unable to eat. What will she do now?'

A burden of sadness expressed itself as Jibon spoke. 'There are at least seven or eight-hundred rickshaws around Jadavpur station, the bus-stand crossing, Bijoygarh and so on. If all the men come together, they can have each other's backs at all times. Just think about it. A fund can be created and each person can contribute four annas every day towards that. How much money there would be! Getting those arrested out on bail, getting proper treatment for those who are in hospital, their legal expenses, helping those who are unable to provide for their families—all of that can be done without pinching anyone. What's a mere four annas? The price of a cup of tea!'

Anju asked, 'But who will take up the responsibility of doing all that?'

'Someone like that needs to be found. We have to do it ourselves. If we don't, then those who are in jail and in hospital will all die.'

Anjali smiled wryly, and taunted Jibon, 'Are you going to enter the "netagiri" game now!'

'Do you have any objections if I do that?'

Jibon was silent for a little while. Then he said enthusiastically, 'I think I'm the perfect person for this work. My name has appeared in the newspapers. I'm a hero among the rickshaw-pullers. Tell me, am I not a hero? If I propose something, most of the people will consent. Don't you think they'll agree?'

Anjali poured water over his grand plans. 'You'll know what a big hero you are once you fall into the police's clutches. As soon as they hear you've come to Jadavpur, they'll swoop down and take you away. Why have you come here to die? You could have stayed a few months wherever you were. My heart is trembling! Tell me— what'll happen if anyone saw you coming here?'

'Nothing will happen! If any of the poor folk of this shanty colony saw me, there's no harm in that. If any babus saw me, that could be dangerous. But how could they have seen me now? They're all indoors.'

'What about the police?'

'Do the police know my face? How will they know who Jibon is?'

'Just you see, someone or the other will point you out!'

Jibon was silent for a while and then, speaking slowly, he said, 'What can one do about that ... In the line I've entered, one has to finally die, whether lying on one's face or on one's back. There's no option but death, if not today then tomorrow. So there's no point in being scared. I had gone to a fishery. I was there for only two nights. What can I tell you—there's gunfire and country-bombs exploding all the time. So why should I leave Jadavpur to die anywhere else?'

'Go home then!'

'Where's home?'

'Where your parents live!'

'Would I have come back to West Bengal, amidst all this danger, if I could have stayed there?'

Who knows why, but Anjali was greatly worried about Jibon. She said, 'So where will you stay now?'

'Where else will I stay? I'll stay near the station, or in the hospital compound, or near the bus-stand crossing.'

'Won't you be scared?'

Jibon replied in a wounded tone. 'What else have we learnt other than to be scared! All my life, I've only learnt to be scared. I couldn't make anyone scared instead. After all, I didn't learn that. But now I've realised that if one mistakes a rope for a snake, then the rope will actually raise its hood and stand in front of you. But if I hold even a snake firmly, as if it's a mere rope, then the snake does turn into a rope out of fear! Tell me, how many were they? I took down one, and all the others fled with their tails between their legs.'

Jibon was silent again for a while. Then he said, 'Remember something I'm telling you. It's something I learnt from my own life. If you're not afraid of dying, and if you're not afraid of killing, all the bastards will be scared of you. Do you know why? Because everyone is afraid of dying. All those who wish to live will then pay obeisance to you. You don't need anything else, just give up the fear of death and confront them.'

Hearing Jibon's words, Anjali was silent for a while. Finally she said, 'You're a prize idiot!'

'Why do you say that?'

'Do you think they got scared and ran away? That they won't return? Just you see, if they ever catch you unawares, they'll exact revenge alright!'

Jibon said, with an air of effortless ease, 'Let them do that if they can, who's stopping them! After all, this is a game!'

'A game?'

'A game between tiger and hunter. Sometimes the hunter gets the tiger, and sometimes it's the tiger that gets the hunter.'

'Are you the tiger or the hunter?'

Jibon laughed. He said, 'I see myself as a tiger. Do you know why? You'll never hear of a tiger that leaves the forest and comes to the city to hunt humans. It's the hunters who go to the forest and kill tigers for no reason. And even when a tiger kills a human, it's not without reason. I'm the same. If anyone comes to kill me, I'll kill him if I can.'

'Whatever you do, you'll have to do alone. Those rickshaw-puller bhais of yours—when danger arrives, you'll see there's no one beside you.'

'I know that. When someone is unable to eat unless he works, how can he stand beside another?'

'So what will you do?'

'I didn't get you.'

'Do you know what happened in Kasba? A rickshaw-puller, I forget his name, he had a quarrel with a passenger over the fare. A few days later, a passenger got into his rickshaw to go to the canalside in Rajdanga. He killed him and threw him into the canal. The same will happen to you if you pull a rickshaw.'

'I can't pull a rickshaw anymore!'

'Then how will you eat?'

Jibon burst out laughing. He said, 'You'll feed me!'

Anjali responded to Jibon's joke with one of her own. 'Marry me then! People feed their wives, so let me feed my husband!'

'You want to get into a boat that's sinking?'

'But I'm already in deep waters! I'm clutching at whatever I can find, so that I can reach the shore ...'

'What about your son? Surely he wouldn't want to call me "Baba". I've been his "Mama" so far.'

All this talk was entirely in jest. That was the nature of the relationship between Anjali and Jibon, which was to be found in our country between a bridegroom and his wife's younger sister, or between a bride and her husband's younger brother. The two of them were friends. And good friends at that. Anjali viewed this locality around the Jadavpur railway station as a sanctuary of leering, lustful rapists and rascals of that ilk. There was no way she could trust anyone at all. One never knew when the mask of decency would be shed to reveal a violent animal preying on female flesh. Jibon was the only trustworthy male in this jungle. If he were ever to arrive one night and find Anjali lying drunk and naked, he would cover her up with a sari, shut the door behind him and sit outside guarding her.

Taking a look at Jibon now in the dim light streaming in from the lamp-post afar, Anjali said, 'How can you make such jokes at such a time?'

Jibon replied, 'But who started it?'

'There's no sword of danger hanging over my head. But there is, over yours.'

Jibon took Anjali's hand and pressed her palm on his waist. He said, 'This is called a "one-shot". The bullet that's inside this is called "three-nought-three", the same as in police rifles. I'll kill at least one before I die. There were plenty of these in the bloody fishery. I made off with one. I took about a dozen bullets too. That's how I've been able to come to Jadavpur.'

Her eyes agape in astonishment, Anjali kept gazing at this hitherto unknown face of Jibon in the darkness of midnight. Had another star risen in the firmament of hoodlumism in the locality around the station?

⊙⧓⊙

Sona used to work as a porter in the Jadavpur railway station. Later, he lost his right arm in a bomb explosion, and came to be known as Haat Kata Sona, or 'one-armed Sona', in Jadavpur. When Sona was a porter, the most well-known mastaan of this locality was Sadhan Dey, the elder brother of Mona Dey. Once, for some reason, he had thrashed Sona, who was skinny and only five feet tall. After he was thrashed, Sona waited in the wings for an opportunity to take revenge. A few days later, when Sadhan Dey was on his way home one night in a state of intoxication, Sona suddenly came running and plunged a knife into his back. A stab from a very ordinary knife, which was less than three inches deep. But with that stab, Sadhan Dey's name slipped from the peak of respect and fame. And Sona's ascended, as if to light.

After that, for a few years, his name was sung in victory chants everywhere. Finally, one day, someone called Kana Bagha—Deaf Bagha—stabbed him to death. A few days later, someone killed Bagha, and to date, no one knows who did that. Some said it was the police, some others said it was the Naxalites, and yet others said it was the CPI(M). If Jibon could fill the vacuum left by Kana Bagha, he would be in the limelight—as long as he wasn't wiped out by someone else.

Those who used to rule the roost so long on this side of the rail track, the Naxalites, were all gone now. And those who ruled on the other side, the CPI(M), had also fled the area. The might of the Congress in Bijoygarh was also confined to the other side of Raja Subodh Chandra Mullick Road. They had not really formally taken over the area around the Jadavpur station. The only one here was the drunkard, Sadhan Dey, who was run-down on account of age. And there wasn't even any emerging mastaan in the area. Therefore, in a sense the station was devoid of a guardian. Jibon could achieve hegemony without any hindrance. The opportunity had come to him. But both the police as well as old enemies would target him, in order to retain their hegemony, as well as for their own safety. That was the only thing to fear.

After some time, Anjali said, 'Listen carefully to what I tell you. Don't go on the same road twice. When you go somewhere by a particular route, take another route while returning. Don't sit in one place for more than five minutes. Don't tell anyone where you sleep at night. Change the place every few days, if you can. Look all around you, in all directions, when you walk anywhere. Stay away from crowds. Always sit with your back to a wall. Don't drink liquor. People become incautious when they get intoxicated. Be alert at all times.'

The clock in Jadavpur University sounded again, twice this time. Anjali had not lit any lamp in her room. Two shadowy figures sat next to each other in the bit of light that entered from outside. They spoke in hushed tones, almost in whispers.

After a while, Jibon asked, 'Where does the booze in the dens in Taltala come from, re Anjali? Is it from Hussainpur or Charan?'

'Why do you ask?'

'Mention my name and tell the suppliers that just like they make weekly payments to the police and excise folk, they have to pay me something too, something at least. Or else, I won't let them carry on their business. And they should leave the payment with you.'

Anjali's sleepy eyes were now shutting. She lay down on the torn mattress spread out on the floor. Her pillow shifted a bit, and the knife kept under it for self-defence was exposed. Anjali put it back under the pillow and said, 'Lie down next to me and get some sleep. There's a long time left for daybreak. Wake up and leave in time for the first train.'

'What if I don't wake up on time?'

'I'll wake up on time even if you oversleep. Don't worry. Go to sleep now.'

'There's no one else here, just you and me.'

'So what?'

'Aren't you afraid?'

'Afraid of what?'

'Let's say I can't control myself ...'

'Tell me what you'll do after that.'

'Let's say I ... you can guess the rest.'

Anjali laughed out aloud and moved her pillow. 'Take a look at this. I'll cut the whole thing off! You'll become a eunuch! No girl will even piss on your face!'

Jibon lay down next to Anjali and said slowly, 'The day Babua died, I was there at the final moment. He was full of sadness when he died. He told me, "Jibon, I'm dying without even having seen or touched a woman's body, that's the worst part." That's what I'm thinking too now. If I die tomorrow, I'll never have known the secret pleasures hidden in a woman's body.'

Anjali said, 'Stop talking and go to sleep. If I try to fulfill your wishes, and then another enemy enters my womb—what will I feed him? How will we survive? And why on earth should you die? I pray to God you live for a hundred years, and that you see your grandchildren and great-grandchildren!'

The clock sounded once again. It was three. The first train would arrive in another hour.

⊰⊱

There's no estimate of how many hundreds of people arrived at the railway station and city pavements to lay down their heads to rest, after fleeing drought or floods or famine, or for so many other reasons. To this had been newly added the crisis of Partition. Those who once had shelter of their own had lost everything and were squatters in stations and on the pavements. A new family had arrived a few days ago at the Jadavpur railway station. A widow, accompanied by her minor son, and adult daughter.

Perhaps they did not know that, come night, a poor girl of that age wasn't safe in any rail station in the country. Or else, the mother would not have had the courage to take such a big risk. They were crouched under the stairs of the bridge on Platform No. 2, with their cooking utensils, bedding and mat. Perhaps they were ruing their fate.

Jibon was a creature of the night nowadays. He spent the whole day sitting or lying down in an abandoned, broken-down brick platform behind the sweepers' quarters in the hospital premises. A gambling group used to assemble in front of that. Illicit liquor was also sold there. Jibon came out to the road only at night. But today he had to leave his safe cave and come out during daylight. He wanted to take the train from Platform No.2 to go to Garia station. Nitya, from Shikhonda, had invited him today—'Jibon bhai, you must come! I'll wait for you at the station.' Who knows why, for no reason at all, Nitya was fond of Jibon. He had a fruit stall at the TB Hospital gate.

Jibon could not go to the station directly. Taking a roundabout route, and through twists and turns, he arrived at the station and stood furtively under the bridge. That's when he noticed the woman nearby. At once, he felt as if he had stepped on a live wire; the hair on his body stood on end. Despite the widow's garb, and the stamp of acute hardship all over her eyes and face, he recognised Subol Sutar's wife, Tulsi. And beside her was Kusum. Next to Kusum was Bishwo.

'What's this, Kakima? How come you're here, in this condition?'

Tulsi was struck dumb and stared at him, overwhelmed. It was a long time before she could speak. Coming upon one's own right next to her, a rush of tears overcame her. At length, she said, 'It's all our fate! Our fate has brought us here. I had told Bishwo's father so many times, don't go anywhere, let's remain in Dandakaranya, whatever happens to everyone will happen to us too. But he did not heed that. He went and died, and now he has left us to die here. Where do we go now? What are we to do? With a grown-up daughter ... what a danger it is!'

Jibon asked Tulsi, 'Where were you people all these days?'

Tulsi replied, 'After leaving Dandakaranya, we went to Bongaon. We built a shanty beside the railway line and lived there. After that Kusum's Baba said, let's go to my brother's house and seek his help. What a mistake we made by going there!' Tulsi's eyes brimmed with tears once again. 'Kusum's kaka wasn't happy to see us. But because it was his elder brother, he couldn't say anything. He let us stay. As soon as his brother passed away, he drove us away.'

'What happened to Subol Kaka?'

'What can I say ... He had loose motions three or four times one day, and he vomited a few times. He was dead before night fell.'

Kusum sat inertly with her back resting against the metal railing on the platform. She was very embarrassed, as thousands of lustful eyes gazed at her blooming body. As if a mighty diffidence had wrapped itself around her like a python. It was as if in her shameful plight, she was praying inwardly—*Dharani dwidha how!* O Mother Earth, split open!

Tulsi said, 'Even a stranger isn't driven away the way Kusum's kaka drove us away. After the partition of the country, people's souls have been partitioned too. No one has mercy, pity or a feeling of oneness any more. If we remained there, they would have to spend on our food. The girl's come of age, and so the bother of getting her married. By driving us away, he freed himself of all such bother. Only God knows where we'll go now, and what we'll do ... We were in Canning for three days. Someone said, go to Jadavpur. Our country folk are there, you'll be able to work and survive if you go there. I heeded their words and came here. But now that I'm here, I can't figure out anything.'

Kusum! Oh, the same old Kusum! It was as if she had just removed her slough and stepped out, and that she would wilt if any breeze so much as brushed her. Begin to droop if exposed to sunlight, and melt if any man touched her. As if she was a soft, tender, precious treasure. From some distant star, a divine melody struck his ears. The fragrance of a forestful of rajnigandhas suffused all his senses. You've come! You've come, my dear! But why did you come so late?

Behind Tulsi were just a few household possessions. Which were so meagre that even thieves wouldn't take them. But something very valuable was in her custody. Why only thieves, even a king would snatch that away, given the opportunity. Tulsi said, 'What dangers we've fallen into by coming here! The greatest of them is regarding Kusum. Even if I shut my eyes for a moment, men close in. They call out to her. They say unthinkable things.'

Jibon said, 'This is a station. Those who stay here put up with everything. You'll have to put up with it too. Why did you just arrive here out of the blue?'

'What else could we have done? How much more abuse and berating could we bear? They wouldn't stop until they drove us out.'

Expressing his despair, Jibon said, 'But what am I to do now? How can I go away leaving you here like this? And if I take you away—where can I take you?'

It was as if Tulsi was being carried away by floodwaters, and by finding Jibon here, had something at hand to cling on to. She said, 'Wherever you stay, Jibon, please let us stay there for a few days, or else Kusum will be destroyed!'

Jibon thought inwardly—at least nothing is destroyed yet. But come night, how does one know that claws and fangs won't tear up and devour Kusum! Parul used to come to the city from Gobindopur to wash kitchen utensils. One rainy night, she stayed back on the platform after the last train was cancelled. The next morning she was found in an empty wagon of a goods train. Naked and unconscious. It was heard that four constables of the railway police had taken Parul away on suspicion of being a thief. After that, they looted everything and dumped her in the goods train.

Helpless. Jibon felt extremely helpless today. Life was no longer worth a whit now. It was no longer the time of Partition and the terrible communal riots. The responsibility of governing the country was now in the hands of a democratic, secular ruling party. The police force, nurtured by the salaries paid by the same government, deliberately and cruelly raped the Bagdi girl, Parulbala, and left her to a fate worse than death. Were the communal rioters any more inhuman than that? Then why was all blame pinned on a specific community?

But what was Jibon to do now? He himself was homeless. Some of his nights were spent on the roof of the morgue, or some under the culvert in Loharpara, and sometimes inside the large drain pipes around there. And here was Tulsi asking him for shelter! Shelter for Kusum! Jibon hadn't been able to save Parul. Neither had he been able to protect Shikha Mondal of Gosaba, who had run away from home after being scolded by her step-mother. She was looted of everything in an empty train compartment. In mortifying despair, she had thrown herself on the railway line.

What if something like that happened to Kusum? ... But Jibon could not figure out what he ought to do. He lamented his own incapability now. He remembered someone's words— *'Maarnewale se bachanewale ka taaqat zyada hota hai*, the one who protects is mightier than the one who attacks'. That was true. It was easy to kill someone, but protecting someone was extremely difficult. It was even more difficult for Jibon now, given his circumstances. How could someone who was homeless provide shelter to others?

Tulsi said once again, now with a hopeful tone, 'I never imagined I would find you at such a frightening time. God made us meet!' When she stopped speaking, she knocked her hand on her forehead in pious devotion.

Jibon was thinking that if he could get hold of a few bamboos and some matting, he could erect a shanty beside the rail line, at the spot where he had earlier planned to make one and bring over his parents. They could at least stay there for a while. But for that he needed both money and time. How about keeping them for about ten days with Anjali? He should talk to her. After all, she lived alone. Wouldn't she be able to put up with a bit of inconvenience for a few days for Jibon's sake?

Kusum sat with her head leaning on the metal railing, gazing at the sky. She had not said a word in all this while. As if all that she had to say had died. A flock of vultures circled around in the sky. Had a cow landed in the carcass dump beside the rail line?

Jibon looked at Kusum out of the corner of his eye. Kusum, who had no one to protect her now but her mother.

Tulsi enquired, 'What work do you do here, Jibon?'

'Work!' Jibon smiled wryly, and replied, 'Mad dogs, you know, the ones that bite people … I catch those dogs.'

'What kind of work is that! How much do you get paid?'

'I've not become permanent yet. But whenever I get work, I get paid well.'

'Take care of us for a few days. I've heard that there's work available in babu homes here. Once Kusum and I find work, we won't bother you.'

Kusum now turned her face to look directly at Jibon. It was a look full of distress and tears. Did she want to say something? It was as if hidden within her gaze were hundreds of things she wanted to say, but which could not be expressed in words.

Jibon suddenly remembered, and he asked, 'Have you eaten anything since morning, Kakima?'

'We ate muri with alur-dam. Where shall I cook? What can I cook? We've been like this for three or four days. It's not difficult for me. But Bishwo can't bear it anymore.'

As she spoke, Tulsi's eyes brimmed with tears once again. Tears were extremely unfeeling. They did not know when they should pour out. Jibon was completely penniless. He himself was going to eat two stations away, in another pauper's home. But then he said, 'Let Bishwo and Kusum come with me. I'll feed them rice at an eatery. You can also go when they return. Look after your things until then.'

Tulsi said, 'I have some rice with me. I could boil that in your house …'

'I have to attend to various things before you can do that. Eat something before that.'

Jibon mentally calculated that it would cost at least six rupees for three people to eat. He owed six rupees from before. Chhechan would flatly tell Jibon that he could not eat without paying. He allowed him credit out of simple trust. When Jibon had money, he paid off his dues too.

Kusum's face betrayed no eagerness at the mention of rice. It was as if she was unable to mentally accept as normal the wound of fate, and the unbearableness of the world around her. Maybe that was why she could not talk to Jibon. Everything seemed false, illusory and dream-like to her.

Jibon said again, 'Eat properly first, and then we can think about other matters. Bishwo, Kusum, come with me. Let Kakima wait here.'

Bishwo became eager at the mention of rice. He pulled Kusum by her hand, 'Come on, Didi!'

'You go. I won't go, I'm not hungry.' Kusum spoke for the first time. It was as if it wasn't words but lumps of grief that escaped her lips.

Tulsi said to her, 'Why don't you go, Kusum? Jibon is one of us, after all. He's our own boy. You haven't eaten for three or four days. He's calling you, go.'

After being told several times, Kusum finally stood up. She held Bishwo's hand and began walking with hesitant steps. Jibon walked ahead. His watchful eyes surveyed all directions. He was walking like this, at this time, in broad daylight, after many days. While getting off the end of the platform via the incline, the famished Kusum's tired legs slipped. Just as she was about to fall on her face, she grabbed hold of Jibon from behind.

Jibon's whole body was electrified by the unimagined close embrace. He had never before felt so deeply the pleasure of being held so firmly. It was as if some terrified gourd creeper had clutched a strong tree in order to survive a cyclonic storm.

Jibon said, 'Did you get hurt, Kusum?'

'Thank God, you were in front of me!' Kusum steadied herself and began walking. The way ahead was still slippery, and so she held Jibon's hand firmly with her hand. Both the hands seemed to be trembling. As if opening his heart to a soulmate, Jibon said, 'I always thought that I'd definitely meet you, one day or the other. The day you people went away from Dandakaranya—what can I tell you, it was as if I could see nothing but darkness in front of my eyes. It was as if I was surrounded by emptiness. I'm so lucky that I found you again! I must never lose you now!'

Kusum did not say anything. She merely squeezed Jibon's hand hard. She did not care about who was looking at her, or what anyone was thinking of her. She conveyed all she had to say through the firm bond of her hand.

⁂

Chhechan's eatery was extremely crowded at this time. There was no other eatery in this locality which was as cheap. All the porters, labourers, cart-pullers and rickshaw-pullers ate here. Jibon wouldn't be able to get a place unless the crowd thinned. The three of them stood across the road from the eatery, under the shade of a guava tree, leaning against the metal railing of the railway quarters. Bishwo gazed ardently at the steaming rice on the plates. Jibon consoled him, 'Just wait a bit. As soon as those who are eating get up, we'll sit down.'

It was almost 2 p.m. now. The sun blazed overhead. The breeze seemed to carry waves of fire. Chhechan's shop had a tin roof, and there were no fans in it. The people seated on the benches to eat were dripping with sweat. As if in a stupor, they weren't able to eat quickly.

The streets were usually devoid of people at this time. No one was outside except those citizens who absolutely had to be there. A rickshaw-puller was returning to the bus-stop crossing along the desolate road. His name was Jahar. Spotting Jibon, he said in a muted tone, but sharply, 'Come here, quickly!'

Jibon hurried towards the rickshaw stand. Jahar said to him, 'Run! Pal babu has parked the police van in front of the TB Hospital and is heading in this direction!' There wasn't time to hear any more! Irrespective of whether the report was true or false, he could not afford to take any risk. But in which direction would Jibon flee? Anjali had counselled him not to stay long in any place. Perhaps because he had been standing here for about an hour, visible to hundreds of eyes, somehow word about him had reached the appropriate quarters. There was no more time. He could not say anything even to Kusum. He ran, jumped over the hospital wall, and entered the compound. He ran ahead breathlessly.

Kusum and Bishwo waited under the scorching sun, in the hope of eating rice. They kept waiting. And waiting. One batch finished eating and rose, and another batch sat down to eat. That batch finished and another batch sat down. But Jibon was unable to return.

15

The Station Netherworld

There were some boys between the ages of sixteen and twenty-two who lived in the Jadavpur rail station, about whom Kali babu, who had a newspaper and magazine shop, said— *'Ma baaper naam jaane na, hoteley khaay, footpathey ghumaay.* They don't know who their parents are, they eat in eateries, and sleep on pavements.' That was one hundred per cent true. Except in one case, and that was the case of the brothers Amal and Bimal, who knew who their father was, but didn't know who their mother was, because she died when they were very small. Their father, who was a day labourer, made the two brothers sit in the railway station one day—and then, who knows where he disappeared. Ganesh did not have an arm, hence he was widely known as Haat Kata Ganesh. His father died when he was very small. His mother abandoned him and set up home with someone else. No one knew who the parents of Bhola, the porter, were. He himself had no clue. Then there were the two Gopals: Boro Gopal and Chhoto Gopal. One was from Taldi, and the other was a Lakshmikantapur boy. But they never went there. They never spoke to anyone about those who lived there. Nor did those with whom they lived in the station ask them about such personal details. They had no interest in such matters. Bangaal Naran was from Khulna district in East Bengal. It was said that he was separated from his family while crossing the border and coming over to this side under cover of night. Ghoti Naran was a Medinipur boy. He had come to Calcutta to work as a servant in a tea-shop. He had risen from that to become a rickshaw-puller at the stand at Jadavpur Station now. Kaliya's father was a rickshaw-puller too, and his mother was mentally ill. His father had married again for that reason. Kaliya lived in the railside shanty settlement with his sick mother. But that was only at night. He spent the whole day in the station. Sheltered in the station in the same way, after some calamity or the other, were Shibo, Mota, Bishu and several others. Almost all of them were assembled beneath the station's water tank now. Something that had never happened in this station before, something no one ever imagined would happen, had actually happened. Everyone was hanging their head in shame. They had assembled to discuss and decide how the disgrace could be wiped away, and how their ruined dignity could be restored.

There was a dumping ground on railway land, near the signal-post on the western side of the station. All the dead cows of the locality were brought and dumped there. Those dead cows belonged to Jalodhar Nayak. He was the one who had leased the land for the dumping ground from the railway authorities. Jalodhar had the hides of the cows skinned by his men, and took them to Park Circus, where he sold them. Besides that, Jalodhar had two more businesses, one of which was selling liquor. That was not illicit liquor. He purchased English liquor from the licensed shop in Jodhpur Park, stored it discreetly in his house, and then sold it at a higher price to the affluent drunkards of the locality. Just as he earned a little bit from that, he also saved the drunkard babus time and effort. Because Jalodhar sold expensive liquor, he was like a kulin Brahmin of a businessman among liquor sellers. His third business was money-lending. All the rickshaw-pullers and small traders of the locality borrowed money from him, at an interest of ten per cent per month.

Anyone who had money also came to wield some influence and power. And so Jalodhar was an honourable person of the locality. Sanyasi Das was a flunky of Jalodhar's. Sanyasi was lame in one leg. He was from the marshlands of the Sundarbans. He had stepped into the river to catch fish long ago, when a turtle sank its teeth into his leg. He survived the attack, but he was crippled for the rest of his life. Sanyasi wore a kurta printed with the Lord's name, and he went around the whole locality with a bag slung on his shoulder, a tilak on his forehead, and a kartal in his hand, begging, as he sang, *'Bhojo gobindo, koho gobindo, loho gobinder naam he, je jon gobindo bhoje shey hoy amar praan re.* Chant Gobindo, say Gobindo, o take Gobindo's name, the one who chants Gobindo becomes my very life ...' The man was a religious soul. Which was why, whenever he got the chance, he fed ripe bananas to the most sacred creature in the Hindu religion, the cow.

There were a lot of cows nowadays in the Jadavpur area, not only in the fields, but also sitting, lying and standing on the roads, obstructing people and vehicles as they chewed cud. The roads functioned as their pasture as well as cattle shed. Looking at them, one would think they were free, omnivorous and omnipresent. No one ever claimed ownership over them. But they were far from being unclaimed. If a cow butted a pedestrian, its owner might not be found. But if any vehicle hit a cow, one could never say whether an owner wouldn't pop out from among the bus passengers or the nearby lane or tea-shop, or from anywhere else.

Jalodhar had inducted Sanyasi to serve all these creatures of Lord Krishna. The bananas were paid for by Jalodhar, and Sanyasi's task was to make sure no one saw him as he held out a banana in front of the meek creature. Sanyasi was not to blame, neither was the banana supposed to be at fault.

The blame lay in the cow's fate. The blame lay in being born a cow. Within ten minutes of consuming the banana, the cow died. In the last month or so, forty or fifty cows from the locality had died in this way, of some unknown malady. And as usual, these cows landed on Jalodhar's carcass-dump. As a reward for his pious work, he also dropped a bit of whatever he earned from selling the hides into Sanyasi's bag.

This enterprise was carrying on, and it would have continued until all the cows died, leaving the roads completely vacant. But Sanyasi's fate was awful, and so, somehow or the other, Kaliya spotted him. He caught him and found five poison-laced bananas in his possession. He was brought to the rail station and tied with his hands behind to one of the pillars of the water tank, with his own kurta that bore the Lord's name. Everyone was unanimous that he was to blame, and that he ought to be punished. The only difference was in regard to what the punishment should be.

Jatadhari guru, who practised palmistry on Platform No. 2, and sold talismans and amulets, had declared, 'We are Hindus, the cow is our Mother Incarnate. The one who feeds poison to and kills the cow commits matricide. The only punishment for that should be hanging him at the crossroads. But that's not possible nowadays. What's possible is to make him eat all the five poison-laced bananas. If he doesn't eat them on his own, he can be fed by force.'

Bilal Mollah was the owner of the cycle-rickshaw repair shop near Chhechan's eatery. He could not agree with the first part of Jatadhari guru's declaration. A cow was actually merely a cow. How could it be a mother? Cow flesh was nutritious food. After all, Bilal himself ate it. How was it possible to get cow meat without killing the cow? But he had no objections to the final part of what Jatadhari guru said. He agreed that the crime of poisoning cows called for a suitable punishment. He also added to that, saying, 'If Sanyasi doesn't agree to eat the bananas, laying him on the rail track, with his hands and feet bound, should solve all problems!'

Kaliya did not like what Bilal said. He said, 'For the kind of sin the bastard Sanyasi has committed, simply killing him will be no punishment at all! Let both his hands be chopped off instead. He won't be able to do something like that again if he no longer has the hands with which he poisoned and killed so many mute creatures.'

'Kaliya is right!' shouted Ghoti Naran. 'He won't be able to play the kartal and sing 'Chant Gobindo' either. He won't be able to utter the name of Gobindo from the mouth with which he ate food purchased by selling those cows' hides.' Of course, Bhola, from the tea-shop, did not want any of these terrible punishments. His view was—'Let him be handed over to the police. Let them do what they like with him.'

'No, it's no use handing him over to the police,' said Boro Gopal. 'What do you think will happen if he's given over to the police? Do you think Jalodhar is short of money? He'll pay two- or five-hundred and get Sanyasi released. Sanyasi is his goose that lays the golden egg. Hasn't Sanyasi killed plenty of cows? Who got rich thereby? In my opinion, Jalodhar too should be brought here.'

'Who'll catch Jalodhar and bring him here? You? Will you be able to do that,' someone or the other said.

'Why just me? What if all of us went together?'

'It's not necessary for everyone to go,' said Haat Kata Ganesh. 'Let Kaliya, the two Gopals and Jibon-da go. They'll get the bastard out even if he's hiding in his mother's womb!'

At the mention of Jibon's name by Haat Kata Ganesh, everyone realised that the one whose presence was most necessary wasn't there. He hadn't been seen since morning. Where was he?

'Where's Jibon-da, re?' Haat Kata Ganesh asked Boro Gopal. 'I haven't seen him even once all day. Have any of you seen him?'

'I saw him once yesterday. No one knows where he stays nowadays! He seems to have changed. Sometimes he speaks in the Bangaal language, and sometimes just like a school-educated babu's son. And sometimes what he utters makes him seem a champion in profanity. The most terrible thing is that come evening, he can't remember what he said in the morning. I saw him standing at the Naskarpara crossing one day. So many enemies there! Just imagine, if someone had spotted him,' exclaimed Boro Gopal.

Moving Haat Kata Ganesh aside a bit, Boro Gopal now asked the gathering, 'Didn't you notice all these changes in him?'

'I did,' said Haat Kata Ganesh. 'You brought it up and so I'm saying this, or else I wouldn't have. I don't know why, but I think Jibon is actually two people. I mean, the Jibon we used to know has been split into two and become two Jibons.'

Boro Gopal said, 'There are two Kana Ajits. One lives at Baghajatin, and the other at Lal Gate. One is blind in the left eye, and the other in the right eye. Both are with the Congress. Both are mastaans. Although their behaviour and activities are the same, their appearance is different—one can tell them apart. Similarly, there are three Balak-das, all three are with the CPI(M). One lives in Loharpara, one in Bijoygarh, and one in Santoshpur.'

Someone said, 'Balak-da from Bijoygarh was shot and killed by Suresh Pal.'

Boro Gopal said, 'He may have killed him, but they were three different people! The most dangerous among them is Balak-da of Loharpara; the one from Santoshpur is a bit less dangerous than him. And coming to Balak-da of Bijoygarh—look, if one is involved in the party's work and such like, one has to do some killing and thrashing, but despite that, Balak-da of Bijoygarh was a good man. He knew the pain of the poor. But be that as it may, one could tell each of them apart. But coming to our Jibon-da, if there are really two of them, then it's difficult to tell them apart since they look the same.'

'Why do you think it's two people? Why do you think that?' asked Haat Kata Ganesh.

'It seems that way to me.'

'It seems that way to me too.'

Pausing a bit and smiling, Haat Kata Ganesh said, 'I had seen it in the cinema once. Was it *Ram Aur Shyam*?'

'No man, it was a Bengali film, what was the name ... *Bhranti Bilash*. With Uttam Kumar and Bhanu Bandopadhyay in double roles. Who knows whether or not we are in a *Bhranti Bilash* situation!'

From the crowd, Kaliya called out to Haat Kata Ganesh and Boro Gopal, 'Aeyi, come here! Do what you have to quickly! If you're going to take his hands off, do that. Or if you're not going to do that, then let him go. We can't afford to waste an entire day over one problem.'

Haat Kata Ganesh asked, 'How would it be if we let him go?'

'No,' said Kaliya, 'we can't let him off. No one can accuse a single boy from our rickshaw-stand in this station of being a thief or cheat. Everyone sweats it out all day in order to have food to eat. But just because of Sanyasi, everyone has been disgraced. If he was eager to do crooked things, he could have left the station and gone away, and then done that. None of us would have said anything. Hara, Monta and Bisha are pickpockets, Bhoja and Badal rob homes. But do we tell any of them anything? The bastard Sanyasi could have gone and stayed in their basti and done whatever he wanted. If he does terrible things while living among us in the station—whoever else may spare him, we won't let him go! This station is like where we were born, and it's where we'll die too. It's a question of our pride, we won't let anyone take over this place.'

'That's fine, but unless Jibon-da arrives ...' concluded Boro Gopal, on a note of hopelessness, 'we can't do anything. Chopping off his hands is two minutes' work. But the situation that will arise after that—do any of us have the power to handle that? Do you think Jalodhar will keep quiet? He knows the police, the mastaans, and so many more people. Who knows whether he isn't sitting in the police station right now!'

'But there's no news of Jibon-da. I heard that apparently he's found a new place in the Kalighat crematorium. If he's living there, then it's unlikely he'll come here today.'

Those who needed Jibon badly now weren't able to find him. But it was someone who wasn't looking for him who found him. That was Naru.

There was a stretch of vacant space between the canteen of the TB Hospital and the Hundred-Bed ward. Although it was vacant, it wasn't really empty; it was full of trees and shrubs of various kinds. Some thick clumps of morning glory, bushes of jungle tulsi and so on, which gave the place a wooded appearance. Jibon lay in concealment on a bit of clearing on the far side of that jungle, deep in daytime slumber.

⁂

Hara, the pickpocket, lived in one of the shanties near Sandhyabazaar, adjacent to the Jadavpur rail station. He wasn't just a pickpocket, but also a master psychologist. With his amazing knowledge, he had the ability to figure out where people had hidden money on their persons. It was a weakness in people that they kept touching the place where they had hidden something. This excessive carefulness proved to be their undoing when someone observed them closely, and thus discovered where the secret stash lay.

Today, employing this power of observation, Hara had discovered that there was a good amount of money in a pouch hidden in a passenger's groin. He was going to Bowbazaar to buy provisions for his shop. After that, whatever had to happen happened. When the train was between Garia and Jadavpur, Hara slit the pouch with a blade and removed the money. But he could not escape. Someone saw Hara's handiwork. He caught hold of the collar of Hara's shirt and screamed out, 'Pickpocket!' The moment he screamed, the others in Hara's gang, who were called 'thekbaaj', abandoned Hara and disappeared.

The weak creatures of the dark netherworld used some symbolic words in order to hide their professional identities from the people at large. For instance, in their argot, 'tingbaaj' was the general name for a pickpocket. And the one who did the main job, that is, the one who removed money from the pocket, was known as a 'mistri'. And the others, meaning those who carried out the task of surrounding and pressing into the one whose pocket was to be picked, and thus helped in carrying out the job, were known as 'thekbaaj'. The one who picked the pocket was the one who took the greatest risk, and so he alone took half the pickings. The other half would be shared by four or six 'thekbaajs'. Among the 'mistris', the one who was adept at using a blade to cut the pocket and remove the money was like a kulin Brahmin among pickpockets. His prestige was immense. Another name for him was 'ghaubaaj'.

Similarly, the thief who broke the lock of a house and robbed it at night was known as 'gabbabaaj'. The one who pilfered luggage from trains was called 'dholbaj'. The one who lay waiting on a train or platform, and when he got the chance, fled with everything belonging to a sleeping person, was known as 'podibaaj'. In the same way, they had given the name 'lohar chaka' or iron wheel to the train, and likewise, 'rubber wheel' was a car. The breast-pocket of a punjabi was 'bukkhal', the hanging pockets were 'nichhchhaal'. A wrist-watch was 'chorki', a neck-chain was 'shuto'. Currency notes were 'chitta', coins were 'hechki'. A ten-rupee note was 'dosha', and a fiver was 'panjon'. An eight-anna coin was 'taali', and a four-anna coin 'masha'. The house that was to be robbed was called 'gabba', while the lock was called 'phool', meaning flower. And the crowbar with a pointed end, with which the lock was broken, was known as 'gamchha'. The one who bought stolen goods was called 'khau'. The police were 'khonchor'. 'Andar' meant jail. To be caught was to be 'ladaan'.

Hara had undertaken his 'ghaubaji' today, just before the train reached Jadavpur Station, and pinched two-and-a-half-thousand in cash from the 'aenrkhal', the pocket in the man's groin, amidst the crowd and bustle of boarding and alighting passengers. Right then, because his fate was against him, he became 'ladaan'. The public was belligerent. They pounced upon Hara. A fierce storm of blows landed on him at once. Within ten or fifteen minutes, his lip was bleeding, his chest was covered in blood, and his eyes were swollen like potatoes. It was said that a thrashing by the public was the turn for the whole world to join in. If the public did actually do that, it wouldn't matter. But they wanted to do more than that, something worse than that. They wanted to hand him over to the GRP. That meant the loss of a major part of Hara's hard-earned pickings over the last two days. If they didn't accept a bribe and free him, they would send him to court. In that event, the money would be taken away legally, by some lawyer. Hara would then have to pick the pockets of even more people in order to pay for the legal expenses. The upshot was that, in a roundabout way, it was the same public that was harmed.

Those who were permanent residents of the station, those who toiled to feed themselves, did not really like Hara. But not Jibon. He was of the view that although thieving was very bad, compared to those who adulterated life-saving medicines, those who sold documents pertaining to national security abroad, those who won elections on the promise of serving the people and accumulated millions upon millions of rupees through illegitimate means—it wasn't that bad. And besides, who would pronounce judgement on Hara's crime and punish him? The police, the court, the judge, the jailor, the jail superintendent? If it was said that the first stone should be cast on Hara by someone who had never done anything wrong—not a single person would be found. After all, this was the great country where people sold off orphan children abroad for money.

For some reason or the other, Jibon had reached the eastern side of Platform No.1 just then. At once he noticed the crowd baying for blood. Going near, he spotted Hara. Seeing Jibon, a fervent appeal for help was writ large in Hara's eyes. And what did Jibon do? He advanced and landed two or three punches in succession on Hara's bloodied, cut and swollen face, and then threatened him, '*Shala, shuorer baachcha!* You've come again to this station of ours to pick pockets! No one can save you today!' 'Hand him over to the police,' said someone. 'Who said that?' Jibon shouted out. 'He must be a member of their gang. He knows that if he's handed over to the police, his life will be saved! Ki re, don't you have an understanding with the police? Do you think I'll hand you over to the police? I won't do that! All the money of the person whose pocket you picked will remain in the court's custody. He won't get it back until the case is settled. I won't get into that trap. I'm going to break your arms and legs and cripple you for life. You won't be able to pick anyone's pocket ever again!'

Running his eyes over the crowd, Jibon spotted Raghu the porter. He shouted out to him, 'Raghu, go and get a hammer from Bilal's workshop. Get two bricks as well. I can't break his arms and legs in the station. I'm taking him to the siding. Meet me there!'

The crowd of people who had alighted from the train had various jobs to go to. After all, how much time could one spend on a thief? They implicitly entrusted the responsibility of the thief to Jibon and left for their respective destinations. To the man whose money was saved just as it was about to disappear, Jibon said, 'There's nothing more for you to do here. Leave now, and go and make your purchases. I'll take care of this chap.'

Jibon made Hara stand up, held him firmly by the waist of his trousers so that he couldn't escape, pushed him ahead and took him out of sight, behind the mound of stone chips at the railway siding. From there, he took him to a doctor's clinic in Palpara. After Hara's cuts were dressed, Jibon accompanied him to his hut. In gratitude, Hara stuffed a blue note into Jibon's hand. 'I don't have any more, Jibon bhai, have some cha-biskoot with this.'

A hundred rupees was not a small amount. Even if Jibon ate fish curry and rice twice a day at Chhechan's eatery, it would see him comfortably through ten or twelve days. But instead, he had a hearty meal of mutton curry and rice, and then, out of sight under a tree in the hospital premises, he had spread out his gamchha and fallen into a deep sleep.

16

Srimati

Jibon usually ate at Chhechan's eatery if he managed to get some money. But today, he didn't feel like eating the same old mixed vegetable dish of rotten potatoes, worm-eaten egg-plant and withered pui-spinach served by him. Buoyed by the strength of the hundred rupees Hara had given him in gratitude for saving him, he had gone to the Hema Malini Eatery, which was next to the timber-yard behind the bus-stand crossing. The food here was one-and-a-half times or twice as expensive as that in Chhechan's place. Yet there was a crowd spilling over. The food was good, but even better was Hema. Her beauty, and the way she smiled and spoke, more than made up for the price difference. When she brushed against someone and lovingly asked, 'There's some fine pona fish today—shall I give you some?'—unless one's heart was made of stone, it wasn't possible for them to disregard her request.

After all, there was something called business policy. It wasn't enough to simply display the wares in one's shop, one had to have the skill of selling them too. That's why the big and fancy hotels in Chowringhee and Park Street did not stop at merely serving mouthwatering things to consume. Beautiful, scantily-clad dancers and waitresses also assembled there. They also kept comely maidens who would spend the night in bed for a price. Had all these small eateries on the city fringe, with their tiled roofs and walls of matting, also been inspired by that to keep one or two women who were deft in the art of deception?

After having eaten his fill at the Hema Malini eatery, Jibon had lain down under the safe shade of a tree in the TB Hospital field, and embarked on a journey in the land of the slumber fairy. His slumber was suddenly cut short by the loud report of Naru's voice: 'Aeyi Beimaan, get up!'

The name 'Beimaan', meaning crook, had been affectionately bestowed upon Jibon by Naru. He was the one who had taken Jibon to Kanti babu, the rickshaw owner, and got him a rickshaw to ride. That was long ago. Around that time, Jibon had left Naru behind one day, and gone and seen a movie at Pradip Cinema, in Tollygunge. That had seemed 'crooked' to Naru. He called him 'Beimaan' ever since, instead of his proper name. Notwithstanding all the subsequent treats of food and movies, the name 'Crook' stuck.

Jibon looked at Naru and was taken aback to see that he wasn't alone; there was an unknown face with him. The face belonged to a fifteen- or sixteen-year-old girl, who could deliver a scorpion's sting in any youth's heart.

Naru said, 'What's this deathly sleep at an untimely hour? I was looking for you for so long! My throat's gone hoarse calling you! Get up! Get up and see who I've brought along. You'll go crazy!'

Jibon kept gaping. Who was this? Jibon's eyes seemed to not want to blink. How old was she? No one could really say. Her face had the gracefulness of a wildflower that had blossomed at dawn, wet with dew. Her large black eyes seemed to be brimming over with a tide of gaiety and joy. Eyes which silently communicated a lot without speech! There were small scars and signs of poverty all over the girl's body. Despite that, it was as if transcending all deprivation, a ruby-coloured island had arisen in the sea of her body. The fierce lustre of that ruby dazzled the eye. Every curve, bulge and fold of her body was fulsome. Nothing was incomplete, or inadequate, or absent.

'Who's this?'

'Her name's Srimati.'

'Who's Srimati? Tell me her full name.'

'That's her full name, Srimati. There's nothing before or after that. She lives in the Talbagan basti. Her mother sells ganja, her father's a drunkard. She has a brother and a sister. Her parents are still young. So the number of her siblings might increase.'

Perhaps Naru would have said more. But after Srimati landed a slap on his face, he was compelled to stop. 'Why did you hit me?' he shrieked.

'Serves you right! If you act cheeky, I'll slap you again!'

What could Jibon say! Unable to figure out anything, he remained sitting on the gamchha laid out on the grass. The girl then looked at Naru with a mischievous gleam in her eyes and said, 'So this is Beimaan!'

'Yes, it's him, he's Beimaan,' stuttered Naru.

'What do you mean "He's beimaan"?' Jibon asked, feigning anger.

Pausing for a while, Naru then continued, in order to provoke Jibon. 'It's just my rotten fate that I got a friend like him. Someone who's crooked from the hair on his head to the nails on the toes of his feet!'

Srimati began to titter at Naru's manner of talking. He turned towards Jibon and continued. 'Here's a man, who to all appearances seems perfect, who walks and talks like a man, he eats in the eatery, sleeps in fields and jetties, and it's in the fields that he sh ...'

'Stop! Don't say any more. I know what you're going to say!'

'What am I going to say?'

'I told you, I know.'

'You don't! You thought I'd say, "shits". But I wouldn't have said that. Does anyone say such things in front of a girl! Anyway ... so after hearing so much about you from me, Srimati told me that she's been to the zoo and seen all the tigers and apes there.

Apparently, she also saw a ghost there once. But she's never seen a crook. That's why I brought her along, to show her a full-size crook!'

Srimati said, 'I've seen him a few times before too.'

'Where?'

'Where else! At the station, or inside the hospital premises. He's been to our basti too, once or twice.' Srimati was about to say something more, but she stopped.

Naru laughed out aloud and said, 'Thank God it was you who saw him and he didn't see you! Or else, one can't say whether I wouldn't be the one lying here and he the one who brought you along to show me—"Look, here's Naru Gopal!"'

Jibon got a bit angry at Naru's needling and said, 'Now that you've shown me to her, why don't you take her along and go wherever you're going?'

'What are you going to do now?'

'I'm going to sleep for some more time.'

'And what will you do all night then?'

'Do you think I sleep at night like you? How can I sleep?'

Srimati said to Naru, 'I think your friend's angry.'

'Yes, I woke him up, didn't I!'

'So he has night duty, does he?'

'Yes, he stays up at night and guards us,' said Naru, and laughed.

It was almost evening now. In a little while, the vacant fields in the hospital premises would not be so desolate. The children from the employees' quarters would come to play football. The patients and their family members would walk around. But right now, there weren't any people in this part. There never were. Only a few cows grazed here, and there were some mangy mongrels. A few plump pigs, and one or two people of the sweeper class too. Besides one or two people like Naru and Dilip—who ran Nanu's illicit liquor den—no one really knew that Jibon came here in the afternoons to sleep. Once it became more widely known, he would have to change his location again.

Seeing that Jibon was trying to lie down again, Naru gave him a hefty shove. 'Don't play hard to get! Get up! Sit up now! I have something to tell you!'

'About what?'

'I'll tell you! Why are you in such a hurry?' said Naru, as he pushed Jibon aside and sat down on his gamchha. Srimati then asked with an injured air and an aggrieved tone, 'Am I supposed to remain standing like a tree?'

'Why, why don't you sit down?'

'Where shall I sit?'

'There's such nice grass here, sit on the grass,' said Naru.

Srimati scowled in disgust. 'There's pig shit and cow-dung everywhere, and what a terrible smell! I'm sure there must be leeches too hidden in the grass. Do I want to die! Let's go somewhere else, some secluded place where we can sit for a while.'

Jibon thought to himself: where will you go, you stupid girl? Is there any place left for us to sit in seclusion, or for that matter, even to die? Someone or the other has snatched away from people and taken over all the land on the plains of the world, all the hills, all the rivers, the entire sky. There's nothing left anymore for us to call our own. The most safe and peaceful place for a person is called home. I don't even have a home where I can take you and ask you to sit ...

Before Jibon could express what was in his mind, Naru caught hold of his arm and pulled him hard. 'Come on!'

'Where?'

Jibon realised that although Naru's acquaintance with Srimati was a recent one, it was not all that new either. In the time that they had been together, they had more or less moved beyond the stage of mutual liking, and were advancing towards a strong ground of mutual trust. They needed privacy at this time, which would only be interrupted by the presence of any third person.

He said, 'Why don't you people go, what will I do going with you? Haven't you heard the expression *"kabab mein haddi"*? That's what I am now!'

Was there an injured tone in Jibon's words? The scorch of some painful remembrance? Inner anguish? Which had been left behind by a half-bloomed flower called Kusum? Whose very name brought Jibon an ocean of agony?

Srimati had no clue about what was in Jibon's mind. She thought he was annoyed because they had arrived there. She said, 'If I'd known you'd be angry, I wouldn't have come. Naru told me, "Come, let's go and meet my friend." I've heard a lot about you. That's why I thought I'd come. Let it be, I won't come any more.'

Angry! Jibon surely had the right to be a bit angry. But that was with Naru. They had been friends for so long, they talked about so many things every day. But who knows why, he had never, even by mistake, mentioned this girl called Srimati. Why hadn't he done that? Why had he kept the news about such a big accomplishment secret for so long? Would Jibon have gobbled up the girl had Naru told him?

Srimati continued, 'Whenever I meet Naru, half of whatever he says concerns you. My friend Jibon is like this, he's like that ... I listen to him and wonder who he is. He's not at all like the Jibon I'd seen a couple of times. I told Naru not to tell you anything about me. I never got the time to come and meet you, and find out for myself the truth of whatever he told me. I got the time today—but now you're angry.'

'I'm not angry with you.'

'Who are you angry with? Naru? Why? He's very fond of you! I think that if you had been one of Naru's girls, he would have fallen in love with you and married you too already.'

Naru interrupted her, 'Love's fine, but if we were married, it wouldn't have been a happy marriage. Can't you see I'm always quarrelling with him? We can't get along at all!'

Srimati said, 'There's a couple like you in our basti. The husband beats his wife and the wife beats him back. They fight and scream at each other all the time. But if any outsider goes and tells either of them anything, the two of them gang up and give him hell. They say, "Whatever we, as husband and wife, may do—what's it to you? Do you feed or clothe us that you've come to poke your nose in our business?"'

Jibon too had had a similar experience. Of course, at that time the character named Jibon had not yet become as widely known in the locality as he was today. The people in the sweepers' quarters hadn't yet started doing what they had got used to doing whenever they encountered an influential person, that is, knocking their right hand against their forehead and saying, *'Namaste bhaiya!'*. The people at the rail station and the railside squatter colony did not run to him, as a trusted protector, to settle their quarrels and fisticuffs.

During that time, Jibon was walking one day to the station from Raja S.C. Mullick Road, going along the canalside and through the hospital premises. In front of the sweepers' quarters, he came upon a sweeper's wife. She was being beaten mercilessly with the handle of a spade by her drunk husband for the outrage of retaining her monthly wages from working in various houses, and thereby depriving him of his right to drink. The woman was lying on the ground, weeping, screaming and hurling abuses at him. Although many people were witnessing the scene, no one was stopping him. Jibon could not bear to see it. The worm began wiggling inside his head. The one that said, 'Stand with the weak'. And so, Jibon jumped into the fray. He pushed away the drunk husband. The woman then sprang up to her feet angrily. Like a wounded tigress, she attacked Jibon! 'My man beat me. I am his wife. My man can hit me and cut me as much as he wants. Why did you hit him? What did he do to you?' Had Nanu not arrived that day at that crucial moment, the tigress would definitely have torn open Jibon's throat!

Nanu was a party man, and besides, he was an upcoming mastaan. He was a hospital boy and a friend of Jibon's, and so, Jibon was saved from great danger that day.

Jibon stood up now. He wanted to explain to Srimati that he wasn't angry with her, and that he never ever got angry with any girl. He shook off the dust and grass from the gamchha that he had spread out and lain on, tied it at his waist, and covered it with his panjaabi. He straightened out the creases on his lungi. He combed and straightened his hair using his fingers. After that he said to Naru, 'Let's go! Where do you want to go?'

Naru replied, 'Let's go anywhere. Let's go somewhere we won't come across any known faces.'

'Where will you find such a place? The rickshaw-pullers from the station go in all directions. Someone or the other is bound to see us.'

'Oh they're one of us. There's nothing to worry about with them. I'm only afraid about Srimati's dad. He's a real *maal*, I swear.'

'What did you say?' There was anger as well as astonishment on Srimati's thin red lips. You called my father *maal*! Do you know what the word means?'

'It just slipped from my mouth!'

'If you ever say such things again, I'm telling you, I'll break your face!' Rolling her large eyes, Srimati continued, 'Whatever he may be, he's my father, someone to respect.'

'Wonderful, so I just said *maal* and you immediately turned red with anger, but when you roundly abuse him seven hundred and seventeen times a day, I suppose there's nothing wrong with that!'

'Do you have to abuse my father just because I do?'

'No, if you forbid me then I won't.'

'Don't do it!'

'Never ever?'

'I told you never to abuse him.'

The three of them now began walking in silence. They went over the semi-broken hospital boundary wall and arrived at the wide road where buses plied. There were known faces everywhere. There was amusement and curiosity in those eyes. Yes, there was a lascivious gaze too from some eyes. It was as if they wanted to devour Srimati's freshly bloomed body. The gaze was extremely annoying and intolerable, something that incited rage.

Jibon said, 'How people are staring ...'

'They're plain jealous!' Naru said. 'All the bastards are just burning!'

Casting her eyes in all directions, Srimati said, 'Tell me where we can go! There's just men and more men everywhere!'

Naru asked, 'Would you like to go to the Dhakuria lake, Srimati? There aren't such crowds there.'

'Death!' burst out Srimati. 'Do you think I want to die by going to the lake? If you want to go there, go ahead, but I'm not going there.'

Naru protested, 'Why, what'll happen if you go to the lake? It's such a beautiful place. We can sit there without any disturbance. So many boys and girls go there.'

Srimati replied, as testily as before, 'I know the lake is a very beautiful place. I know that boys and girls go there, I know who goes there and also why they go. Death!'

'Is that so? Then tell me why people go to the lake! To die?' Naru asked vehemently, as if it was an examination.

'Don't try to teach me about whether they go there to live or to die! I'm a Taltala girl, mind it! I know more than you about the lake! Get it?'

All this was useless talk. But at this age, at this time, all talk wasn't with reason or logic. That was the business of calculating folk, and so Naru picked up the thread again. 'When you know so much about the lake, then please tell us why so many boys and girls go to the lake.'

'They go there to do love marriage!' said Srimati angrily. 'Do you know what love marriage is? Love and intimacy. *Chhee*, are we going to do that, so we need to go to the lake?'

After stifling his laughter, Naru said in a serious tone, 'So what are we going to be doing now, Srimati Devi?'

'We are going to roam around, what else are we going to do? I like roaming around a bit with you. I'll roam around, observe people, and then I'll return home.'

'And what about that thing you said—love marriage? How about going to the lake and doing a bit of that? When you've been born a girl, you'll have to do all that one day or the other. So why should you delay that? Come, let's finish that today!'

The girl from Taltala basti turned red in embarrassment. With her head cast down, she said softly, '*Jaah*, do you think I'm old enough to do all that! I'll do all that when I'm grown up.'

'When will you be grown up?'

'There's a year, or a year-and-a-half left. I'm seventeen now.'

Heaving a deep sigh, Naru said, 'Just make sure that I don't die and turn into a ghost while you're still growing up.'

After a pause, Naru continued. 'The old days were really great. A girl was grown up at the age of eight or ten. She was married off, and by the time she was twenty, she would have one child on her bosom, one on her lap and one in her belly. A real accomplished housewife!'

Srimati's response to this was—'You're a brute! Just because there's no tax on speech, you think you can say whatever you like!'

Jibon was walking ahead. Naru and Srimati were walking side by side behind him. The slanting rays of the sun from the west fell directly on their faces. Who knows why, the unforgettable memories of the bare hill in Dandakaranya, the disused runway and the jujube clumps of Bankura, and the desolate platform of Jadavpur Station tormented him greatly. The sal forests of Bankura, the bare hill in Dandakaranya and even Jadavpur Station—all these places were associated with joyful memories because someone was there beside him at those moments. The two of them had walked in step together one day, knitting a web of dreams. Only a girl named Kusum and a boy named Jibon knew about that.

No, one other person knew. That was Jatadhari guru, who sat under the stairs at the Jadavpur rail station, smoked ganja, read people's hands and sold amulets and talismans. He had told Jibon, 'If you can keep your mind as clear as water, then you'll suffer less pain in life. Don't you see, there's no stain on water. Throw a stone, it shimmers a little, there'll be some waves, but a moment later, it's as it was. Forget whatever happened. It wasn't your fault. Just think of it as your fate. Forget about it.'

Jibon too wanted to forget. But where was that happening? Again and again, the sad, virginal face came and stood in front of his mind's door. For no fault of Jibon's, she thought he was a wrongdoer and left. Gone now to the other side of a moat, from where it was difficult to bring her back.

They walked southwards along the wide road. Going past the bus-stand junction, on the left was the muddy road going towards Bijoygarh, with stones jutting out like teeth. Walking down this road for a while and going past Bijoygarh on the left, Bikramnagar lay straight ahead. But there was no seclusion there either. Where new lives could hold hands, sit and gaze at one another and coo for a little while, evading the razor-sharp gazes. Where they could open the doors of their beings and laugh in joy.

These were all refugee colony localities. This wasn't central Calcutta. All around were the eyes of predators lying in wait, searching for chinks. All around were eyes of predators who pounced as soon as they spotted an opportunity. The belligerent sons of the elderly social reformer uncles had already observed them. In their suspicious eyes, two lungi-clad chhotolok boys, accompanied by a shameless girl, were looking for a secluded spot. That could only mean they were going to do something dirty. Whatever they did would definitely not be anything like the pure love portrayed in Bengali cinema, and so all the frowns had only one message: None of that here! Run, or else you'll be thrashed!

Not finding any place to sit or even stand, they walked through lanes until they reached the main road. This road was called Prince Anwar Shah Road. They now walked westwards along that. Buses, lorries and taxis sped along the road, raising a cloud of dust. It was about 4 p.m. now. The day's scorching heat was a bit less at this time. They did not have any difficulty walking. After they had walked awhile, Naru said to Jibon, 'Do you have money re, Beimaan?'

'Why?' retorted Jibon. 'What business do you have with my money?'

'No ... I mean, we can then get into some cinema hall for the six to nine show. I can't walk any more. My legs are aching. We'll be able to sit for a while. No one will be able to gape at us either in the darkness.'

Jibon was about to utter a swear word—fucker, you're the one who's romancing, and it's my pocket that you'll empty out! Do you think I'm such a big idiot? But before he could say anything, Srimati said, 'Who'll save me from my dad's anger if I return home late because I went to the cinema?' Hurling the question at Naru, she looked at Jibon and said, 'My dad's told me, "You can go wherever you want during the day, but you have to be back home by sunset. Or else, you'll get a thrashing."'

After walking a few steps, Srimati continued, 'After all, I'm of a tender age. I think maybe my dad's afraid that I might go off somewhere with someone at night and do love marriage or something like that. Hadn't Sonali of Taltala got a baby in her womb? Her dad had to spend seven hundred rupees to get rid of that!'

The real meaning of what the girl from Taltala called 'love marriage' was finally clear to Jibon. It was a beautiful word, but who knows how it had transformed to mean something so ugly ...

But Naru was thinking about something else. He spoke out what was on his mind. 'Aeyi Srimati, does your dad hit you?'

'No, he doesn't hit me, he worships me!'

'How can anyone raise a hand against such a big girl?'

'Go and ask him that!'

Remembering her dad and his behaviour, Srimati's sparkling, jovial demeanour vanished and was replaced by anguish. She said, 'Can a man remain in his senses after hitting the bottle? Can he tell what's good and what's bad ...' She clutched the hair on her head in the throes of some agony. Her eyes glistened with tears. 'My Ma's a complete fool! Who knows why she went and got married to such a man, knowing all about him! Tell me, wouldn't she have found someone better than him? Is my Ma bad-looking?'

Naru felt like laughing, but he couldn't laugh. One shouldn't laugh at someone's sorrows. So he suppressed his laughter, and donning a sombre mien, he said, 'Tell me, can you really blame your Ma? Even fine, upstanding folk lose their head when it comes to marriage. They end up doing what they should never do. But you should have stopped her. After all, whatever you might be, you are her daughter. She's not just anybody, but your own Ma. Giving good counsel to one's Ma is any child's duty.'

Srimati said, 'We explained everything to her.'

'Who's "we"?'

'My Dada and I. What can we do if she refuses to listen to us? Dada left for Burdwan in rage. He doesn't come home any longer.'

'How old were you when your Ma got married?'

'I was very small then, only about eight or ten years old. Dada is four or five years older than me. There was a sister between Dada and me. She died.'

Usually parents witnessed their children's marriage. But a child who witnesses her mother's marriage—without doubt, that was a unique experience for anyone. Srimati had gone through such an experience. Because her Ma had got married a second time.

She said, 'Dada and I are from her first husband. There's no one as yet from this husband. That'll come after two or three months.' Affecting a happy smile, she said, 'I'm going to have a little brother.'

'How do you know it'll be a brother, what if it's a sister?'

'It can't be. If there's a boy in the womb, he doesn't move about so much. If it's a girl, she moves a lot. There's no movement in my mother's belly. Just you see, it's a bhai I'm going to get.'

The values manifest in the life and society of a shanty settlement beside the rail track had an impact on people's consciousness. Such a precocious explanation on such a serious matter from such a young girl of that social class of people had no social authorisation; it wasn't in vogue. What this seventeen-year-old girl had said effortlessly, would be jarring and unbecoming to the ears of educated, decent people, people of taste. Something unimaginable, and entirely inappropriate given her age. But Srimati had been raised in the environment of the railside settlement called Taltala, into which the light and fresh air of education or culture had never had the chance to penetrate. As a result, in this habitation of rootless, low-income folk, deprived of education, with diverse mentalities derived from various places, there were no social customs, norms, rules or laws; no codes of decency and honour were observed in personal and kin ties. No one really cared or felt for anyone here. Everyone was caught up in an animalistic, primitive life where the fight for survival was paramount. Another name for the malady of irresponsibility that such socially excluded, unrestrained folk were afflicted by was wantonness. The matted walls of the shanties here were so thin that one could easily hear the conversation on the other side. The walls were so tattered that one couldn't help seeing many things even without wanting to. No child could remain a child in such an environment. They learnt about significant matters that were strictly of an adult nature long before attaining puberty.

When two kids from the shanty settlement—naked, their bellies distended, noses snotty—quarreled and fought, their profanities expressed the immense threat of raping each other's mothers: 'I'll fuck your mother!' This wasn't their fault. It was the ill-mixed, misbegotten situation that was to blame. It was the abnormal life pattern that had caused it.

Naru asked Srimati, 'Your earlier baba ... where's he? Is he dead?'

'I don't know.' After a pause, and with a fierce ring to her voice, Srimati continued, 'A cunning slut from the house in front of ours ran away with him. The slut's man couldn't satisfy her. There's been no news of them since.'

'But your Ma already had two nearly grown children. Why did she get married again?'

Srimati was now transported from the present to an almost forgotten, grey chapter of the past. She spoke, slowly, as if in a monotone. 'My Ma was very good looking then. She had mothered three children, but you couldn't guess that by looking at her. All the rickshaw-pullers, hawkers and porters of the railway station used to gawk at her.'

'Your Ma is still very good-looking.'

'So you can guess what she was like six or seven years ago. Who knows why my Baba left such a wife and ran off with that dark, fat slut, Sabitri! Believe me, I don't remember my parents quarrelling even once. How things changed! That day, he left for work in the morning, like every day, and never returned. The same night, we learnt that Sabitri hadn't returned from work either. My Baba was a mason, and Sabitri used to work with him as an assistant.'

Naru did not think it was appropriate to interrupt Srimati by saying anything now. Someone was drowning in sorrowful memories, he did not want to make jest of her by cracking a joke.

Srimati continued, 'Dada and I were small then. We could not do any work. Ma was in a hot mess. She didn't have a husband. How would she eat now, and how would she keep us alive? She had no relatives or friends nearby who would stand by her in such times.'

Srimati stopped speaking and gazed into the distance. It wasn't clear what her eyes were searching for.

In front of them was Kolabagan bazaar. At the entrance of the market, a vendor was selling jackfruit pods, which were laid on a banana leaf inside a basket. He was weighing out measure after measure. The air was redolent with the sweet aroma of the jackfruit. It had turned dark by now. The flies were blind at this time, yet bunches of blue-bottle flies that were born in filth smelt the fruit and arrived there, buzzing, and sat on top of the uncovered juicy pods. It was the job of flies to swoop upon food and they would do that come what may. It wasn't possible for the vendor to thwart them.

'Why are you silent? What happened after that?'

'What else could happen? Whatever happens when there's no man in the house happened. Ma could not sleep any more at night. Drunkards came and banged the door at the dead of night. They used to say all kinds of dirty things to Ma. Some men wept and thrust money into her hand. Finally, one day, Ma declared, "I can't go on like this. *Petey nai bhaat nanger utpaat!* No food in the belly, and the men are horny! Instead of being at the mercy of assorted men, it's better to die at the hands of one. Say what you will, but I'm going to get married again." Dada had argued a lot with her. But Ma did not heed him at all. She did what she had decided to do. She's paying the price for that now. He doesn't do any work whatsoever, just sits and feeds off Ma's earnings.'

'How does your Ma earn? What does she do?'

In reply to Jibon's innocuous query, Naru whispered to him, 'I don't know what she used to do earlier, but now she sells pellets of ganja.'

Srimati resumed. 'So many people have wonderful babas. I don't hope for something like that. Naru, do you know Mamata? Mamata too got married twice. Mamata's daughter is the same age as me. She says her new baba is apparently ten times better than the earlier one. If only my Baba was a bit human, nothing else ...'

Naru once again returned to his fickle self. 'I got it now. So this Baba of yours is not human.' Not being able to catch his ribbing, Srimati said, 'Inhuman! Simply an animal! Can a drunkard ever be human? He says things to people which shouldn't be said. He goes and lies down where one shouldn't even sit. Worse than even a dog!'

The evening sky was clear, cloudless and sparkling. But black clouds appeared from somewhere and covered the entire sky. A gusty wind blew. Srimati's hair began blowing in the wind. Dust began getting into the eyes. But it did not last long. After a few gusts, it became still. Srimati then asked, 'Do you know what he did one day?'

'You didn't tell me! How would I know ... '

'He was drunk, and he caught hold of a person and arrived home with him. He said he would marry me off to him. You know how old the man was? I wanted to thrash him with a broom and exorcise the ghost of marriage out of his head. Tell me, tell me the truth—do you think I'm old enough to get married now?'

'No, you aren't, not at all!' Naru said emphatically. 'Getting someone married before eighteen is against the law.'

'That's what Ma said too,' continued Srimati, picking up the thread of what she had been saying. '"My daughter's just a little girl, what does she know about running a household and family? Why on earth should she get married now?" But would my dad listen to that? Apparently he had taken a lot of money from that man by showing me to him. Now he was pressuring my dad to either give him his daughter, or to return the money with interest. How can he return the money? He has drunk it all away!'

A trafficking racket had been active for long in this locality. Agents kept close watch over railside and canalside shanty settlements to see whose daughter was coming of age and blossoming. They allured poor parents, who were burdened with the responsibility of getting their daughter married, by spinning a web of words. Your daughter's grown up now, don't you want to get her married? Let us know if you want to. I know of a good groom. Who has at least one-hundred-and-fifty or two hundred bighas of agricultural land! The land is farmed using a tractor. They have sugarcane fields, tobacco gardens and also a rice mill. A two-storeyed concrete house, something like a zamindar's actually. But the only problem is that he is non-Bengali. Haran Naskar's daughter, Putul, was married to someone in his village. Ever since he laid eyes on Putul, the boy had his heart set on her. Said if he'll get married, it will only be to a Bengali girl, or else he'll stay a bachelor for the rest of his life! So if you're agreeable, I can begin the mediation. Dowry? Oh no, they won't demand any dowry and such like—why should they ask for that? Are they short of money or gold? The boy's gone so far as to say that if a nice girl is found, he'll be the one who'll give one or two thousand rupees in cash to the girl's father. Your daughter is of marriageable age now. You won't get a groom without dowry in Bengal. So if you send your daughter to Delhi ... What more can I say? Think about it and let me know.

If the girl's parents swallowed the money-bait, the agents carried out a marriage ceremony with someone, for appearances' sake, complete with the recitation of the mantras and so on. After that they left with the unfortunate girl for Bihar, or Uttar Pradesh or Maharashtra. Some were trafficked to even more faraway places. In that distant land, where she did not know a soul, a band of flesh-hungry beasts, comparable to vultures and jackals, tore the girl to shreds and devoured her. Finally, when they had had enough of her, they sold her to some brothel. There was a great demand in brothels for underage girls. People believed that hard-to-heal venereal diseases were cured by sleeping with them.

Who knows whether the one whom Srimati's step-father had brought was a recruiter or middleman of that trafficking racket.

'What happened after that?' Naru asked.

'What else ... quarreling and fighting between my parents. I ran away from home in that melee. I got into a train and went to Sealdah—where else could I go ... After all, I don't know any places farther than that. I sat on a bench in the station there and began to cry.'

'Did you start crying or did the tears flow on their own?' Naru asked.

Jibon chided Naru, 'Don't ask for such minute details. Let her speak!'

'Okay, carry on.'

'Finally, an old woman saw me crying and took me along with her. I used to go with her to Kolay market, forage vegetables, sell that and buy something or the other to eat. And we slept on the pavement. She loved me like a daughter. She watched over me. I had run away from home out of fear of my dad, only to find even more fearful dads here. But the old lady was of strong mettle. No one's dad had the guts to come anywhere near me. I was with her for two or three months. Ma traced me somehow, and brought me back home.'

'Doesn't your dad mention the subject of your marriage now?'

'How can that be? After all, he's taken money. Why would those who paid him spare him? But he can't do anything because of Ma. She fights back. She says, "You put an enemy in my womb, and why was that, because you want a child of your own! If she's not around now, who'll fetch twigs and suchlike for fuel, who'll cook and wash, and who'll trudge two miles to fetch water?"'

Jibon asked, 'So until you get a brother or sister, there's no great danger as such. Is that right?'

Perhaps Srimati didn't hear him. She continued saying something else. 'Ma says girls grow as fast as banana palms. How long is it before I'm grown up? Once I'm a bit older, I'll have learnt to know what's good and what's not. Won't I? Just watch, I'll run away with someone then, like Bisakha did.'

Arriving at a crossroads, Srimati suddenly came to a halt. It was as if her feet had got stuck to the earth. In front was the thing that made only girls crazy. She said, 'I want to eat phuchka!'

Naru looked in the direction of Jibon and said with a magnanimous air, 'Sure, who's stopping you? Isn't Jibon here? He's really large-hearted. He's not one to flinch even if he has to spend ten rupees.'

Jibon whispered into Naru's ear, 'However much you try to pump me, I'm not giving you a penny! I'm telling you in advance! You have to do the spending!'

'*Chhee, chhee,* Jibon! Aren't you ashamed to say something so nasty? I've not been able to ride the cycle-rickshaw properly for the last seven or eight days. On top of that, I've lost at cards three days in a row. Who knows why the fucking cards are simply acting up! Five rupees on two days and seven on the third. I've lost seventeen rupees in all. And you! Even without any gambling, you're sitting pretty, having won a blue note in the morning, and now you're asking me to pay for phuchkas! *Chhee!*'

Not paying any attention to Naru's gestures and dialogue, delivered in the argot of the station residents, which would have made a skilled actor proud, Jibon said, 'You brought the girl to roam around with her. I didn't. I just happen to be with the two of you. Whatever is spent now is all yours. Why should I pay?'

The whispered exchange wasn't so hushed that people standing two or three feet away couldn't hear it. Even if Srimati couldn't hear them, it wouldn't have been difficult for her to get the drift from the movements of their hands and lips.

She said, 'You people don't have to worry, I have money, I'll pay whatever's necessary. I'll pay for you too!'

'You have money! Where did you get it, re? You didn't have any yesterday.'

'I went to get stuff in the morning. I earned five rupees.'

'Stuff' meant ganja. Srimati's mother was in the ganja trade. Which she had taken up in order to fend for her family after her first husband ran away. That business was doing quite well now. She sold forty or fifty pellets every day, worth a rupee each. With what remained after paying off the excise and local police, she was able to eke out a living. The stuff was available wholesale in Park Circus. She had to go and get it from that shanty every other day. Earlier her Ma used to get the stuff. But it was difficult for her to move around now because she was pregnant. This trade could only be undertaken by women. They had plenty of space to hide the stuff in their pubis and inside the brassieres. No one's dad had the gall to put his hands in all those places to pull out the stuff!

Srimati was somewhat buxom for her frame, she couldn't keep stuff there. On account of her age, she couldn't pretend to be pregnant either. A young girl in a pregnant condition would arouse suspicions, not only among the excise and police, but also in the public at large. And so, she was compelled to take the risk and carry the stuff in a bag. As a result of which, she was able to earn some money every few days.

Seeing that Srimati was now going to spend her hard-earned money, Jibon said, with an air comparable to that of a bank manager, 'Oh not at all, why should you pay? All expenses today are on us. After all, you're our guest today!'

Affecting a tone as if he was the one who was going to pay for everything, Naru said, 'That's the rule! When a girl goes out with a boy, all the expenses are from the boy's pocket. Keep your money, you'll need it later. Jibon will pay for everything today!'

Like an experienced and shrewd traveller, Srimati said, 'I know about all those rules, moshay. Charu and Sushila from our basti go out with boys. They come and tell me about all that they get them to buy. Although she pretended to say "no", Charubala got as many as five fine saris, and Sushila was even able to get earrings made for herself.' After this Srimati declared her fundamental defensive decision. 'The way they extract saris and jewellery from boys, and how they do that—I'll never ever do that! I'll never take anything from anybody!' Addressing the phuchka-seller, she said, 'I'll have one rupee's worth.'

'Why re? asked Naru in astonishment. 'After all, girls have a birthright to boys' money. Why do boys earn? So that they can blow it up on girls! Do you want to deprive yourself of that right?'

Srimati responded, 'Do you know the saying, *jibh jaar nun khaay mon taar gun gaay*—singing praises of the one who feeds you? I'll have something today, some more tomorrow, and by doing this again and again, do you know what'll happen? I'll get attached, and then there'll be love. Suppose there's love marriage—then what'll happen to me?'

'What will happen? If the thing you mention happens, what's the harm in that? Let it happen! It's not as if you're being eaten alive by a tiger or bear!'

'It's worse than that!'

'What's so bad about that?'

'Won't people say Amrito Sapui's daughter has become too fast? That she's going around doing "love"? Do you think I want to sully my Baba's name? I'll do all that after I'm married.'

Jibon was silent now. One could not make out what he was thinking. But Naru was very happy now. He felt light-hearted and everything seemed colourful. The cloudy evening seemed to be very precious. He felt as if he had been granted the greatest boon today. He thought that if he squandered his entire life's savings at such a time, there was nothing to regret. Who knows whether there was a God or not, and if there was, who knows where he lived. But if this evening was granted out of your mercy, thank you for giving me such an unimaginable gift!

The phuchka-seller was Bihari. He was in his forties. He had been in Calcutta for twenty years. He lived in a rented room in Bondel Gate. It was probably for the first time that he was seeing a girl who had come out with two strapping youths having phuchkas with her own money, eight for a rupee. They each had a rupee's worth and then continued to walk ahead. Navina Cinema was visible in the distance. Beyond that, farther ahead, was the Tipu Sultan mosque. For a long time, no one said anything. They walked silently and slowly in that direction. After a while, Naru said, 'All this while, all along the way, I was just joking with you. Now I'm going to ask you something serious. Think about it properly and then give me an answer.'

'Go ahead,' said Srimati.

'When you're grown up, I mean a year or a year-and-a-half later. When you'll be ready to love someone— will either of us two friends get a chance?'

Creases appeared on Srimati's brow. After all this was a matter calling for deep thought. Maybe Naru was always flippant, but his question was not a joke at all. The question required a carefully thought out answer.

Srimati had firmly decided that she would never marry someone her dad brought. She would pick someone she liked, and it was only to be expected that her dad would not like him. She would have to run away then. So these two boys, whom she was more or less acquainted with now, would not be too bad. Either one of them could definitely be selected.

She said, 'It's alright.'

'What's alright?'

'I'll love the two of you.'

After a pause, Naru continued, 'But even if you love both of us, you'll have to select one of us to get married to. Who'll you select? Who'll be the fortunate one?'

Srimati said, 'Both of you are nice.'

'How do you know that?'

'Girls know.'

Jibon realised now that the girl was quite immature. She had only grown physically. Had she been mature, she would talk and act differently. She wouldn't be so likeable then. She was an exception. Or else, given the environs she lived in, she should have been extremely seasoned. There was a difference here between Kusum and Srimati. Kusum was at least five years ahead of her age, while Srimati lagged behind by five. Whatever Kusum said and did, she did with the awareness of their outcomes and consequences. But what Srimati said and did, was all like childish play, which did not bear the stamp of any mindfulness.

17

The Temple of the Gods

Jibon returned to Jadavpur Station after that day's haphazard wanderings with Srimati and Naru and all the nonsensical talk. He found out that after having waited for him for long, the tired and dejected Haat Kata Ganesh and Boro Gopal had arrived at the best decision they could think of regarding the cow-killer, Sanyasi. After a good dose of thrashing, his hair was shaved off on one side, his face was tarred, and he was paraded around the entire locality adjoining the station like that. And then he was driven out of his residence in the station.

Two Jibons resided now on the two platforms of the Jadavpur railway station. One of them could be found after evening at Sandhyabazaar, or at the railside shanty settlement, or at the railsidings; or if it was late at night, under the stairs of the overbridge. It was difficult to accurately say where exactly he was during the day, or what he did then. It was said that he had a spot in the Kalighat crematorium, beside the area where the wood-pyres were lit, near the Krishna-Kali temple. Shankar Mallick, the brother of hangman Nata Mallick, Radheshyam Roy, a warder in the Central Jail, and a few doms from the crematorium were Jibon's friends and companions there. There was also a sadhu, who had recently been released after a ten-year jail sentence, who had decided to forsake his earlier ways and taken up sanyas, coming to the crematorium and setting up an ashram nearby.

Just the way a kite flies all over the sky but has to return to the reel at the pull of the string, however this Jibon might spend the daylight hours, come night, he immediately returned to his spot beneath the stairs on Platform No. 2. His eyes would be red then, under the influence of ganja, or his feet unsteady because of liquor.

This was the Jibon who had arrived at this station as he was wandering around after fleeing from Dandakaranya. After that, drawn by that soil and his attachment to the people there, he had not been able to leave. He remained in the station, as one of the people there, sharing in their joys and sorrows.

Sadhus, sages and scholars contend that it is the position of the planet and stars in the heavens at the time of a person's birth that determines what the person's life will be like. And that people do not have the power to change what has been determined by the planets. The lives and actions of everyone are controlled by those infallible, unseen forces. This Jibon, who was a duplicate of another Jibon, did not know how much of truth there was to that belief, or whether there was any truth to it at all. He had never tried to know about that either. He never had the opportunity that people needed to obtain education, intelligence and knowledge. He didn't have it now either. Given his present and uncertain future—when on earth would he do anything about all those matters pertaining to a higher plane?

For the same reason, Jibon hadn't been able to bother about gods and ghosts and suchlike either. 'I don't believe what I don't know' was what he felt, and there was also a thin plaster of atheism on his mind. If there is anyone called God, so what, what's it to me? When he never felt the need to find out about me, why on earth should I know about him?

All those who knew Jibon were unanimous in saying that however many times he might go to Kalighat, and however much he hung out with sadhus, he would never become a sadhu himself. That was just not in his zodiac. Because if it had been, some indications of that would surely have found expression by now. There was a saying, *jaar noye na hoy, nobboiteo hoy na*, if one doesn't have it at nine, he won't have it at ninety either.

Jibon himself knew that it would not be possible for him to become religious in his lifetime.

How could a mad dog ever become noble? But Jibon did not know that even if he didn't want it, his fate would make him do something that would grow to become a great hub for religious folk, pious acts, and recitation of the Name. One couldn't say whether for his act, after a century or two, his name wouldn't evoke, to people of the Hindu faith, the same reverence with which the name of Raja Rajballabh was spoken of, notwithstanding his having been a companion of Mir Jafar. It was said that this king, who was an ally of the British, had set up ninety temples in different parts of the country.

⁂

The road from the station curved a bit to the left and went all the way to Raja Subodh Chandra Mullick Road. In front of the ticket counter on Platform No. 1, on the left side, was an ancient banyan tree. In front of which were rows of many empty rickshaws, waiting for passengers. Because this was a rickshaw-stand, everything that happened in the rickshaw-stands in the city and the suburbs was to be found here as well. If one looked a bit closely, one would observe that some people were sitting behind the parked rickshaws and puffing ganja from a chillum. One could see people sitting on gamchhas and gambling with cards; this would often culminate in scenes of shouting, quarrels and fisticuffs. Also to be found here was the enticing *satta* gambling, or numbers game, which artfully took away the money earned by men through their labour and sweat.

There was space to keep about fifty rickshaws in the rickshaw-stand. But except at night, there were never that many rickshaws there. Some would be in the stand, while the others were out on the streets with their passengers. The rickshaws used to be parked in a haphazard manner earlier, the riders hailed and called out to get passengers, and the disorderly way in which the rickshaws were parked greatly impeded the movement of the passengers who had got off the train and stepped out of the station. Jibon had laid down the rule: it would no longer be disorderly, the rickshaws would have to be parked in an orderly fashion, in a queue, and passengers would be picked up one by one. It wasn't correct that one rickshaw-puller made ten trips while another didn't get even a single trip. Jibon had said in a voice choked with emotion, 'We are all poor folk, we don't have the power to wipe out anyone's hardship. But do try to see that another poor man's hardship is not increased because of what you do. Do try to see that ten people sharing one person's hardship allows him to survive.'

Partly on account of fear, and partly by virtue of affection, everyone agreed to Jibon's proposal and picked up their passengers in turn, following a queue. And they were astonished to find that when they counted their money at the end of the day, it was not at all less than what they were making earlier. Coming to the station one afternoon to observe whether the queueing rule was being followed, Jibon saw the porter Raghu carrying a huge basket of green coconuts, and calling out frantically. But there was no rickshaw-puller present to help him unload his burden at either the first, second or third rickshaw parked there. The load of coconuts was extremely heavy, it wouldn't be less than a quintal. Only the one carrying a mountain-like load on his head knew how difficult it was to carry that in this heat even for ten seconds.

Just a few of those who rode rickshaws here lived in Jadavpur. Most of them were from the 24-Parganas district, which lay to the east of Calcutta. Kedar and Sitaram were from Bihar. They genuinely wanted to feed their families by earning whatever they could by riding their rickshaws. They had no ill intention of leaving their rickshaws unattended and roaming around here and there. They always sat waiting for passengers on their rickshaw, but who knows why, once their rickshaw moved ahead in the queue and approached the base of the banyan tree, they did not stand anywhere near the vehicle. They could not stand there. They left the rickshaw in the queue and went far away. Very far away. What was the reason for that? The reason was none other than the afternoon's southerly breeze. A pungent odour that burned everyone's nostrils wafted in through the strong breeze. No one had the guts to bear that stench and remain there.

More than a hundred trains arrived at Jadavpur Station throughout the day. All were local trains. There was no toilet facility on them. There was a toilet of sorts on Platform No. 2, but none on Platform No. 1. Consequently, all those who alighted on Platform No. 1 or boarded a train there, relieved themselves under the shade of the banyan tree before boarding the train or after disembarking from one. Our national trait is imitation, and when it comes to negative traits, it is twice what it is in case of positive ones. As a result, as soon as anyone spotted someone standing under the banyan tree with his fly unzipped, or lungi raised, he was impatient to give him company and follow in his footsteps. For no reason at all, the sprinkling of water was taking place at the banyan tree, without letup, and without any opposition.

Opposite the ticket counter on the platform was a tea-stall. Almost every day, as a matter of routine, there were quarrels between the people at the tea-stall and the water-sprinkling masses. One side complained that because of the stench from and obscenity of the watery release, their business suffered. Women didn't even want to stand there, let alone have tea. The other side's reasoning was extremely simple. They were railway passengers and the spot belonged to the railway authorities. It was not as if it belonged to anyone's dad. It could be argued that their forefathers, by virtue of being train passengers, had been granted the human right to discharge urine there long before the tea-stall came up. So chucking water at them now, in order to deprive them of that right, was not only unfair, it was also extremely inhuman. When the railway authorities were not preventing them, why would they heed anyone else?

One Jibon did not know about this wrangling that had been going on for long. The other Jibon may well have known about it. But he too went and stood there from time to time—and because he was compelled to do that, he could not pick a side in the fight.

At one time, the CPI(M) leader Montu Sen had enlisted all the rickshaw-lines in the Jadavpur locality and established a rickshaw union. After Montu babu fled the locality, that became defunct. Now the rickshaw-pullers in all the rickshaw-stands made their own laws and rules, formed small independent unions and plied their trade. They solved whatever problems arose locally. The rickshaw-pullers at Jadavpur Station too had established a union, which existed only notionally, with Mona Dey, the brother of Sadhan Dey, the mastaan of the TB Hospital, as president.

One could say that Jibon, the nocturnal vagabond Jibon of Platform No. 2, was plucked out from the darkness and brought to the fore by some rickshaw-pullers. They told him to become the secretary of their union. 'Bearing in mind the way you stand beside the rickshaw-pullers in times of danger and adversity, everyone wants you to take up the position.'

Even if a request could be disregarded, an instruction couldn't be, especially Mona-da's. He said, 'There's nothing more to be said, you're the secretary. It's the people's demand. This demand ought to be respected.'

So in order to respect that demand, Jibon became secretary. And as soon as he became secretary, he issued his first diktat—everyone had to form a queue and pick up passengers one after another. 'That's the rule from today!' Anyone who broke the rule would be 'suspen' for three days. The subjects on which the newly elected secretary Jibon laid particular emphasis in his victory address, delivered in the style of a seasoned political leader, were patriotism and public service. 'Look, bhai, you have to build a nice relationship with all those who board your rickshaws. No one should behave improperly with them. Why would you do that? After all, they are the ones who grant you sustenance. Shopkeepers view their customers as Goddess Lakshmi incarnate. The passengers are really like Goddess Lakshmi to you all, and so, whatever little you can do to make things convenient for them, I mean, without harming yourself in any way—if you do that, you would only gain from that.'

'Can anyone gain if no one loses anything in the bargain?' Nimai Master blurted out.

Nimai Master was the master of a jatra squad. He was from across the Matla river, in Gosaba. Jatra was his passion from the time he was a child. He had fond hopes that he would become a big jatra star like Sonai Dighi and Swapan Kumar one day. And in that quest, he sold the two bighas of ancestral land he had inherited, and set up the Bon Bibi Opera with the neighbourhood boys. He could not stage more than four shows with the money he got from the land sale. Nor did Nimai Master gain any fame from the four shows with which he had hoped to rival Swapan Kumar. After having squandered his land and inheritance on his jatra dreams, Nimai now rode a rickshaw in Jadavpur in order to eke out a living. Although jatra had left him, the moniker 'master', that is to say the infamy, was still attached to his name.

He was considered the only educated creature in this rickshaw-stand, because his handwriting was 'pearl-like'. And so, he exercised his right to proclaim the piece of wisdom that no one could gain without harming someone else. Sanyasi used to kill cows by feeding them poison. Someone was the loser, but Jalodhar was the one who profited.

Jibon flared up and reprimanded Nimai loudly. 'Master, stop reciting your jatra role! All that is the false reasoning of educated scoundrels. They say that because they are wicked fraudsters. It can be done if one wishes to do so—one can definitely help people without harming anyone else.' Pausing for a while to look at everyone, Jibon continued, 'None of you will come to harm in any way. Just stand in front of your rickshaw when the train arrives, people will benefit from just that. Don't I see, people come out of the train with heavy loads, or accompanied by children, and come and stand in front of the rickshaws and shout out, asking, "Who'll go"—and the rickshaw is in the queue but the puller is nowhere to be found. Just think about it. If you're carrying a load of a maund-and-a-half on your head and you have to stand waiting with that, how difficult it is! And so, from today, the new rule is that the rickshaw-pullers of the first four rickshaws in the queue have to be seated on them. If the driver of the first vehicle is absent, the second rickshaw will take the passenger. If the driver of the second is not there, then the third. And if the third isn't there, then the fourth. And all those who are not there to take passengers will be "suspen" for the whole day.'

Jibon did not pull a rickshaw, so how would he know why things were the way they were. Nimai Master was quick to challenge him, 'Can you do it?'

'Do what?'

'Will you be able to sit on the rickshaw in the afternoon, when the sun is beating down, and a southerly breeze comes in?'

'What if I can?'

'Do it first and show us!'

Jibon had made the rule. There was a saying in Bengali, *apni aachari dhormo porke shikhao,* teach your faith to others through your conduct. Consequently, he had bound himself to the duty of demonstrating it himself.

'How long shall I sit?'

'As long as there's no passenger.'

'Alright, tomorrow then.'

'Why tomorrow, let's do it today!'

Jibon had not yet realised why exactly Nimai was being so mulish. He thought it was because of the sun. The sun! Oh you crazy fellow, how much sun, rain and cold this body has withstood, nothing could harm even a hair on it. What can the May sun do to me!

Jibon climbed into the first rickshaw in the line and sat down with a smile on his face. He was able to sit there for only about a minute. Once the breeze changed direction, his nose, lungs and stomach began to feel like they were on fire, as if someone had poured a bottle of ammonia down his nostrils. Unable to bear the deadly stench, Jibon ran southwards towards the far side of the banyan tree, opposite the rickshaw-stand. The much used, beloved address of annoyance and embarrassment, 'Oh fuck!', slipped out of his mouth entirely involuntarily. Anil Ghorui was the former secretary of Montu Sen's rickshaw union. He was as dark-skinned as a buffalo, he was always chewing paan, and his whole body was covered in perspiration and prickly heat. Anil burst out laughing. 'You made a rule, now see how you feel!'

What was Jibon to do now? It was said that a bullet shot from a gun and words spoken by the mouth could not be retracted. How was Jibon to save the people from that deadly stench-missile? How would he preserve the honour of his victory address?

That very night, he called an emergency meeting with some specific rickshaw-pullers in a corner of the station platform. 'Please tell me, what can we do? We have to put an end to the stench by any means whatsoever.'

Anil Ghorui said, 'So many heavyweights couldn't do a thing, and now you think you can solve the problem?'

'How can we do what even Montu babu couldn't?'

'We can, we surely can.' Kalicharan, whose head was somewhat large in proportion to his body, and who splashed saliva every time he spoke, said, 'If you can do as I say, there won't be any more stench.'

'Do what?' asked everyone in chorus.

'As soon as you spot someone pissing, go kick him on his backside. If they get kicked like this a few times, no one will piss there out of fear.'

'Who'll kick them? Can you do it?'

'I can.'

Jibon replied, 'Have you ever hit anyone? It's not so easy to hit anyone. You'll kick him once, but the public will catch you and kick you ten times in return.'

'Won't you guys be there with me?'

'No, bhai, count me out of any fighting,' said Nimai Master. 'I take passengers here and there, night and day. What if someone catches hold of me and thrashes me till I forget my dad's name?'

Earthen cups of ten arrived from the tea-stall. The tea was to be paid for from the subscriptions collected by the union every month. For now, it was on credit. Together with the tea arrived special flat-top Lal Shuto beedis, i. e. tied with red thread, made by hand by workers from Ghutiari Sharif, with strong, aromatic tobacco from Nepal and Gujarat. Beedis were lit in every hand. Beedi smoke was extremely helpful in unraveling knots in the brain. Ganja was even better than beedis. That's why people had given the name '*buddhimasto*'—brain-head—to the ganja chillum. But now, the 'brain-head' had been put aside. If anyone smoked ganja on the railway platform, the GRP would haul them away under the Narcotic Drugs Act.

Now Doctor said, 'What if a board is put up on the trunk of the banyan tree, in which it'll be written in large letters, "Do not urinate here"? If we do that, I don't think anyone ...' This 'Doctor' was not the kind of doctor who pressed patients' stomachs and examined them. This was a 'horse-doctor'.

He knew all about the actual condition and horoscopes of all the horses on the race course. No knowledge was to be had for free. All the capital of his provisions store had been squandered in his quest to amass this great store of knowledge. He was forced to give up his shop and now rode a rickshaw. He plied the rickshaw and dreamt that someday, he would make his calculations and come up with five numbers for that day's races. He would hit a jackpot. And then he would return, with goods from Burrabazaar stacked in a lorry, to his shanty in Madanpur. His shop would be full of wares once again.

The rickshaw-pullers present in the meeting unanimously adopted the proposal that a board should be put up. After that began the debate on the budget. The money that would be required to prepare a board and have it written on was not at all a small sum. Where would the money come from? Who would pay that?

Someone called Gokul expressed the opinion that the current rickshaw fares could be raised slightly; the expense of the board could be extracted from the passengers.

'Can't do that,' said one among the attendees. 'That will only lead to problems. The passenger who arrives here in the morning from Bijoygarh, by paying a particular fare on a rickshaw from the Bijoygarh stand, would not want to pay the additional fare in the evening while getting into a rickshaw from our stand. That will lead to a quarrel. They may beat us up too.'

'So what's to be done?'

Matha Mota Kalicharan—who was considered a blockhead, and was hence named so—expressed his heart's desire. 'The gambling squad that assembles at night in the station—let's beat them up and take away the money.' Kalicharan would gladly do this task if Jibon and Jibon's strongmen, Gona, or Ganesh, and Gopal were there behind him. If he had the moral support of all the rickshaw-pullers, he was willing to do the job even if it meant taking the risk of landing up in the hospital.

Finally Jibon said, 'There's no need to get into so many complications for a simple matter. Let's do what's simple and straightforward. Let all fifty rickshaw-pullers contribute eight annas each. If necessary, that amount can be deducted from the monthly subscription.'

Who would collect the contribution? Anil Ghorui, who had prior experience in such matters, gravely declared, 'Collecting contributions from rickshaw-pullers is the same as snatching food from a tiger's mouth!'

'No one has to collect it, I'll do it myself,' said Jibon. After a few days, a shining tin board, red-and-green in colour, was nailed to the banyan tree. On which was the unforgettable and historic exhortation, 'Do not urinate here'.

All those daily passengers who habitually urinated here were greatly impressed seeing the pleasant sight of the new board as they stood under the shade of the banyan tree. Many of them did not know how to read or write, and so they did not know what exhortation, by which sage, was written on it. But observing the excellent use of colours, they imagined it to be a great piece of art. They could not help praising the artist: this must be the handiwork of none other than that 'Kaku' from Panchanantala, who painted trees, flowers and birds on the rear of rickshaws.

The artworks of the great artist of Panchanantala who was known by the name 'Kaku', graced the rear of many rickshaws of Jadavpur. He painted not only trees, flowers and birds but also self-composed ditties on the body of the rickshaws. *Phool hai gulab ka, khushboo leke jaaiye, gaari hai gareeb ka, kiraya deke jaaiye.* Here's a rose, enjoy the fragrance; the vehicle's a poor man's, pay the fare. *Nahana hai to dariya mein ja, kinara mein kya rakkha hai, paar karna hai to direk bol, ishara mein kya rakkha hai.* If you want to bathe, go to the river, what's there in the bank; if you want to go somewhere, say that directly, what's with the gestures. They were all his poetic creations. Perhaps the travellers thought the new board on the banyan tree too had some modern poem scripted in a secret language, whose meaning could not be fathomed by people at large.

But there was no sign of the stench diminishing. Rather, it actually increased. Acharya Rajneesh had said: Prohibition means invitation. Just write on the door of a house, 'do not peep'. You'll see that whoever comes across the notice will definitely stare intently at the house. His curiosity about why it is prohibited will compel him to stare. That is man's eternal nature

A lot of passers-by did not know that they could urinate here. Now, as a result of the board being put up, they too came to know about the reason for the board. Consequently everyone became engrossed in the deadly game of violating the prohibition. A few days later, it was discovered that one dark night, when everyone was asleep, someone, or some people, seized the opportunity and conspired to wipe out the word 'not' from the board. As a result, what was earlier prohibited now became a written appeal—'Do urinate here'. Whatever little reluctance arose earlier on seeing the board, was brushed aside and like before, all the people seemed to have obtained the moral right to urinate there enthusiastically and gleefully.

One night, Jibon had gone with a rickshaw-puller by the name of Abhimanyu to a place called Viveknagar. It was quite late by the time he completed some important work there. It was about ten minutes to midnight. The streets were completely desolate. Because of the police and the party boys, people did not remain outdoors after nine at night. While returning in the darkness, Jibon's eyes suddenly went towards the semi-dark, south-western corner of the football field of Viveknagar Sporting Club. A young woman draped in a sparkling white silk was sitting there, all alone. Who knows who she was waiting for! Looking from afar, Jibon thought she wasn't bad-looking, her body was comely too. Her two saucy, chubby breasts pierced the darkness and lay awake like undiscovered islands. But all alone here, like this! Why?

'Stop the rickshaw!'

After Abhimanyu halted the rickshaw, Jibon got down and hesitated for a while. He could not decide what he ought to do. He had seen some women standing like this by the roadside once it was evening, along the National Highway, or on Harkata Gali and in Sonagachhi, as if waiting for someone. But this was not that kind of a neighbourhood. A girl, all alone, here, at this time! What was it all about?

Finally Jibon found the courage to advance towards her. He had to find out, come what may. O Hari! Jibon was astonished when he went near the girl. What she was sitting on in the darkness was a donkey. Not an ordinary donkey, but one that neither moved, nor ate grass, nor drank water. It just stood there.

Jibon had gone to the house of Chowdhury, the lorry driver. His host had not only provided him dinner, of tarka and rotis, before he sent him off, but also offered him two glasses of undiluted cholai, or illicit liquor. Jibon had been mistaken on account of his intoxication. This was no woman of flesh and blood. What was called 'basanto' in the Hindu religion, was not the 'basanto', or spring, when even the tone deaf broke out in melody, singing *ore bhai phagun legechhe bone bone*, o brother, the forests are aflame with spring. This basanto was smallpox, a deadly malady which set one's entire body on fire. Sitala was the goddess of smallpox, who had no other work besides killing and blinding people with this disease. She was a goddess whose immersion in water like Kali or Durga—saying *'dur haw'*, 'be gone'—was not prescribed in the shastras. It was the custom to chant *'aschhe bochhor abar hobe,* once again next year', and then lovingly sit her down in an open space.

It was a difficult time now. Let alone a clay mother, nowadays people did not want to be saddled unnecessarily with the burden of looking after even a real mother for a year. Even during that mythic Dvapara Age, when rivers of virtuousness flowed on earth, Yudhishtira, the son of Dharma, had sent his mother off to the forest, together with the parents of his arch-enemy, Duryodhana. The three aged folks were burnt to death in a forest fire. There was no one nearby to save them. And now it was Kolijug, the Age of Kali. An age of utter darkness. Consequently, once the Sitala Puja was over and the prasad was consumed, someone, or some people, had, under cover of the darkness of night, placed the Mother who had just been worshipped in a corner of a desolate field, so that the Mother of clay could disintegrate into the earth under the sun and rain.

Confronting the lone woman in the silent night, a devious design suddenly popped up in the head of the atheistic and intoxicated

Jibon. He looked around, and when he was absolutely certain that no one was watching, he grabbed hold of the Sitala idol. He looked like someone who possessed the infinite courage arising out of the rapist mentality of a debased man. He carried her all by himself and placed her in Abhimanyu's rickshaw, and said, 'Let's go!'

'Where to?'

'Where else? Straight to Jadavpur Station!'

'What will you do with this?'

'You'll see what I'll do. Let's go!'

Once they reached the station, Jibon quietly said to Abhimanyu, 'Go and fetch four bricks from somewhere. Look in front of Bilal's shop, you'll find it there.'

After that, Jibon placed the four bricks on the slime of yellow liquid under the banyan tree, and installed the image of Mother Sitala, bestride her vehicle, the donkey, as 'Kancha Kheko Devi', the divine devourer of the weak. There were no witnesses to this other than the two of them. The installation of this image was most beneficial. At dawn the next morning, as soon as the train halted at the station in semi-darkness, those who unzipped their trousers or lifted up their lungis and stood there, rubbing their sleepy eyes, as was their permanent habit—immediately fled in the opposite direction! That was only because those who were Hindu by faith were not mentally prepared to take the risk of being completely destroyed, together with their families, by urinating on the body of Kancha Kheko Devi. While those who were Muslims were entirely unwilling, at this moment, to become victims of communal rage by denigrating a Hindu goddess. And those who were neither Hindu nor Muslim, but only humans, only men, felt extremely weak and helpless at the prospect of exposing and brandishing their male organ, especially in front of a woman, and drawing shame and indignity thereby for descending into uncivilized conduct. As a result of all three factors, after a few days, the soil turned dry. The stench vanished. Those who had initially been enraged by the distressed plight of the goddess were now voluble in praise for that misdeed. The vagabond Jibon was now entranced by his own discovery. No one knew and no one fathomed who this foremost devotee of the epoch-making Ma Sitala was, who alone truly knew how great the name of Sitala was.

After several days, a pedestrian walking by saw an eight-anna coin lying unceremoniously in the dust of the street. It was only fifty paise, if it had been fifty or a hundred rupees, that would have been something. He had a big shop in the Jadavpur market. He was well known here. So he was reluctant to pick up this measly coin in front of everyone and put it in his pocket. The demands of culture and civility prevented him from doing so. He picked up the eight-anna coin from the dirt with two fingers, as if he was picking up some dirty object, and as if by the contaminating touch of money, his mind and body were becoming impure. After picking up the coin, he looked in all directions, to see if he could spot any destitute to donate it to. There was nobody around. Beggars did not come out for their rounds so early. That's when his eyes fell on the idol of Sitala. Here was a worthy place! He flung the eight-anna coin in front of the idol, with the zeal of someone freeing himself of a burden of sin, as if he was immersing himself in the holy Ganga itself.

The pious Brahmin, Harinarayan Chakraborty, who scribbled numbers and recorded bets on the satta pad, had just sat down then at his counter at the base of the banyan tree. He was lighting incense in his workplace in propitiation of deities. The clinking of the coin flung in pious offering seemed to shake him to the core. It was as if the sound echoed at the base of his Brahmin brain and awakened him from a century-long slumber. This was the first time he realised how sweet a sound could be. Perhaps that's why sound too was called Brahma, the creator. With the miraculous touch of the awareness of Brahma, his inner eye saw a door of opportunity opening. It was the grand wish of none other than the Lord, the creator, that seemed to be behind this feeling and awakening. God surely wanted to have his deed done by him. Harinarayan Chakraborty was beside himself with joy.

He rose from where he was seated and picked up the fifty-paise coin. Adding another fifty paise from his own pocket, he went and bought a packet of fragrant incense. He implored the flower-sellers to give him some flowers. And an offering-plate was purchased on credit from Roy babu's brass and bell-metal utensils shop. After all, the offerings would need to be dropped on that. Duli's mother, the beggar, lived in the station. She was lame in one foot. Harinarayan called her and explained to her with great tenderness, 'Look, this is Ma's work. It's a sin to say "no" when it's Ma's work. Go and get a broom. Get a bucket of water and some cow-dung. Plaster Ma's image and smoothen it. Ever since Ma manifested herself here, she has been suffering neglect. All of you'll be ruined if she becomes enraged!'

After Duli's mother finished her sweeping, plastering and smoothening, Harinarayan lit the incense and placed the flowers and the offering-plate in front of the idol. After that, he went to all the rickshaw-pullers, hawkers and shopkeepers. 'Two rupees, five rupees, please give whatever you can in the name of Ma. She has been suffering neglect and disregard for a long time. That's not good for anyone. Can anyone know in advance exactly who Ma Kancha Kheko will cast her scornful eye on? What with the various ailments and diseases all around, care and service to her is absolutely vital. Last night, Ma appeared in my dream and instructed me. "Perform my puja!", she said.'

That day, even if there wasn't much pomp, the puja was performed in accordance with the shastras and customs. Harinarayan recited mantras after a long time. Which he had almost forgotten in the course of writing on the satta pad. Everyone consumed the prasad. Not all of the money that had been collected was spent. Whatever remained went towards Harinarayan's dakshina. In arithmetical terms, it was not less than what he got by writing on the satta pad the whole day. That was already there, so now he had the additional amount too, thanks to the boundless compassion of the Almighty.

One major problem with Sitala puja was that there could be no more than a single puja in a year. Perhaps the goddess could afford that, but how could the priests afford that? Where was the fun then? What was required was a puja that would be performed every day. With this in view, Harinarayan Chakraborty formed a queue of idols, with Shani, Kali, Shiva, Manasa and various other gods and goddesses, as well as Paramhansa Sri Ramakrishna. Before one knew it, a temple sprang up there, first built with bamboo matting and then with bricks. A collapsible gate was installed at the entrance. A large box for offerings arrived, secured with a chain.

The money intended for Mother Kali could no longer be kept on the plate for offerings. A hungry child passing by could insert his hand through the gap in the collapsible gate and take away a fistful of coins. And if someone saw him doing that, he would grin and ask, 'Will God keep it all for himself?'

As soon as it was dusk, the assembly of the band of devotees grew ever larger. And as the night advanced, there was more and more ganja smoke in the air. Everything that happens in religious places was soon to be found here as well.

Jibon observed the temple and thought to himself—perhaps one day, some immense temple that touches the very sky, might come up here. All the big temples in the country, wherever they were, had all begun one day in this fashion. The shrine that some bandits had made one day in the middle of a forest was today revered as a great pilgrimage site. Who knows whether or not this temple too would become like that someday? This temple that was set up by a rascal only to eliminate the stench of piss!

NEW FRIENDS AND OLD

18

Kamake Khane Wali

The intolerable heat of summer, which was good for ripening mangoes and jackfruits but tormented the lives of humans, departed. After a whole day of scorching sun, the sky turned black in the evening as dark clouds gathered. Such clouds had been gathering for a few days, but they dissipated at night. But today, the rain suddenly descended in the evening like a shower of arrows, accompanied by thunder, lightning and terrific gusts of wind. A thick branch of the ancient banyan tree beside the Jadavpur railway station, under which was the cycle-rickshaw-stand, snapped and fell with a crashing sound. The electric cables slung from the post snapped and lay sprawled on the road. The tin roof of a shop was blown off by the gale, and it spun like a veritable sudarshan chakra before crashing down in front of Chhechan Sahu's eatery. Fortunately, there was no one standing there at the time, or else who knows what might have happened.

Although there was a furious gale, the rain wasn't so heavy. Pushed by the strong wind, the rain slanted down like a barrage of stinging pellets. On the station platform, this was the time when the crowd of passengers waiting to catch a train was at its peak.

The people waiting there had gathered on one side, near the ticket counter, to escape the pinprick assault of the gust-driven rain. There was a tea-stall and a wall there, and some cover. So the spray from the rain wasn't so bad.

Jibon was in the station at this time, near the same ticket counter. He had found a corner and lit a Charminar cigarette with a very luxurious air. The strong tobacco helped to rouse him a bit. He couldn't go anywhere until the rain stopped. He needed to go to the Jadavpur bus-stand crossing. But he didn't think that would be possible now.

He finished the Charminar and flicked the stub away into the rain outside the shed. And then, when he turned his head, his eyes went in the direction of Selim and Bisha, the pickpockets, who were standing there. The moment Jibon spotted them, blood rushed to his head. Why were they strolling around on Platform No. 1? The crowd of people were in a harassed state, pressed closely together because of the rain. None of them were really keeping tabs on their pockets or belongings. Capitalising on such an opportunity—who knows how many people they would destroy before they slipped away!

Jibon pushed through the crowd and headed towards them. And then he asked in a menacing tone, 'What are you lot doing here?'

Seeing Jibon's belligerent mien, Selim was at a loss for words. 'Oh, nothing at all,' he said fearfully. 'We're here just like that!'

Jibon realised that whatever he wanted to say would have no effect if he said it in his own language. That language was very sick, weak, malnourished. Perhaps one could trigger tears with that language, but one couldn't make someone tremble. He had to communicate in a powerful and strong language. Which was the only language they understood. Jibon said loudly in the language they perforce knew. 'If you slip your hands into anyone's pocket here, I'll thrash the two of you and break your necks, I warn you!'

Selim at once whispered in an amicable tone, 'Why are you saying such things unnecessarily in front of the public? We were standing here because of the rain. Do you think we're here to do all that? Alright, since you say so, we're going away.' The two of them then got off the platform, crossed the railtrack and climbed onto Platform No. 2. Jibon knew they would not stand there either. Even if they did, they wouldn't do anything. What was the point? When their pickings would have to be returned? After all, the bastard Jibon had spotted them! When Jibon turned his face away to return to his corner, his eyes fell on someone who looked familiar. But he could not remember where exactly he had seen this person, or when. It was a woman.

Jibon had this problem almost all the time. Seeing the crowds in Calcutta, some people likened it to a sea, a sea of people. It occurred to Jibon that the women in this deep sea were as unrecognisable as the silver-colored hilsa were. But why only the hilsa of the sea? Punti fish from a pond, or shung and magur from a fetid puddle, were all difficult to tell apart. Just like it was difficult, even after looking at a punti a hundred times, to find it once it was thrown into a basketful of them, because each one looked the same. Whenever Jibon saw a woman, he felt he had seen her before.

But why did the girl start smiling when she looked at him? There seemed to be a clear admission of prior acquaintance in the smile. 'Dada, don't you recognise me?'

Jibon shook his head, 'You look familiar ... But I can't exactly place you.'

'What do you say! Don't you remember?' The girl seemed very surprised. How could this person forget such a big incident, which was how they became acquainted? But she could remember vividly. And that's why, although she had met the helpful boy only once, she could easily recognise him.

It was as if the creator of the world had a fierce apathy towards rail stations. Whether it was in West Bengal, Bihar, Assam or Uttar Pradesh, a hub of anti-social activities always grew around the stations. So how could Jadavpur station be an exception? Here, everything in one's pockets could be pilfered while boarding or alighting from a crowded train. One's salary, necklace and wrist watch could be snatched from an empty carriage at night. A helpless woman could have her body and all her honour ravaged if she had to spend the night in the station after missing the last train. But if Jibon happened to be there when any such incident occurred, he could never remain neutral or peaceable; he inevitably lost control. He had to take a side. And the side he took was necessarily that of the helpless and weak. That was on the basis of an arithmetic of disparity. By the same arithmetic, if twenty or twenty-five people had surrounded a man and were subjecting him to wholesale thrashing because he was a pickpocket, Jibon stood in support of the alleged pickpocket. He saved him from the hands of the public in whichever way he could. Similarly, if five scoundrel youths surrounded a solitary, helpless, meek, poor girl and began misbehaving with her, he turned into the girl's brother and protected her. He thrashed the scoundrels. If he was unable to do that by himself, he called Ganesh, Boro Gopal and Kaliya to assist him.

For all these reasons, the porters, workers, rickshaw-pullers, vendors, local unemployed youths and daily train commuters all knew Jibon. They viewed him somewhat differently, and some people were fond of him too. At a dangerous moment one night, this woman who stood before him now, calling him 'dada', had accidentally found him beside her, as a rescuer. His face became indelibly etched in the mirror of her mind that day. A face that would never be wiped out or forgotten.

⚭

That was also a stormy night like this one. After three or four days of uninterrupted rain, all the roads in the city were inundated. Which meant hell for people. The girl had waded through knee-deep water all the way from Bijoygarh that day, and arrived at the station. But once she reached there, she found herself in a soup. There were no trains available to go where she wanted to. The rail tracks had been flooded in various places. Neither the Up nor the Down trains could run until the water receded.

What was she to do now?

The girl worked in a babu household, something that was an inseparable part of babu culture in the city of Calcutta. Without girls like her, the middle-class housewives of the beautiful city were thrown into a physical as well as a mental crisis. They were needed, for sure, but these girls were not as valuable to them as their crystal ashtrays or porcelain teapots, which needed to be wiped clean and placed in their designated spots in the house. They were a lot like an earthen teacup, or a wooden ice-cream spoon or a sal-leaf cup, something meant to be thrown away like a waste product after use. Wring them like a sugarcane-crushing machine for as long as necessary, and after that—go away, get lost!

These maidservant girls were not complete idiots, they were well aware of their standing in the eyes of the babus and bibis. That was why, even after five or ten or twenty-five years of daily proximity on both sides, no fat of humanity and fellow-feeling could form. A toothy exchange of measured and mechanical civility was all that prevailed between the employer and employee.

And so that day, when she finished her work in the evening, seeing the fierce rain outside, the maidservant enquired anxiously, 'Didimoni, how will I get home? The streets are all flooded. There's lightning ...' The house-mistress's calculating mind had realised what the cost of allowing her to stay the night would be. That's why she had smiled softly and replied in a tender voice, 'Will you be able to make it? I can see a lot of people going about. You have an umbrella, don't you? If you don't, take that old umbrella from the room below the stairs. But remember to bring it back tomorrow ...'

Although she had not worked very long in this particular household, she had worked for several years in quite a few households. So she knew that besides getting work done and throwing some money at her at the end of the month, the babu-folk had no place in their hearts and minds for any other weakness. A maidservant was after all only a maidservant, so how did she matter? The same people did not hesitate to turn their parents out of the house once they became old, and send them to an old-age home. The calculus of the babus' wives was extremely straightforward—only I, my children and my husband matter, everything else other than that is an unnecessary hassle.

Surrendering to fate, the girl had descended to the flooded street. When she reached the station after somehow ploughing through three or four kilometres, her eyes searched frantically for some known face from her village. But she could not find anyone. Where was Harimoti? Where were Potol's Ma, Anga Pishi, and all the folks from her village? They had all left by the train they went back on everyday. This girl had reached the station late.

It was getting darker, and the girl grew anxious as she scanned the platform. The rain too grew heavier as the evening advanced. The darkness all around them grew thicker. And yet there seemed to be no sign of any train arriving. Feeling extremely helpless, the solitary girl bundled herself up and lay down on a bench in the middle of Platform No. 2, with the intention of spending the night there. In this locality on the fringes of the city, such a night was extremely lawless, terrifying and full of dread. In its darkness, the peaceable, harmless, meek visages visible in the light of day underwent a fundamental transformation. The violent fangs and claws they kept secret were bared. Those fangs and claws tore apart resistance, hymen, chastity and dignity.

Last year, on a night exactly like this, a band of brutes had devoured a fourteen-year-old girl from Piyali village in an empty carriage of a goods train. Those who were associated with that incident were not any seasoned criminals; some were porters in the station, some were rickshaw-pullers, some ran petty-businesses. Eight or nine men were involved.

The girl in our story knew about that incident. It was out of that fear that she had lain down right in the middle of the lighted section of the platform, where there were a few people. Although they were extremely powerless, weak, aged folk, she still felt somewhat assured, on the assumption that people stand by others in times of danger.

Late in the night, as the fury of the rain lessened a bit, she felt sleepy. After all, at the end of a whole day of work, it was sleep that night was meant for. If this mishap had not happened, that is what she would have been doing by now, under a thatched roof in her small hut, in a rural area called Taldi. Because the rain had lessened, she stopped shivering from the spray of the rain and began dozing off. Suddenly, near her ear, there was a lustful voice speaking in whispers, and the touch of a brutish hand on her body. 'Aeyi, why don't you get up!'

'Who's that?' The girl sat up at once and looked. Three of four hazy figures had surrounded her. There was a strong odour of liquor on their breath, their eyes were red, and their voices were threatening. 'Don't you dare shout or scream! Get up and come with us quietly. Or else...' The old beggar woman lying nearby opened her eyes. She shut them again at once. She was a homeless beggar. Many years of her life had been spent under the shed of Platform No. 2 in this station. At one time, there had been some youthfulness in her body too. She felt the dreadful, harmful breath of power close to her. She knew what was about to happen now. Keeping eyes, ears and mouth shut at this time was a sign of prudence. At such a time, not being like Gandhi's monkeys meant putting oneself in the path of danger. Now she would not see any bad sights, hear any bad sounds, or say anything that would have a bad outcome. She took a vow and became mute, deaf, dead.

But the girl could not play dead. She felt a ghastly hand taking stock of her body. In terror and dread, she pushed the hand away from her body. And then she burst out in her rural dialect— *'Togar ghore ma bon neiko? Ja, shekhane ja!* Don't you have mothers and sisters at home? Go there!'

The owner of the hand did not get angry at the girl's words. He melted in humility. '*Lokkhi sona,* precious one, don't make trouble!

Tell me, what's the use of making trouble for no reason? Come along with us instead! I swear on my mother, we'll leave you within an hour, okay? You don't have to come for nothing! Tell me how much money you want, we'll give you that too.'

The girl said, 'Get out from here! Or else I'll scream!'

'So what if you scream? No one's going to come.'

It was true that no one would come. This was a time at which no one stood beside someone in danger. There was a GRP outpost on Platform No. 1. But the Naxalites had once raided the outpost, killed six or seven policemen, and taken away all their rifles and ammunition. What if they attacked again? Fearing that, the men on duty too now lacked the courage to come out of the camp late at night. But the real truth was that there were no more Naxalites in this locality. Some were dead, some were rotting in jail, and the rest had fled. The CPI(M) activists too had fled, out of fear of the Congress and the police.

As a result, some miscreants, anti-socials, goondas and scoundrels had now raised their heads in the vicinity of the station. Earlier they had been compelled to lie low out of fear of the boys from those political parties. But now some small groups of louts had sprung up around the station. They did just as they pleased. This band was one of those. They robbed and snatched, and pounced on women when drunk.

The girl saw, once again, the loathsome hand advancing towards her. Accompanied by two more assisting hands, which wanted to grab and carry her away.

It wasn't just a girl, this was a feast of flesh. Waves of undiluted cholai liquor had lashed their primitive senses. The rain-drenched, desolate wee hours had lent a stormy velocity to those waves.

Compared to other days, very few people were sleeping at the station tonight. So this young woman was even more unprotected. The whole city was asleep then in the pleasant weather brought on by the drop in temperature. A night like this was a wonderful and opportune time to commit robbery, rape and whatever one wished.

And so, as soon as a hand grabbed her forcefully, the girl screamed out for life. '*Banchao!* Help!' After a single scream, someone pressed a hand over her mouth.

Hearing the scream, the old woman sleeping beside the bench turned to the other side. Nothing was happening. Nothing would happen. It was a question of merely one night. Shut your eyes and ears, grit your teeth and bear it, ma. What else can you do, tell me? All this is simply what fate has in store for us, ma.

Using both her hands, the girl pushed away the hand covering her mouth and screamed once again. '*Banchao!* Help!' The scream floated away in the rain-drenched darkness. After that came another kind of sound. It seemed to be an *Aah! Aah!* kind of moaning sound, coming out through the cracks between the fingers of the hand covering the mouth. And just then, a boy jumped down from the opposite platform, crossed the rail tracks and climbed onto this platform. He roared out, '*Kon shuorer bachcha re!* Who's the son of a swine! Let her go!'

'Who the fuck are you?', said one of the men. 'If you want to stay alive, get out from here! Don't poke your nose in our affairs ... Or else you'll die!'

The boy who had crossed the rail tracks and arrived realised that it was futile to exchange words with these men. He advanced and suddenly landed a powerful punch on the face of the one threatening him. The man lost his balance under the force of the blow and fell on the platform. Seeing the turn of events, the remaining accomplices ran away, tottering, in whichever direction they could.

After that the boy said to the girl, 'There's nothing to fear, go to sleep, I'm here. No one can harm you as long as I'm there.'

That incident had taken place quite some time ago.

⊘

Humanity is absolutely helpless in the face of time. Time turns even a pauper into an emperor. The one who was a great soldier yesterday lies in the dust today with his bones scattered. Again, the one who was a lover of truth and beauty yesterday, for which everyone accorded him respect and honour, walks in the opposite direction today. Who knows, perhaps it was time that caused the lapse, flinging him into the slime at which people spat in hatred and rebuke.

There are thousands of examples like this. Perhaps that was why, thanks to the blows and counterblows of time, for this girl, who the other day had filled the night air with her cries of distress, all that had today become extremely trivial and commonplace, a matter of nominal value only. Now she did not tremble in fear at the prospect of being raped. She offered herself willingly to be raped at the beds of lustful men. She was no longer a maidservant washing utensils in babu homes; she was now a whore who sold her body. She commuted on the train in search of customers. Sometimes she had to alight at Jadavpur Station too. She had to be there for a while. And after all, one couldn't be sure about when one needed assistance, so she had to be acquainted with the dadas of the station. This dada was already known to her. Time seemed to have cast some dust over his memory. She had to renew the old acquaintance now, for business reasons.

She said, 'I used to come to your station earlier. Don't you remember, you saved me one night from some drunk goonda-types?'

Jibon could not remember. Maybe it wasn't him, and he was receiving compliments for something undertaken by another Jibon. And so, he wanted to steer the conversation in another direction. He asked her if she was well, and what she was doing in these parts now. Was she returning after work?

'I don't work in babu homes anymore. I do other work. I earn and feed myself. *Kamake khane wali!* That was a euphemism. Even if its meaning was not understood by all people, all those who were not quite so ordinary knew it—they knew who or what the girl was. That's why Jibon wasn't startled. He knew there was nothing in this to get startled about. So many people's occupations had changed in recent times. Kalua used to ride a rickshaw earlier at the bus-stand crossing. Now he had opened an eatery. Haren Ghosh used to have a vegetable shop earlier, now he was a rickshaw-puller. So by the same rule, the girl who was seen selling flowers in the market yesterday, today stood at Harkata Gali, with cheap powder and lipstick on her face, and glass bangles on her wrist, to sell herself.

By way of justifying herself, the girl said, 'Dada re, I don't know what sins I committed that I was born a girl. The fuckers... hundreds of people gape at this body like vultures. As if it's not a woman, but a dead carcass lying there. Tell me, how long can one survive trying to protect oneself? Wherever you look, wherever you go, people are waiting with gaping mouths to devour you. Instead of all that, I'm doing fine now. Come and take what you desire, I say! As long as I get my price, there's no other grief or worry.'

After she had had her say, the girl made a face and laughed in an ugly way. As if she was mocking herself and the men around her.

Even if he was unable to recognise her, Jibon knew plenty of *kamake khane walis* like her. They looked to all appearances like female workers employed on weekly wages in some small factory. No one knew about their occupation in the villages where they lived. As if they were leaving home for work, they carried an umbrella, a handbag and a lunch-box and set out in the afternoon. After that, they went around railway stations, bus-stands, cinema halls and other crowded places, and by sitting, standing, talking, smiling and signalling with eyes and gestures, they conveyed—I'm cheap and available. Just like they looked for customers, customers too looked for them on the streets and railway stations. Once there was a meeting of eyes, they agreed on the rate and left for the duration agreed upon. One could rent a room at any time in Harkata Gali, Kalighat, Ghutiari Sharif, Diamond Harbour and so on.

Jibon felt no attraction towards the girl. But he thought that instead of standing there like an idle idiot, waiting for the rain to stop before he went away elsewhere, there was nothing wrong in whiling away the time chatting with her. Whatever it was, and however it was, after all she was a woman. She wasn't bad-looking either. Besides, since women in this profession were less afraid of men compared to others, they were also easy-going, brave and fond of intimacy. No, one shouldn't object to such a companion at this time. And especially someone lashed by the tides of his hormones at this hour.

Jibon asked her, 'Ei, what's your name, re?'

Smiling and almost falling over him, the girl replied, 'Why do you need to know my name? If you want to do something, tell me that!'

'Still ... one needs a name to call someone by. What shall I call you?'

'Why don't you think of some name? Which you like.'

'Won't you tell me your name?'

'What's the point! If I tell you a name, how will you know whether that's real or false?'

'You tell me. I'll think about the rest.'

'Fine, then call me Golapi.'

19

Gurupado's Liquor Den

The rain was pouring down now, and lightning was crashing in the vicinity with peals of terrifying thunder. One struck really close by. The flash was blinding. The raindrops driven by the furious wind lashed one's body. It was a bit chilly too. The shadow of anxiety was writ large on the faces of all the people on the station platform. Would one be able to make it home tonight?

After a while, the girl who told Jibon her name was Golapi spoke. 'I'm completely wet. As soon as the rain lessens, I'll head home. I don't think there'll be any customers today. Business has been really bad. It's the third successive day I'll be returning empty-handed. Will you buy me some tea, dada?'

'Where do you live?'

'In Taldi.'

'In which village in Taldi?'

'I won't tell you that. I've never told anyone. *Baapre!*' Becoming animated suddenly, Golapi continued, 'Do you know what happened once? I was new in the trade then. I knew nothing about what should be said and what shouldn't. After being with a man for a few days, I had a weakness for him. In the course of conversation, I told him the name of my village. That bastard then suddenly appeared in our village one day, drunk on toddy, because he hadn't seen me for a few days. You tell me, won't the people there thrash me if they came to know what I do? That's why I never tell anyone where I'm from. Let acquaintances of the street remain on the street. Tell me, can I ever get married once my name is sullied in the local community?'

Whatever the girl's profession was, there was still a rustic simplicity in her speech and language. There was no complicated twist or knot in what she said, one did not have to wrack one's brains to gather what she was saying. Who knows why, but Jibon liked the girl. He felt cheerful and chirpy, just like how he spontaneously felt good in the company of good folk.

'So you want to get married ... Do you still desire that?'

'O Ma, of course I'll desire that! What are you saying? I've been born a woman, can I carry on being a *baarmukhya* for the rest of my life? Do you know, if a woman dies unmarried, there's no place for her even in hell? I have to marry someone, whoever and however he might be.'

'Then why don't you find someone and marry him right away? You can set up home with someone without doing whatever you're doing. I think that's far better than this!'

Golapi said, 'I don't know whether to laugh or cry at what you're saying!'

Jibon stared at her blankly. Had he said something wrong?

'Dada re, which land do you belong to? Can any girl get married nowadays unless she has money? The better the lad, the greater the price—bicycle, watch, gold, silver, cash, and even after all that, so much more. Tell me, how can my poor dad and brother gather so much money? Whatever they earn for their labour isn't enough even to feed everyone!'

Squinting her eyes and flashing a meaningful smile, she continued, 'That's why I entered this trade. I'm saving money. In just two or three years, I've saved a thousand-and-a-half. Once I've saved another thousand-and-a-half, I'm done. I'll leave the trade and get married.'

Jibon was astonished, he could not help smiling sardonically. 'The way you're saving money, doing what you're doing ... the groom you buy with the money is truly unfortunate! There's no doubt about that.'

'If he's unfortunate, what can I do about that, tell me? Grief poured out in Golapi's words. 'I'm not all that bad-looking, right, tell me? But no one wants to marry me empty-handed. Sons of whores! They crave the real thing and take money too, can you believe it! Has anyone ever found a cow that eats little and yields lots of milk! So come now and lick the soiled plate, what else can you do!'

Jibon felt his heart corroding as he heard the outpouring. There was a deep agony underlying all that she said, there was hostility and there was powerlessness. And there was the mental trauma of daily humiliation.

In an endearing tone, Jibon said, 'Look, let me tell you something, if you listen to me, it'll be good for you. Please leave this trade. See how so many poor girls protect their honour and work in small factories. Some wash utensils in babu homes, so many sell fish and vegetables. See how they are content with the little bit of money they earn thus. I tell you, do something like that. I'll help you. That'll be good for you.'

'Like hell it'll be good for me!' Golapi retorted angrily. 'Didn't I work in babu homes earlier? Have you forgotten that? Why do you think I stopped doing that? All the bastards are decent only on the surface. Actually all the fuckers are sons of whores!'

'Ooh, don't use foul language!'

'Do you think I enjoy using foul language? ... It was bhadralok babus who destroyed me first. I'd go to the babus' homes to work, and there, once the house was empty, they'd pull off my clothes ... On the train, in the station, on the playfield, or on the paddy-field, wherever I go, someone or the other pounces on me. It's a woman's body that's her greatest enemy! Forget about others, even one's own relatives don't spare you, if they get the chance. Dada re, in all my years, I haven't seen a single lad who lets you go once he gets a chance! So how am I to save myself? I realised there's no use living in fear all the time. So I entered the trade. Now I won't take my clothes off at someone's will, or because I'm forced to. I'll get naked according to my own wishes and my own needs. This body is mine, I am its owner. So why should someone else snatch my body? Whatever I do will be at my own will.'

Golapi's eyes were like a dry sea now. On which there was no wave, ripple or stirring. A huge, peaceful, dull, salty mirror. The mirror in which no shadow or image could settle. Both the past and the present had slipped away, without any dreams. What remained now was a harsh reality that mocked her. After a long pause of silence, she suddenly began laughing. Not heartily, but somewhat bitterly. She said, 'Forget all that! What good is it knowing about me? Buy me some tea?'

The tea-stall was nearby. They went and stood there, and took a lot of time to finish their tea. There wasn't any sign yet of the rain stopping. It poured down torrentially on the tin-roof of the rail station with a crashing sound. Every now and then, a spray of water blew in with a gust of wind. The people there got drenched. There was a wall behind where Jibon and Golapi were standing. To their left was the counter of the tea-stall. And in front of them and on their right side was a human wall. So the spray from the rain could not reach them.

Standing in front of them and also drinking tea was Jogai, the barber who worked on the pavement at the bus-stand crossing. Seeing Golapi having tea with, talking to and laughing with Jibon, he squinted his eyes and looked fixedly at them for a while. He felt the scorpion sting of desire in his heart. *Eesh*, isn't it that *maal*? She used to go to work in Bijoygarh. Had the fucker Jibon hooked her? And so, after some time, he gestured with his hand, calling Jibon some distance away. 'I swear, it's a great day today! Are you going to roll around with that *maal* tonight?'

Jogai's language, gestures and the look in his eyes made Jibon burn. He retorted angrily, 'Do you have any objections?'

'What?'

'Do you have any objections if I sleep with her? If you do, tell me!'

Jogai realised Jibon was annoyed. He said, 'Why would I have any objections? Who is she to me?'

'Then why are you talking about her?'

'For your good! Or else, why would I say anything?'

'For my good!'

'I know her. She has syphilis. If you sleep with her, you'll get it too.'

'How did you find out about it? Have you got it or what? When did you sleep with her? Has your wife got it from you?'

Jogai realised the conversation was turning in a nasty direction. After which would come a thrashing. It was difficult to prevail over people like Jibon with fisticuffs. Because they were constantly ready for fisticuffs. It wasn't unusual for them to possess a knife or suchlike, who knows there might be a revolver too. That's why it was important to step back to protect one's dignity. And so, forcing a bit of loudness into his voice, he said, 'I don't run behind such useless women. My wife is ten times more beautiful than her.'

'Then why did you think it necessary to lend me your wisdom? Do you think you're very clever? And that everyone else is an idiot?'

Jogai mumbled, 'What's clever and idiot got to do with it ...?'

'Go away from here! Go before I count to three! Or else ...!'

Jogai said hesitantly, 'I mean ... I mean, I told you something thinking you're a friend. Why else would I ... You're getting angry for no reason at all ...'

'Will you leave? I'm asking you again, will you leave?'

Jogai realised that leaving now would be good for his health. As if nothing had transpired, he said, 'It doesn't look like the rain is going to stop, what's the point of waiting here ...' And then he ran in the direction of the bus-stand crossing, getting drenched in the rain.

As soon as Jibon returned to Golapi, for some reason, she asked, 'So, can I leave?'

'Are you asking for my permission? *Pagli* ... where can you go? The way it's pouring, and the crowd that'll be there once the train arrives—will you be able to get into the train in that terrible crowd?'

'Then what shall I do now?' This wasn't a question, it was an expression of despair.

⁂

An altercation had taken place. And Jibon seemed to be unable to wipe that away and return to his normal self. He was burning with rage at what Jogai had said, and especially his vulgar gestures. The veins on his forehead were throbbing. That suppressed rage wanted to explode. And so, as if denying and scoffing at everything, all the people around, known or unknown, all the long-standing values, regulations, culture, customs, laws and edicts of society, Jibon said loudly, 'You're not going to be able to go home tonight. But I'll arrange something for you!'

'Where shall I stay in this storm and rain?'

'Wherever I take you! That's my business. Won't you come?'

'Of course!' Golapi said, with a worried look. 'I'll go. But why do you want to put me up for the night?'

Jibon replied, as angrily as before, 'Observing me, what do you think, that I'm celibate?'

'No, but ...'

'A eunuch?'

'Rubbish!'

'If you don't want to go, tell me.'

Golapi shook her head. She would go. The word 'no' wasn't supposed to be uttered by any girl in her profession. There weren't supposed to be any personal likes or dislikes either. Here, saying 'no' to someone and sending him away was akin to kicking away food. However clever the reasons one cited were, the one who did that invited the rage of Ma Annapurna, Ma Lakshmi and Baba Ganesh.

They wouldn't get any customers all day, not a single one. They had to return home empty-handed and broken in spirit at the end of the day. A man was as good as gold. Whether he was crooked or straight made no difference, as long as he paid the price.

Seen from that perspective, Jibon was a gem of a boy. There was no stench of liquor on his breath. His behaviour too was quite humane. Besides, he had jumped into the dangerous predicament Golapi was in one day, completely unselfishly. That debt had not yet been repaid. Maybe that could be settled today.

But will he really come with me? Or is he simply brushing away the anger from his altercation with that man by being loud? Golapi was unable to understand.

※

Rain continued to pour down. There was no sign of any letup. And there was lightning, accompanied by the ear-splitting sound of thunder. If it rained like this all night, the whole city would be inundated. *Baapre!* What calamitous rain! No one had ever seen such rain in the last twenty years. It seemed to be an intimation of some impending catastrophe.

There was no light anywhere now. The electric cables had snapped. Trees had been uprooted and they blocked the roads. Vehicles were unable to move. They stood motionless on the roads, in the water. The railway tracks were submerged, so the train service was suspended until the water receded. Everything all around was brimming with water. Drains and roads were indistinguishable. All the filth and garbage was floating away in the current of the floodwaters. But the darkness was not so dense at this time. It looked like there was a largish moon hidden behind the clouds. The colour of the clouds was therefore not black but almost white, like a crane's feathers. That was the reason for fear. There was a rustic saying, *hansha megh phanshay,* swan-coloured clouds trap you. That's why it looked like this city would go under today. The rain had begun long back, in the evening, and now it was late at night! And as the night advanced, so too did the fury of the rain grow. All the homeless people of the station—forget about sleeping, it was doubtful whether they would even find a dry spot to stand on. The platform was packed with hundreds of train passengers who had not been able to return home. Everyone was drenched with the spray of rain. The small space in front of the ticket counter seemed to be the most crowded, because the spray from the rain was somewhat less there. If the rain did not lessen, if the train service did not resume, this crowd would be there all night. A couple of trains had run in the evening, although they were delayed. But now they had come to a complete halt. They would have to wait until morning for sure, but if the water did not recede, it was impossible to say how much longer the train service would stay suspended.

Jibon and Golapi stood there for a long time. When it became clear that this caprice of nature was going to continue, Jibon said, with bitterness in his voice, 'I see that what I said in anger then has turned out to be true re, Golapi. It looks like you have no option but to stay with me tonight!'

Golapi grimaced and responded with a practised retort. 'I've been standing for four long hours. I couldn't even find a place to sit for a while. My legs are aching badly. If it's going to be like this all night, what's the point of staying here?'

Scratching his head, Jibon said, 'There's a room where one can stay, it's not so far away. There aren't any doors or windows, but there's a concrete roof. Come, let's go there. It's just a question of one night, you'll be able to squeeze in there. Let the rain abate a bit.'

'Don't hope for the rain to lessen. Let's go now. I can't stand here anymore.'

'Let's wait a bit more.'

But the rain did not lessen, and the night advanced as they waited. In the meanwhile, they had some cakes and biscuits from the tea-stall. That was tonight's meal. Because of the calamitous storm, no fire had been lit in the kitchen of Chhechan's eatery. He was worried about what the restaurant workers would eat. The tiles on the roof had given way and water had poured down into the eatery, and the floor was one big puddle. The oven was drenched, the fire had gone out and it was stone cold now. It was best not to hope for any rice there in such a situation. Jibon did not have any problem with that. It was fine if he could get something. He had no objection even if there was nothing.

After a while, Jibon arrived with a plastic sheet which had been tied in front of a rickshaw to keep away the spray of the rain. Taking cover somehow under the plastic sheet, they went across the field beside the water tank, walked a bit along the lane going from behind the stationmaster's quarters to Loharpara, and arrived at the broken boundary wall of the TB Hospital. The two of them crossed over the broken wall and entered the hospital compound. Making their way through knee-deep, dirty water from the overflowing drain, they reached Gurupado's liquor den. On other days, the den ran till ten or ten-thirty at night. Given the rain this evening, he must have shut shop early and left. Various signs of Gurupado were scattered all over this unused room of the hospital now. In one corner were a few empty liquor bottles. Beside that was a pot for storing water. Used glasses were washed with that. Next to that was a coconut shell, in which the customers were given some slivers of ginger with salt. And beside that were a few bricks. The customers sat on those while they drank. Who knows for what purpose this room had been built at some point in this expanse, a jungle of tall grass and morning glory flowers, between the main building and the wide sewage drain in the south. Pigs grazed there, and the room was occupied by Gurupado now. He was a ward boy in the hospital. He could not sustain his family with his salary. He got some additional income from this liquor den. The room lay empty once he finished selling liquor. No, it wasn't empty every night. Some people came here in secret. Because of which Gurupado had given it the name 'Prem Bhawan' or Love Mansion. There weren't any houses nearby. And there was only a dark alley leading there.

Having come here and found a place to lay one's head to rest, Jibon and Golapi felt at ease. It was still raining as hard as before, but the floor of the room was dry because there was a wall on the side from where the spray of the rain would have come. But because hundreds of people had walked there through the day, it was full of dust. Jibon searched the room and found a torn bit of sack-cloth. He wiped the floor with that. After that, in a cheerful mood, he said, 'At least we found a place to stay the night. It's better than an empty wagon of a goods train, isn't it?'

And so she began. Although there was no need to say it, Golapi responded. 'If the GRP ever catch me in an empty wagon, they'll destroy my very flesh and bones. Tell me, can I suffer four or six *medos* and *khottas* with this body of mine? The bastards don't see their wives' faces for ages. They grab you like Yama does. They don't care about whether the person is dead or alive. Do you know what happened once when I was new in this line?'

Jibon finished wiping off the dust, stood up straight and said, '*Chup!* Don't ever describe such things to me! I don't like to hear it!'

Golapi looked at Jibon in astonishment. She could not understand why he reacted like that. After all, she wasn't saying anything particularly bad. She had been caught by the GRP once. Everyone knew what they did if they found a woman alone in the darkness. So what was wrong about saying that? After all, it was true. And Jibon was not a dada or bhai or kaka or mama or anyone from the village and hamlet. So why this reaction?

After sitting silently for a while in a dark corner of the room, Jibon finally said, 'Whatever has happened was in the past. But now, just think that you've never done any bad deed with anyone, willingly or unwillingly, knowingly or unknowingly.'

'Is there any point in thinking like that?'

'There is. If you think like that, then you'll see the outcome. It's the mind that's the real thing. Imagine you are a virgin, completely sinless and pure. That no one has ever touched your body till today.'

Golapi laughed. But she did not say anything. Jibon came near and placed his arm on Golapi's right shoulder with utmost tenderness and intimacy. This arm was strong and dependable. Golapi felt she could hold such an arm and journey a great distance.

Jibon asked, 'Do you ever dream, Golapi?'

Golapi replied, 'Everyone dreams. Girls dream a bit more than boys.'

'But those are joyful dreams. I'm not talking about that. Have you ever had a bad dream? Just imagine that everything that happened so far in your life was only a terrible dream. None of which that is true.'

'Then what's the truth?'

'The truth is this!' Jibon pinched Golapi's arm. 'Tell me, doesn't it hurt? That means the fact that you and I are together now is what's real. Anything else that was there is rubbish, false, lies, a nightmare.'

On this night of drenching pouring rain, it was as if a lover of life was sitting on an uninhabited island, cut off from the world, weeping out of thirst for the elixir of life. Only the one with a thirsting heart could fathom the meaning of the cry. Someone from whose hands the wine-cup had slipped out. Who had no option but to imagine the empty cup was full, and wait.

'Golapi, re, for you and me, and all the people like us ... There are thousands of hurdles on the way to surviving by doing right and staying good. No one will allow you to stay well, however hard you try. And one can't survive the wrong way. There's only one way to survive and remain good, and that's by not being bad in any way. Whatever's bad, whatever's not good, should not even be admitted. Think always that nothing bad could ever touch you. What do you think—did whatever happened in your life not befall anyone else? Go from house to house and find out. If they talk, then you'll come to know how much humiliation and oppression has taken place in the lives of thousands upon thousands of women.'

Jibon paused for a while and then continued. 'I can't tell you everything today. But you should know that no less has happened in my life too. What could I do, I was small, I was weak. The strong will forever oppress whoever is weak. Either be strong, or suffer oppression!'

After a while he continued, 'I don't remember all those old things. I don't want to remember them either. When I remember all that, I feel like a dog. I won't be a dog anymore, re Golapi. If anyone even tries to make me a dog, he'll find out what I do to him and regret it.'

The room was an illicit liquor den. The stench of cheap liquor suffused the entire room. Had Jibon become intoxicated by the very stench? He suddenly said,—'Tell me, Golapi, will you marry me? Will you set up home with me?'

Flabbergasted by this sudden enquiry, Golapi said, 'I can't figure out what you're saying ... What can I say ...'

Slowly, Jibon said, 'For a long time, I've been feeling the need for a companion. I can't carry on otherwise. I'm telling you, please don't mind. All day and all night, it's as if Ravan's pyre is burning inside my body. I feel terribly empty inside. Which I just can't bear. Besides, no landlord in the city wants to rent a place to a single person like me, so I have to stay in the station or on the pavement. For that reason too, I need a companion. Will you marry me?'

Words are not always mere words. Sometimes it's a recitation, sometimes it's a mantra, or a eulogy, and sometimes it could be delirium. Or it could be gossip or rubbish. Golapi was unable to understand what this was. Jibon said, 'You'll wait for me at home and cook to your heart's content. You'll serve me the food lovingly. If I'm late returning home, you'll be waiting, gazing at the road. And you'll stay up all night with me as we exchange stories. You'll share some of my sorrows and hardships. I'll share yours. When I think of all these things, I feel like starting a family. Tell me, will you stay with me all your life?'

Golapi stared blankly at Jibon's hazy face for a while, and then asked him, 'Have you had ganja or bhang?'

'Why?'

'People talk all kinds of nonsense when they are intoxicated, and once the buzz fades and they are out of the stupor of intoxication, the don't remember any of that. I've seen so many men saying all kinds of things at night. Once it's morning, they want to run away, as if their very lives depended on that!'

'I don't consume ganja or bhang.'

'Liquor?'

'Only sometimes, but although I didn't drink liquor today, I feel intoxicated. This is called the intoxication of love. The intoxication of setting up home. Who knows why, I feel like loving you very much. If you're willing, tell me!'

'But I'm a bad girl. You know everything about me. Does anyone knowingly play with fire like this?'

'Again the same talk!' Jibon pressed his hand on Golapi's mouth. 'Didn't I tell you to forget about all the old things! You never did anything wrong. Then how could you become a bad girl? I'm the first man in your life. I am the first person to touch you. If that's bad, then it happens in every girl's life. If it doesn't, then she's an unfortunate soul!'

'Na, re.' Staring at the roof, Golapi said in a tone of hopelessness, in a broken and choked voice, 'Even if a person consumes snake venom unknowingly, he can digest it. But no one can digest poison if they swallow it knowingly.'

'I can.' Jibon was quiet for a while, and then he said, 'It's because you told me everything about yourself openly that I came to know about your secrets. If you didn't tell me anything, would I have known anything? I wouldn't. Suppose there's another person whom I marry, another woman, one day or another. ... Would she ever be able to tell me about herself as frankly as you did? She won't. So I'll never be able to know who or what she is. Isn't it? Maybe the one I set up home with, thinking she's as good as gold, is actually base metal. Instead of that, if I knowingly bring the base one home, then there's no fear of being cheated later. And if base metal turns into gold later, that's only a gain! You say you're bad, but what kind of washed tulsi leaf am I! Who's a pure one today?'

Hearing Jibon's words, Golapi sat in the darkness like a tree struck by lightning. She had some reason to be taken aback, but she no longer possessed the emotion to be moved. She had heard a lot of babbling like this earlier, on many occasions, on many nights. Many enticing promises like this had showered down. A frenzied man would rise and speak at specific times, and was wont to say a lot of things like this. But later, he could no longer comprehend the meaning of those words. He felt ashamed of himself.

But it was true that even if all those people offered enticements of sari, jewellery, cash, a holiday in Digha—none of them had claimed to want to marry her. Even if they were tottering in their drunken state, none of them had said, 'I'll make you my wife and take you home.' Even if they belonged to the race of drunkards, they were fine when it came to the real thing. Their minds did not totter. They knew—one could have fun with such girls outside one's home, but one couldn't set up home with them ... what would people say!

So in that sense, there was definitely something novel in what Jibon said.

It was as if Jibon had descended into a deep meditative trance. From there, came his voice that sounded crazy. 'In my whole life, I could never be of any use to anyone. So many years have been wasted. If I can be of any use to you now, I can take solace in the fact that I did something worthwhile. My life would not have been entirely wasted.'

Golapi was a whore. Her ears had turned sour hearing such lovely words from the mouths of men. Yet she listened to him, because she liked to hear it. Everyone knew that whatever happened in a jatra, or cinema, or play, was all false; it was only acting, with a time-span of only two-and-a-half hours. Yet people were captivated by those false dialogues. They wept at the hero's and the heroine's sorrows and rejoiced in their joys, because it was far away from the harsh realities of the present. For a time, it took them away to a world where their imaginary desires found fulfilment.

Perhaps the time-span of all such emotional laments on the part of Jibon was only one night, but right now, in this rain-drenched darkness, as soon as Golapi heard his words, there was a wrench in her heart. She wanted to believe him. It was supposedly a sin to lose faith in humanity. She wanted to believe that Jibon was a man who had a heart.

A tiny little bud, whose parents had named her after a flower. The flower that had not been laid in offering in a temple for worship of the deity. Even before spreading out its petals and blooming in fullness, it had been scorched by the lustful breath of men. Suspicion and disbelief had accumulated in the recesses of her scorched heart. A man—meant a barbaric creature. Yes, for the sake of her profession she did surrender to men's embrace. But the bitter experience of the past held her back, and so an entrancing love did not awaken, which, once awakened with deep conviction, enabled even a poisonous snake to be worn on the neck like a garland. But when there was suspicion, even a rope could appear to be a snake.

Nevertheless, she did not prevent Jibon. She let him speak, so long as the intoxicated excitement was inside him. How long would that be? Once the night was over, so would the talk end. Let it burn like a sparkler's multi-hued splash of colour before it is spent. Let it go on, let the night be a bit illuminated and honeyed. When an actor wept during his act, after all the tears did flow from his eyes. For that time, those tears were not false.

Jibon had not yet been freed from his trance. He said, 'Tell me, Golapi, speak, don't be silent! Tell me, will you start a family with me? After all, you want a home, a husband. I want to give you all that. Tell me, will you accept?'

In Jibon's words, in his touch, there was none of the aggression of the pouncing men, who didn't give a damn about feelings and simply possessed the body. They behaved terribly. As if they could thereby cruelly extract every bit of the price paid. This was another kind of man. It was as if he had the fatal desire to melt like wax, a death wish. Which beckoned her almost-dead heart to drench itself in a new feeling, completely denying the harsh reality. This invitation brought the touch of an untasted excitement in her mind and body. The eternal feminine being within her, which was crushed under the loud life of a prostitute, became very distressed. It was a great insult and humiliation to her femininity. Today that precious treasure had arrived, unsolicited, and was knocking on the door—Open the door! I'm here! Golapi stood with her hand resting on the shut door. It could be opened with a single push. But where was she being able to open the door? After all, the thorn of a suspicion was pricking her terribly. What was that thorn?

Golapi wondered—not once is this man saying, if you come into my life I would benefit, I would be blessed, I would be fulfilled! He wants to fulfil my life. But didn't the heart feel despair, fatigue and exasperation seeing the emptiness underneath all the help, pity and magnanimity? Unless a solid ground of love, mutual generosity, respect and dependence between two people grew, could a relationship of donor and donee be stable and survive for long?

Golapi thought about waiting some more, she wanted more proof of trustworthiness from the man. It was meaningless to give an opinion without seeing the end of it. It was also unpleasant, humiliating and a matter of ridicule. Who could say whether, like many others, he too wouldn't say—there goes that *maal*, whom I lied to and made her dance to my tune all night!

Outside, the rain continued to pour without interruption. The transformed nature had two different kinds of impact on the two minds in the room. One person was keen to smash himself to pieces, while the other wanted to bring together the scattered pieces. Now, Jibon's hand placed over Golapi's shoulder steadily abandoned the soft, gentle role and began turning strong and brave. In a dark room in a desolate flooded field, the hand wanted to gather something. It was a firm, spirited hand of a youth. The pressure of the hand broke down the wall of balance, rules and restraint.

20

Intimacy and Distance

'Tell me, Golapi, say something. Whether good or bad, but say something.'

Golapi laid all the weight of her body on Jibon's heaving, hot chest and said in a voice choked with anguish, 'Don't be mad, re! And don't turn me mad too. Let me be as I am and how I am. Don't destroy me, re. You say you'll start a family with me, you'll love me—don't tempt me so badly, re. Girls like me seek a babu, but they only want me for their debauchery. They don't want me for a wife. If you stay with me for some days, once your passions have cooled you'll see that you feel revulsion for me. You'll bite your own hand that day for this mistake.'

Jibon had never before been as intimately close to a girl like Golapi, someone so devoid of complications and arrogance. The hot touch of each body was now on the other. Perhaps the female body was not entirely unknown to him. But, for some strange reason, there was a latent inner conflict about justice and injustice in that limited knowledge. Which impeded any satisfaction. In Golapi's case, there was nothing like that. And so now, a strange breeze of peace, contentment and bliss blew through Jibon's being.

He was no longer eager to hear and know what Golapi was saying, or what she was thinking. What she would do tomorrow—was her affair. But this night belonged to Jibon. Today, life was trying to tell Jibon something, which, if it remained unsaid, would make life futile, one's youth futile, and one's very birth futile.

But his heart trembled and his voice quavered to say that. Had any words been invented yet with which that inner feeling, which he yearned to express, could be said?

Now Jibon felt that at times saying nothing said more than saying anything. Time itself speaks a lot through silence. Where language had lost its way, there a sexualised woman's ardour itself was capable of and successful in expressing the unexpressed distress of the human mind.

And so, wrapping his arms around Golapi and holding her close, Jibon sat silently, listening to the sound of the rain outside. The shafts of rain pouring down from the sky seemed to be whispering something into the earth's ears. What were they saying? The earth would become soft, tender and full of potential on receiving this bounty of water. The promise of becoming green, of becoming vigorous would arise in her body. The joyful pride of overcoming the annual obstacle and bringing forth an abundance of crops.

After a long time had passed, Jibon felt he should say something to Golapi. The exhausting and shaming feeling from the past of having been wronged was striking its claws and fangs at her ribs now. The shadow of those poisonous fangs lay on the doorway to her hopes and dreams for the future, and the long-cherished bridal chamber. Now she needed a centre of support, the touch of the empathic heart of a trustworthy man.

After much thought, slowly, in a voice full of tenderness, he said, 'Listen, Golapi, the one who is lovable can never be revulsive. If you can stay close to the person, all your inner ailments are healed. I've fallen deeply in love with you, re Golapi. The more I look at you, the more the love grows. I feel as if you're the girl whom I've been searching for all my life. Who I've finally found today. Now that

I've found you, I don't want to lose you. I think if I lose you, I'll lose the very joy of living.'

'How can someone suddenly fall in love like that? One has to first get to know the person, understand her. If her qualities outweigh the faults, then one likes her. After that, when one goes around with her—that's when it happens.'

'No, no ...' Jibon protested loudly. 'Anything done so calculatingly can never be love. Wise folk say love is blind. It can't go around making all the calculations, searching for faults and qualities. The one who's destined to fall in love—it happens to him suddenly. And the one who's destined never to—even if he tries all his life, it's not going to happen.'

'Where did you learn all this?'

'Why do you ask?'

'It's like a teacher's talk! I used to work in a teacher's house. He used to talk like that.'

'He used to talk to you?'

'Why should he talk to me? He used to talk to his students. Those who used to come to him to study.'

Jibon laughed and said, 'I never learnt anything from anyone. Whatever I've learnt is all by myself, from myself. My life is my guru. You should know that all the so-called knowledge and education is utterly false and useless.'

The same sound of uninterrupted rain pouring outside the room. It seemed the world and all creation was drowning under the frenzied rain-dance of a million water sprites. A tiny dinghy with two lost souls floated away amidst the ferocious, billowing waves of an inundating deluge. The runaway vessel without a helmsman rocked in the waves.

A sluggishness began to cling to Golapi's eyes. Sleep, cold as death, began to seep into every pore of her body. The blood in her veins turned icy. Her legs were unable to support her. Like a tree cut at its stumps, she rolled over from her sitting position and lay on the dust-covered floor. She said, 'Say it once more ... once more ... tell me once more that you love me ...'

'I do, re Golapi. I really, really love you. I can't tell you how much I love you. If I get the chance, I'll prove it and show it to you.'

A wail burst out from Golapi's throat. 'No one ever spoke to me of love! So many people have said so much about my breasts and my body and so much more. But no one wanted to buy the entire person, or her heart. Which only a woman can give. You're the first man to say you love me. Say it again! Say it again and again, let me die hearing you say you love me ...'

Lightning struck somewhere, with a terrible crashing sound. A huge flash of light lit up the whole sky. The tiny room quaked. It seemed as if a chunk of the sky had fallen on the roof of the shed. Jibon's entire body and soul trembled. There was no one anywhere. It was as if only these two creatures were alive after the final cataclysm, in earth's aboriginal cave. One of whom was male and the other female. What didn't the female possess? She had everything that other women possessed. Which men wished and yearned for and also found satisfaction in. All other women, perhaps now, on this night, were floating on the honeyed rhythm of coital pleasure as they slept with their beloveds. If the dark night wanted to terrify them with rain and lightning, a man whom she could hold tight and feel fearless was right next to her. But this girl, with the same possessions, lay in disaffection and humiliation in the ankle-deep dust of an illicit liquor den. There was not a single trustworthy man anywhere near her to whom she could give herself up entirely. The one whom she would trust and surrender herself to, who would not enjoy her body as he wished and then go away, throwing her into the garbage-pile like an empty clay-cup. Who knows how many men had gone away like that. Perhaps because of that, suspicions and disbelief regarding men had accumulated in her mind. Perhaps her life had taught her—men are selfish, greedy and lustful. Don't let his words make you forget that. He will defraud you, get what he wants and slip away.

Jibon realised he had to rid her of this apprehension.

Jibon tried to observe Golapi closely in the bit of light coming into the room through the stratus of clouds. But his gaze was thwarted; there wasn't sufficient brightness in the room for anything to be clearly visible. And so in the darkness, like a blind man using the touch of his hand, Jibon tried to get a complete sense of Golapi. This was her head, this the hair. A chignon made of her long hair, tied with a string. Jibon undid the string. Golapi's hair was wet from the rain. The smell of cheap coconut oil on her undone hair. Jibon's hand was stroking Golapi's forehead. There was a bindi on her forehead, who knows what colour it was. Here were her eyebrows, and these her eyelids. Jibon remembered that there was kohl in the girl's eyes in the evening. Now both her eyes were shut. He could sense that it was not sleep, but the pleasure of passion, which lay midway between sleep and drowsiness, that sealed her eyes.

The hand slid down over her nose and descended upon her lips. They were not thin like orange peels. A bit thick, somewhat dry and rough. And swollen, as if in a pout, at many offences. No loving kiss had ever been planted on these lips. Whatever had been planted was only ugliness wrapped in the saliva of lust. Maybe that explained the sense of offence.

After that Jibon stroked Golapi's cheek. Using four fingers, he pressed to test the suppleness of the flesh. This was the cheek that had borne so many hundreds of lustful kisses, so many bites from sharp teeth, under cover of night. But there was not a single sign of love that had stayed permanently. Perhaps it was the agony of not getting that which made her downcast, which made her lip pouty out of offence.

His hands descended to her neck. There were a bunch of thin imitation-gold necklaces, and similar imitation-jewellery on her ears. A girl in her trade had to be adorned in all this imitation-jewellery, and stay awake at night in imitation-offering. Oh you dear unfortunate one!

Jibon's breathing now became rapid. Hot steam seemed to emanate from his mouth and nostrils. His throat was dry. His heartbeats sounded without pause, like a clock. It was as if his whole being was burning in the heat of a fire. He planted his hot lips gently on Golapi's. With merely a kiss he conveyed what the eunuch Vatsayana could not in his thousand-page book.

Oh Golapi! You've seen clay dolls, don't you know what the image of the Goddess is? You've seen lustful dogs, but you don't know what a lover is like. You've heard a lot of shouts, you've heard plenty of loud talk, you've seen many greedy, selfish, deceitful demons, but you've not heard the silent sweet melody of submission. You never found a single love-crazed, entranced man's heart! You don't know the difference between rape and love-making. Tonight, I'll take you far away from the world you know to that unknown world. I'll stay awake all night and keep you up too all night long. I'll stay awake with you, as will every cell of my body.

His hand descended lower and moved away the drenched cloth covering her breast. Beneath that was her brassiere. Right now, in this darkness, Jibon wanted to remove all bonds. His hand trembled a little. As if he was the first man on earth to touch that forbidden fruit. Like someone who had no experience at all. The safety pin on the blouse pricked the tip of his finger. 'Ooh!'

'What happened?'

'The pin pricked my finger!'

Golapi was a prostitute. A prostitute knew what she had to do, and when. She opened her blouse herself, and held out her hidden treasure. After that she said in a whisper, 'Shall I tell you something?'

'Yes.'

'Will you believe me?'

'I know you'll never lie to me.'

'I've never let anyone touch them until today.'

'What do you say!' Jibon was astounded. 'How did you manage to protect them from the hands of the *rakkhosh*?'

'I'm telling you the truth. I can swear to that on the name of anyone you ask me to. I once lost a good customer of mine because of that. He used to pay twenty rupees for a night.'

'Why did you do that?'

Golapi's eyes shone in the darkness. In a voice choked with emotion she said, 'I'll have a child in my womb one day or the other. Tell me, won't I? Will I be able to put the breasts soiled by so many men into its mouth then? How do you think I'll feel then? That's why I don't let anyone's touch soil what's sacred. Even if there's dirt and slime all over my body, my breasts remain clean.'

Startled, Jibon removed his hand from Golapi's breast. Golapi asked, 'What happened? Did you get angry?'

'No, not at all!'

'Then?'

'It's for your children!'

Golapi giggled. She pulled Jibon's hand and pressed it down on her breast. 'You're different from all of them. You aren't a customer.' Her voice trembled with emotion. 'You said you loved me! That you'll marry me and make me your wife. There's no fault or sin if a wife gives anything to her husband.'

Jibon filled the palm of his hand with that ocean of divine elixir, and squeezed excitedly as if he was going crazy. Running his cheek on this sacred, spherical breast reserved for her child's consumption, he felt as if the joy of winning an entire empire, and the happiness of climbing the peak of a tall mountain and touching the sky, had all been attained in full measure. Winning a woman's heart was a far more difficult task than winning a battle. He had won over a woman's heart today. There was no greater victory than that.

The much-abused girl named Golapi was very surprised today. Was there still so much sensitivity left in this body that had been ground by the embraces of so many men? How come? Never before had she felt blood coursing through her veins at this pace. There had never been such pure obsession and entrancement that broke all the barriers of her mind. This fatal longing to give herself away entirely and become empty was a first. What was there in this man's touch which no one else had? Had she fallen in love with Jibon and begun to trust him? That's why the Vesuvius sleeping inside her for so long had finally awakened. The volcanic eruption had begun, a stream of hot lava was streaming out. Was that why the desire of her flesh was submitting to the desire of her heart—possess me, plunder everything of mine with everything of yours, I shall not resist!

Jibon's hand slipped from Golapi's breast to her stomach, and then descended further. After circling around the deeply-set navel a few times, his fingers squeezed a lump of soft flesh. He released it—and squeezed again. After that, it was as if the hand pushed its way upstream. It touched the breast and again slipped downwards. Golapi shivered and trembled to the squeezes of the male hand. Perhaps this was what was called horripilation. An all-destroying coital hunger seemed to raise its hood in every fibre of her body.

In the course of the play of his hand, Jibon removed all the clothes from Golapi's body. He did not leave a single stitch on her. He removed the bangles on her wrist, the earrings on her ears and the necklaces around her neck. He freed her from all the imitation-adornment. He made Golapi as naked as a village girl playing in front of her ramshackle hut. After that, his ten fingers moved in a spiralling curve over the smooth warmth of each and every fold and curve of her unclothed body. No, there was no flaw anywhere, no scar anywhere. Her body was unalloyed, perfect and complete in itself. After going all over, Jibon ran his hands again and again over her face, her breasts, her stomach, her groin and her buttocks. All this is mine. She isn't anyone else's. From today, she is mine and mine alone.

At the touch of Jibon's strong hands, Golapi shivered like a creeper touched by a breeze. Lightening seemed to be erupting all over her body. As if there was a strange horripilation on every inch of her body. Like from a river in spate that had overrun both its banks, uncontrollable waves lashed the shore. She could remain still no longer. In fierce passion, using both her hands, she pressed Jibon down upon her swollen breasts, and like a crazed soul, planted kiss after kiss on his cheeks and lips. Without shame, she pleaded in distress, 'I feel like dying today, re. If I die today, I won't have any sorrows left. Kill me today!'

Didn't Jibon feel like dying as well? Never before had he seen such a perfect body. Never before had he got the chance to know that such excitement arose in one's flesh and soul at someone's touch. It was as if all of nature and the environment were giving him company today. This thick darkness, the sound of pouring rain and this desolation were all on his side. Women are compared to flowers. Golapi was no flower now. She was like a spark of fire. Which was waiting for kindling to turn into an inferno. She was like a living idol crafted by the labour of many artists with honey and alcohol, fire and dynamite. Which had been created out of a part of an apsara like Urvashi or Tilottama, in order to be a playmate for adult children. Would Jibon be able to show his prowess now in this play of bodies? Someone had said, given the right time, opportunity and a companion after one's own heart, no man could remain a celibate. All three of these were within Jibon's reach now. But now—it was also the time to be tested by oneself. Just as there was the delight of accepting the invitation, sometimes there is delight hidden in non-acceptance as well.

Golapi was half-sitting and half-lying. She pressed Jibon's face to her own. Her hot breath scorched Jibon's neck. Every pore of Golapi's body seemed to be intoxicated with the masculine smell of the sweat on Jibon's body. In the fierce lust for the bliss of union, with all the bolts and barriers of heart and soul being released, she beckoned the beloved man. Come, come closer. Strike me with all the weapons you have and take away everything of mine. Take possession of the so-called impregnable fort.

But why was Jibon still so restrained? Golapi could not fathom why. When would he come racing, like a wild buffalo that had broken its chains, flaunting its horns? How much longer? When would he release himself and seek the divine elixir? Seek and give?

Golapi grew tired of waiting. She was dejected, in despair. After a while, the bond of her impatient and tired arms loosened. The tide of the river that had rushed in, drawn by the moon, began its return journey. Ebb set in in her heart. Her defeated body slumped once again on the bed of dust. A sigh of futility escaped her lips and flew away into the wind around. Two drops of tears streamed down her cheeks from her anguished eyes. There was no witness to those tears. The dust on the floor of the room soaked up the tears at once.

Jibon's blazing eyes were then searching Golapi's body for something. Golapi shrivelled under his gaze. For the first time, she felt terribly ashamed. Now she felt, not unclothed or uncovered, but naked. She had become aware of that nakedness after she suffered rape at the hands of a man her father's age, while walking across a field. She had become aware of the nakedness one desolate afternoon in the bathroom of a babu's house. She could not bear her own nakedness now. Feeling around in the darkness, she searched for her clothes and covered her body. In exactly the way a dead body was covered in a shroud. After that, she lay down and turned aside.

Jibon did not know about the upheaval inside Golapi. He asked, 'What happened re, Golapi?'

'Oh nothing!'

'It seems you're angry.'

'Who shall I be angry with?'

Now Jibon realised that for some reason Golapi had been pained by his conduct. To placate her, Jibon once again became tender. 'Don't get me wrong.' These words uttered by him now sounded to Golapi's ears like a joke. It was as if he was giving the final kick on the chest of a defeated, fallen foe. Golapi burst out in agony and agitation, 'Did you bring me here in order to make fun of me like this?'

'Why do you say I made fun of you? When did I make fun of you?'

'If you had been a woman you would have known what you did and what you didn't do!'

As soon as Jibon tried to say something, Golapi said, 'Let it be. You don't have to say anything more. I've understood all there is to understand. Just like doctors can touch a patient and say whether the fever's high or low, we too can know from a man's behaviour what he feels inside. After all, I've been in the trade for a while. I've seen hundreds of men saying no. Don't take me for a fool.'

Jibon was now wounded by the arrows of Golapi's words. He had thought the night to be heady and unforgettable in every way, but the unsolicited floodwaters of a misunderstanding had arrived, wanting to wash away all its sweetness, wanting to wreck the monumental palace of his dreams.

The economic, social and cultural environment in which a person lives affects every level of his thinking, contemplation and assessment. The person carries this in his mind, unknowingly, all his life. This was a virus which could not be destroyed. Neither of them could examine themselves because both of them continued to stand by their feelings and decisions. The misunderstanding had arisen because of that.

Golapi lay on her back now, gazing at the ceiling. Her swollen breasts, tilted upwards, rose and fell, smarting from the scorch of the unbearable insult. An unbearable torment of having lost lay in the secret pulse of her heart. Never before had she faced such a big defeat. Only a woman could fathom how large this defeat was.

After a long time was spent like this, in complete silence, Golapi turned towards Jibon, keeping some distance between them. 'Will you tell me the truth? You are repulsed by me, isn't it?'

'Of course not,' Jibon said with a start. 'Why should I be repulsed?'

Golapi smashed and flung away her normal soft, tender feminine demeanour of all this while. The touchstone called love whose touch could turn base metal to gold was no longer faithful. How then could Golapi hold on to tenderness? And so, she was now an extraordinarily provoked tigress. Which had no desire to gain anything and no fear of losing anything. There was only a desire for bloody vengeance. She said, 'What did that son of a whore tell you then? You think I didn't hear that? That I have syphilis? Wait till I meet him! Just see if I don't hit him on the face with my slipper!'

Jibon mumbled, 'But I didn't pay any attention to what he said, or else would I have come here with you?'

'Then why did you shrink back like this?'

Jibon looked at Golapi. His whole face was shrouded by darkness. In the darkness, he appeared to be the collapsed pillar of some great palace built of precious stones, under which the joyful nuptial bed that had been laid out lay crushed. Jibon was responsible for that. Unknown to him, he had committed a grave crime. What could he say at such a moment to console her? How could he wipe away her humiliation?

When Jibon had brought Golapi here, he did not really have any particular objective or plan. Where would the girl go on such a calamitous night—and so, he had brought her along. Only a woman could cast a spell of entrancement. A woman—means the one who is the mistress of that extraordinary power that can turn stone to water. In the special atmosphere tonight, whatever had to happen after talking so long with Golapi happened. Jibon began to like her. Which, with the passing of time, was transformed and resulted in love, and then the companionless bereft heart lying in wait inside his breast cried out—She's the one! The one I had gone around searching for on the streets of the whole world. She's the one I want for the rest of my life, inseparable like a shadow.

There was no flaw in Jibon's thinking thus far. The mistake came after that. When she is the one I want to make my wife, then why should I take advantage of her destitute helplessness tonight, at this time, and do what all men have done? The thought had entered Jibon's startled mind at the peak of intimacy. Where's the difference then between me and all those men who, like dogs, had torn, dug into and bitten Golapi's soft flesh in the darkness of night? I had said to her I would prove myself, so here's the appropriate moment for that proof.

Jibon said, 'Golapi, I'm not going to be a dog, and I'm not turning you into a bitch. When two hearts have become one, how long can it take for our bodies to become one? Only a day, after all, only twenty-four hours. I'll take you to Kalighat tomorrow and apply sindoor on your forehead. After that, there will no longer be any social, religious or legal hurdle to bathe in that ocean of bliss. No one will have anything to say if I adhere to custom and bring my wedded wife home in front of everyone and then shut the door. But now, until I apply sindoor in your hair, this is wrong. Wise people have said that the conclusion of anything begun in wrongdoing is never beautiful.'

But Golapi was not in any mental condition to hear or understand all this abstract talk. Her life stood upon a harsh reality. In every layer of that reality there was only suspicion, distrust, duplicity and deception. The relationship between people here was that of commodity and consumer. There was a calculating buyer-seller relation. In this terrifying forest, where would Golapi find the eyes to recognise a person as a human? How would she understand why Jibon had retreated? Who would tell her that this retreat of one step by him was only in order to advance two steps?

Jibon realised that it would take a while to make Golapi understand the real reason. And the way the situation had turned now, it would be quite a task at this time to bring back her dead hopes to life. No more talk now. Let the night pass. There would be a lot of time the whole day tomorrow to wipe away this small mistake.

⁂

Golapi turned and lay on her stomach, with her head buried in the dust, like a camel in a desert-storm. She wept silently. The couple of drops of her tears were lost among the millions of drops of water of the rain-drenched night. No trace of which was meant to be anywhere. There was nothing more Jibon could do now. Inwardly he said, I realise you're hurt at my behaviour, but believe me, I did not pay the slightest heed to what that idiot, Jogai, said.

Golapi heaved a deep sigh. Who knows what that sigh meant. Maybe with the sigh, she blew out all the dreams and hopes she had woven so long into the night, unburdening her heart. Now she would sleep. Like on so many nights, after another wasted night, she needed a bit of sleep.

⚬⚘⚬

Jibon did not realise when he fell asleep. When his eyes opened, the storm and rain had stopped, and the reflection of the huge early morning sun floated like a golden dish on the water. All around the shed there was only water and more water. He cast his eyes to look for Golapi. She was nowhere to be seen. The room was empty, it seemed to gape back at him. There was a broken glass bangle where she had been lying. But the girl was not there. Amidst the vast stretch of water all around, the room seemed like an island now. All the access roads lay under water. Where had the girl gone wading through the water? There was no sign of where she may have gone. It seemed everyone would disappear from Jibon's life in this way, leaving behind no trace at all. Why was that?

Jibon gazed at the water. Tiny ripples were created by the soft breeze. But there was no other mark. No marks were ever left behind on water. Were the hearts of women like Golapi also as spotless as water, Jibon wondered.

Who would provide the answers to all these questions to Jibon? Life meant battle. It meant battling continuously with some seen and many unseen enemies who were all around, and standing firm in the battlefield, so as to defeat them.

Life also meant an ocean of experience. One had to advance, filling one's empty sack all the while, with every kind of information, theory and knowledge derived from the bends, crossroads, events and accidents of each day. Life was a journey too. One had to walk one step at a time, endlessly, towards death. Death completed the circle of life that had begun at birth.

Life was an agony, too, for sure. Getting wounded and bloodied by the knocks and blows encountered on the way, carrying a mountain of hurt on your back, like a camel's hump, and tramping the streets of the world—was also another name for life.

21

The Morgue

The person in whose life this great assemblage of journey, battle, pain and experience had occurred—as it happened, his name too was Life, or Jibon. Who was called Chandal Jibon by some, and Bangaal Jibon by some. The latter was because he spoke in the Bangaal or East Bengali language. But he was Chandal for two reasons. The first was because he was prone to anger. And once he was angry, he completely lost his senses. He was also angry most of the time. He became hot-headed on the flimsiest of grounds. Say, on the nearly-empty minibus plying from Rabindra Sadan to Jadavpur, a checked-lungi-clad middle-aged man, with the stench of liquor on his breath, was continuously bumping into a girl. Like all others passengers, he too ought to have shut his eyes and sat meditating on 'not having seen anything'. But he was unable to do that. He stepped up to the man and pushed him aside—'Move, move away, or else I'll rid you of your intoxication with one slap.' The lungi-clad Hindi-speaker was compelled to get off. But he did not go away; he stood on the pavement, flashed a razor and heaped abuse for a while. Hearing that, Chandal Jibon became enraged and was about to get off the bus with the intention of fighting. But the girl stopped him. 'Don't go! They're scoundrels, you can't fight them!'

There were countless such incidents in Jibon's life. Which were all the acts of an angry or thick-headed fool. In the shastras, it had been said that anger was 'chandal'. For that reason, it was his name.

The other reason was that under the chaturvarna, or 'four-caste', system of Hindu religion and society, Jibon belonged to the Namasudra community, which was one step below the sudras. One doesn't really know why, but until the year 1911, the high-caste folk used to call them 'chandal'. Most Namasudras, if reminded that they were once called chandal, felt deeply pained. They shrivelled up. They felt humiliated. The only exception was this Jibon. He was proud to call himself a chandal. I am the Jibon whom people earlier called chandal! And I have no pity at all for anyone who commits injustice!

It was a biological fact that the contents of every person's brain was different, and so each person's decision-making and analysis, their definitions or conceptions of justice and injustice, too, were all different. Because of which, whatever Jibon did, thinking it was merely fair, was often considered by many to be against the law, or anti-social. They did not see him as a social worker or a friend of the people. Rather, they viewed him as an anti-social scoundrel, a hoodlum.

There was another Jibon like this Jibon in the Jadavpur station locality. There were so many words for such a concurrence. Dummy, duplicate, clone, double, twin ... Although both of them looked the same, the two of them were different people, and they also thought and acted differently in some respects. Even if the two Jibons actually lived in the same station precincts, and even if sometimes there were differences of opinion between them—until now they had never been so opposed to each other that one of them annihilated the other. Like it hadn't happened between Balak-da from Loharpara and Balak-da from Santoshpur. Or between Kana

Ajit from Baghajatin and Kana Ajit from Kayastha Para. Or Joga of Bijoygarh and another Joga from near the timber warehouse. In the same way that the two Balaks, the two Jogas, and the two one-eyed Ajits were two persons despite subscribing to the same ideology and being fellow-travellers along the same path, the two Jibons too carried on with their own personal decisions, thinking, outlook and preferences, and were living in more or less peaceful coexistence in the same station. The two Jibons existed within one and the same physical body.

The Jibon who had spoken once again in the Bangaal language just this afternoon, and had also attached 'Chandal' before his name, came and sat in the shade-shrouded semi-jungle near the Hundred-Bed ward building and the hospital canteen in the TB Hospital compound. He wasn't alone, Naru too was with him, because Srimati was coming. After roaming around the other day, the three of them had of course returned to their respective addresses. Who knows what the others thought after that, but Jibon had felt that his presence had been completely pointless. And useless. But the very next day, he had roamed around with them once again, like before, for no reason at all, and also again the following day. It was as if he had become addicted to wasting his time doing nothing. There was no storyline. There was no specific side, no seat to sit on. No ground to stand upon! Only walking, and laughing, and moving on. Which seemed to Jibon to be without reason. Naru liked Srimati. Any reason or action was all his. Jibon was the third one there.

Roaming around like this one day, they had gone to the Baro Bhooter Mela, 'Carnival of Ghosts' fair, in the field beside Srinath Colony. They had taken a ride on the giant wheel, eaten papad, and while returning, when they were right in the middle of Lalu Kaka's field, Naru had asked Srimati, 'Tell me, Srimati, whom do you prefer between the two of us? Look, I want to see you happy. Even if you like Jibon, tell me! I won't mind at all. But you have to choose one of us today. So tell me whom you like!'

As soon as Naru finished speaking, Jibon said, 'But I have something to say …'

Naru knew what Jibon might say. He interrupted him. 'You have nothing to say now. It's Srimati who must speak first. Didn't you say the other day that you'd give your heart and soul to do whatever's best for Srimati? Then what more's there for you to say now? Srimati should know what's best for her better than you. Tell us, Srimati!'

Srimati had to make the final decision. But even today, after a-year-and-a-half of acquaintance, she wasn't able to make up her mind. Jibon was in good health, he was brave, and had hundred-rupee notes in his pocket. But Naru was hard working, honest and wonderfully mirthful. One could say his laughter was worth a thousand rupees. But he gambled a lot on cards. He blew up all his earnings on that. Jibon did not gamble, but he drank sometimes. Taking everything into account, both of them were almost the same on the scale of good and bad. And both of them loved Srimati dearly. Whom should she leave, and whom should she embrace? Whichever hand one cut off, the pain would be hers. Having gone through such an inner examination, Srimati realised she had the same weakness for both of them. A problem which had no solution. And so, after thinking for a long time about Naru's question, she finally said, 'I like both of you!'

'You can't say that. If you have to get married and set up home, you have to choose one person. Either Jibon or me.'

'I won't get married.'

'Then what will you do?'

'The three of us will live together. You and Jibon will go out to work and bring back provisions from the market. I'll stay at home and cook. And I'll feed you when you return home. Tell me, won't that be fun?'

'Yeah, it'll be fun! People will show you the fun! We can't live like that.'

'Why not? Why can't we?'

'I can't explain that to you. You have to be the wife of either one of us. Look, that's the rule of society.'

Srimati said, 'But how can that be? I want both of you. I like both of you. How can I make one person happy and leave the other to weep?'

But it seemed as if Naru could not be at peace until he got the answer to his question. As if his very life and death hinged upon this question. But Jibon was unmoved. He did not want to think about this subject too much. Once before, someone had wanted to attach her life to Jibon. What a heart-rending plea there had been in her eyes. What a turmoil there had been in her heart and soul to give herself away entirely and unconditionally. But after waiting patiently, she finally went away empty-handed. Her memory brought a lot of pain, even now. He could never forget her pretty face, darkened by humiliation. He wouldn't be able to find her now. He had no hope or faith that she would return one day. She had crossed over to the other side of a very difficult trial. The sky turns red before the sun rises. But there was only dense darkness enveloping Jibon's sky. He was reluctant to tie himself up once again with bonds of pain. But Naru's mind was like a blank sheet of paper. There was no mark, blow, wound, or blood clot there. He wanted to see Srimati happy. That's why he asked her again and again, 'Tell me who you like! Who will you be happy and cheerful with?' It was as if Naru's life and death, the fulfilment of his very life, was hinged to her answer. He wanted to hear the clear utterance in Srimati's own voice. If she made him her husband, Naru would consider himself blessed. If she selected Jibon, he would not be anguished, nor would he be angry. Why would he? He loved Srimati. Naru's own happiness lay in her well-being. But Srimati had to say that herself. And it could not be deferred.

After stifling her laughter for long, Srimati burst out laughing and finally said, 'If I must get married, then I'll marry both of you. Or else I won't marry anyone.'

Naru said, 'You crazy girl, you can't do that!'

'Why can't I do that,' asked Srimati. 'How could Draupadi Mashi do it then?'

Naru promptly shot back another question, 'Is Draupadi your mashi?'

Srimati said ingenuously, 'We live in the same basti, one has to call people by some name, that's why I call her mashi. Do you know how many husbands Draupadi Mashi has?' She stuck out her two thumbs, and said, 'Two! 'Rampal Mesho is Bihari, and Dharanidhar Mesho is Oriya. Both of them are watchmen in a factory in Narendrapur. When one of them goes to work, the other stays at home. The two husbands get along very well. On holidays, Mashi sits between the two of them on the cycle-rickshaw, and they go to the cinema. Whoever sees them thinks—a man's two wives never get along with each other, but look how these three get along!'

'What do your mashi's children call them? Are both of them called "baba"?'

'Mashi's had the operation, so how can she have children? Mashi has two sons back in the village, from her earlier husband. They never come to Calcutta. Neither does Mashi bring them over. But she goes to the village sometimes to meet them.'

'Doesn't anyone in the colony say anything?'

'Does anyone have the guts? Poncha from our colony opened his mouth once. Mashi gave him an earful. She said, "What's up, Poncha, so you're grown up enough to be a libertine, are you? Who do you think you're speaking to? What does your own sister do? A new man every month! I've kept whoever I've got, whether he's Bihari or whatever. I didn't leave them, did I? And how many women do you yourself have? Do you think you can do whatever you like, and have five or seven women, just because you're a man? But if a woman has two men, your eyes pop out of your head! Why is that? Set your own house in order and then point out others' faults!"'

After a pause, Srimati continued, 'Everyone in the colony has shit on their bum, no one is pure as milk, so no one can say anything to anyone!'

Naru made a final attempt to make Srimati understand and bring her on track. He said, 'Your mashi's had an operation and so she can't have any children. But you'll have children, won't you? What'll happen then?'

'What'll happen?'

'Who'll they call dad?'

'Why, both of you!'

'How can that be?'

'Big Dad and Little Dad!'

'Who's big and who's little?'

Srimati smiled mischievously. 'There's plenty of time to think about it. I'll tell you after a few days.'

In a voice dripping with despair, Naru retorted, 'So many days have gone by with you saying "I'll tell you" ... Tell me when you'll decide! I think I'll be dead and gone before I hear what you have to say!'

'Don't say such inauspicious things! Why on earth should you die? May your enemies die! Who the hell are you in debt to, that ...'

Srimati stopped midway. A nocturnal bird or creature of prey had swooped down upon the peaceful, blissful nest of some bird in a hollow of the solitary ancient tree that stood, in dense darkness, exactly in the middle of Lalu Kaku's field. The terrified, alarmed mother bird screeched plaintively in mortal terror. Perhaps its chick had been snatched and gobbled up. The night air suddenly turned heavy with the plaintive cries of the mother bird.

It was at least ten-thirty now. There was no light as such on Lalu Kaku's field. Ordinary folk were not brave enough to come to this field so late in the night. But they—and especially Jibon—were not at all ordinary. Those who took over the field once darkness set in, like Tonai, Anjan and Kishan, were all his friends. They knew what kind of creature Jibon was.

They crossed the field slowly, arrived at Raja Subodh Chandra Mallick Road, and after walking along that for a bit, they took the narrow path beside the canal, behind the TB Hospital. They could reach the railside shanty settlement called Taltala through this route.

When they arrived at the bank of the pond in which Babua had fallen after being shot dead, Bangaal Jibon finally spoke after all this time. 'Srimati, I hope your baba won't thrash you for returning home so late.'

'He's not at home tonight. Or else do you think I would ... *ooh, baapre!*' Srimati let out a terrible scream and flung herself into Naru's arms.

'What happened?'
'What happened?'
'A snake!'

At the vibrations of their approaching footsteps, a sleeping water-snake which had coiled itself peacefully across the path, slunk away annoyedly into the fetid canal beside.

June, July and August seemed to pass very quickly. Actually, it wasn't moving any faster than other months; it was just that when times were joyful, time passed by swiftly. It was times of grief that pressed down on one's chest like an unmoving mountain.

On the tenth of June, at the end of the unbearable scorching heat of summer, heavy rain descended on the city. It looked like the whole city would be washed away by the fury of the rain. The streets were flooded because the city's drainage system was not in order. The vehicles ploughing through the flooded streets had the appearance of watercrafts. One morning, floating face-down on the rainwater were the corpses of five youths. Their throats were slit and their hands and feet were tied.

Death was no big deal in the suburbs of Calcutta. It was a daily affair nowadays. It did not rattle people anymore, it did not upset them or make them shiver in horror. But the difference was that, while earlier, one or two people were murdered—now, people died by the dozen. And that was what was a matter of annoyance.

Apparently, all of last night, some people had been racing through the city, screaming threats, while some others were shrieking in terror and running for their lives through the flooded streets. It was five of the latter who were seen floating on the dirty water flooding the city this morning. With single swipes of a knife, those who, even twelve hours ago, were human, who had names too, were left with nothing at all—they had become corpses. They had become mere numbers—one-thousand-eighty-four, one-thousand-eighty-five …

Under government regulations, all unclaimed bodies were subject to a post-mortem examination prior to cremation. The bodies made the rounds of the police stations and hospitals before being piled up on the floor of the morgue in Mominpur. That was where the cutting and slitting and stitching took place.

Among many such dead people—no, they were not exactly people—among the rotten, decomposed pieces and limbs of bodies lying on the floor of the autopsy room, Naru lay nearly naked on his back. He had worn a lungi and a shirt yesterday; the doms had removed all that, and he only had his underwear on now.

Jibon had never seen such an ugly manifestation of the misery of death before. The dead bodies were bloated and decomposed, and the whole place was smelling so foul it made living people vomit. The eyes of some were missing, someone's abdomen was slit, someone's face had been smashed with something heavy, someone's whole body was so badly burnt that it was doubtful whether even their loved ones would be able to recognise it. Someone's only garment was a rag, while some lacked even that. Men and women—altogether, there were twenty or twenty-two corpses, piled up obscenely, one over another. White maggots were bunched around some bodies. Who knows how long ago they had been thrown into the pile. The stench from this place made the whole locality think of hell.

Of course, Naru wasn't decomposed, he was freshly dead. After being admitted to the hospital at ten or half-past-ten last night

night, he had died at dawn, at about four o'clock, and his body had been lying on the cement floor of the morgue since ten in the morning. It would lie like that for some more hours because the doctor had not yet arrived, and also because of a delay in paying the hundred-and-fifty rupees demanded by the doms, who handled the bodies, towards their refreshments. It would be a while before it was taken to the crematorium. All told, about twenty or twenty-five people from the Jadavpur bus-stand crossing, where Naru gambled every night and where he was a rickshaw-puller, had come as pall-bearers to participate in his last rites. There was no one from Naru's family though. None of them knew about Naru's death. And how would they know? Naru himself did not know their whereabouts. So how could anyone inform them? But someone claiming to be Naru's sister had come. She wept tearfully, and asked everyone there whether Naru had any money saved, and if so, who might have it, and how it could be obtained.

Among the twenty or twenty-five pall-bearers were two whose names were Baowa and Bhutto. Of course, they had never been Naru's friends. In keeping with Chanakya's policy of an enemy's friend being an enemy, Naru was their enemy. Nonetheless, they had come because they believed that Naru's death was not really a normal death. This was definitely a pre-planned murder. The name of Beimaan Jibon was at the centre of their suspicion and belief: it was Jibon who had killed Naru, as a result of a love triangle. Jibon was their arch-enemy. Here was an opportunity to witness the end of the enemy. They were unable to keep themselves away from what could potentially be a joyful event for them. And that was why one of them left his illicit liquor den and the other shut the recycling shop where he bought stolen goods, and rushed to the morgue in Mominpur.

☙

Naru's death wasn't such a matter of sorrow to anyone that they were stunned into grief. Or even sat and wept. The pall-bearers talked and laughed loudly. They were laughing about something foolish Naru had done sometime. Poor Naru! There wasn't even a single person whom he could call his own, who would shed real tears for him. The miserable death of a life lived without friends had thrown him with great disaffection on the dirty floor of the autopsy room.

Jibon stood all alone, far away, in a corner. No one said anything to him. Everyone stayed far away from him. Everyone seemed to be pointing an invisible finger at him, sharp as a spear: It's you! You're the one responsible for Naru's plight! You killed him!

The first one to point a filthy finger with a dirty nail, standing in front of the main gate of Bangur Hospital, had been the illicit liquor seller Baowa. 'I know why Naru was killed. I know who killed him. But I won't tell anyone anything now ... Let the postmortem report be out first, and then I'll tell the police everything.'

It was about eight in the morning. Kalua ran the eatery at the bus-stand crossing. He used to stay up at night with Naru to play a couple of hands of cards. The game was called *andar-bahar*, 'inside-outside'. Standing at the Bangur hospital, Kalua suddenly felt the need to smoke a cigarette. He declared in an officious tone, 'It's going to be a while before the body is released. The doctor won't arrive before nine. We can't get the body until the doctor issues the death certificate. Come Baowa, instead of hanging around here uselessly, let's go and have tea and a smoke.'

Baowa wasn't a fool. He knew very well what Kalua meant. He followed Kalua, crossed the main road, and stood somewhat furtively at a tea-shop beside the shops opposite the hospital selling biers and water-pots. Kalua said, 'Tell me, Baowa, what really happened? How come a healthy, robust chap suddenly died? Naru was like a younger brother to me. Tell me whatever you know.'

Baowa sipped his tea, took a deep puff on his No.10 cigarette, blew out a lungful of smoke, and then slowly said, 'Kalua-da, I'll tell you. But please don't tell anyone now. If the fucker realises we know, he'll run away. How can anyone find him once he runs away?

We folks have a home, family, wife and kids. He has nothing in Jadavpur, he sleeps wherever he happens to be at night.'

'Oh, don't worry, I won't tell anyone anything. Tell me without any fear,' Kalua assured Baowa.

'You know Bespati, don't you? Arey, she's the one who sells vegetables in the Jadavpur market. I had been trying to catch that fish for a long time, you know. The bitch just wouldn't swallow the bait. The same old drama, "If your wife finds out she'll thrash me". But after a lot of effort, I finally managed to net her yesterday. So I'd netted her, but where would I go with the *maal*? Where would I lay her down and fuck her? So I finally took her to the Dhakuria lake. You know how desolate it is on the stretch along the rail track at Gobindapur. There's a bit of jungle too there, and besides, it was dark. So I was sitting there, and had just started fondling the *maal* and warming her up—when who do you think I suddenly spotted? I saw Naru and Jibon strolling around beside the lake.'

'Didn't they see you?'

'How could they? We were sitting in the darkness, next to the jungle. They were on the road, under a lamp-post. We could see them, but they couldn't see us.'

'What time was it then?'

'It must have been eight or nine in the evening. I didn't look at my watch, I'm guessing.'

Kalua made a mental calculation. If Jibon and Naru had been strolling at the lakeside at eight or nine o' clock, and if Naru was taken to the hospital at about ten-thirty at night, then what was it that happened in the hour or hour-and-a-half in between, that turned the fully-alive Naru into a corpse?

He asked, 'What happened after that? What else did you see?'

'I didn't see anything else. They walked ahead. I got the news when I returned to Jadavpur station at night ... Tell me, Kalua-da, how can a person who was walking around two hours ago, who wasn't suffering from any kind of ailment and was hale and hearty, suddenly die? Do you know what I think? No, I don't just think so, I'm certain—it's Jibon who murdered Naru.'

It wasn't as if such a suspicion had not entered Kalua's mind. Why just him, everyone had the same notion. But the person they suspected had 'Chandal' before his name, and so, no one had the guts to say it openly. Baowa was saying so now, he did have guts.

Without revealing his own thoughts to Baowa, and with the intention of getting him to reveal whatever he knew, Kalua pretended to be shocked. 'What are you saying?'

'I've trusted you and told you what I saw, please don't tell anyone ...'

'It's all right, I won't tell anyone.'

'But whatever I'm telling you is the truth. You'll know as soon as the post-mortem report arrives.'

'Rubbish! It's all nonsense. Why would Jibon kill him? They were good friends. They never even had a petty quarrel. Jibon has fed Naru at least fifty times in my eatery.'

'Oh, all that's only on the surface. You know, Kalua-da, all of you have been taken in by appearances. None of you know anything. They were sworn enemies inwardly. I know everything. Being together, staying together, eating together—was only for show.'

'But why?'

'What do you mean why?'

'Why kill Naru?'

'Why else? For a girl! Is that anything new? It's been happening from the days of the Ramayana and Mahabharata. Can one ever put a number to the murders that have been committed because of a girl?'

Baowa took a final puff on the No. 10 stub, flicked the butt far away, and then continued. 'Do you know Srimati, Amrito's daughter, who lives in Taltala? Jibon and Naru were both having an affair with her since a long time. The girl's a looker. The bitch could be Helen's younger sister! There was a lot of animosity between them about who would climb over the other's head and get her. *Ek*

Phool Do Mali—that's exactly how it was!' Baowa tittered and then said, 'If it's *Ek Phool Do Mali* then there has to be hustle!'

Kalua was keen to know the details of this juicy tale. 'When they were strolling near the lake, was the girl, what did you say her name was, with them?'

'I didn't look so closely then. I don't think she was there. Do you think Jibon is so foolish that he'll murder Naru in front of a witness? I think he planned to kill Naru and that's why he took him to the lake. There's no one outside even on the main streets nowadays once it's evening, and this was the desolate Dhakuria lake! He did his job there ... Wasn't Jibon with the Naxalites in Palpara earlier? Murder is child's play for him!'

The colour of Kalua's skin was like a buffalo's, and he was fat. But his mind was sharp. He thought for a long time about what Baowa had said. If it was true, that would provide a simple, rational and adequate explanation for Naru's sudden death. Or else everything was vague, and so now, rather than being mere suspicion, the matter was a proven truth, based on supporting documentary evidence. After all, even the court had to heed Baowa's testimony.

It happens, such things happen often. For age after age, so many wars had been fought, there had been so much bloodshed, so much of destruction, death and disaster, all for possessing and enjoying the female body. One knew that just by watching jatras and films, and by reading the daily newspaper. Kalua was a great fan of jatra and cinema. He had seen the jatra performance *Sonai Dikhi* thrice and the film *Naya Daur* twice. *Baapre!* What calamities, all because of a girl!

Baowa continued, 'Do you know what I think, Kalua-da? I think Jibon hit him suddenly from behind with something heavy—something big like a crowbar, or maybe even a hammer—yes, it must have been a hammer. If he had been carrying a rod or crowbar, there was the risk of Naru seeing it. A hammer is small, easy to conceal. He hit him hard on his head from behind. He chose the spot well—and with just one blow ... what do you think?'

Kalua lit another cigarette. He felt giddy. There was a veritable storm of thoughts in his head. How the world had changed! Men were dying like dogs or goats everywhere. Brother killing brother, son killing father, father killing son, friend killing friend, party members killing other party members ... Corpses and more corpses everywhere. This was a very difficult time indeed. Who could one trust in such times ... No! There were no more people in this world whom one could trust. Everyone was dishonest, everyone was a murderer, a butcher, an executioner! O Jibon, alas Jibon! How easily you took away the life of the one who until yesterday was your dearest friend! Why did you do that? For a girl? A girl—when one could get four of them for a rupee, with a fifth thrown in free! Just imagine!

Standing afar, observing the mood all around, Jibon had surmised that they were not willing to accept Naru's death as a normal one. It wouldn't have been easy for anyone to accept how it had really happened. It was a murderous, destructive time now. Suspicion was perfectly natural. After all, was Jibon himself being able to accept Naru's death quietly? How could it be that the person who had been hale and hearty until yesterday, the one with whom so many plans were made and so many webs of dreams spun, was no longer there now?

It struck Jibon once again now that human life was utterly weightless, small and meaningless ... When a tree was uprooted in a storm, the earth trembled at its fall. But humans fell dead in sheer silence. Jibon tried to recall once more what exactly had happened yesterday—which incident was it that had invited another incident, which incident was it that wouldn't have been possible unless a preceding incident had taken place ...

Baowa had told whatever he knew to his best friend, Bhutto. And so, a jubilant Bhutto had dropped all his work, and after a visit to the hospital, headed straight for the morgue in Mominpur. It was a joyful day today. An arch-enemy of theirs would meet his end. Even if he wasn't hanged, who could stop him from getting life imprisonment? A lot of fine people were in deep waters trying to deal with a case under Section 302 / 34 of the Indian Penal Code, and this Jibon was only a pavement dweller after all.

❦

Yesterday. It was noon then. There had been a spell of rain a little while ago. Jibon and Naru had washed their shirts and lungis at the pond in the TB Hospital precincts, using 501 soap, and then bathed. After that they ate egg curry and rice to their fill at Chhechan's eatery, and came to the verandah of the Hundred-Bed ward. It was quite secluded there. There were no visitors at this time. All the patients were asleep in their beds. Jibon and Naru weren't sleepy. They were waiting. When would the crazy girl come, flitting about like a bird? This place was desolate everyday these days. Birds dozed on the branches of trees and tired cows sat under the trees and chewed cud. Srimati came to meet Naru and Jibon everyday, at exactly this time, escaping her devilish father's clutches. Her childish words strung garlands of adult thoughts. A few days ago, she had said a sister was born. Apparently she looked just like her.

Being true to his form, Naru had teased her by saying, 'So your dad's like, what do they say, *angul phule kolagachh*—gotten rich overnight—isn't it, Srimati? He's already got what he could by selling you, now it's a done deal for him to sell the next one and booze for free for some more days.'

'No, my dear, he won't do that. After all, he gave birth to that one.' Twisting her lip, Srimati had said, 'He's buying Horlicks for his own daughter. And if I ask for a rupee, he asks, "Does money grow on trees?"'

Srimati had arrived somewhat later than usual yesterday. And after she came, she was silent. There was no smile on her face, she seemed listless. In a choked voice, she said tearfully, 'I can't come to see you any more.'

'What happened?' Naru asked ardently. 'Why are you like this today? Did your dad beat you up?'

Srimati began to cry. She said, 'He beats me almost everyday. I don't tell you people. What's the point in telling you, it'll upset you for no reason. After all, he's not just anyone, he's my dad. I think the son of a bitch has lost his head after all his drinking. He wants to sell me off so that he can settle his debts. Apparently, if he gets me married right now, they're willing to pay him another thousand. As it is, he's angry with me because I'm not consenting, and besides, someone's told him I keep meeting the two of you. So, for those two reasons ...'

'He hit you?'

A stab of anguish pierced Jibon's chest, his breathing became laboured. The palms of his hands turned sweaty. A wild, untamable buffalo bellowed in his mind. He clenched his sweaty hands in rage. He wanted to do something just now, something he shouldn't do. What kind of father was he? Was he a father or a butcher? There would be no sin in cutting up the son of a pig and throwing him on the rail track.

Naru tried to calm Jibon. 'Aeyi Beimaan, keep your head cool! Anything you do hot-headedly will be wrong.'

'How can I remain calm,' protested Jibon. 'Even a butcher doesn't slaughter his own children.'

'Am I his own child,' Srimati said sorrowfully. 'He's got his own one now, I'll see what he does to that one.'

Although Jibon did not want it, the dynamite of his rage exploded. Which even Srimati was shocked to hear. 'Just tell me to go Naru ... I'll cut the son of a bastard and go to prison! Jatadhari Guru told me that I have the prison line on my palm. Let me go and spend a few years there!'

'Nothing's to be gained by that!' Naru retorted. 'Forget all that. Think of something so that the snake dies and the stick has no clue ...'

Turning towards Srimati after that, Naru said, 'You tell us what you want to do!'

'What can I say and what am I to do?' In a hopeless tone she said, 'I don't have any other option, re. I must either agree to getting married, or I'll have to throw myself on the railtrack ...'

'No! Don't say a word about dying!' said Naru. 'Why should you die? Can't you see the people all around, how so many people are struggling to survive? All of them hope their suffering will come to an end one day, and that they will know good times. Don't lose faith, your good times will also come one day. But if you die—everything will be finished.'

'It's my father who's my enemy. Tell me, how can I survive? He's going to send me off to Bihar, or who knows where ... that's worse than dying.'

The shadows of the trees kept moving. A slice of sunlight fell on Srimati's face through a gap between the leaves. The impression of the five fingers of a hand was visible on her cheek.

After a while, Naru said, 'Don't be afraid, Srimati. Aren't the two of us there? As long as we're alive, no one can harm you. Go home and lie low for now. Come at this time tomorrow, we'll arrange something or the other by then.'

'What will you do?'

'We'll take you and go away.'

'Where to? Where will you keep me if you take me away? If my dad finds out where you've taken me, he'll drag me back by my hair. The two of you will be in danger if he informs the police.'

'That's for us to worry about. Be ready to leave when you come tomorrow. You don't have to live with that devil anymore.'

'Do you really mean that?'

'Do you think I'm lying?'

'Then I'll come tomorrow.'

'Do that!'

After Srimati left, Naru said to Jibon, 'There's no time to waste. Let's go!'

'Where to?'

'Where else? To find a room! Don't we need a room where we can keep her? We have to find a place to rent and take it today.'

'Will we be able to find a place in such a short time?'

'We have to find it! Come on! Isn't it said that if you search, you can find even a needle in a haystack? So why won't we find a room?'

22

The Accident

Jibon and Naru set out to find a room at a cheap rent. Such rooms were available only in the squatter settlements of the poor along the canal or the railway line. But what misfortune! Naru had hoped he would easily find a room in some squatter settlement or the other, but after they went around Kasba, Rathtala and Ramlal Bazaar, where thousands of labouring folk, rickshaw-pullers and handcart-pullers lived, he realised it wasn't so simple. There were plenty of reasons for not finding such a room. But the principal reason was that two youths, who at the very first glance did not exactly appear to be very decent, who were apparently rickshaw-pullers, wanted to rent the room. Let them take it. But the problem was that another person would also stay with them, and it was a girl. Who wasn't their mother or sister or aunt or anyone. So it was problematic, to say the least. The times were terrible nowadays. There was danger lurking at every step in such times. Would anyone invite trouble onto themselves? The rising mastaans of the neighbourhood, or the police from the local police station, or the girl's father or brother—who could say where the danger would come from! 'No, baba, please excuse me. To hell with the rent, I don't want any trouble. No, there's no room available!'

That's why even after finding a room for twenty rupees a month at the canalside in Rajdanga, they were finally unable to get it. Although it was on the bank of a canal and the land belonged to the West Bengal government, nevertheless, each of the occupants here owned two or three rooms. The owner Naru and Jibon had approached lived in one of them with his family, and rented out the others for twenty rupees a month. Naru and Jibon had gone to meet him after hearing about the place from a rickshaw-puller they knew. 'We heard that you have a room available?'

'I do.' The houseowner had long hair, and his eyes were bloodshot. 'Two on the cot, and two under. It's a large room, big enough for four people. The rent is only twenty-five rupees. But if it isn't paid by the tenth of the month, I'll put a lock on the door. A month's rent in advance as a deposit. But you can't bring anyone here—no family, friends or acquaintances. You can drink if you like, there's no restriction on that, but if there's any shouting or commotion, you have to leave the next day. What more do you want to know?'

'No, nothing else,' Naru said cheerfully, 'I'll take your room.'

'When will you come?'

'Tomorrow evening.'

'Five rupees for the six days of this month and twenty-five for the deposit of a month's rent. Will you pay me now or tomorrow?'

Naru thought for a moment and then replied, 'I'll pay you tomorrow morning.'

'When in the morning? At what time?'

'Say, at about eight? I'll buy a stove and some other stuff and keep it here.'

'You haven't told me how many of you are there?'

'Three. Me, my friend here, and a girl.'

'A girl!' The houseowner's eyes widened. 'The one who'll stay with you is a girl? Not anyone's wife?'

'No, I mean, not a wife, I mean, not yet. Once she's married, she'll be a wife. The marriage couldn't take place yet because a room wasn't being found. Now that we've found one, we can go to Kalighat one day ...'

'Who will she marry?'

And that was where, in their hurry, they made a terrible mistake. Naru pointed towards Jibon, while Jibon pointed towards Naru. And both of them said, 'Him, he'll be getting married.' Who knows what the houseowner surmised or didn't from that, but he responded angrily—'There's no room!'

'Please hear me out. Please try to understand that we are two friends who love the same girl. She too loves both of us. As long as any one of us puts sindoor on her forehead, there's no problem, right? What do you say?'

The houseowner replied, 'I've fathered as many as five daughters. It's not for nothing that the hair on my head is grey. You won't get any room for all that here. This isn't Ghutiari Sharif or Diamond Harbour, where such things happen. This is a neighbourhood of householders, do you get that!'

After failing to find a place in Rajdanga, they walked and walked in search of shelter, and reached Gobindapur via Kasba. They lacked the means to take a nice room on rent. And so, the only room they could find had to be a decrepit one, with walls of matting. But they were crazed by hurry now, they had to find it by any means whatsoever, and they had to find it today. Srimati would come tomorrow afternoon.

The girl had run away in order to survive, with a skyful of hope in her bosom, and appeared on the doorway of the difficult and deceived lives of two unfortunate souls named Naru and Jibon. Her laughter, her talk, her vanity and pride were all as fresh as the fluttering breeze. Which now depended on the life and death of the trust and breath of the two unfortunate youths. If she was excluded, a lifelong void and misery would be created, and there was nothing at all with which that gap or chicanery could be filled or overcome. That was why they could not lose her. Not at all. It was their solemn duty to hold on to this precious treasure at any price or condition.

They searched hard for a small room with a low rent in every nook of the railside settlement at Gobindapur. But their appearance and demeanour, and the unreasonableness of what they said, did not escape experienced eyes.

They roamed around frantically as afternoon turned into evening. In a tone of despair, Naru said, 'There's no point in searching any more today. We'll look in Garia and Sonarpur tomorrow. There should be plenty of rooms available there. Many of the rickshaw-pullers we know live there.'

'The outcome will be the same however many rooms there might be. There's no way anyone will give us a place,' Jibon said with annoyance. 'If it was a babu neighbourhood or the prostitutes' district, you could get a place if you paid more money. They don't care who lives with whom. But in our poor neighbourhoods, there are a hundred problems.'

Realising the essence of what Jibon was saying, Naru said thoughtfully, 'So what's the option now? Unless we find a room ...'

'There is an option.'

'What's that?'

'Marrying Srimati and making her a wife. After that, all the houseowners will willingly give us a room.'

'So do that then.'

Both Jibon and Naru fell into deep thought now. If Srimati had to become a wife, one of the two had to be the husband. Who would that be? After all, a woman could not have two husbands. That was against social norms. What Draupadi had done in the Taltala slum could not be done elsewhere. But Srimati wasn't at all declaring whom she liked. However many times she was asked, her answer was the same—'I like both of you'.

After some time, in a voice that was weary with doubt, Jibon said, 'If Srimati selects you, everything will be taken care of, there won't be any more problems. If she stubbornly insists on marrying me, then that will make things very difficult.'

'Why, what difficulty? In what way is the girl any worse than you?'

'I didn't say she was worse, but ...'

'But what?'

After some thought, Jibon said, 'Given my situation, I shouldn't be taking on such a burden on my shoulders. First of all, I don't have any stable livelihood. I'm surrounded by enemies. Even if I want to drive a rickshaw like you, I can't. Besides, there's no certainty that I won't land in jail or get killed.'

Naru listened closely to Jibon and then said, 'You don't have to worry about that now. Let her come tomorrow. Let's explain everything to her. What if, even after hearing everything, she wants to make you her husband? I don't think she'll do that. If you think about it, I love her more than you do. Love melts girls' hearts. Let's see what happens.'

Tomorrow meant time, tomorrow meant an unknown, unseen, unimagined world on the other side of a curtain of terrifying darkness. Neither of them knew the news that tomorrow was waiting to deliver them.

Now it was time for them to head back towards the Jadavpur station. Two pairs of crestfallen, dejected and defeated feet advanced in that direction. The hopes and plans that had been budding in their hearts all this while had vanished. Everything had to be begun anew, and in a new way, tomorrow.

Jibon wanted to walk along the railway line to Dhakuria, climb up to the bridge, and then walk along the main road to the station. But Naru said, 'Aeyi, Jibon, I don't feel good, re. Come, let's go and sit for a while by the lake. Maybe the breeze will cheer me up a bit. We don't have any work right now. We can leave after about an hour.'

Dhakuria Lake. A history of hundreds and thousands of broken and joined hearts carpeted every blade of grass of these grounds. There were lots of couples of united bodies and hearts seated hand-in-hand on the grass now. Peanut shells were being cracked amidst the buzz of webs of dreams being spun by humble folk. A mound of empty clay teacups grew. Whatever was pleasurable was as good as elixir. In a corner of that carnival of pleasure, Naru and Jibon sat like still idols. They had nothing to talk about, nothing to dream about, no reason to laugh either. All around them was the tortuous darkness of a mysterious black night. After a long time, in an emotional and mysterious voice that seemed to emanate from the other side of life, Naru had said, 'Let's go now.'

In hindsight, it seemed to Jibon that in Naru's expression 'let's go now', there lay a cruel, purposeful illumination. No one knew then, after he said they should leave, about the outcome towards which Naru's feet advanced. Perhaps some anonymous bird that had built its nest on a branch of a tree within the darkness had sensed that. For it had let out a terrible screech, *chaen-chaen,* at that very moment.

The two of them walked through the lakeside grounds and reached the Panchanantala bus-stop at the northern end of the Dhakuria bridge. They planned to hop on to a bus and get off at the Jadavpur crossing. And walk from there to the Jadavpur station. Eat at Chhechan's eatery and then go to sleep. But that didn't happen.

⊱⊰

Jibon still vividly remembered every moment. One bus after another arrived, but they were all terribly crowded. There wasn't space even to plant one's foot on the footboard of the bus. Who knows why, but Naru suddenly became impatient. He ran and held on to the rod at the front entrance of a crowded, moving bus and hung on. He shouted out to Jibon—'Get on quickly!'

Jibon knew how to get onto a moving bus. He boarded it, or rather one should say he hung on to the grille on the window beside the rear entrance. The grip of his hand was very strong; the crowd wasn't strong enough to break that grip and push him off. But Naru's sweaty hand slipped. He fell from the moving bus. The back of his head hit the concrete slab at the edge of the pavement along the Dhakuria bridge. There was a sound like an earthen pot being smashed. Within moments, Naru lost consciousness and went limp.

'Aeyi, stop the bus!'

By the time the speeding bus came to a halt, it had reached the next bus-stop. But Jibon had jumped off the bus and picked Naru up. He splashed water on his face and head from a pedestrian's water-bottle. But Naru did not return to his senses.

Jibon hadn't been able to tell anyone about what happened. Where did he get the chance to? All by himself, he had got into a cycle-rickshaw and taken Naru to the emergency ward at Bangur Hospital in Tollygunge. Jibon had spent the whole night sitting there. But bad news never remains suppressed. It flies in the wind. The news from Bangur Hospital spread wings and reached Jadavpur. People from the Jadavpur station and bus-stop crossing arrived there in a group. Some of them were distressed on account of Naru, and some were eager to see Jibon in dire straits.

Now it seemed everyone's suspicion-laden gazes was piercing Jibon. They thought this was clearly not just a road accident. It was the end result of Jibon's artful plan to remove the hurdle on his way. Which was the inevitable outcome of a love triangle.

Those who had come to accompany the dead body to the crematorium now split up into small groups, and were having whispered conversations among themselves. They were also somewhat afraid that if they spoke loudly and Jibon heard them, they could become embroiled in some hassle. After all, the man was not at all what one could call 'decent'. One had heard that he had killed some people earlier too.

One person who was unconvinced said, 'From what you're saying, I gathered that in order to get the girl, what's her name, Jibon took Naru under some pretext to the lake, took him to a dark spot, and hit him on the head with a crowbar, or stone, or something, and killed him. If that's what happened, then he should have left the body there and fled. But instead of doing that, why did Jibon bring Naru to the hospital? Bhai, I can't think of any explanation for that.'

Another person responded, 'What's that spider's web you're spinning? You see so many films and you don't know about this?

What's the story made up by Jibon? That Naru fell off the bus. After that he took him to the hospital, maybe spent ten or twenty rupees buying medicines, sat there with a sad face, maybe he cried a bit when required. So would anyone be able to suspect that it was he who killed Naru?'

Another person said, 'The way he says Naru fell off the bus—no one dies if they fall like that. If a vehicle had run over his head or something, that would be different. There's no cut or breakage, only some swelling in the head. I think it wasn't a crowbar or anything, but some poison in the food. They would have found out if they tested the vomit.'

Jibon could not remain standing there. All around him was a zone of invisible suspicion. Although no one would say anything to his face, the look in everyone's eyes were like waves of doubt, disbelief, hatred and terror lapping the room, like a carpet of worms or maggots. Jibon felt compelled to stand as far away as possible. He moved away on the pretext of going to drink tea. Almost at once, Kalua turned towards Baowa, winked at him, and said, 'Follow him. See that he doesn't give us the slip and get away.'

As Jibon turned around after asking for a cup of tea, he found Amal standing beside him. This was the same Amal whom the people from Laskarpara beat up for no fault of his with their cricket bats and stumps. And Jibon was the only person who had stood up to protect him, grabbing Chhechan Sahu's fish-cutting bonti and risking his own life. That was a long time ago. Times were very different now. Who knows why, but Jibon thought that perhaps Amal too had joined the opposite camp. Perhaps he had come and stood near Jibon only in order to keep a watch over him.

He said rudely, 'What's up, Amal? Why are you hovering around me?'

Amal said, 'I'm keeping a watch over you.'

'Why?'

Amal was no longer the fifteen- or sixteen-year-old boy, he was a seventeen-year-old youth now. He said, 'You need someone to stand beside you at this time. After all, I can fathom at least something of the danger you are in. Neither Ganesh-da nor Gopal-da are here, but I'm here. You had jumped into the fire for me one day. If required, today I'll jump!'

Young Amal's words warmed Jibon's heart. He had heard from someone somewhere that those who came and stood beside someone at a time of danger in the royal court and in the crematorium, were the ones who were real friends. Now Jibon's life was in danger. The post-mortem report—a small error in it on the part of the doctor could destroy him. Whoever took Jibon's side then would also be in danger.

After a while, Amal said, 'Although I shouldn't say this, but can I tell you something, Jibon-da?'

'Tell me.'

'You won't mind, will you?'

'If it's not something to mind, then why would I?'

Looking all around once, Amal said, 'I know how much you loved Naru. Let people say what they like, but I don't believe that you could kill him. But the situation is not in your favour now. Baowa is inciting people. He wants to avenge his old grudge against you. People are like mad dogs nowadays. You never know what someone might do any time. And that's why I say, for your own good you should go away for now. I'm here, I'll get the body cremated.'

'What are you saying, Amal! Do you think I'll leave Naru at the final moment and run away for fear of false accusations?'

In a final bid to convince Jibon, Amal said, 'It's only human to make a mistake. The one who does the post-mortem is also only human. Suppose he somehow submits a wrong report? A huge calamity will then strike you. Don't you remember the incident in Selimpur?'

A girl used to work in a babu's house in Selimpur. The people in the house had strangled her to death and hung her by a sari from the fan. That murder was stated to be suicide in the post-mortem report.

Amal said, 'If murder can be made into suicide, then it's not difficult for an accident to be made into a murder.'

Jibon replied, 'Whatever happens will happen. Let me also wait and see what finally happens. But if something like that happens, you'll get dragged into this if you support me.'

With fierce determination in his voice, Amal said, 'One day, my life was saved because of you, so it's fine if it's lost for you.'

After a while, Jibon and Amal saw the entire group of seventeen-, eighteen-, nineteen-, twenty-year-old boys, about whom people said—thrashed by his mother, driven out by his father, eats in eateries and sleeps on the pavement. Whose names did not appear in the voters' list or in the list of ration-card holders, or in the census records. Deprived of citizens' rights, surviving and growing up like weeds—Gona, Ganesh, Kaliya, Boro Gopal, Kalo Gopal, Bheem, Kalachand, all of them arrived and surrounded him. Jibon realised that no conspiracy of Baowa and Kalua could penetrate this human armour and reach him. They had come to stand up against any danger whatsoever and protect their Jibon-da.

Jibon enquired, 'Do you guys have some money? Give me whatever you have. We'll need to pay twenty rupees to the doms to get Naru's body. I don't have that much money.'

Gona replied, 'As soon as we got the news, we collected money. We've raised a hundred and eighty rupees.'

Turning towards Ganesh and Boro Gopal, Jibon said, 'If the doctor's here, go and see if they'll release Naru's body now. Who knows how much we'll have to pay the doms who do the autopsy. We'll pay whatever is required. Make sure Baowa and Kalua don't get a chance to show their compassion.'

After that, Naru's body was taken in a three-wheel van-rickshaw from the hospital to the morgue in Mominpur, and by the time it was cut and bared and then stitched up, five or six hours had passed. The eager pallbearers were all annoyed now. It was already evening by the time all the formalities were completed.

Kalua went up to the doctor responsible for the post-mortem, who had a register under his arm. 'How did the boy die, saar? He was in good health. Could you detect anything?'

The doctor replied, 'Brain haemorrhage, death because of a head injury.'

Looking in the direction of Kalua, Baowa blinked his eyes. 'So what do you think that means? Didn't I tell you then that it must have been a rod or something like that, do you believe me now? But why haven't the police arrived? Why haven't they arrested Jibon? The fucking police haven't filed any complaint. It's clear they must have extracted a good amount of money from Jibon. I think he must have gone and paid off the police station last night itself. The police are not friends of anyone. They vote for the one who pays them, so they've voted for Jibon. Poor Naru doesn't have anyone of his own, so there's no one to take up and pursue the matter. If there had been anyone like that, would Jibon have gone scot-free today? He would have been arrested at once, and then, either the noose, or life imprisonment. That wouldn't have been wrong at all. The bastard has got away!'

'What's the point of sitting around uselessly here now? We know what's happened.' Baowa called out, 'Aeyi Bhutto, let's go, a waste of a day. Kalua-da, we're leaving.'

'Wait, I'm coming too.'

After Kalua left, everyone left one by one. The whole joy of cremating a body had been turned to ashes. Only Jibon and his companions, a band of vagabonds, stayed back.

※

When they reached Jadavpur Station after cremating Naru in the electric crematorium in Kalighat, it was quite late in the evening, about nine or nine-thirty. None of them had bathed or eaten all day. Jibon took a long bath, using soap, at the lake in Garfa. And then in a melancholy state of mind, Jibon came and sat on the platform erected around the base of the banyan tree at the rickshaw-stand outside the station. Everything around seemed terribly desolate to him.

Jibon felt joyless and companionless. There was an emptiness inside him which could never be filled up by anyone else. The one who had filled that had suddenly gone, without any advance intimation. So many days spent together, so many things said, so many songs, so much laughter, so many quarrels, so much of bickering. All those were mere memories now. Naru had entered Jibon's life like a sudden storm on an imperilled, dark, new moon night. Nestling him like a bird chick in his breast, he had helped him cross terrifying dark times. And with the passing of the night, he had disappeared without a word. No sign of him remained any more. Jibon was truly unfortunate. Why was it whoever he formed deep and close friendships with, got lost in the twists and turns of life's road? Maran, Raja, Naru—one by one, all of them had gone away, each one leaving behind the scar of a wound in his heart.

Jibon was alone now, completely alone. Gona, Ganesh, Kaliya, Boro Gopal, Kalo Gopal, Jatadhari guru—none of them were with him. But even when they were there, were they really one with him? Each one had his own life, own problems, own reality, feelings, thoughts and expressions. Even if they lived together in the same place, each one was of a different temperament. To the extent that the vagabond Jibon, and his spitting image, Bangaal Jibon, weren't identical and undivided either. And so, there was no one who could share Jibon's anguish. He sat in one corner now, his heart burdened with tears like a skyful of rain.

Suddenly he spotted Srimati. She was no longer a human figure of flesh and blood; she was like a disorderly, alarmed picture of grief. Her eyes were swollen and red from weeping. Her hair was dishevelled and flying wildly in the breeze. Her whole body was trembling with unbearable suffering. Appearing in front of Jibon, she looked at him for a few moments and then again burst into tears. 'What have you done? Is that what you had in mind? You went and killed Naru?'

Jibon felt as if the earth beneath his feet had split open in an atomic explosion and he was being sucked into the hot bottomless pit of lava. There was no light there, no air, no relief, no life.

Like someone who was sick with poison, Srimati said in a voice distorted with agony, 'Baowa-da told me everything. What did you think? That by killing Naru, you'll have me all to yourself? Wrong, you were wrong, re Beimaan! What's the value of or need for a mirror for one who's blind? I used to love you because of Naru. Without Naru, you're not worth the slightest bit to me. Instead of taking the hand of a murderous butcher like you, it's a million times better for me to tie a rope around my neck and die.'

Jibon was trembling now. He felt as if he couldn't breathe. A soul caught in a death-trap cried out—'You too! You too think ...?'

Had Jibon plugged his ears with his fingers to defend himself against the hateful words that shot towards him like cannon balls? Did he shut the lids of his eyes like a crow to protect himself from the terrifying slight? Or had he lost all his senses for a little while? When he regained his sight and his audition, he saw that he was completely alone. There was no living being anywhere near him. There was only an all-encompassing darkness, black as pitch. The darkness that had pervaded the entire universe millions and billions of years before the birth of the sun! Rocked by buoyant waves in that great ocean of darkness, a life floated on, gathering the curses of the universe from the moment of birth.

The next day, Amal arrived with the news. 'Srimati Didi got married last night. Her husband is Bihari, he's very good looking. Apparently he has a hundred and fifty bighas of agricultural land in the village, and a two-storeyed pukka house. They're leaving now. They'll take the train to Bihar from Howrah.'

Amal had thought that Jibon-da would ask him to say more about Srimati's wedding. But instead he asked, 'Where's Baowa now?'

Amal had told Jibon about Srimati at about eight in the morning. At eight that night, he found out that the police were looking for Jibon. And that Baowa's brother Bulton too was looking for him.

⁂

Somehow or the other, another six unbearable months for Jibon passed by. Now the soldiers of the tricolour brigade had descended with full strength, not just in Jadavpur, or in Calcutta, but in all the small and large towns, as well as all the rural areas across West Bengal. Thousands upon thousands of jawans of the central paramilitary forces had arrived from New Delhi to assist them. Their violence could be compared only with that of Hitler's Gestapo. The whole country was scorching in the fierce flames of a dance of destruction orchestrated by the partnership of the non-violent tricolour party and the armed central forces. The situation in West Bengal was the most terrifying. At home, on the street, in the office, at school or college—no life was safe anymore anywhere. The brutal members of the joint forces of the police and party fell upon people whenever they wished, wherever they wished, and in any way they wished. In the name of crushing terror, wives were raped in front of their husbands, daughters were raped in front of their mothers, and mothers were raped in front of their children. Female political activists were taken to the police station, where boiled eggs and greased rulers were inserted into their private parts. Lit cigars were stubbed on them. Bullet-riddled bodies of youths lay on fields and playgrounds, lanes and pavements. Nowadays it was no longer just one or two bodies, murders were committed on a mass scale. A dozen at a time somewhere, a lorryful elsewhere. In Diamond Harbour, twelve decomposed bodies, with their arms and legs tied, were found stuffed in sacks. In Kashipur-Baranagar, in the course of a day, there were killings just like at the time of the communal inferno, and the bodies were piled into and carted on tempos, hand-carts and rickshaws and thrown into the river. One would never really know the exact number of people who were killed. Some said it was two hundred, others said four or five hundred.

Unable to survive in the face of this immense assault, Balak, Mohan and all their party-boys had fled Loharpara long ago and gone underground. The boys in Palpara had left the locality even earlier. But because Bijoygarh, the main stronghold of the Congress, was quite far away from Jadavpur, the locality around the station had not come under their control. All these localities were controlled not by any political party now, but by some rising mastaans.

It is a strange law of nature that no grass or weeds grows beneath a large tree. As soon as the big trees in Loharpara and Palpara exited, some small-time mastaans had begun to come up around the station. In the railside squatter settlement in Taltala, it was Shibua, in the TB Hospital, Chhoto, and in Palpara, Mintu, the younger brother of Katu, whose hand had been blown away. Each one vied with the other to be the latest and the greatest.

In this scenario, Jibon too was successful in carving out a distinct identity. Although that identity had not made such a deep impact on the minds of people at large, for a few people in the station, like rickshaw-pullers, hawkers, porters, and ordinary daily commuters on the train, it was a great assurance. That was why one day, the girl who looked for customers at various stations, arrived in Jadavpur and told Jibon, 'Dada, I come to your station from time to time. I sell my body to feed myself. Please keep an eye on me, dada.'

Jibon kept an eye on her. A fish-seller in Jadavpur market spent the night with the girl in an empty wagon of a goods train, and then slipped away at dawn without paying her. The next day, his fish-scales were grabbed and the agreed-upon sum of twenty rupees was extracted. Jibon also had to look out for someone who worked in a shop in Sealdah. He came and pleaded, 'I've fallen into great danger, Dada. I was coming by train with my salary for the month in my chest-pocket. The money was in my pocket all through the journey. As I was getting off the train at Jadavpur, I was pushed at the door and fell down. And the money was no longer there. What am I to do now! What will I feed my wife and child all month?'

Jibon knew well how agonising it was to go without food. In order to rid the man of his anguish, Jibon had to go to the den of Hara, Monta and Bisha. They had their den at the Bondel rail-gate earlier. The public thrashed them and drove them away from there. After coming to an arrangement with the GRP, they now operated in the Dhakuria–Jadavpur–Garia stretch. Hara and Monta heeded Jibon's rebuke, and although they were unable to return the entire amount, he did not return empty-handed either. They apologised to Jibon and returned whatever was left after they had splurged on booze and so on.

Jibon was not alone any longer, he had a band. Amal, Bimal, Boro Gopal, Kalo Gopal, Gona, Ganesh, Ghoti, Naran and Kaliya—some of them were rickshaw-pullers, some cleaned fish in the market, some worked in liquor dens, or were porters in the station, while some smuggled rice concealed under the train wagons.

23

Seth Bagan Lane

The only people who could survive now were those who knew how to kill the killers. Not tears or languishing, but fierce retaliation. There was no alternative to retaliation at this time. Jibon had learnt this truth in the course of his own life. It was futile to expect any mercy from a mad dog.

Once upon a time, huge dinosaurs roamed the earth. Where did they go? They were destroyed, they disappeared, they are mere legend now. Because they were in no position to strike back. In the same way, the elephant too failed to strike back. That's why a five-foot tall mahout can sit on its back with his legs resting on its head. For the same reason, men use bullocks to plough the earth and pull carts, and donkeys to carry loads. Or slaughter goats and sheep for food. But the tiny ants, wasps and bees don't submit to anyone. No one can control them. They counter-attack at the first opportunity. That's why they were not destroyed like the dinosaurs. They are still alive today, independent and brave.

Jibon thought about such things nowadays. Dwelling in such thoughts, he was walking towards the disused morgue so that he could hide himself for the night, among the rats and cockroaches behind the mountain of discarded, undisposed torn blankets, quilts and mattresses of tuberculosis patients. The hospital compound was always quite secluded. The desolation was even more acute at night. Now the huge white buildings looked like giant tombstones. Everything was silent and still. Only some mangy mongrel dogs roamed around everywhere. Long ago, an ancestor of these dogs had bitten off a chunk of Jibon's flesh and then died after being hit on the head with a rod. Who knows, perhaps remembering that sad family history, none of them chased him or barked at him now.

Taking the road in front of Gurumohan babu's and Mona Dey's quarters, and walking southwards for a bit, he came upon the field, and walking eastwards through that, he came to the Hundred-Bed ward on his right. Going past the ward associated with the poet Sukanta, and walking through the vacant fields, Jibon came to a halt near the waste incinerator. He looked all around cautiously, and when he was certain that no one was following him, he slipped into the jungle of morning glory shrubs, full of shit and piss, behind the incinerator. Owing to the frequent passage of people, a narrow path had formed in that jungle. Walking along that, Jibon reached the morgue. There were no doors there now. There used to be doors when the morgue was functional. There had also been watchmen on duty then. They were taken off duty two months after the corpses stopped coming here. Someone or some people had then removed the doors and taken them away.

But entering the disused morgue now, Jibon was astonished. The hospital employees seemed to have left a dead body in this doorless, dark, unguarded morgue. Jibon felt dejected at the disregard meted out to a dead person. How could they do that? After all, jackals would devour the body if it was left there! The dead body lay on the concrete shelf along the southern wall, wrapped up in a sheet. Jibon too slept wrapping himself from head to toe like this. There were too many mosquitoes here.

What was Jibon to do now? How could he sleep peacefully tonight in the same room where a dead body lay? He was still thinking of a way out when the dead body moved. Jibon clearly saw the dead man scratching his head. So the dead body was not really dead, it was someone alive. Jibon's hand shot to his waist. To the single-shot 303 tucked in there. If it was a friend, that was fine. But if it was an enemy ... who knows, perhaps it was Jibon that he was waiting for.

Holding the grip of the one-shotter firmly, Jibon slowly poked the ribs of the sleeping person. 'Aeyi, who are you?'

The one who was lying there recognised Jibon's voice. Without moving, he replied, 'Hey, take away the gun, Jibon, it's me, Nanu.'

Nanu! Jibon was shocked. 'Why are you lying here like this?'

Nanu replied, 'I went to my neighborhood in the evening. Some people saw me there. What if one of them went and reported that to the authorities? I'll be killed if I sleep at home!'

'Why did you come back here suddenly?'

'I didn't come suddenly, I had to come. Have you heard about my elder brother?'

'No! What's happened to Debu-da?'

Nanu sat up now. 'You're my friend. What's the point in hiding anything from you? My brother has bad habits. The moment he has money in his hands, he drinks and spends all his time in the whore quarters. A girl was found, and he was married off in the hope that he would change his ways. You've seen Boudi, haven't you? Tell me, doesn't she look just like Ma Durga? But he's abandoned a wife like that and he's back to his old ways. It's only me who Dada fears a bit. But taking advantage of the fact that I was away, he opened Boudi's trunk one day, took all her jewellery, and ran away to the whore. That was ten or twelve days ago. He's putting up there. We have to bring Dada back now, by any means. Who knows whether Boudi's jewellery is still there. We have to bring that back too if possible, and return it to Boudi.'

'Where has Debu-da gone? Is it Sonagachhi?'

'No, it's Seth Bagan. Do you know where Ganesh Talkies is? It's near there.'

'Then let's go there tomorrow. We'll persuade Debu-da and bring him back.'

'You won't be able to persuade him. We've got to bring him back by force. Do you know about the whores there? Just like a snake catches frogs, they catch men and swallow them up. Dada can't fathom that they'll make much of him only as long as he has money. Once the money's gone, they'll kick him on his arse and throw him out in the street.'

After a pause, Nanu continued, 'If we have to bring Dada back from there, we have to be fully prepared when we leave. The police, the neighborhood mastaans and landlords, all get a share of whatever the whores earn. They've trapped someone of means now. Dada has five or six tolas of gold. Do you think they'll let him go so easily? Do you have any country bombs? One can threaten them with the one-shotter, but after all, you can't use it. What if someone gets killed and all that? That's why country bombs are best. People panic more when there's a loud explosion. Do you have any?'

'If it was anyone else, I'd have said no. But I won't tell you that. Will four do?'

'Four bombs and a one-shotter. And I have a dagger.'

'What happened to that six-shooter of yours?'

'Which six-shooter?'

'The one which you had poked in my spine?'

'Oh, that belonged to the party. I had to give it back.'

Nanu fell silent for a while and then resumed. 'We'll manage with what we have. What we need is a vehicle and two more boys. We need at least four people to do the job. I have Dilip. Although he's a kid, he has guts. At least he won't slip away in fear. We can get a car too if we ask Madan-da. A metred taxi. If one digit of the number on the number plate is smeared with mud, there won't be any problem. But who else can we get? There's no one in the neighborhood.'

'I'll get someone.'

'Who's that?'

'Either Ganesh or Kaliya from the station. But they need to be trained before we take them.'

'So that's it then. Be ready. I'll speak to Madan-da, and let you know about when we'll go.'

⁂

A couple of days later, at seven on a Monday morning, Madan, the taxi driver, arrived with his taxi at the desolate area beside the thick undergrowth behind the TB Hospital canteen. The car did not belong to him, he was only the driver. He would take two hundred rupees. He had not concealed the number on the number plate but skillfully altered it with grease. The locality Nanu's older brother Debu was in was full of lanes and alleys and got crowded once it was evening. But it was likely to be empty in the morning as no one woke up before ten or eleven after working all night.

Nanu, Jibon, Kaliya and Dilip got into the car. The taxi driver Madan delivered shipments of illicit liquor to various parts of Calcutta. He knew the city like the back of his hand. And so, avoiding the crowded parts of the city, and going through lanes and bylanes, the experienced driver finally dropped them off safely at their destination, which was Seth Bagan Lane. After they got down from the car, Madan said, 'I'll turn the car around and park it near Girish Park. Find Debu-da and bring him there.'

Seth Bagan Lane was eight- or ten-feet wide. There was a paan and cigarette shop at the very beginning of the lane. There were more packets of condoms than cigarettes on the shelf of the shop. There were pictures of nude and semi-nude male and female bodies making love on the condom packets. A captivating song was playing on loudspeakers from a cassette-player, *Ek ankh marun to chhori patt jaaye* ... This was not the time to hear songs. The battleground lay ahead. Their breathing became quicker. Wild buffaloes had begun to rumble in their chests. The four of them walked ahead with the conviction of soldiers. Nanu was in front, and behind him was Jibon. Nanu had been here a couple of times before, so the address was known to him. They entered the lane, went past two houses on the right side, and stopped at the next one, a dirty two-storeyed house from olden times. This was where their target was. Nanu's brother, Debu.

The house was a pukka one only till the first floor. Above that was another floor, with a tin roof, which one had to climb up to using a wooden staircase. As one went through the door at the entrance of the building, there was a long verandah on the right hand side, along which were six ten-by-ten rooms. After three rooms was the narrow staircase going up to the first floor. Going past the stairs, Nanu, Jibon and the others walked along the long verandah towards the room at the far corner of the ground floor. There was a small wooden chouki on the verandah in front of the room. Nanu's elder brother, Debu, was sitting on that platform.

It was close to nine in the morning now. Debu was already drinking leisurely at this early hour. Everything was laid out in front of him—a roundish bottle of liquor, glasses, some peanuts and slices of cucumber, and a packet of cigarettes. It was a terrible custom of drinking, which all those who drank knew, that if you drank a lot at night, unless you drank a bit again in the morning, you couldn't get rid of the hangover.

Three or four feet away from the wooden chouki, a concealed space had been created by erecting a three-feet-high wall. The occupants of the six rooms, and the babus who came to visit them, used that space as a 'toilet', where they cleaned themselves. There was a large bucket and a plastic mug in that toilet space. A woman was scooping water out of the bucket with the mug, and pouring it on her head and body. She had short hair and her skin was as dark as printing ink. She had a flat nose and big teeth, one of which was half-broken, perhaps after she had slipped at the tap sometime, or perhaps after someone punched her face. She was about five feet and three inches tall, and almost as broad. She looked to be thirty-five or thirty-six years old. The gamchha she had wrapped over herself as she bathed was highly inadequate in relation to the size of her body. As Debu drank, he gazed at the woman squatting and bathing in the hovel in Seth Bagan as if he was sitting on a sea beach, watching some stunning beauty bathing. This was no luxury hotel, yet the woman in the tiny bathroom in this brothel made his eyes light up as if she were nothing less than a five-star swimming beauty. Nanu went up to the chouki and looked closely. It was Dada, wasn't it? Yes, it was him. Debu was about to take a sip from his glass, but his hand stopped midway. Seeing a group of strangers at this untimely hour, Debu lost his temper. As if he was the lord of this house, he thundered in imperious rage, 'What the hell are you doing here? Get out!'

'We've come for you!' said Nanu, stepping forward. 'Don't make a scene, Dada, just come along quietly with us. Ma and Boudi are very worried about you. They can't stop crying. Come along.'

Who knows, perhaps in his drunk state, the word 'boudi' triggered off some reaction. Debu screamed out in rage, 'Go away! Get out, all of you! I'm not leaving! No one can keep me away from Sonka! Go away! Get out!'

Jibon intervened, 'Aeyi Debu-da, what's this? You leave behind a goddess-like wife at home and stay with this witch! *Chhee!*'

'Don't you dare say *'chhee'*! Don't call Sonka a witch! Yes, she doesn't have looks. But what do I care about looks! Shall I wash the looks and drink the water? What Sonka has, you can't buy even for a million rupees!'

'What does she have?'

'What can I tell you people about what she has? If I could replace your eyes with mine, perhaps you'd have been able to see. She may be a girl in the trade, but no one has her nature and her love. And what's your boudi? She's like an inedible fruit, lovely in appearance but nasty within. Her looks have gone to her head, she doesn't even think of me as human!'

'Then why did you marry her?'

'I didn't do that. Baba and this Nanu got me married forcibly. I wasn't willing. Let them face the music now!'

'Where are the ornaments?'

'Which ornaments?'

'Boudi's ornaments, which you took away!'

'I didn't bring any ornaments.'

Like the leader of a gang of bandits, Nanu ordered Dilip and Kaliya, 'That box, the bed, the cupboard, search everywhere. He didn't go anywhere else, everything has to be here!'

'Aeyi Nanu, don't mess up the room, I tell you! There's nothing here.'

Debu's loud voice made a couple of frightened, annoyed and curious faces from the adjacent rooms peep out to look. Nanu grabbed Debu firmly by the waist of his trousers and pulled him down from the platform. He pulled out the dagger from his waist with his other hand, and said, 'I can't bear to see Boudi's tears anymore. If you don't come along quietly with us, I'll chop you right here and leave. I don't need a brother like you!'

Jibon stepped forward and grabbed Debu's shirt. 'Let's see how he doesn't come! I've given my word to Boudi that I'll bring Debu-da back. How can I show my face to her if I don't take him back? Get up, Debu-da, start walking!'

Dilip took out a bomb from the jute bag he was carrying and gave it to Kaliya, and took another one in his hand. The unsightly one-shotter was in Jibon's hand. True, it did not exactly fill one with confidence regarding native artisans, but still it was something to fear. A single shot from that could kill even a tiger, let alone a man. Seeing all this, Debu realised that they had come well prepared to take him away. There was no point in refusing to go now. If he did, he could come to harm. If a brother was also a friend—an example of what he would be like was Lakshman. And if he was a foe, a specimen of what he could do was Vibheeshan. They were like the two sides of a coin.

Feeling helpless, Debu meekly surrendered now, and turning to Jibon, he said plaintively, 'Listen to me, bhai. Where will you take me? To that house? Please don't take me back to that hellhole.

I'll run away again and come back here. I don't have anyone there whom I can call my own. There's an ogress there who's eating up my flesh and bones. Let me go! Let me live in peace here!'

Jibon shouted back, 'How can I do that when I've given my word?'

The alcohol had risen to Debu's head by now. He began to weep mournfully. 'What will happen to poor Sonka when I'm gone? She has no one else in the whole universe other than me. Who'll look after her, who'll love her like me? She doesn't have looks, she's not so young, no one comes to her room. How will she survive? What will she eat? How will she pay the rent? Will she be able to survive?'

'Don't make a scene! Come along now!'

Jibon and Nanu had not come here to listen to a drunkard's raving. They were within the dangerous boundaries of the red light district. Murder and violence without a second thought were part of the daily routine here. Hearing the commotion, a crowd was gathering in the lane in front of the building. If they wasted any more time listening or speaking, it could become complicated for them to exit the place. Nanu had already pulled Debu down from the platform. Now Jibon pushed him from behind towards the door.

Nanu asked Dilip and Kaliya, 'Did you find the ornaments?'

'No!'

'Did you search everywhere? Bring that bag down. See what's inside.'

The woman named Sonka was bathing. At first, she had been terrified seeing the intruders. But some of her courage had returned now. As soon as she saw them taking away the black bag—in which she had hidden the ticket to her future—she let out a deathly scream. '*Ore baba re!* They're killing me! Thieves! Thieves! Aeyi Bhutto, Chandu, Gabbar—where have you gone? Come here at once!'

Bhutto, Chandu and Gabbar were the goondas of this lane. They were the protectors—as well as the consumers—of the sex workers of the lane. Nanu and Jibon realised that resistance was imminent now. Dilip walked ahead of the others with the bag of bombs in his hand. There was nothing better than bombs to disperse a crowd. Jibon pushed Debu with one hand and brandished the single-shot gun with the other, and shouted out a warning: 'Get away from the door!'

Sonka was no longer alone. The five women from the five other rooms on the ground floor, as well as some of their tiny kids, also added their screams to hers. 'Thieves! Help! They're killing us!' From somewhere, others too joined the group. The screams grew louder. The lane had been vacant when they arrived, except for a crowd of freshly-bathed and made-up harlots standing, for no reason, in front of the main doors of the houses. From all along the lane, they screamed out in fear and panic. 'Bhutto, Gabbar, Chandu! Come quickly! There are thieves in Sonka's place!' There were three rooms on either side of the flight of stairs going up to the first floor. Girls of various ages began spilling out from the first and second floors down those stairs. As if the building had caught fire. As if they had to flee. They were disorderly and not even fully clothed when they rushed out anxiously to find out what all the screaming was about. What had happened? In whose room? This wasn't late at night, it was broad daylight. Robbery, murder, fights—were all nocturnal affairs. So what was it then?

Suddenly, as his eyes went in the direction of the stairs, Jibon was startled seeing a pair of terrified eyes. Those eyes and their distressed gaze were very familiar to him. Who was it? Who? Who possessed those big, black entrancing eyes?

Debu turned around once again, and cried out, 'Jibon, let me go! Have pity on me!'

Pity! Who pities anyone at a time like this! Losing patience, Jibon poked Debu in the back with the barrel of his one-shotter. 'Not one word! Just keep walking!' After that, he pushed him out of the verandah and down the steps at the entrance into the lane outside.

༺༻

Some idlers were sitting on the elevated red-floored *roak* in front of the building and gambling. Hearing the women's screams, they threw down their cards and ran to help. This was their neighborhood. They were born in this lane and would die there too. The entire responsibility of taking care of everything here was theirs. That's why the girls paid them a share of their earnings from working their bodies. How could they tolerate outsiders coming into the lane and throwing their weight around? Would they have any dignity or worth left in that event? No, they had to offer resistance. Picking up whatever they could find around them, which had been obtained and kept in advance for just such a situation, they ran in. Lathis, rods, swords and so on were within reach. Fights were a daily affair in this locality. They had no option but to keep weapons ready.

There was no more room for delay. The advance of the hooligans had to be halted. Jibon brandished the one-shotter and threatened, 'Nobody move! Or else I'll shoot you!' Dilip chucked two bombs in succession. He didn't want to injure anyone, that wasn't necessary either, and so he threw them into a vacant spot. There was a terrific explosion, smoke and the acrid smell of gunpowder filled the lane. The group of advancing youths moved back in fear. The terrified girls rushed back into their rooms and shut the doors. The lane became empty. The shutters of the paan shop at the end of the lane came down with a loud crash. Within a few minutes, Nanu and gang had dragged Debu and put him into Madan's taxi. Madan had kept the engine running. As soon as they were inside the car, it moved ahead.

Then—suddenly, Jibon remembered. The one who possessed those dark, helpless eyes! Those were Kusum's eyes! It was no one else but Kusum! No one else had those eyes!

⸎

Jibon was correct. Those eyes were indeed Kusum's. After Jibon left her standing in front of Chhechan's eatery and ran away in fear of the notorious police officer, Pal babu, he had not been able to return to the station the rest of the day. All kinds of rumours were going around—for instance, that the area in and around the station was full of plainclothes policemen. That's why Jibon had been afraid. And Kusum—after standing hungrily in front of Chhechan's shop for a long time, she and her brother had returned to the platform of the station, full of disappointment, and feeling terribly slighted by Jibon. They did not know why Jibon had run away.

Later, when Jibon was able to return to the station, Kusum, her Ma and brother, Biswo, were no longer there. There was no sign of them, or any clue which would help him find them. And so, once again, for the third and final time, Jibon had found and then lost Kusum. After that, Jibon's time had been spent in various attacks and reprisals. He had not been able to think about a lot of things because of the difficult times. But he had never been able to forget Kusum's entrancing, distressed, black eyes. Which knew him to be a wrong-doer. For an error that there was no way of correcting.

The same evening, Basona had spotted Kusum. She used to live in the railside squatter colony in Salampur. After the settlement was demolished, she went to Piyali town, bought land and built a house there. Basona went up to Tulsi to strike up a conversation. 'Where are you from? What led you to coming here?' After such stray talk, she came to the main issue.

She said, 'Didi, it's not good to be at the station with a grown-up daughter. There are goondas around, the police are around too. If your daughter falls into their clutches, she'll lose all her honour for sure. She may be killed too.' After that Basona told Tulsi about Parul and Behula, who worked in babu homes. About how they had been cruelly raped while they were at the station after missing the last train, one by a policeman, and the other by goondas. 'Nothing happened. Nothing happened to anyone, Didi. Tell me, who do poor people have? Everyone blamed the girls instead: "Why were they in the station? Would they have been in the station unless they were fallen women?" Tell me, Didi, is the station anyone's father's property that people can't be there when they miss the train? And when they're there, can they be in peace?'

Having instilled some fear in Tulsi with her tales, and won some trust after spending some of her own money to buy them muri-ghugni, Basona said, 'After all, I too am a woman, Didi. Being a woman, how can I bear to see another woman in trouble? Although we're strangers, we're both from the same land. You're from Barisal, while we are from Khulna, on two sides of the river. What kind of person would I be if I didn't stand beside you in such a time? Come with me to my house. I have three vacant rooms. You can stay there until you find a shelter. I'll take ten rupees a month as rent. You don't have to pay me that now. Give it to me when you are able to. And if you can't, then don't pay me.'

With such talk, Basona convinced Tulsi and company to come to her house. Under the circumstances, the simple and naive Tulsi did not even realise that she was being pushed by circumstances from the frying pan into the fire.

Tulsi did not know Basona, but everyone in Salampur knew that she was a recruiter in a female-trafficking gang. She had trafficked innumerable girls to many parts of the country. She was well-versed in the tricks, subterfuges and devices of trafficking.

She would first get close to the parents of poor girls of marriageable age and gain their trust in various ways. Once she had won them over, she would suddenly announce one day that she knew a potential groom. He had at least five businesses to his name. A pukka house, the only son of his parents. But he had only one fault—he wasn't Bengali, but Bihari, and he lived in Delhi. 'If you can overlook that single fault—then all the responsibility for your daughter's marriage is mine. You don't have to pay a single paisa for dowry. Actually, if you want, I can get them to pay you one or two thousand. Just like we have the custom of paying a dowry and getting a son-in-law, they have the custom of paying a bride-price and taking a girl. So what do you say? Do you agree?'

Once the girl's parents consented, the date was decided upon. The groom appeared. His appearance was indeed captivating. A priest was called, mantras were recited, and the marriage ceremony too took place. After that the groom went away with the bride. If they wanted, the girl's father or brother could accompany them too. They too could then see for themselves where the girl was going. But after that, a few days after the girl's kin returned—only the unfortunate girl knew where she went. She became ensconced in the red light district. Without anyone to call her own, in a faraway province, in the darkness of night, on and on—she was taken apart, in mind, body and soul, by a horde of lustful men. Even if her tears wet her pillow, no one came to wipe the tears of that unfortunate creature.

It wasn't just one, there were plenty of routes to reach there. Some girls were married and brought, while some were tempted with the offer of a well-paying ayah job. Some went to do dance programmes. But no one was able to return. Four immense mountains stood in the way. Politicians, the police, mastaans and landlords. All of them devoured the girls' blood, flesh and vaginal secretions.

Debu was a man. It was somewhat easy to bring him out from that lane. But taking any girl out in the same way was not so easy. Men went there voluntarily, merrily, but girls were brought there through trickery. A lot of money changed hands in the course of bringing them there. The police station, goondas and mastaans, pimps, agents, recruiters, madams, politicians—all kinds of vested interests of a host of people were tied to the fate of the girl. They wouldn't let her go. And even if she managed to get away, they would not let her live in peace.

But right now, it was a great mystery why Basona had not sent Kusum to Delhi or Mumbai or Dubai, but consigned her instead to a tiny cell in Seth Bagan Lane in the heart of Calcutta. Had she done that because Kusum came voluntarily to this death-trap for a handful of rice? Jibon was at a loss to fathom how and why such a turn of circumstances had taken place. He had to find out the truth. Someone had said, 'Know the truth. Only truth will set you free.' Given the acute distress Jibon was suffering now, he would not be free of it unless he knew the truth. He had to know the truth—and he had to tell the truth as well. He had to say— Believe me, I didn't leave you behind and run away willingly.

Jibon reflected—if after hearing me out, Kusum wants to be free of that hateful environment, if she wants to return to normal life, with all my powers, and if need be, through bloodshed, I have to free her and that too right now! One day meant twenty-four hours. In twenty-four hours—who knows how much humiliation, how many rapes Kusum would have to suffer ...

Jibon had spotted Kusum in a brothel in the red light district. He had not seen her in anyone's room in a compromising situation. The sages had counselled—do not believe anything you don't see with your own eyes. Jibon had not seen anything. He could not believe that anyone had touched Kusum. For Jibon, she was, even now, just like before—pure, sinless, sacred. But if there was any more delay, perhaps something terrible might happen. Kusum would be finished. He could not take any risk. He could not waste even another minute. If any harm came to Kusum, life itself would become tasteless, ghastly and utterly meaningless for Jibon.

Madan's vehicle was about to enter a lane. Another Jibon, one who knew no hindrance, or bonds, or fear of death, was being born inside Jibon now. A terrifying Jibon, a Jibon who had no past, no future. Who had only the present, the illusory present, broken into pieces, crushed and ground! Standing on the slippery ground of that present, Jibon roared out loudly, 'Madan-da, stop the car! I'm getting off!'

Startled, Nanu asked him, 'Why?'

'I have to go to that lane again.'

'Why?'

'I left something very valuable there in the hurry, re Nanu!' As he spoke, tears welled up in Jibon's eyes, his voice choked. He said, 'I'll go and bring her along. I came to help you, didn't I? If you want to help me now, come along. Or else go away. I'm not going back without her.'

Jibon opened the door, got out of the taxi and snatched the bag of bombs from Dilip's hand. 'Give me that!' Two of the four bombs had been spent. Two more were left.

Nanu too got down, and held Jibon's arm firmly. 'Have you gone mad, Jibon? You want to jump back into the fire we set off? Who's there? Tell me why you want to go there.'

'There's no time to tell you, Nanu. Come along if you want!' As soon as he said that, Jibon turned around and began running in the direction of the fire set off by them. Nanu ran behind him. 'Listen, listen ...' But Jibon did not hear him. He ran and re-entered the lane. Nanu was quite some distance behind. Suddenly, Nanu heard the loud sound of a bomb exploding. Smoke filled the lane, and so, Nanu did not know what exactly happened. Had Jibon tripped on his lungi while running with the bag of bombs and fallen on them? Or had someone from the other side thrown a bomb at him? Not fathoming what had happened, Nanu came to a halt at the beginning of the lane. It was enveloped in thick smoke. He didn't feel brave enough to venture in. When the smoke cleared a bit, there was no sign of Jibon. Nanu turned around and ran towards the car.

www.ingramcontent.com/pod-product-compliance
Lightning Source LLC
LaVergne TN
LVHW010307070526
838199LV00065B/5466